Y

VOLUME 2

This new series by famed anthologist Terry Carr is
an entertaining collection of haunting and surprising stories, and far more: it is the definitive selection
of the very best of the imaginative story-teller's art,
masterworks of our decade that you will want to
keep and read again.

Fantasy: the most ancient, and most continually
new, of literature's arts. Here you will find
explorers, discoverers, shape-shifters, and word-
slingers, and above all else *entertainers.* . . .

Berkley Books Edited by Terry Carr

THE YEAR'S FINEST FANTASY
VOLUME 2

EDITED BY
TERRY CARR

A BERKLEY BOOK
published by
BERKLEY PUBLISHING CORPORATION

Berkley Publishing Corporation
200 Madison Avenue
New York, New York 10016

SBN 425-04155-7

*BERKLEY BOOKS are published by
Berkley Publishing Corporation*

BERKLEY BOOK ® TM 757,375

Printed in the United States of America

Berkley Edition, JULY, 1979

Table of Contents

Introduction

FANTASY FICTION IS in the midst of a renaissance this year. There was a time when publishers shied away from fantasy as though there were a curse on it—and in truth one couldn't blame them, for even the most conscientious efforts in fantasy magazine publishing met with disheartingly poor sales. One after another, magazines such as *Unknown Worlds*, *Weird Tales*, *Fantasy Fiction*, and *Beyond* were forced to suspend publication.

Only two fantasy magazines survived, and even they had to add liberal doses of science fiction to their offerings in order to attract readers. In 1949, *The Magazine of Fantasy* was launched under the editorship of Anthony Boucher and J. Francis McComas—and almost instantly (by the second issue) its name was changed to *The Magazine of Fantasy and Science Fiction*, as it remains to this day. In 1952, along came *Fantastic*, edited by Howard Browne, who used a large budget to present fiction by writers of the caliber of Bradbury, Sturgeon, and Leiber in combination with fantasy paintings from the Museum of Modern Art; but by the third issue, *Fantastic* was featuring the byline of Mickey Spillane in a desperate attempt to attract readers. The magazine's budget was soon trimmed, liberal doses of science fiction were added, and *Fantastic* survived into the 1970s.

In recent years, *Fantastic* has returned to an all-fantasy policy—and the most recent information I have is that the magazine will either fold or fall back on reprints from past issues.

The record is discouraging. However, there are brighter signs for the future.

If the magazine field is untenable for pure fantasy, the book field certainly isn't. Three original-fantasy anthologies are now being published: *Whispers*, edited by Stuart David Schiff; *Shadows*, edited by Charles L. Grant; and *Swords Against Darkness*, edited by Andrew J. Offutt. As the titles suggest, the first two are devoted to horror fiction, the third to sword-and-sorcery adventures.

In addition, there's an interesting hybrid called *Ariel: the Book of Fantasy*, which is published twice a year in a large-format, slick paper edition—at a price of $7.95. It features excellent color paintings, which are backed up by fantasy stories both old and new.

So the impending loss of *Fantastic* as a source of new fantasy stories is balanced by the advent of these new publications. And, of course, there are dozens and dozens of fantasy novels on the stands and in preparation—for a more complete report on these, see Susan Wood's "The Year in Fantasy," included in this collection.

If most of the fantasy novels published this year are simple-minded sword-and-sorcery adventures, this needn't be any more discouraging to adult readers than is the large number of space-opera science fiction novels. Each form attracts younger readers who will graduate to its parent genre in time, and meanwhile we can enjoy the rich fantasies of novelists like Stephen King, Fritz Leiber, and Stephen R. Donaldson who are able to devote craft and care to their work because of the higher payments available to the best fantasists writing today.

The situation is likely to improve, too. There's already a large fandom devoted specifically to fantasy; its members hold regular conventions, present fantasy awards equivalent to science fiction's Hugos, and support a surprising number of quality semi-professional publishers. There's a feeling of excitement in this field, of growth and success both monetary and literary: the next few years may well present us with an explosion of major fantasy works.

Remarkable fantasy fiction is appearing right now, of course, and the present volume gathers a selection of the very best: stories that startle and delight, tales of love and revenge . . . and yes, some that may indeed haunt you.

—Terry Carr

Gotcha!
by Ray Bradbury

Since the beginning of his career, when he was making a name for himself in the pages of Weird Tales, *Ray Bradbury has been a master of the quiet horror story. He doesn't need graveyards or vampires to provoke an air of fright; on the contrary, he does his best work in ordinary modern settings—such as the following tale of two lovers playing a game. Of course games can be frightening, but... between lovers? Oh yes, oh yes.*

They were incredibly in love. They said it. They knew it. They lived it. When they weren't staring at each other they were hugging. When they weren't hugging they were kissing. When they weren't kissing they were a dozen scrambled eggs in bed. When they were finished with the amazing omelet they went back to staring and making noises.

Theirs, in sum, was a Love Affair. Print it out in capitals. Underline it. Find some italics. Add exclamation points. Put up the fireworks. Tear down the clouds. Send out for some adrenalin. Roustabout at three A.M. Sleep till noon.

Her name was Beth. His name was Charles.

They had no last names. For that matter, they rarely called each other by their first names. They found new names every day for each other, some of them capable of being said only late at night and only to each other, when they were special and tender and most shockingly unclad.

Anyway, it was Fourth of July every night. New Year's every dawn. It was the home team winning and the mob on the field. It was a bobsled downhill and everything cold racing by in beauty and two warm people holding tight and yelling with joy.

And then...

Something happened.

At breakfast about one year into the conniption fits Beth said, half under her breath:

"Gotcha."

He looked up and said, "What?"

"Gotcha," she said. "A game. You never played Gotcha?"

"Never even heard of it."

"Oh, I've played it for years."

"Do you buy it in a store?" he asked.

"No, no. It's a game I made up, or almost made up, based on an old ghost story or scare story. Like to play it?"

"That all depends." He was back shoveling away at his ham and eggs.

"Maybe we'll play it tonight—it's fun. In fact," she said, nodding her head once and beginning to go on with her breakfast again, "it's a definite thing. Tonight it is. Oh, bun, you'll love it."

"I love everything we do," he said.

"It'll scare the hell out of you," she said.

"What's the name again?"

"Gotcha," she said.

"Never heard of it."

They both laughed. But her laughter was louder than his.

It was a long and delicious day of luscious name-calling and rare omelets and a good dinner with a fine wine and then some reading just before midnight, and at midnight he suddenly looked over at her and said:

"Haven't we forgotten something?"

"What?"

"Gotcha."

"Oh, my, yes!" she said, laughing. "I was just waiting for the clock to strike the hour."

Which it promptly did. She counted to twelve, sighed happily and said, "All right—let's put out most of the lights. Just keep the small lamp lighted by the bed. Now, there." She ran around putting out all the other lights, and came back and plumped up his pillow and made him lie right in the middle of the bed. "Now, you stay right there.

You don't move, see. You just...*wait*. And see what *happens*—okay?"

"Okay." He smiled indulgently. At times like these she was a ten-year-old Girl Scout rushing about with some poisoned cookies on a grand lark. He was always ready, it seemed, to eat the cookies. "Proceed."

"Now, be very quiet," she said. "No talking. Let me talk if I want—okay?"

"Okay."

"Here goes," she said, and disappeared.

Which is to say that she sank down like the dark witch, melting, melting, at the foot of the bed. She let her bones collapse softly. Her head and her hair followed her Japanese paper-lantern body down, fold on fold, until the air at the foot of the bed was empty.

"Well done!" he cried.

"You're not supposed to talk. Sh-h."

"I'm sh-h-h-ed."

Silence. A minute passed. Nothing.

He smiled a lot, waiting.

Another minute passed. Silence. He didn't know where she was.

"Are you still at the foot of the bed?" he asked. "Oh, sorry." He sh-h-h-ed himself. "Not supposed to talk."

Five minutes passed. The room seemed to get somewhat darker. He sat up a bit and fixed his pillow and his smile got somewhat less expectant. He peered about the room. He could see the light from the bathroom shining on the wall.

There was a sound like a small mouse in one far corner of the room. He looked there but could see nothing.

Another minute passed. He cleared his throat.

There was a whisper from the bathroom door, down near the floor.

He glanced that way and grinned and waited. Nothing.

He thought he felt something crawling under the bed. The sensation passed. He swallowed and blinked.

The room seemed almost candlelit. The light bulb, one hundred and fifty watts, seemed now to have developed fifty-watt problems.

There was a scurry like a great spider on the floor, but

nothing was visible. After a long while her voice murmured to him like an echo, now from this side of the dark room, now that.

"How do you like it *so* far?"

"I . . ."

"Don't speak," she whispered.

And was gone again for another two minutes. He was beginning to feel his pulse jump in his wrists. He looked at the left wall, then the right, then the ceiling.

And suddenly a white spider was crawling along the foot of the bed. it was her hand, of course, imitating a spider. No sooner there than gone.

"Ha!" He laughed.

"Sh-h!" came the whisper.

Something ran into the bathroom. The bathroom light went out. Silence. There was only the small light in the bedroom now. A faint rim of perspiration appeared on his brow. He sat wondering why they were doing this.

A clawing hand snatched up on the far left side of the bed, gesticulated and vanished. The watch ticked on his wrist.

Another five minutes must have gone by. His breathing was long and somewhat painful, though he couldn't figure why. A small frown gathered in the furrow between his eyes and did not go away. His fingers moved on the quilt all to themselves, as if trying to get away from him.

A claw appeared on the right side. No, it hadn't been there at all! Or had it?

Something stirred in the closet directly across the room. The door slowly opened upon darkness. Whether something went in at that moment or was already there waiting to come out, he could not say. The door now opened upon an abyss that was as deep as the spaces between the stars. A few dark shadows of coats hung inside, like disembodied people.

There was a running of feet in the bathroom.

There was a scurry of cat feet by the window.

He sat up. He licked his lips. He almost said something. He shook his head. A full twenty minutes had passed.

There was a faint moan, a distant laugh that hushed

itself. Then another groan ... where? In the shower?

"Beth?" he said at last.

No answer. Water dripped in the sink suddenly, drop by slow drop. Something had turned it on.

"Beth?" he called again, and hardly recognized his voice, it was so pale.

A window opened somewhere. A cool wind blew a phantom of curtain out on the air.

"Beth," he called weakly.

No answer.

"I don't like this," he said.

Silence.

No motion. No whisper. No spider. Nothing.

"Beth?" he called, a bit louder.

No breathing, even, anywhere.

"I don't like this game."

Silence.

"You hear me, Beth?"

Quiet.

"I don't like this game."

Drip in the bathroom sink.

"Let's stop the game, Beth."

Wind from the window.

"Beth?" he called again. "Answer me. Where are you?"

Silence.

"You all right?"

The rug lay on the floor. The light grew small in the lamp. Invisible dusts stirred in the air.

"Beth ... you okay?"

Silence.

"Beth?"

Nothing.

"Beth!"

"Oh-h-h-h-h-h ... *ah-h-h-h-h*!"

He heard the shriek, the cry, the scream.

A shadow sprang up. A great darkness leaped upon the bed. It landed on four legs.

"Ah!" came the shout.

"Beth!" he screamed.

"Oh-h-h-h!" came the shriek from the thing.

Another great leap and the dark thing landed on his chest. Cold hands seized his neck. A white face plunged down. A mouth gaped and shrieked:

"Gotcha!"

"Beth!" he cried.

And flailed and wallowed and turned but it clung to him and looked down and the face was white and the eyes raved wide and the nostrils flared. And the big bloom of dark hair in a flurry above fell down in a stormwind. And the hands clawing at his neck and the air breathed out of that mouth and nostrils as cold as polar wind, and the weight of the thing on his chest light but heavy, thistledown but an anvil crushing, and him thrashing to be free, but his arms pinned by the fragile legs and the face peering down at him so full of evil glee, so brimful of malevolence, so beyond this world and in another, so alien, so strange, so never seen before, that he had to shriek again.

"No! No! No! Stop! Stop!"

"Gotcha!" screamed the mouth.

And it was someone he had never seen before. A woman from some time ahead, some year when age and things had changed everything, when darkness had gathered and boredom had poisoned and words had killed and everything gone to ice and lostness and nothing, no residues of love, only hate, only death.

"No! Oh, God! Stop!"

He burst into tears. He began to sob.

She stopped.

Her hands went away cold and came back warm to touch, hold, pet him.

And it was Beth.

"Oh, God, God, God!" he wailed. "No, no, no!"

"Oh, Charles, Charlie," she cried, all remorse. "I'm sorry. I didn't mean—"

"You did. Oh, God, you did, you did!"

His grief was uncontrollable.

"No, no. Oh, Charlie," she said, and burst into tears herself. She flung herself out of bed and ran around turning on lights. But none of them were bright enough. He was crying steadily now. She came back and slid in by him and put his grieving face to her breast and held him, hugged him, patted him, kissed his brow and let him weep.

"I'm sorry. Charlie, listen, sorry. I didn't—"

"You *did*!"

"It was only a game!"

"A game! You call that a game, game, game!" he wailed, and wept again.

And finally, at last, his crying stopped and he lay against her and she was warm and sister/mother/friend/lover again. His heart, which had crashed, now moved to some near calm. His pulses stopped fluttering. The constriction around his chest let go.

"Oh, Beth, Beth," he wailed softly.

"Charlie," she apologized, her eyes shut.

"Don't ever do that again."

"I won't."

"Promise you'll never do that again?" he said, hiccuping.

"I swear, I promise."

"You were *gone*, Beth—that wasn't *you*!"

"I promise, I swear, Charlie."

"All right," he said.

"Am I forgiven, Charlie?"

He lay a long while and at last nodded, as if it had taken some hard thinking.

"Forgiven."

"I'm sorry, Charlie. Let's get some sleep. Shall I turn the lights off?"

Silence.

"Shall I turn the lights off, Charlie?"

"No-no."

"We have to have the lights off to sleep, Charlie."

"Leave a few on for a little while," he said, eyes shut.

"All right," she said, holding him. "For a little while."

He took a shuddering breath and came down with a chill. He shook for five minutes before her holding him and stroking him and kissing him made the shiver and the tremble go away.

An hour later she thought he was asleep and got up and

turned off all the lights save the bathroom light, in case he should wake and want at least one on. Getting back into bed, she felt him stir. His voice, very small, very lost, said:

"Oh, Beth, I loved you so much."

She weighed his words. "Correction. You *love* me so much."

"I *love* you so much," he said.

It took her an hour, staring at the ceiling, to go to sleep.

The next morning at breakfast he buttered his toast and looked at her. She sat calmly munching her bacon. She caught his glance and grinned at him.

"Beth," he said.

"What?" she asked.

How could he tell her? Something in him was cold. The bedroom even in the morning sun seemed smaller, darker. The bacon was burned. The toast was black. The coffee had a strange and alien flavor. She looked very pale. He could feel his heart, like a tired fist, pounding dimly against some locked door somewhere.

"I . . ." he said, "we . . ."

How could he tell her that suddenly he was afraid? Suddenly he sensed that this was the beginning of the end. And beyond the end there would never be anyone to go to anywhere at any time—no one in all the world.

"Nothing," he said.

Five minutes later she asked, looking at her crumpled eggs, "Charles, do you want to play the game tonight? But this time it's me, and this time it's you who hides and jumps out and says, 'Gotcha'?"

He waited because he could not breathe.

"No."

He did not want to know that part of himself.

Tears sprang to his eyes.

"Oh, no," he said.

The Lady in White
by Stephen R. Donaldson

Stephen R. Donaldson burst onto the fantasy scene just two years ago with the publication of his epic fantasy trilogy The Chronicles of Thomas Covenant the Unbeliever. *He's reported to be working on another trilogy, but in the meantime here's his first published shorter story: a tale of love and mystery, magic and bravery.*

I am a sensible man. I have been blacksmith, wheelwright, and ironmonger for this village for seven years; and I have not seen the need to believe in magic, no matter what that loon, mad Festil my brother, says. I have not had need of magic. I am a man who does what he wills without such things—without such nonsense, I might once have said. This village is small, it's true, but not so small that Mardik the blacksmith does not stand as tall as any man here, fletcher or stonemason or vintner. I have all the work I choose to do, and my asking is fair because I have no need to ask for more. There is no woman here, widow or maid, who scorns the touch of my hands, though it's true my hands have the grime of the smithy in them and are not like to look clean again. Men listen when I speak; and if they do not hear me well, they can hear my fist well enough, and better than most. For my sake they treat mad Festil with respect.

Yet that respect is less than his desert. Loon that he is, he is wise in his way, though the village does not see it. He is younger than I, and less of stature by a span of my hand, but when he smiles the look in his face is stronger than fists, and many are the angers he has brought to an end by gazing upon them with his blind eyes. For this I esteem him more than our village can understand. And for one thing more. Mad Festil my brother came to me when I

11

was in need, brought close to death by the magic of the
Lady in White.

Magic I call it, lacking another name for the thing I do
not understand. Fools speak of magic with glib tongues
that have no knowledge; they seek a respect that they
cannot win with their own hands. Children prate of magic
when they have taken fright in the Deep Forest. Well, the
Deep Forest is strange, it's true. The trees are tall beyond
tallness, and the gloom under them is cunning, and men
lose their way easily. Our village sits with its back to the
mighty trees like a man known for bravery, but ofttimes
tales are heard of things which befall those who venture
into the Deep Forest, and in storms even the priests gaze
upon that tall darkness with fear. And fools, too, are not
always what they seem.

But fools and children speak only of what they hear
from others, who themselves only speak of what they hear
from others. Even the priests can put no face to their fear
without consulting Scripture. I am neither fool nor child.
I am not a priest, to shudder at tales of Lucifer. I am
Mardik the blacksmith, wheelwright, and ironmonger;
and I make what I will, do what I will, have what I will. I
fear not Satan nor storms nor black trees.

I speak only of what I have seen with my own eyes, and
I was not struck blind by what I saw as Festil was. I have
kissed the lips of the thing I do not understand and have
been left to die in the vastness of the Deep Forest.

I say I do not believe in magic, and I hold to what I say.
Mayhap for a time I became ill in my mind. Mayhap, all
unknowing, I ate of the mushroom of madness which
grows at night under the ferns far in the Deep Forest.
Mayhap many things, none of them magical. I do not say
them because I cannot say them and be sure. This I do say.
For a time under the spell of the Lady in White, I had need
of a thing that was not in me; and because I had it not, I
was left to die. If that thing had another name than magic,
mad Festil knows it, not I. He smiles it to himself in his
blindness and does not speak.

He was fey from his earliest youth, like a boy who knew
that when he became a man he would lose his sight. My

remembering of him goes back to the sound of his voice in the darkness of our loft-room. Though sleep was upon me, he would remain awake, sitting upright in the strawbed we shared, speaking of things that were exciting to him—of dragons and quests and arcane endeavors, things mysterious and wonderful. He spoke of them as if they were present to him in the darkness, and the power of his speaking kept me awake as well. I cuffed him more than once, but often I listened and let him speak and laughed to myself.

At times when the excitement was strong, he would say, "Do you believe in magic, my brother? Do you not believe in magic?" Then I would laugh aloud. And if the excitement was very strong, he would become stubborn. "Surely," he would say, "surely you believe that there is some witchery in the Deep Forest?" Then I would say, "A tree is a tree, and paths are few. It does not need magic to explain how fools and children lose their way. And if they come back to the village with strange tales to excuse their fear and foolishness, that also does not need magic." And then if he pressed me further, I would cuff him and go to sleep.

For this reason, I did not esteem Festil my brother as we grew to manhood. And for other reasons, also. I have no wife because I have no need of wife. No woman scorns me, and I take what I will. It pleases me to live my life without the bonds of a wife. But Festil has no wife because no woman in the village, be she ripe and maidenly enough to make a man grind his teeth—no woman pleases him. I believe he is virgin to this day.

And when our father, the blacksmith before me, died, I did not learn to esteem my brother more. He was a dreamer and a loon and understood less than nothing of the workings of the smithy. So all the labor came to me, and until I grew strong enough to bear it, I did not take pleasure in it.

Also his speaking of our father's death was worse than anile. Our father died from the kick of a horse whose hooves he was trimming. A placid plowbeast that gave its master never a moment's trouble suddenly conceived a desire to see the color of our father's brains. To this Festil cried, "Bewitchment!" He took a dagger and spent long hours in the Deep Forest, seeking to find and slay the caster of the spell. But I looked upon the beast when it grew calm again and found that our father's trimming blade had slipped in his hand and had cut the frog of the hoof. Bewitchment, forsooth! I saw no need to treat mad Festil with respect.

Yet he was my brother, kind and gentle, and willing in his way to help me at the forge, though it's true his help was often less than a help. And at times he fought the fools in the village for my sake when he would not fight for his own. I grew to be glad of his company and tolerant of his talk. And I knew that a matter to be taken seriously had arisen when he came to me and said that he had seen the Lady in White.

"The Lady in White!" he said softly, and his eyes shone, and his face was full of light. I would have laughed to see any other man act such a calf. But this was Festil my brother, who had not so much as touched his lips to the breasts of any woman but his mother. And in past days I had heard talk of this Lady in White—as who had not? The men who had seen her had told their tales until no ear in the village was empty of their prattle. For three nights now, every tankard of ale I took at the Red Horse was flavored with talk of the Lady in White. I cannot say that I was partial to the taste.

Fimm the fruiterer had seen her, with Forin his son, who was almost a man. Forin had gone senseless with love, said Fimm, and had crept away from his father in the night to follow the road taken by the Lady—into the Deep Forest, said Fimm. For two nights now Forin had not returned, and no one in the village had seen him.

"Well, lads are wild," said I, "and a Lady in White is as good a cure for wildness as any. He will return when she has taught him to be some little tamer."

But, nay—Fimm would not agree. And Pandeler the weaver was of the same mind, though Pandeler does not take kindly to nonsense. He himself had seen the Lady in White. She had come to his shop to buy his finest samite, and there his two sons, the twins Paoul and Pendit, had seen her. They had come to blows over her—they who were as close to each other as two fingers in the same fist—and Paoul had gone away in search of her, followed soon afterward by Pendit, though they were both of them under the banns to be married to the ripe young daughters of Swonsil the fletcher.

Yet that was not the greatest wonder of it, said Pandeler. Neither of his sons had been seen in the village for two days—but that also was not the greatest wonder. Nay, the wonder was that Pandeler himself had near arisen in the black night and followed his sons into the Deep Forest, hoping to find the Lady in White before them. He had only refrained, he said, because he was too old to make a fool of himself in love—and because, if the truth were known, it would be that he was altogether fond of Megan his wife.

"What is she like, then," said I, "this Lady in White?" It was in my mind that any woman able to lead Pandeler the weaver by the nose would be worth a look or twain.

But he gave no answer. His eyes gazed into his tankard, and if he saw the Lady in White there, he did not say what he saw.

Then other men spoke. If all the tales were true, this Lady had already consumed some half dozen of our young men, and no one of us knew a thing of her but that she came to the village from the Deep Forest and that when she left she took herself back into the Deep Forest.

Well, I thought of all this often in my smithy—and not with displeasure, it's true. If our young men were fool enough to lose themselves in the Deep Forest—why, soon the village would be full of maidens in need of consolation. And who better to console them than Mardik the blacksmith?

But that look in Festil my brother's face stood the matter on other ground. When he came to me and said that he had seen the Lady in White, I put down my hammer and considered him seriously. Then I took a step to bring myself close to him and said, "It's come to that, has it? When will you be after her?"

"Now!" he said gladly. It pleased him to think that I

understood his desire. "I only came to tell you before I left."

"You are wiser than you think, my brother," said I. And because I am not a man who hesitates when he has made his decision, I swung my fist at once and hit mad Festil a blow that stretched him on the dirt of the smithy. "I have no wish to lose my only brother," I said, though it's true he was not like to hear me. Then I bore him sleeping to our hut and put him in his bed and contrived a way to bolt his door. When I was sure of him, I went back to my forge.

But I was wrong. The blood of our father flows in him as well, after all, and he is stronger than he seems. When I returned home at midday, I found him gone. He had been able to break the wallboard that held my bolt in place. Without doubt, he was on his way into the Deep Forest.

I went after him. What else could I do? He was a dreamer and a loon, and he knew more of witches than of smithing. But he was my brother, and no other could take his place. Pausing only to slip my hunting knife into the top of my boot, I left the house at a run. It was my hope to catch him before he managed to lose himself altogether.

I ran to the stables and threw a saddle onto Leadenfoot, the grey nag that draws my wagon when I go to do work at the outlying farms. Leadenfoot is no swiftling—what need has a blacksmith's wagon for swiftness?—but when I strike him hard he is faster than my legs. And he fears nothing, because he lacks the sense of fear—which is also an advantage in a blacksmith's nag. So he heeded the argument of my quirt and did not shy as many horses do when I sent him running down the old road into the Deep Forest.

That road is the only way which enters the forest, and all the talkers at the Red Horse had agreed that when the Lady in White left the village she walked this road. It began as a wagon track as good as any, but it has been long disused and no longer goes to any place, though surely once it did in times so long past that they have been forgotten by all the village. Now only mad priests claim knowledge of the place where the old road goes. They say it goes to Hell.

Hell, forsooth! I have no use for such talk. Yet in its way Hell is as good a name for the Deep Forest as any. As I ran Leadenfoot along the road at his best speed, the trees and the brush were so thick that I could see nothing through them, though the sun was bright overhead; and birds answered the sound of Leadenfoot's shoes with cries like scorn. I called out for Festil, but the woods took my voice and gave back no reply.

And in a league or two the road grew narrower. Grass grew across it, then flowers and brush. Fallen limbs cluttered the way, and the black trees leaned inward. Leadenfoot made it clear to me that he would not run farther, though I hit him more than I am proud to admit. And nowhere did I see any sign of Festil.

How had he eluded me? I had not left him alone more than half the morning, and he had been sleeping soundly when I had bolted his door. He could not have awakened immediately. He could not have broken the wallboard without effort and time. He could not have outrun me. Yet he was gone. The Deep Forest had swallowed him as completely as the jaws of death.

Railing against him for a fool and a dreamer, I left Leadenfoot and searched ahead on foot. Shouting, cursing, searching, I followed the road until it became a path, and the path became a trail, and the trail vanished. Almost I lost my way for good and all. When I found it again, I had no choice but to return the way I had come. All about me, the birds of the Deep Forest cried in derision.

At the place where I had left Leadenfoot, I found him gone also. This day everything was doomed to betray me. At first, I feared that the senseless nag had broken his reins and wandered away off the road. But then I found his shoe marks leading back down the road toward the village. I followed as best I could, and now there was a fear in me that darkness would come upon me before I could escape these fell trees.

But in the gloom of sunset, I gained a sight of Leadenfoot, walking slowly along the road with a rider upon his back.

I ran to catch the nag and jerked the reins, pulling the rider to the ground. Mad Festil.

"Mardik," he said. "Mardik my brother." There was joy in his voice, and there was joy in his face, and all his movements as he rose to his feet and clasped me in his arms were as certain as truth. And yet he was blind. His eyes were gone in a white glaze, and I did not need the noon sun to see that there was no sight in them.

I held him with all the strength of my anger and pain. "What has she done to you?" I said.

But my grip gave him no hurt. "I have seen her," he said.

"You are blind!" I cried at him, seeking to turn aside the joy in his face.

"Yet I have seen her," he said. "I have seen her, Mardik my brother. I have entered her cottage and have won through its great wonders to the greatest wonder of all. I have seen the Lady in White in all her beauty."

"She has blinded you!" I shouted.

"No," he said. "It is only that my eyes have been filled by her beauty, and there is no other thing bright enough to outshine her."

Then I found that I could not answer his joy, and after a moment I gave it up. I did not say to him that he was mad—that there was no cottage, no place of wonder, no Lady who could blind him with her beauty unless she had seduced him to eat the mushroom of madness and had done him harm by choice. I stored these things up amid the anger in my heart, but I did not speak them. I put Festil onto Leadenfoot's back and mounted behind him, and together we rode out of the Deep Forest in the last dusk.

That night, with mad Festil sleeping the sleep of bliss in our hut, I went to the Red Horse as was my custom. Nothing I said of my brother's folly—or his blindness. I listened rather, sifting through the talk about me for some new word of the Lady in White. But no word was said, and at last I spoke my thought aloud. I asked if any of the young men who had followed the Lady into the Deep Forest had returned.

The older men were silent, and the younger did not speak, but in his own time Pandeler the weaver bestirred himself and said, "Pendit. Pendit my son has returned. Alone."

I saw there in his face that he believed his other son Paoul dead. Yet I asked him despite his grief: "And what says Pendit? How does he tell his tale?"

With head bowed, Pandeler said, "He tells nothing. No word has he spoken. He sits as I sit now and does not speak." And in the firelight of the hearth it was plain for all to see that there were tears on the face of Pandeler, who was as brave a man as any in the village.

Then I returned to our hut. Festil my brother slept with a smile on his mouth, but I did not sleep. My heart was full of retribution, and there was no rest in me.

The next morning, I spoke with Festil concerning the Lady in White and the Deep Forest, though it's true that all the speaking was mine, for he would say nothing of what had happened to him. Only he said, "My words would have no meaning to you." And he smiled his joy, wishing to content me with that answer.

But when I asked him how he had come to be riding Leadenfoot out of the Deep Forest, he did reply. "When I had seen her," he said, "I was no longer in her cottage. I was in the dell that cups her cottage as a setting cups its gem, and Leadenfoot was there. I heard him cropping grass near at hand. He came to me when I spoke his name, and I mounted him and let him bear me away. For that I must ask your pardon, my brother. I knew not that you had ridden him in search of me. I believed that the Lady in White had brought him for me, in consideration of my blindness." Then he laughed. "As in truth she did, Mardik my brother—though you scowl and mutter to yourself at the thought. You are the means she chose to bring Leadenfoot to me."

The means she chose, forsooth! He spoke of magic

again, though he did not use the word. And yet in one way
he had the right of the matter, despite his blindness. My
scowl was heavy on my face, and I was muttering as I
mutter now. Therefore I swore at him, though I knew it
would give him pain. "May Heaven damn me," I said, "if
ever again I serve any whim of hers." Then I left him and
went to the smithy to bespeak my anger with hammer and
anvil. For a time the fire of my forge was no hotter than
my intent against this Lady in White.

But all my angers and intents were changed on an
instant when a soft voice reached me through the clamor
of my pounding. I turned and found the Lady herself
there before me.

She bore in her hands a black old pot which had worn
through the bottom, and in her soft voice she asked me to
mend it for her. But I did not look at the pot and gave no
thought to what she asked. I was consumed utterly by the
sight and sound of her.

Her form was robed all in whitest samite, and her head
was crowned as if in bronze by a wealth of red-yellow hair
that fell unbound to her shoulders, and her eyes were like
the heavens of the night, starbright and fathomless, and
her voice was the music that makes men laugh or weep,
according to their courage. Her lips were full for kisses
but not too full for loveliness, and her breasts made
themselves known through her robe like the need for love,
and her skin had that alabaster softness that cries out to
be caressed. Altogether, she struck me so full with desire
that I would have taken her there in the dirt of the smithy
and counted the act for treasure. But her gaze had the
power to withhold me. She placed her pot in my hands
with a smile and turned slowly and walked away, and her
robe clung cunningly to the sway of her hips, and I did
nothing but stare openly after her like the veriest calf.

But I am not a man who hesitates; and when she had
left my sight among the huts on her way back to the old
road and the Deep Forest, I did not hesitate. I banked the
fires of my forge and closed my smithy and went home.
There in my room I bathed myself, though I do not bathe
often, it's true; and when I had removed some of the grime

of smithing from my limbs, I donned my Easter garments, the bold-stitched tunic, and the brown pants with leather leggings which the widow Anuell had made for me. Thus I readied myself to depart.

But when I turned from my preparations, I found Festil before me. He was laughing—not the laughter of derision, but the laughter of joy. "A bath, Mardik!" he said. "You have seen her."

"I have seen her," I said.

"Ah, Mardik my brother," he said, and he groped his blind way to me to embrace me. "I wish you well. You are a good man. It is a test she gives you now. If you do not falter or fail, she will fulfill your heart's desire."

"That is as it may be," I answered. But in my own heart I said, Then I will not falter or fail, and you will not be blind long, Festil my brother. I returned his embrace briefly. Soon I had left our hut, and the village was behind me, and I was walking along the old road into the Deep Forest, and there was an unwonted eagerness in my stride.

Striken with desire as I was, however, I did not altogether lose sense. I took careful note of the passing trees on my way, finding landmarks for myself and searching for any path by which the Lady in White might have left the road. I discovered none, no sign that any Lady lived near this track, no sign that any Lady however white had ever walked this way. In a league or two, my heart began to misgive me. Yet in time I learned that I had not missed my goal. For when I neared the place where I had tethered Leadenfoot the day before, I came upon a branching in the road.

A branching, I say, though I do not hope to be believed. I will swear to any man who asks it that no branching was there when I came this way in search of Festil. But that is not needed. It is plain to all who dare travel that road that there is no branching now. Yet I found a branching. That is sure. If I had not, then none of the things that followed could have taken place.

In my surprise, I walked along this other road and shortly came to the dell and the cottage of which Festil my brother had spoken. And he had spoken rightly. Safe and

sunlit among the gloom of the trees was a hollow rich with
flowers, soft with greensward, and cupped in the hollow
was a small stone cottage. Its walls had been whitewashed
until they gleamed in the sun, and all the wood of its
frames and roof had been painted red. White curtains of
finest lace showed in the windows, and beneath the
windows lay beds of columbine and peony. Faint white
smoke rose from the chimney, showing to my keen desire
that the Lady was within.

I went with heart pounding to the red door, and there I
paused as if I, Mardik the blacksmith, were unsure of
himself, so great and confused were my lust and my anger.

But then I recollected myself, put aside my unseemly
hesitation. With my strong hand I knocked at the door,
and there was both confidence and courtesy in the way I
summoned the Lady in White.

The door opened, swung inward, though I saw no one,
heard no one.

Then in truth began the thing for which I have no other
name but magic. Many things in the world are strange,
and magic is not needed to explain them. But in this thing
I am beyond all my reckoning, and I know no explanation
other than that I became ill in my mind or ate of the
mushroom of madness or by some other means lost
myself. But Festil my brother, who is wise in his way, says
that I am neither mad nor ill, and I must believe him when
I cannot believe the thing of which I speak. He was there
before me, and this thing named magic cost him his sight.

But magic or no, I have chosen to speak, and I will
speak. My word is known and trusted, and no man in the
village dares call me liar or fool, though at times I seem a
fool to myself, it's true. This, then, is the thing that befell
me.

As the door opened, I stepped inward, into the cottage,
so that no effort could be made to deny me admittance.
Within, the air seemed somewhat dark to my sun-
accustomed eyes, and for a moment I was not certain that
I saw what I saw. But beyond question I did see it, just as it
was. Behind me through the doorway was the sunlight
and the green grass of the dell that cupped the cottage. But

before me was no cottage room, no cozy hearth and small kitchen. I stood in a huge high hall like the forecourt of an immense keep.

The ceiling was almost lost to sight above me, but even so I could see that its beams were as thick as the thickest trees of the Deep Forest. The floor space before me was all of polished grey stone, and it was large enough to hold a dozen cottages such as the one I had just entered. A stone's throw to my left, a stairway as wide as a road came down into the hall from levels above mine. And an equal distance to my right, a hearth deep enough to hold my smithy entire blazed with logs too great for any man to lift. The light came from this fire, and from tall windows high in the wall behind me. And all about these prodigious stone walls hung banners like battle pennons.

Two of these held something familiar to me. Woven large in the center of one was the weft mark of Paoul son of Pandeler the weaver. And displayed across the other was a great big apple. At this I ground my teeth, for it was known in all the village that Forin son of Fimm the fruiterer look pride in his apples.

Now in truth there was no hesitation in me, though this high castle hall sorely baffled all my reckoning. My hands ached to entwine themselves in the bronzen hair of the Lady, and my mouth was tight with kisses or curses. When my eyes were fully accustomed to the keep-light, I espied an arched entryway opposite me. It had the aspect of an entrance into the less public parts of this castle, and I strode toward it at once. As I moved, the air thronged with the echo of my bootsteps.

Surprised as I was by the strangeness of this place, and by the meaning of the pennons about the walls, I had at first failed to note a small table standing in the very center of the hall. But as I neared it, I considered it closely. It was ornately gilt-worked, and it stood between me and the arched entryway as if it had been placed there for some purpose. When I came to it, I saw that on it lay a silver tray like a serving dish, polished until it reflected the walls and ceiling without flaw. All its workmanship was excellent, but I saw no reason for its presence there, and so I stepped aside to pass around the table toward the far entryway.

At my next step, I struck full against the outer door of the cottage. Of a sudden there was sunlight on my back, and my eyes were blurred by the brightness of the whitewashed walls. The dell lay about me as fragrant as if I had not left it to enter that place of witchery, and the red door was closed in my face.

Then for a time I stood motionless, as still as Leadenfoot when the fit comes upon him and he stops to consider the depth of his own stupidity. It seemed to me that the mere taking of air into my lungs required great resolve, that the beating of my heart required deliberate choice, so unutterable was my astonishment. But then I perceived the foolishness of my stance and took hold of myself. Though the act gave me a pang akin to fear, I lifted my hand and knocked at the door again.

There was no answer. As my enstupidment turned to ire, I knocked at the door, pounded at it, but there was no answer. I shook mightily on the handle, kicked at the door, heaved against it with my shoulder. There was no answer and no opening. The door withstood me as if it were stone.

Then I ran cursing around the cottage and strove to gain entrance another way. But there was no other door. And I could not break any window, neither with fist nor with stone.

At last it was the thought of the Lady in White that checked me. I seemed to feel her within the walls, laughing like the scornful birds of the Deep Forest. So I bit my anger into silence, and I turned on my heel, and I strode away from the cottage and the dell without a backward glance. And through my teeth I muttered to her in a voice that only I could hear, "Very well, my fine Lady. Believe that you have beaten me if you will. You will learn that you scorn me at your peril."

But when I regained the old road, I ran and ran on my way back to the village, wearying my unwonted fury until I became master of myself once again.

When I returned to our hut, I found Festil my brother

sitting in wait for me on the stoop. Hearing my approach, he said, "Mardik?" And I replied, "Festil."

"Did you—?" he said.

"I failed," I said. I had become myself again and was not afraid to speak the truth.

For a moment, I saw a strange pain in my brother's face, but then the gaze of his blindness brightened, and he said, "Mardik my brother, did you take the Lady a gift?"

"A gift?" said I.

Then Festil laughed at my surprise. "A gift!" he said. "What manner of suitor are you, that you do not take a gift to the lady of your heart?"

"A gift, forsooth!" I said. "I am not accustomed to need gifts to win my way." But then I reflected that mad Festil my brother, loon and dreamer though he was, had had more success than I with the Lady in White. "Well, a gift, then," I said. Considering his blindness and his happy smile, I asked, "And what was your gift?"

His laugh became the mischievous laugh of a boy. "I stole a white rose from the arbor of the priests," he said.

Stole a rose? Aye, verily, that had the touch of mad Festil upon it. But I am not like him. I am Mardik the blacksmith, wheelwright, and ironmonger. I had no need to steal roses. Therefore I slept confident that night, planning how I would make my gift.

Dawn found me in my smithy, with the music of the anvil in my heart. The blade of a discarded plowshare I put into the forge, and I worked the bellows until the iron was as white as sun-fire. Then I doubled the blade over and hammered it flat while the smithy ran with bright sparks as the impurities were stricken away. Then I tempered it in the trough and put it in the forge again and worked the bellows so that the fire roared. Again I doubled it, hammered it flat, tempered it. Again I placed it in the forge. And when I had doubled it once again, hammered it to the shape I desired, and tempered it, I had formed a knife blade that no hand in the village could break.

To the blade I attached a handle of ox horn, and then I gave the knife a keen edge on the great grindstone made by our father in his prime, when Festil and I were young. And all the while I worked, my heart sang its song, using the name of the Lady in White for melody.

My task was done before the passing of midday. With the new blade gleaming in my hand, I determined at once to assay that cottage of bewitchment without awaiting a new day. I returned to our hut to take food. I spoke pleasantly with Festil my brother, who listened to my voice with both gladness and concern in his face, as if the hazards of the Lady were as great as the rewards. But when I sought to learn more from him concerning the "test," he turned his head away and would not speak.

Well, I felt that I had no need of further counsel. He had told me of the gift, and that was enough. I put the new knife in my belt and went just as I was, begrimed and proud from the smithy, to visit again in the dell and the cottage of the Lady in White.

On my way between the dark and forbidding tree walls of the Deep Forest, my confidence was weakened by a kind of dread—a fear that the branching of the road would be gone or lost. But it was not. It lay where I had left it, and it led me again to the dell of flowers and grass and the cottage of white walls and red wood.

At the door I paused, took the blade from my belt and held it before me. "Now, then, my fine Lady," I muttered softly, "let us see if any man in the village can match such a gift as this." With the butt of the knife, I rapped on the door.

Again the door swung inward. And again I saw no one, heard no one.

I entered at once and found myself once more in that huge high hall, castle forecourt spacious enough to hold a dozen such cottages. But now I did not waste time in wonder. Though the image of the Lady in White filled my very bones with desire—and though the pennons of the dead (young men consumed by whatever hunger drove that cruel and irrefusable woman) did not fail to raise my anger—still I had not lost all sense. I knew my time was short. If I were to fail another test, I meant to do so and be gone from this place before day's end. No man would choose to travel in the Deep Forest at night.

So I strode without delay across that long stone floor toward the table in the center of the hall. The light was dimmer than it had been the previous day—the afternoon sun did not shine into those high windows—and this dimness seemed to fortify the echoes, so that the sound of my feet marched all about me like a multitude as I approached the table. But I did not hesitate. Nor did I trouble myself to make any speech of gift giving. I held up the knife so that any hidden eyes might see it. Then I placed it on the silver tray.

There was no response from the castle. No voices hailed my gift, and the Lady in White did not appear. I stood there before the table for a moment, allowing her time for whatever answer seemed fit to her. But when none came, I took my resolve in both hands and stepped around the table toward the arched entryway at the far end of the hall. Almost I winced, half expecting to find myself in the dell once more with the cottage door shut in my face.

But I did not. Instead, another thing came upon me—a thing far worse than any unexplained vanishing of hall and locking of cottage door.

Before I had gone five paces past the table, I heard a scream that turned the strength to chaff in my limbs. It rent the air. It echoed, echoed, about my head like the howling of the damned. A gust of chill wind near extinguished the blaze in the hearth, and some cloud covered the sun, so that the verges of the hall were filled with night. I spun where I was, searching through the gloom for the inhuman throat which had made that scream.

It was repeated, and repeated. And then the creature that made it came down the broad stairs from the upper levels—came running with murder in its face and a great broadsword upraised in its foul hands, shrieking for my blood.

It was fiend-loathsome and ghoul-terrible, a thing of slime and scales and fury. Red flames ran from its eyes. In the dimness its broadsword had the blue sheen of lightning. Its jaws were stretched to rend and kill, and it ran as if it lived for no other purpose than to hack my heart out from between my ribs for food.

The fear of it unmanned me. Even now, looking back on things that are past, I am not ashamed to say that I was lost in terror—so much lost that I was unable to take the knife from my boot to defend myself. The creature screamed as it charged, and I screamed also.

Then I was lying on the greensward of the dell, and the afternoon sunlight was slanting through the treetops to glint in my eyes. The cottage stood near at hand, but the door was closed, and the windows had a look of abandonment. Only the curling of smoke from the chimney showed that the Lady in White was yet within, untouched by any desire or anger of mine.

Stricken and humbled, I left the dell and returned to the old road. As the sun drew near to setting, I went back through the Deep Forest toward the village.

But there was another thing in me beyond the humbling, and I came to know it soon. For while I was still within the bounds of the forest, with the hand of the coming night upon me, I met a man upon the road. When we drew near enough to know each other, I saw that he was Creet the stonemason. He stood tall in the village, and it's true that his head overtopped mine, though mayhap he was not as strong as I. We were somewhat friends, for, like me, he had done much wooing but no marrying—and somewhat wary one of another, for we had only measured our strength together once, and there had been no clear issue to that striving. But I gave no thought to such things now. For Creet the stonemason was walking into the Deep Forest at dusk, and there was a spring of eagerness in his step.

Seeing him, the other thing in me was roused, and I shifted my path to bar his way. "Go back, mason," said I. "She is not for you."

"I have seen her," he replied without hesitation. "How can I go back? Mayhap you have failed to win her, blacksmith. Creet the stonemason will not."

"You speak in ignorance, Creet," said I. "She has slain men of this village. That *I* have seen."

"Men!" he scoffed. "Paoul and Forin? They were boys,

not men." Clearly, he did not doubt himself. He placed a
hand on my chest to push me from his way.

But I am Mardik the blacksmith, and I also can act
without hesitation when I choose. I shrugged aside his
hand and struck him with all my strength.

Then for a time we fought together there in the old road
and the Deep Forest. Night came upon us, but we did not
heed it. We struck one another, clinched, fell, arose to
strike and clinch and fall again. Creet was mighty in his
way, and his desire for the Lady in White was strong
beyond bearing. But the other thing in me had raised its
head. It was a thing of iron, a thing not to be turned aside
by failure or fear or stonemasons. After a time, I struck
Creet down, so that he lay senseless before me in the road.

Thus I chose my way—the way that brought me near to
dying in the end, lost in the maze of the Deep Forest.
From the moment that I struck down Creet the
stonemason, I gave no more thought to humbling or fear.
I was Mardik the blacksmith, wheelwright, and ironmonger. I was accustomed to have my will and did not
mean to lose it at the hand of any lady, however strange. I
lifted Creet and stretched him across my shoulders and
bore him with me. So I became the first man in my lifetime
to find his way out of the Deep Forest in darkness.

I bore my burden direct to the Red Horse, where many
of the men of the village were gathered, as was their
custom in the evening. Giving no heed to their surprise, I
thrust open the door and bore Creet into the aleroom and
dropped him there on a table among the tankards. He
groaned in his slumber, but to him, also, I gave no heed.

"Hear me well," I said to the silence about me. "I am
Mardik the blacksmith, and if Creet cannot stand against
me, then no man in this village can hope otherwise. Now I
say this: the Lady in White is mine. From this
moment forth, no other man will follow her. If your sons
see her, lock them in their rooms and stand guard at the
door. If your brothers behold her, bind them hand and
foot. If your friends are taken with the sight of her,
restrain them with shackles of iron. And if you wish to go
to her—why, then, tell your wives or your maidens or

your mothers to club you senseless. For the Lady in White kills whom she does not keep. And I will be no more gentle to those who dare cross my way. The Lady in White is mine!"

Still there was silence for a moment in the aleroom. Then Pandeler the weaver rose to his feet and met my gaze with his grief for Paoul his son. "Will you kill her, then, Mardik the blacksmith?" he said.

"Pandeler," said I, "I will do with her whatever seems good to me."

I would have gone on to say that, whatever I did, no more young men of the village would lose their lives, but before I could speak, another man came forward to face me, and I saw that he was Gruel the mad priest. His habit was all of black, and his long grey beard trembled with passion, and his bony hands both clung to the silver crucifix which hung about his neck. "She is the bride of Satan!" he said, fixing me with his wild eye. "Your soul will roast in hell!"

"God's blood!" I roared in answer. "Then it will be my soul that roasts and not the souls of innocent calves who cannot so much as say aye or nay to their own mothers!" Then I left the aleroom and flung shut the door of the Red Horse so that the boards cracked.

Returning homeward, I found our hut all in darkness, and for a moment there was a fear in me that Festil had gone again into the Deep Forest. But then I recalled that Festil my brother had no need of light. I entered the hut and found him in his bed, awake in the night. When I opened the door, he said, "Mardik," knowing me without doubt, for in the darkness he was no more blind than I.

"Festil," I said. "Again I failed."

"It was very fearsome," he said, and in his voice I heard two things that surprised me—sorrow and a wish to console me. "Do not reproach yourself."

"Festil," I said again. My own voice was stern. There was a great need in me for the knowledge he could give. "What is that creature?"

"A test, my brother," he said softly. "Only a test."

"A test," I echoed. Then I said, "A test you did not fail."

After a moment, he breathed, "Aye." And again there was sorrow in his voice—sorrow for me.

"How?" I demanded. My need for knowledge was great.

"I—" he began, then fell silent. But I waited grimly for him, and after a time he brought himself to speak. "I knelt before the creature," he said, and he was whispering, "and I said, 'Work your will, demon. I do not fear you, for I love your Lady, and you cannot harm my heart.' And then the creature was gone, and I remained." But then of a sudden his voice became stronger, and he cried out, "Mardik, you must not ask these things! It is wrong of me to speak of them. It is not a kindness to you—or to the Lady. You must meet each test in your own way, else all that you endure will have no purpose."

"Do not fear, Festil my brother," I said. "I will meet that creature in my own way, be it beast or demon." That was a promise I made to myself and to the fear which the creature had given me. "Yet I must ask you to tell me of the other tests."

"I must not!" he protested.

"Yet I must ask," I said again. "Festil, young men are slain in that cottage, and it needs but little to make even old men follow the Lady to their graves. I cannot prevent their deaths if I cannot gain my way to speak with her."

"Is that your reason?" he asked, and now the sorrow was thick and heavy in his voice. "Is that why you will return to her?"

Then I answered openly because I could not lie to that sound in my brother's voice. "For that reason also. And for the reason of your blindness. But if I lacked such reason, yet I would go, for I desire the Lady in White with a desire that consumes me."

Still he was silent, but I knew now that he would tell me all he could without false kindness. And at last he said softly, "There is a woman. You must find some answer to her need. And then there is a door." Beyond that he could not speak.

But it sufficed for me. The thing I feared was a multitude of those screaming creatures, but now I knew there was but one. Therefore I was confident. Surely I could satisfy one woman. And as to the door—why, one door does not daunt me. I thanked Festil for his help and left him there in the darkness and spent the night planning for the day to come.

And in the dawn I left to carry out my will. I took a satchel of food with me, for I did not mean to return to the village until I had won or lost, and if I failed a test I would perforce remain in the dell until the next day to try again. Bearing the satchel on my shoulder, I went to Leadenfoot and led him from the stables to my smithy, where I harnessed him to my wagon. Then into the wagon I placed all that I might need—hammers, an anvil, nails, chisels, rope, a small forge of my own making, an urn of banked coals for fire, a saddle and bridle for Leadenfoot, awls, a saw, shears, tongs, an ax, wood, and charcoal— everything that need or whim suggested to me. And to all this I added a pitchfork—a stout implement with tempered tines which I had made especial for a doughty farmer who broke other pitchforks the way some men break ax hafts. Then I was ready. I climbed up to the wagonbench, took the reins, released the brake, and went out through the village toward the old road and the Deep Forest.

I did not depart unnoticed, though the hour was yet early. My wagon does not roll quietly—it is well known that wheelwrights and blacksmiths do not tend their wagons as well as other men—and the squeal of the singletrees told all within earshot of my passing. Families came from their huts to see me go. But they did not speak, and I did not speak, and soon I was beyond them among the verges of the woods.

The Deep Forest was dim in the early light, and the noise of my wagon roused huge flocks of birds that cried out in anger at my intrusion. But I was content with their outrage. They were creatures of this dense and brooding wood, but I was not. I was Mardik the blacksmith, and I was on my way to teach the Lady in White the meaning of my desire. If the ravens of doom had come to bark about my ears, I would not have been dismayed.

Also I was patient. My wagon was slow, and Leadenfoot had no love for this work, but the pace did not dishearten me. There was a long day before me, and I did not doubt that the Lady would be waiting.

And yet in all my preparation and all my confidence, there was one thought that disquieted me. Festil my brother had gone to the dell and the cottage armed with naught but one white rose—and yet he had contrived to surpass me in the testing. "Aye, and for reward he lost his sight," I answered my doubt. It was not my intent to become another blind man.

Thus it was that I came forewarned and forearmed to the branching of the old road late in the sunlight of morning, and I took it to the grassy and beflowered dell that cupped the witch-work cottage of the Lady in White.

There I tethered Leadenfoot, allowing him to crop the grass as he chose, and set about readying myself to approach the red door. From my satchel I removed the food, storing it under the wagonbench. Then into the satchel I placed all the tools and implements that were most like to be of use—rope, hammer, chisels, awls, nails, saw, shears, tongs. With that load heavy on my shoulder, I took the pitchfork in my right hand, hefted it a time or twain to be certain of its balance. I did not delay. I am not a man who hesitates. I addressed that safe-seeming red door and knocked at it with the shaft of the pitchfork.

For the third time, it opened inward to my knock. And for the third time, I saw no one within, heard no one approach or depart.

I entered warily, alert for the creature of flame and fury. But all within that strange door was as I had seen it twice before. The stone hall stretched before me like the forecourt of an immense keep, far dwarfing the cottage that seemed to contain it. The huge logs in the great hearth burned brightly, and the sunlight slanted through the high windows. The pennons of the dead hung from the walls—but if they hung in derision of foolhardiness or in tribute to valor, I did not know. And there in the center of the floor stood the small gilt-work table with the silver tray.

I strode through echoes to the table warily, and when I gained it I saw on the tray the knife that I had made—my gift. Mayhap the Lady in White had declined to accept it. Or mayhap it had been left there as a sign that the way beyond the table was open for me. This also I did not know. But I did not delay to make the trial. I settled the satchel upon my shoulder and clenched the haft of the pitchfork and stepped around the table.

So I learned that my gift had not been refused, for I did not find myself without the cottage with the door locked against me. At once, my wariness grew keener. I walked on toward the arched entryway at the far end of the hall, but I walked slowly. I believe I did not breathe, so strong was my caution and my waiting.

And then it came again, the scream that rent the air and echoed in the dim hall and chilled my blood in the warmest places of my heart. A cold wind blew, and the air became full of shadows. And the creature that made the screaming came down the wide stairs from the upper levels with its broadsword upraised and its eyes aflame with murder.

I dropped my satchel, turned to face the demon.

Again it filled me with fear, and again it would have not shamed me to say that I had been unmanned. But I had found the thing of iron within me now, and I was prepared.

As the creature ran screaming across the floor toward my throat, I swung with all my strength, hurling the pitchfork like a handful of spears.

The tines bit the chest of the creature and sank deep. Such was the force of my throw that the creature was stricken backward despite its speed. Its broadsword fell in a clatter against the stone, and the creature itself lay writhing for a moment on the floor, plucking weakly at the metal in its chest. Then on an instant it seemed to me that the creature was not a demon at all, but rather a woman in a white robe. And then the creature was gone, vanished utterly, taking broadsword and pitchfork with it. I was left alone in the great hall, with the logs that no man could lift ablaze in the hearth.

"God's blood!" muttered I to myself. But swiftly I shook off the wonder. I had not come so far to be unmanned by wonder. I lifted my satchel and walked away toward the arched entryway, and my stride was the stride of Mardik the blacksmith, strong and sure.

But beyond the arch matters were not so certain. The entryway led to halls and chambers of great complication, and there were many passages and doors that I might choose. All were various, some spare and others sumptuous, and all had the appearance of habitation, as if the lordly people of this castle had left it only briefly and would return, but all were made of grey stone and told me nothing of the Lady in White. For a time, I wandered hither and thither, making no progress. When I came upon one of the high windows, I could see by the sun that midday was passing.

Then in vexation I stopped where I was and gave thought to my situation. I was in need of direction. But in this amazed place east and west, inward and outward, had no meaning. Therefore I must either climb or descend. And because that fell creature with the broadsword had come from the upper levels, I chose to go downward. Then at last I was able to advance, for there were many stairways, and many of them went down into the depths of this prodigious keep.

So I descended, stair beyond stair, and the air became dark about me. Torches burned in sconces in the walls to light the passages—burned, and did not appear to be consumed—but they were few and the halls were many. Therefore I took one of the torches, a brand the length of this arm, and bore it with me, and so I was able to continue my descent.

Then of a sudden I came upon a chamber bright-lit and spacious, its walls behung with rich tapestries depicting I knew not what heraldic or sorcerous legends. And there in the center stood a low couch. And there on the couch lay a woman in black.

She turned her head toward me as I entered, but at first my eyes were unaccustomed to the brightness, and I could not see her well. "Ah, man!" she hailed me, and her voice was the voice of a woman in need. "Rescuer! I beg of you—redeem me from my distress!"

"What is your need, woman?" said I, seeking to clear my sight. But I knew already the name of her need. I had heard that need often before in the voices of women. And I saw no harm in it. I was prepared to answer it, for the sake of the Lady in White and her testing.

"Ah, man!" she said to me in pleading. "I am loveless and alone. Life is a long misery, and there is no joy for me, for I am scorned and reviled everywhere. Help me, O man! For surely I can endure no more."

That had an unsavory sound to it, but still I was undaunted. I moved closer to her, blinking against the brightness.

But then my sight cleared, and I saw her, and she was hideous. Her raiment was not a black robe, but rather leper's rags, and her hands were gnarled and reft with leprosy. I saw them well, for she extended them toward me beseechingly. They were marked with running sores, and her arms were marked, and her face, also, was marked. Her hair hung in vile snatches from her head, and many teeth were gone from her gums, and the flesh of her face had been misshapen by illness, so that it seemed to be made all of bruises and scabs. Gazing upon her, I could not say which of them had become the greater, my loathing or my pity—for I was sickened by the sight of her, it's true; and yet the deepness of her misery wrung my heart.

But Festil had said, "You must find some answer to her need." And verily, this was a test to pale all testing of gifts and demon-creatures. Again she cried out, "Help me, O man, I beg of you! Ease my hurt." Now I knew not what answer Festil my brother had given this leprous crone, but some answer he had given, that was certain, for he had not failed this test. And I knew of no answer but one—no answer but one that could stand against this piteous and abhorrent distress. Therefore I bethought me of the Lady in White, and with her image I spurred myself until my hands ached to feel her throat between them. Then I stepped forward to stand beside the couch.

The woman's hands reached pleading for mine, but I

stopped and drew the knife from my boot and thrust it through her heart with one blow of my fist.

Then on an instant it seemed to me that her face softened, and her hair grew thick and bronzen, and her lips became full, and her rags were whitest samite. And then she was gone, vanished as utterly as the demon-creature, and there was neither knife nor couch with me in the chamber.

Then my anger came upon me again, and I vowed in my heart that the Lady in White would answer me for this. In my anger I did not delay. There was only one other doorway to this chamber. Taking up my satchel, I went out that way swiftly, hoping to come upon the Lady before she had prepared another and more foul test.

But that way led only to a lightless passage, and the passage led only to a stout wooden door and was shut. No Lady was there. And no woman, though mayhap she was swift as a deer, could have run the length of that passage to open and close that door before I entered the passage behind her. Yet did I not doubt that I had come to the proper place. For there was light beyond the stout door, light shining through the edges of the lintel and the space along the floor. And across the light a figure moved within the room from time to time, casting shadows that I could see.

Therefore I did not question how the Lady in White had come to be beyond that door. Indeed it's true that in that strange place no swiftness or startlement seemed strange to me. Desire and anger burned in me like iron from the forge, and I gave no thought to matters that any sensible man might misdoubt. I went forward with the sole intent of entering the room beyond the door.

At the door I knocked, but there was no answer. I called out as courteously as I could. Still there was no answer. Soon it became clear to me that there would be no answer. The figure casting the shadows gave no heed to my presence.

At first, I was filled by a need to shout and rage, but I mastered it. Without doubt, this door was the door of which Festil had spoken—another test. A simple enough thing in itself, after the fear and loathing of the tests I had overcome. Yet for a moment I was daunted. I was unsure of my reply to this test.

My unsureness came from my belief that I knew what Festil's reply had been. No doubt he had announced himself there and then had simply set himself to wait, possessing his soul in patience until the figure within the room deigned to take notice of him. And in this cottage I had come to understand that Festil my brother was not unwise. Loon and dreamer though he was, he had within him a thing that met this testing better than I.

But I was Mardik the blacksmith, not Festil the dreamer, and after my meeting with the leprous woman there was no patience in me. I set down my satchel of tools and turned myself to a consideration of the door itself.

It was made of heavy timbers, iron bound and studded. Its hinges were set to open inward, and I could see through the crack along the lintel that it was held in place by a massive bolt which no strength of mine could break or bend. My first thought was to slip the blade of my saw through the crack to sever the bolt, but I did not, fearing that the figure within the room would not permit me to work unhindered. Therefore I turned to the hinges. And there I saw my way clear before me.

There were but two hinges, though they were of thick black iron; and they were secured, high and low in the door, each by but one heavy bolt through the wood. "Aye, verily, my fine Lady," I muttered to myself. "Does all your testing come to this?" For I was Mardik the ironmonger and knew beyond doubt that those two bolts could not stand against me.

In truth the iron of them was old beyond age, and they were no fair test for me. With chisel and hammer I sheared the head from the upper bolt in two blows. And in three the lower bolt failed before me.

Then, using the chisel, I pried the wood toward me until the door slipped from its frame. Here I had need of strength, for the timbers were heavy, but strength I had, and my chisel did not bend. And then light streamed into the passage, and the door was open.

Snatching up my satchel, I entered quickly and found myself in a large chamber like an alchemist's laboratory.

Work tables stood everywhere, and on them were vials and flasks of crystal, small fires that burned without smoke, many-colored powders and medicines, and strange apparatus with a look of witchery about them. There was no source to the light that I could discover. Rather, the very air of the chamber seemed to shine.

And standing at one of the tables across the room from me was the Lady in White.

She was as radiant as my brightest rememberings, as beautiful as the heavens. Her eyes shone starlike and fathomless, and her hair flamed in bronzen glory, and the whiteness of her robe was pure beyond bearing. At the sight of her, both my desire and my anger became as nothing for a moment, so great was the spell of wonder cast on me by her loveliness.

But she regarded me with something akin to curiosity in her gaze and something akin to humor on her lips, and this regarding made her human to me. The hot iron in me awoke. I cast wonder aside and went toward the Lady in White to take her.

Yet I stopped again at once in astonishment. For at my approach the Lady turned to me and shrugged her shoulders, and with that simple gesture her white robe fell from her, and her bronzen hair fell from her, and her loveliness fell from her and was gone. In her place stood a tall man clad in grey. His shoulders were stooped and his beard long, and on his grizzled hair he wore a pointed hat such as wizards wear. Curiosity and humor were there in his face, but there also were scorn and anger.

"Very well, Mardik," he said to my astonishment. "You have won your way to me. What is your desire?"

But I could not have told him my desire. There was a hand of confusion upon me, and I could not have uttered the name of my desire, even to myself. I stared at the wizard like a calf and muttered the broken pieces of thoughts until at last I found the words to say, "Where is the Lady?"

"There is no Lady," he said without hesitation.

"No Lady?" said I. "No Lady?" And then a great shame came upon me, for I had shed blood for the sake of that Lady, and my anger broke from me in a roar. "Then what was the purpose?"

The wizard shrugged a shrug of scorn. "To disguise myself," he said. "I have work before me, and to work my work I have need betimes for things from the village. Therefore I disguise myself so that I will not be known for what I am. I have no wish to be prevented from my work by callow fools, importuning me for spells to make their cows fruitful and their maidens avid, enchantments to speed childbirth and fend off old age."

"Then you are a fool!" I cried, for I was full of rage. "To disguise yourself, you clothe yourself in a form that draws men here to die!—a form that no man can refuse in his desire!"

"Mayhap," said the wizard. But he gave no explanation. He turned from me as if he had no more use for me—as if he had tested me in the crucible and found me to be impure, base metal. And he said, "Nothing that your heart desires exists at all."

Thus he took the measure of my worth and discarded me.

For there was no laboratory about me and no wizard before me. I stood on the grass in the dell, and the air was dim with evening, and the last light of the sun made the white walls of the cottage gleam strangely. All the windows of the cottage were dark, as if that place were no habitation for man or woman, and there was no smoke arising from the chimney.

And the Lady in White stood before me.

"Ah, Mardik," she said gently, "be comforted," and her voice was a music that made my heart cry out within me. "My magic is strait and perilous, but it is not unkind." Gently her arms came about my neck, and when her lips touched mine, all my desire and my anger melted, and I became helpless to meet or deny her kiss.

Then she was gone. The Lady in White was gone. The cottage was gone. Leadenfoot and my wagon were gone. The dell was gone. Even the branching which had brought me here from the old road was gone. The sun itself was gone, and I was left alone in the night and the Deep Forest.

Then I wandered the woods in misery for a time, reft

and lorn. I was lost beyond all finding of my way, and there was no strength in me. My death was near at hand. I wandered among the inquiries of owls and flitted through madness like the flocking bats and stumbled until I became an easy prey for any beast that might hunger for me. Lost there beyond help, it seemed to me that death was a good thing withal, comfortable and a relief from pain.

Yet when I sought the ground and slept for a time and thought to die, I did not die. I was roused by hands upon my shoulders; and when I looked up in the moonlight, I saw blind Festil my brother bending over me.

"Mardik," he said, "my brother," and there was weeping in his voice.

"Festil," I said. "Ah, how did you find me?"

"I followed the trail of your need, my brother," said Festil. "I have traveled this way before you and know it well."

Then weeping came upon me also, and I said, "My brother, I have failed you. For the wizard asked me to name my desire, and I did not ask him to restore your sight."

"Ah, Mardik!" he said, and now I heard laughter and joy through his sorrow. "Do you truly not understand the reason for my blindness? My brother, it is a thing of choice for me and in no way ill. For I also was asked to name my desire, and to this I gave answer: 'It is my desire to gaze solely upon the Lady in White to the end of my days, adoring her beauty.' That desire was granted to me. For her image is always before me, and my eyes behold no other thing."

Then my heart wept. Ah, Festil my brother! You are a loon and a dreamer, and you are a wiser man than I. But I did not speak aloud. I arose from the ground, and mad Festil took my arm and guided me despite his blindness and brought me without mishap to the old road. There I found Leadenfoot awaiting me in patience or stupidity, and my wagon with him. Together Festil and I climbed up to the wagon-bench, and I released the brake and took the reins in my hands, and together we made our way out of the Deep Forest.

● ● ●

From that day to this, I have seen no evidence of magic and have no need of it. I am Mardik the blacksmith, and I stand as tall as any man in the village, though it's true some muttered darkly about me for a time until I silenced them. I do what I will, and none can say me nay. For my sake they treat mad Festil with respect.

And yet I am not what I was. There is a lack in me that ale cannot quench and work and women cannot fill. For I have failed the testing of the Lady in White in my way, and that is a failure not to be forgotten or redeemed. There was a thing that I needed, and it was not in me.

The Lady in White, I say, though I do not expect to be believed. I have thought long and painfully of all that has befallen me and have concluded that the wizard was like the demon-creature and the leprous crone—another test. By means of testing, the Lady in White sought to winnow men, seeking one worthy of her love. This I believe, though Festil give it no answer but his smile and his joy. Well, smile, then, Festil my brother. You have won your heart's desire, though it has made you blind. But I failed the tests of the Lady. Verily, I failed them all, and knew it not. But this, also, I do not utter aloud.

In truth, we do not speak much of the matter. Betimes Pendit the son of Pandeler comes to our hut in the evening, and we three who have endured the ordeal of the cottage sit together in the darkness, where Festil's eyes are as good as any, and better than most. But we do not speak of what we have endured. Rather Festil spins dreams for us in the night, and we share them as best we may, loving him because he sees the thing that we do not.

Her old pot I keep in the name of remembrance, though without mending it is of little use.

There are some who say that we have been blighted, that we have become old and withered of soul before our time. But we are not blighted, Festil and I. For he has gained his heart's desire, and I—why, I am Mardik the blacksmith, wheelwright, and ironmonger; and despite all my failures I have been given a gift worthy of treasuring, for I have been kissed by the Lady in White.

Within the Walls of Tyre
by Michael Bishop

Michael Bishop, whose science fiction novels include
A Funeral for the Eyes of Fire *and* Stolen Faces,
*certainly isn't a household name in the field of
fantasy . . . yet he has begun to venture into tales of the
inexplicable in recent years, and he's likely to become
as great a favorite in this field as he is in science fiction.
See, for instance, the following strange story of a
woman who nurses a secret from the past.*

As she eased her Nova into the lane permitting access to
the perimeter highway, Marilyn Odau reflected that the
hardest time of year for her was the Christmas season.
From late November to well into January her nerves were
invariably as taut as harp strings. The traffic on the
expressway—lane-jumping vans and pickups, sleek
sports cars, tailgating semis, and all the blurred,
indistinguishable others—was no help, either. Even
though she could see her hands on the wheel, trembling
inside beige, leather-tooled gloves, her Nova seemed
hardly to be under her control; instead, it was a piece of
machinery given all its impetus and direction by an
invisible slot in the concrete beneath it. Her illusion of
control was exactly that—an illusion.

Looking quickly over her left shoulder, Marilyn Odau
had to laugh at herself as she yanked the automobile
around a bearded young man on a motorcycle. If your
car's in someone else's control, why is it so damn hard to
steer?

Nerves; balky Yuletide nerves.

Marilyn Odau was fifty-five; she had lived in this
city—*her* city—ever since leaving Greenville during the
first days of World War II to begin her own life and to
take a job clerking at Satterwhite's. Ten minutes ago,

before reaching the perimeter highway, she had passed through the heart of the city and driven beneath the great, grey, cracking backside of Satterwhite's (which was now a temporary warehouse for an electronics firm located in a suburban industrial complex). Like the heart of the city itself, Satterwhite's was dead—its great silver escalators, its pneumatic message tubes, its elevator bell tones, and its perfume-scented mezzanines as surely things of the past as... well, as Tojo, Tarawa Atoll, and a young marine named Jordan Burk. That was why, particularly at this time of year, Marilyn never glanced at the old department store as she drove beneath it on her way to Summerstone.

For the past two years she had been the manager of the Creighton's Corner Boutique at Summerstone Mall, the largest self-contained shopping facility in the five-county metropolitan area. Business had been shifting steadily, for well over a decade, from downtown to suburban and even quasi-rural commercial centers. And when a position had opened up for her at the new tri-level mecca bewilderingly dubbed Summerstone, Marilyn had shifted too, moving from Creighton's original franchise near Capitol Square to a second-level shop in an acre-square monolith sixteen miles to the city's northwest—a building more like a starship hangar than a shopping center.

Soon, she supposed, she ought also to shift residences. There were town houses closer to Summerstone, after all, with names just as ersatz-elegant as that of the Brookmist complex in which she now lived: Chateau Royale, Springhaven, Tivoli, Smoke Glade, Eden Manor, Sussex Wood.... *There*, she told herself, glancing sidelong at the Matterhorn Heights complex nestled below the highway to her left, its cheesebox-and-cardboard-shingle chalets distorted by a teepee of glaring window panes on a glass truck cruising abreast of her.

Living at Matterhorn Heights would have put Marilyn fifteen minutes closer to her job, but it would have meant enduring a gaudier lapse of taste than she had opted for at Brookmist. There were degrees of artificiality, she knew, and each person found his own level.... Above her, a green and white highway sign indicated the Willowglen and Summerstone exits. Surprised as always by its sudden appearance, she wrestled the Nova into an off-ramp lane and heard behind her the inevitable blaring of horns.

Pack it in, she told the driver on her bumper—an expression she had learned from Jane Sidney, one of her employees at the boutique. Pack it in, laddie.

Intent on the traffic light at the end of the off-ramp, conscious too of the wetness under the arms of her pantsuit jacket, Marilyn managed to giggle at the incongruous *feel* of these words. In her rearview mirror she could see the angry features of a modishly long-haired young man squinting at her over the hood of a Le Mans—and it was impossible to imagine herself confronting him, outside their automobiles, with the imperative, "Pack it in, laddie!" Absolutely impossible. All she could do was giggle at the thought and jab nervously at her clutch and brake pedals. Morning traffic—Christmas traffic—was bearable only if you remembered that impatience was a self-punishing sin.

At 8:50 she reached Summerstone and found a parking place near a battery of army-green trash bins. A security guard was passing in mall employees through a second-tier entrance near Montgomery-Ward's: and when Marilyn showed him her ID card, he said almost by way of ritual shibboleth, "Have a good day, Miss Odau." Then, with a host of people to whom she never spoke, she was on the enclosed promenade of machined wooden beams and open carpeted shops. As always, the hour could have been high noon or twelve midnight—there was no way to tell. The season was identifiable only because of the winter merchandise on display and the Christmas decorations suspended overhead or twining like tinfoil helixes through the central shaft of the mall. The smells of ammonia, confectionery goods, and perfumes commingled piquantly, even at this early hour, but Marilyn scarcely noticed.

Managing Creighton's Corner had become her life, the enterprise for which she lived; and because Summerstone

contained Creighton's Corner, she went into it daily with
less philosophical scrutiny than a coal miner gives his
mine. Such speculation, Marilyn knew from thirty-five
years on her own, was worse than useless—it imprisoned
you in doubts and misapprehensions largely of your own
devising. She was glad to be but a few short steps from
Creighton's, glad to feel her funk disintegrating beneath
the prospect of an efficient day at work....

"Good morning, Ms. Odau," Jane Sidney said as she
entered Creighton's.

"Good morning. You look nice today."

The girl was wearing a green and gold jersey, a kind of
gaucho skirt of imitation leather, and suede boots. Her
hair was not much longer than a military cadet's. She
always pronounced "Ms." as a muted buzz—either out of
feminist conviction or, more likely, her fear that "Miss"
would betray her more-than-middle-aged superior as
unmarried...as if that were a shameful thing in one of
Marilyn's generation. Only Cissy Campbell of the three
girls who worked in the boutique could address her as
"Miss Odau" without looking flustered. Or maybe
Marilyn imagined this. She didn't try to plumb the
personal feelings of her employees, and they in turn didn't
try to cast her in the role of a mother confessor. They liked
her well enough, though. Everyone got along.

"I'm working for Cissy until three, Ms. Odau. We've
traded shifts. Is that all right?" Jane followed her toward
her office.

"Of course it is. What about Terri?"

The walls were mercury-colored mirrors; there were
mirrors overhead. Racks of swirl-patterned jerseys,
erotically tailored jumpsuits, and flamboyant scarves
were reiterated around them like the refrain of a
toothpaste or cola jingle. Macramé baskets with plastic
flowers and exotic bath soaps hung from the ceiling.
Black-light and pop-art posters went in and out of the
walls, even though they never moved—and looking up at
one of them, Marilyn had a vision of Satterwhite's during
the austere days of 1942-43, when the war had begun to
put money in people's pockets for the first time since the
twenties but it was unpatriotic to spend it. She

remembered the Office of Price Administration and ration-stamp booklets. Because of leather shortages, you couldn't have more than two pairs of shoes a year. . . .

Jane was looking at her fixedly.

"I'm sorry, Jane. I didn't hear you."

"I said Terri'll be here at twelve, but she wants to work all day tomorrow too, if that's okay. There aren't any Tuesday classes at City College, and she wants to get in as many hours at she can before final exams come up." Terri was still relatively new to the boutique.

"Of course, that's fine. Won't you be here too?"

"Yes, ma'am. In the afternoon."

"Okay, good. . . . I've got some order forms to look over and a letter or two to write." She excused herself and went behind a tie-dyed curtain into an office as plain and practical as Creighton's decor was peacockish and orgiastic. She sat down to a small metal filing cabinet with an audible moan—a moan at odds with the satisfaction she felt in getting down to work. What was wrong with her? She knew, she knew, dear God wasn't she perfectly aware. . . . Marilyn pulled her gloves off. As her fingers went to the onionskin order forms and bills of lading in her files, she was surprised by the deep oxblood color of her nails. Why? She had worn this polish for a week, since well before Thanksgiving. . . .

The answer of course was Maggie Hood. During the war Marilyn and Maggie had roomed together in a clapboard house not far from Satterwhite's, a house with two poplars in the small front yard but not a single blade of grass. Maggie had worked for the telephone company (an irony, since they had no phone in their house) and she always wore oxblood nail polish. Several months before the Axis surrender, Maggie married a 4-F telephone-company official and moved to Mobile. The little house on Greenbriar Street was torn down during the mid-fifties to make way for an office building. Maggie Hood and oxblood nail polish—

Recollections that skirted the heart of the matter, Marilyn knew. She shook them off and got down to business.

Tasteful rock was playing in the boutique, something

from Stevie Wonder's *Songs in the Key of Life*—Jane had flipped the music on. Through it, Marilyn could hear the morning herds passing along the concourses and interior bridges of Summerstone. Sometimes it seemed that half the population of the state was out there. Twice the previous Christmas season the structural vibrations had become so worrisome that security guards were ordered to keep new shoppers out until enough people had left to avert the danger of collapse. That was the rumor, anyway, and Marilyn almost believed it. Summerstone's several owners, on the other hand, claimed that the doors had been locked simply to minimize crowding. But how many times did sane business people turn away customers solely to "minimize crowding?"

Marilyn helped Jane wait on shoppers until noon. Then Terri Bready arrived, and she went back to her office. Instead of eating she checked outstanding accounts and sought to square away records. She kept her mind wholly occupied with the minutiae of running her business for its semi-retired owners, Charlie and Agnes Creighton. It didn't bother her at all that they were ten years younger than she, absentee landlords with a condominium apartment on the gulf coast. She did a good job for them, working evenings as well as lunch hours, and the Creightons were smart enough to realize her worth. They trusted her completely and paid her well.

At one o'clock Terri Bready stepped through Marilyn's curtain and made an apologetic noise in her throat.

"Hey, Terri. What is it?"

"There's a salesman out here who'd like to see you." Bending a business card between her thumb and forefinger, the girl gave an odd baritone chuckle. Tawny-haired and lean, she was a freshman drama major who made the most fashionable clothes look like off-the-racks from a Salvation Army outlet. But she was sweet—so sweet that Marilyn had been embarrassed to hear her discussing with Cissy Campbell the boy with whom she was living.

"Is he someone we regularly buy from, Terri?"

"I don't know. I don't know who we buy from."

"Is that his card?"

"Yeah, it is."

"Why don't you let me see it, then?"

"Oh. Okay. Sorry, Ms. Odau. Here." Trying to hand it over, the girl popped the card out of her fingers; it struck Marilyn's chest and fluttered into her lap. "Sorry again. Sheesh, I really am." Terri chuckled her baritone chuckle, and Marilyn, smiling briefly, retrieved the card.

It said: *Nicholas Anson/Products Consultant & Sales Representative/Latter-Day Novelties/Los Angeles, California.* Also on the card were two telephone numbers and a zip code.

Terri Bready wet her lips and her tongue. "He's a hunk, Ms. Odau, I'm not kidding you—he's as pretty as a naked Swede."

"Is that right? How old?"

"Oh, he's too old for me. He's got to be in his thirties at least."

"Decrepit, dear."

"Oh, he's not decrepit, any. But I'm out of the market. You know."

"Off the auction block?"

"Yes, ma'am. Yeah."

"What's he selling? We don't often work through independent dealers—the Creightons don't, that is—and I've never heard of this firm."

"Jane says she thinks he's been hitting the stores up and down the mall for the last couple of days. Don't know what he's pushing. He's got a samples case, though—and really the most incredible kiss-me eyes."

"If he's been here two days, I'm surprised he hasn't already sold those."

"Do you want me to send him back? He's too polite to burst in. He's been calling Jane and me 'Ms. Sidney' and 'Ms. Bready,' like that."

"Don't send him back yet." Marilyn had a premonition, almost a fear. "Let me take a look at him first."

Terri Bready barked a laugh and had to cover her mouth. "Hey, Ms. Odau, I wouldn't talk him up like

Robert Redford and then send you a bald frog. I mean, why would I?"

"Go on, Terri. I'll talk to him in a couple of minutes."

"Yeah. Okay." The girl was quickly gone, and at the curtain's edge Marilyn looked out. Jane was waiting on a heavyset woman in a fire-engine-red pantsuit, and just inside the boutique's open threshold the man named Nicholas Anson was watching the crowds and counter-crowds work through each other like grim armies.

Anson's hair was modishly long, and he reminded Marilyn a bit of the man who had grimaced at her on the off-ramp. Then, however, the sun had been ricocheting off windshields, grilles, and hood ornaments, and any real identification of the man in the Le Mans with this composed sales representative was impossible, if not downright pointless. A person in an automobile was not the same person you met on common ground.... Now Terri was approaching this Anson fellow, and he was turning toward the girl.

Marilyn Odau felt her fingers tighten on the curtain. Already she had taken in the man's navy blue leisure jacket and, beneath it, his silky shirt the color and pattern of a cumulus-filled sky. Already she had noted the length and the sun-flecked blondness of his hair, the etched-out quality of his profile.... But when he turned, the only thing apparent to her was Anson's resemblance to a dead marine named Jordan Burk, even though he was older than Jordan had lived to be. Ten or twelve years older, at the very least. Jordan Burk had died at twenty-four taking an amphibious tractor ashore at Betio, a tiny island near Tarawa Atoll in the Gilbert Islands. Nicholas Anson, however, had crow's-feet at the corners of his eyes and glints of silver in his sideburns. These things didn't matter much—the resemblance was still a heartbreaking one, and Marilyn found that she was staring at Anson like a starstruck teenager. She let the curtain fall.

This has happened before, she told herself. In a world of four billion people, over a period of thirty-five years, it isn't surprising that you should encounter two or more young men who look like each other. For God's sake,

Odau, don't go to pieces over the sight of still another man who reminds you of Jordan—a stranger from Los Angeles who in just a couple of years is going to be old enough to be the *father* of your forever-twenty-four Jordan darling.

It's the season, Marilyn protested, answering her relentlessly rational self. It's especially cruel that this should happen now.

It happens all the time. You're just more susceptible at this time of year. Odau, you haven't outgrown what amounts to a basically childish syndrome, and it's beginning to look as if you never will.

Old enough in just a couple of years to be Jordan's father? He's old enough right now to be Jordan's and my child. *Our* child.

Marilyn could feel tears welling up from some ancient spring; susceptible, she had an unexpected mental glimpse of the upstairs bedroom in her Brookmist townhouse, the bedroom next to hers, the bedroom she had made a sort of shrine. In its corner, a white wicker bassinet—

That's enough, Odau!

"That's enough!" she said aloud, clenching a fist at her throat.

The curtain drew back, and she was again face to face with Terri Bready. "I'm sorry, Ms. Odau. You talkin' to me?"

"No, Terri. To myself."

"He's a neat fella, really. Says he played drums for a rock band in Haight-Ashbury once upon a time. Says he was one of the original hippies. He's been straight since Nixon resigned, he says—his faith was restored.... Whyn't you talk to him, Ms. Odau? Even if you don't place an order with him, he's an interesting person to talk to. Really. He says he's heard good things about you from the other managers on the mall. He thinks our place is just the sort of place to handle one of his products."

"I bet he does. You certainly got a lot out of him in the short time he's been here."

"Yeah. All my doing, too. I thought maybe, being from Los Angeles, he knew somebody in Hollywood. I sorta told him I was a drama major. You know.... Let me send him back, okay?"

"All right. Send him back."

Marilyn sat down at her desk. Almost immediately Nicholas Anson came through the curtain with his samples case. They exchanged polite greetings, and she was struck again by his resemblance to Jordan. Seeing him at close range didn't dispel the illusion of an older Jordan Burk, but intensified it. This was the reverse of the way it usually happened, and when he put his case on her desk, she had to resist a real urge to reach out and touch his hand.

No wonder Terri had been snowed. Anson's presence was a mature and amiable one, faintly sexual in its undertones. Haight-Ashbury? No, that was wrong. Marilyn couldn't imagine this man among Jesus freaks and flower children, begging small change, the ankles of his grubby blue jeans frayed above a pair of falling-to-pieces sandals. Altogether wrong. Thank God, he had found his calling. He seemed born to move gracefully among boutiques and front-line department stores, making recommendations, giving of his smile. Was it possible that he had once turned his gaunt young face upward to the beacon of a strobe and howled his heart out to the rhythms of his own acid drumming? Probably. A great many things had changed since the sixties....

"You're quite far afield," Marilyn said, to be saying something. "I've never heard of Latter-Day Novelties."

"It's a consortium of independent business people and manufacturers," Anson responded. "We're trying to expand our markets, go nation-wide. I'm not really used to acting as—what does it say on my card?—a sales representative. My first job—my real love—is being a products consultant. If your company is a novelties company, it has to have novelties, products that are new and appealing and unusual. Prior to coming East on this trip, my principal responsibility was making product suggestions. That seems to be my forte, and that's what I really like to do."

"Well, I think you'll be an able enough sales representative too."

"Thank you, Miss Odau. Still, I always feel a little hesitation opening this case and going to bat for what it contains. There's an element of egotism in going out and pushing your own brainchildren on the world."

"There's an element of egotism in almost every human enterprise. I don't think you need to worry."

"I suppose not."

"Why don't you show me what you have?"

Nicholas Anson undid the catches on his case. "I've only brought you a single product. It was my judgment you wouldn't be interested in celebrity T-shirts, cartoon-character paperweights—products of that nature. Have I judged fairly, Miss Odau?"

"We've sold novelty T-shirts and jerseys, Mr. Anson, but the others sound like gift-shop gim-cracks and we don't ordinarily stock that sort of thing. Clothing, cosmetics, toiletries, a few handicraft or decorator items if they correlate well with the Creightons' image of their franchise."

"Okay." Anson removed a glossy cardboard package from his case and handed it across the desk to Marilyn. The kit was blue and white, with two triangular windows in the cardboard. Elegant longhand lettering on the package spelled out the words *Liquid Sheers*. Through one of the triangular windows she could see a bottle of mahogany-colored liquid, a small foil tray, and a short bristled brush with a grip on its back; through the other window was visible an array of colored pencils.

"'Liquid Sheers?'"

"Yes, ma'am. The idea struck me only about a month ago, I drew up a marketing prospectus, and the Latter-Day consortium rushed the concept into production so quickly that the product's already selling quite well in a number of West Coast boutiques. Speed is one of the keynotes of our company's early success. By cutting down the elapsed time between concept-visualization and actual manufacture of the product, we've been able to stay ahead of most of our California competitors.... If you like Liquid Sheers, we have the means to keep you in a good supply."

Marilyn was reading the instructions on the kit. Her attention refused to stay fixed on the words and they kept slipping away from her. Anson's matter-of-fact monologue about his company's business practices didn't help her concentration. She gave up and set the package down.

"But what are... these Liquid Sheers?"

"They're a novel substitute—a decorator substitute—for pantyhose or nylons, Miss Odau. A woman mixes a small amount of the Liquid Sheer solution with water and rubs or paints it on her legs. The pencils can be used to draw on seams or color in some of the applicator designs we've included in the kit—butterflies, flowers, that sort of thing. Placement's up to the individual.... We have kits for dark- as well as light-complexioned women, and the application process takes much less time than you might expect. It's fun too, some of our products-testers have told us. Several boutiques have even reported increased sales of shorts, abbreviated skirts, and short culotte outfits once they began stocking Liquid Sheers. This, I ought to add, right here at the beginning of winter." Anson stopped, his spiel dutifully completed and his smile expectant.

"They're bottled stockings," Marilyn said.

"Yes, ma'am. I suppose you could phrase it that way."

"We sold something very like this at Satterwhite's during the war," Marilyn went on, careful not to look at Anson. "Without the design doodads and the different colored pencils, at any rate. Women painted on their stockings and set the seams with mascara pencils."

Anson laughed. "To tell you the truth, Miss Odau, that's where I got part of my original idea. I rummage old mail-order catalogues and the ads in old magazines. Of course, Liquid Sheers also derive a little from the body-painting fad of the sixties—but in our advertising we plan to lay heavy stress on their affinity to the World War era."

"Why?"

"Nostalgia sells. Girls who don't know World War II from the Peloponnesian War—girls who've worn seamless stockings all their lives, if they've worn stockings at all—are painting on Liquid Sheers and setting grease-pencil seams because they've seen Lauren Bacall and Ann Sheridan in Bogart film revivals and it makes them feel vaguely heroic. It's amazing, Miss Odau. In the last few years we've had sales and entertainment booms featuring nostalgia for the twenties, the thirties, the fifties, and the sixties. The forties—if you except Bogart—have been pretty much bypassed, and Liquid sheers purposely play to that era while recalling some of the art-deco creations of the Beatles period too."

Marilyn met Anson's gaze and refused to fall back from it. "Maybe the forties have been 'pretty much bypassed' because it's hard to recall World War II with unfettered joy."

"I don't really buy that," Anson replied, earnest and undismayed. "The twenties gave us Harding and Coolidge, the thirties the Great Depression, the fifties the Cold War, and the sixties Vietnam. There's no accounting what people are going to remember with fondness—but I can assure you that Liquid Sheers are doing well in California."

Marilyn pushed her chair back on its coasters and stood up. "I sold bottled stockings, Mr. Anson. I painted them on my legs. You couldn't *pay* me to use a product like that again—even with colored pencils and butterflies thrown in gratis."

Seemingly out of deference to her Anson also stood. "Oh, no, Miss Odau—I wouldn't expect you to. This is a product aimed at adolescent girls and post-adolescent young women. We fully realize it's a fad product. We expect booming sales for a year and then a rapid tapering off. But it won't matter—our overhead on Liquid Sheers is low and when sales have bottomed out we'll drop 'em and move on to something else. You understand the transience of items like this."

"Mr. Anson, do you know why bottled stockings existed at all during the Second World War?"

"Yes, ma'am. There was a nylon shortage."

"The nylon went into the war effort—parachutes, I don't know what else." She shook her head, trying to remember. "All I know is that you didn't see them as often as you'd been used to. They were an important commodity on the domestic black market, just like alcohol and gasoline and shoes."

Anson's smile was sympathetic, but he seemed to know he was defeated. "I guess you're not interested in Liquid Sheers?"

"I don't see how I could have them on my shelves, Mr. Anson."

He reached across her desk, picked up the kit he had given her, and dropped it in his samples case. When he snapped its lid down, the reports of the catches were like distant gunshot. "Maybe you'll let me try you with something else, another time."

"You don't have anything else with you?"

"To tell you the truth, I was so certain you'd like these I didn't bring another product along. I've placed Liquid Sheers with another boutique on the first level, though, and sold a few things to gift and novelty stores. Not a complete loss, this trip." He paused at the curtain. "Nice doing business with you, Miss Odau."

"I'll walk you to the front."

Together they stolled through an aisleway of clothes racks and toiletry shelves over a mulberry carpet. Jane and Terri were busy with customers. . . . Why am I being so solicitous? Marilyn asked herself. Anson didn't look a bit broken by her refusal, and Liquid Sheers were definitely offensive to her—she wanted nothing to do with them. Still, any rejection was an intimation of failure, and Marilyn knew how this young man must feel. It was a shame her visitor would have to plunge himself back into the mall's motivelessly surging bodies on a note, however small, of defeat. He would be lost to her, borne to oblivion on the tide. . . .

"I'm sorry, Jordan," she said. "Please do try us again with something else."

The man beside her flinched and cocked his head. "You called me Jordan, Miss Odau."

Marilyn covered the lower portion of her face with her

hand. She spread her fingers and spoke through them. "Forgive me." She dropped her hand. "Actually, I'm surprised it didn't happen before now. You look very much like someone I once knew. The resemblance is uncanny."

"You did say Jordan, didn't you?"

"Yes, I guess I did—that was his name."

"Ah." Anson seemed on the verge of some further comment but all he came out with was, "Goodbye, Miss Odau. Hope you have a good Christmas season," after which he set himself adrift and disappeared in the crowd.

The tinfoil decorations in the mall's central shaft were like columns of a strange scarlet coral, and Marilyn studied them intently until Terri Bready spoke her name and returned her to the present. She didn't leave the boutique until ten that evening.

Tuesday, ten minutes before noon.

He wore the same navy blue leisure jacket, with an open collar shirt of gentle beige and bold indigo. He carried no samples case, and speaking with Cissy Campbell and then Terri, he seemed from the vantage of Marilyn's office, her curtain partially drawn back, less certain of his ground. Marilyn knew a similar uncertainty—Anson's presence seemed ominous, a challenge. She put a hand to her hair, then rose and went through the shop to meet him.

"You didn't bring me something else to look at, did you?"

"No; no, I didn't." He revealed his empty hand. "I didn't come on business at all... unless. . . ." He let his voice trail away. "You haven't changed your mind about Liquid Sheers, have you?"

This surprised her. Marilyn could hear the stiffness in her voice. "I'm afraid I haven't."

Anson waved a hand. "Please forget that. I shouldn't have brought it up—because I *didn't* come on business." He raised his palm, like a Boy Scout pledging his honor. "I was hoping you'd have lunch with me."

"Why?"

"Because you seem *simpático*—that's the Spanish

word for the quality you have. And it would be nice to sit down and talk with someone congenial about something other than Latter-Day Novelties. I've been on the road a week."

Out of the corner of her eye she could see Terri Bready straining to interpret her response to this proposal. Cissy Campbell, Marilyn's black clerk, had stopped racking a new supply of puff-sleeved blouses, and Marilyn had a glimpse of orange eyeliner and iridescent lipstick—the girl's face was that of an alert and self-confident panther.

"I don't usually eat lunch, Mr. Anson."

"Make an exception today. Not a word about business, I promise you."

"Go with him," Terri urged from the cash computer. "Cissy and I can take care of things here, Ms. Odau." Then she chuckled.

"Excellent advice," Anson said. "If I were you, I'd take it."

"Okay," Marilyn agreed. "So long as we don't leave Summerstone and don't stay gone too long. Let me get my bag."

Inevitably, they ended up at the McDonalds' downstairs—yellow and orange wall paneling, trash bins covered with wood-grained contact paper, rows of people six and seven deep at the shiny metal counters. Marilyn found a table for two and eased herself into one of the attached, scoop-shaped plastic chairs. It took Anson almost fifteen minutes to return with two cheeseburgers and a couple of soft-drinks, which he nearly spilled squeezing his way out of the crowd to their tiny table.

"Thank God for plastic tops. Is it always like this?"

"Worse at Christmas. Aren't there any McDonalds' in Los Angeles?"

"Nothing but. But it's three whole weeks till Christmas. Have these people no piety?"

"None."

"It's the same in Los Angeles."

They ate. While they were eating, Anson asked that she use his first name and she in turn felt obligated to tell him hers. Now they were Marilyn and Nicholas, mother and son on an outing to McDonald's. Except that his attention to her wasn't filial—it was warm and direct, with a wooer's deliberately restrained urgency. His manner reminded her again of Jordan Burk, and at one point she realized that she had heard nothing at all he'd said for the last several minutes. Listen to this man, she cautioned herself. Come back to the here and now. After that, she managed better.

He told her that he'd been born in the East, raised singlehandedly by his mother until her remarriage in the late forties, and, after his new family's removal to Encino, educated entirely on the West Coast. He told her of his abortive career as a rock drummer, his early resistance to the war in Southeast Asia, and his difficulties with the United States military.

"I had no direction at all until my thirty-second birthday, Marilyn. Then I discovered where my talent lay and I haven't looked back since. I tell you, if I had the sixties to do over again—well, I'd gladly do them. I'd finagle myself a place in an Army reserve unit, be a weekend soldier, and get right down to products-consulting on a full-time basis. If I'd done that in '65, I'd probably be retired by now."

"You have plenty of time. You're still young."

"I've just turned thirty-six."

"You look less."

"But not much. Thanks anyway, though—it's nice to hear."

"Did you fight in Vietnam?" Marilyn asked on impulse.

"I *went* there in '68. I don't think you could say I fought. I was one of the oldest enlisted men in my unit, with a history of anti-war activity and draft-card burning. I'm going to tell you something, though—once I got home and turned myself around, I wept when Saigon fell. That's the truth—I wept. Saigon was some city, if you looked at it right."

Mentally counting back, Marilyn realized that Nicholas was the right age to be her and Jordan's child. Exactly.

In early December, 1942, she and Jordan had made their last farewells in the little house on Greenbriar Street.... She attached no shame to his memory, had no regrets about it. The shame had come twenty-six years later—the same year, strangely enough, that Nicholas Anson was reluctantly pulling a tour of duty in Vietnam. The white wicker bassinet in her upstairs shrine was a perpetual reminder of this shame, of her secret monstrousness, and yet she could not dispose of the evidence branding her a freak, if only to herself, for the simple reason that she loved it. She loved it because she had once loved Jordan Burk.... Marilyn put her cheeseburger down. There was no way—no way at all—that she was going to be able to finish eating.

"Are you all right?"

"I need to get back to the boutique."

"Let me take you out to dinner this evening. You can hardly call this a relaxed and unhurried get-together. I'd like to take you somewhere nice. I'd like to buy you a snifter of brandy and a nice rare cut of prime rib."

"Why?"

"You use that word like a stiletto, Marilyn. Why not?"

"Because I don't go out. My work keeps me busy. And there's a discrepancy in our ages that embarrasses me. I don't know whether your motives are commercial, innocently social, or.... Go ahead, then—laugh." She was wadding up the wrapper from her cheeseburger, squeezing the paper tighter and tighter, and she could tell that her face was crimsoning.

"I'm not laughing," Nicholas said. "I don't either— know what my motives are, I mean. Except that they're not blameworthy or unnatural."

"I'd better go." She eased herself out of the underslung plastic chair and draped her bag over her shoulder.

"When can I see you?" His eyes were full of remonstrance and appeal. "The company wants me here another week or so—problems with a delivery. I don't know anyone in this city. I'm living out of a suitcase. And I've never in my life been married, if that's worrying you."

"Maybe I should worry because you haven't."

Nicholas smiled at her, a self-effacing charmer's smile. "When?"

"Wednesdays and Sundays are the only nights I don't work. And tomorrow's Wednesday."

"What time?"

"I don't know," she said distractedly. "Call me. Or come by the boutique. Or don't. Whatever you want."

She stepped into the aisle beside their table and quickly worked her way through the crowd to the capsule-lift outside McDonald's. Her thoughts were jumbled, and she hoped feebly—willing the hope—that Nicholas Anson would simply disappear from her life.

The next morning, before any customers had been admitted to the mall, Marilyn Odau went down to Summerstone's first level and walked past the boutique whose owner had elected to sell Nicholas' Liquid Sheers. The kits were on display in two colorful pyramids just inside the shop's entrance.

That afternoon a leggy, dark-haired girl came into Creighton's Corner to browse, and when she let her fur-trimmed coat fall open Marilyn saw a small magenta rose above her right knee. The girl's winter tan had been rubbed or brushed on, and there were magenta seams going up the backs of her legs. Marilyn didn't like the effect, but she understood that others might not find it unattractive.

At six o'clock Nicholas Anson showed up in sports clothes and an expensive deerskin coat. Jane Sidney and Cissy Campbell left, and Marilyn had a mall attendant draw the shop's movable grating across its entrance. Despite the early Wednesday closing time, people were still milling about as shopkeepers transacted last-minute business or sought to shoo away their last heel-dragging customers. This was the last Wednesday evening before Christmas that Summerstone would be closed.

Marilyn began walking, and Nicholas fell in beside her like an assigned escort at a military ball. "Did you think I wasn't coming?"

"I didn't know. What now?"

"Dinner."

"I'd like to go home first. To freshen up."

"I'll drive you."

"I have a car."

"Lock it and let it sit. This place is about as well guarded as Fort Knox. I've rented a car from the service at the airport."

Marilyn didn't want to see Nicholas Anson's rental car. "Let *yours* sit. You can drive me home in mine." He started to protest. "It's either that or an early goodbye. I worry about my car."

So he drove her to Brookmist in her '68 Nova. The perimeter highway was yellow-grey under its ghostly lamps and the traffic was bewilderingly swift. Twilight had already edged over into evening—a dreary winter evening. The Nova's gears rattled even when Nicholas wasn't touching the stick on the steering column.

"I'm surprised you don't have a newer car. Surely you can afford one."

"I could, I suppose, but I like this one. It's easy on gas, and during the oil embargo I felt quite smart. . . . What's the matter with it?"

"Nothing. It's just that I'd imagined you in a bigger or a sportier one. I shouldn't have said anything." He banged his temple with the heel of his right hand. "I'm sorry, Marilyn."

"Don't apologize. Jane Sidney asked me the same thing one day. I told her that my parents were dirt-poor during the Depression and that as soon as I was able to sock any money away for them, that's what I did. It's a habit I haven't been able to break—even today, with my family dead and no real financial worries."

They rode in silence beneath the haloed lamps on the overpass and the looming grey shadow of Satterwhite's.

"A girl came into the boutique this afternoon wearing Liquid Sheers," Marilyn said. "It does seem your product's selling."

"Hooo," Nicholas replied, laughing mirthlessly. "Just remember that *I* didn't bring that up, okay?"

They left the expressway and drove down several

elm-lined residential streets. The Brookmist complex of townhouses came into the Nova's headlights like a photographic image emerging from a wash of chemicals, everything gauzy and indistinct at first. Marilyn directed Nicholas to the community carport against a brick wall behind one of the rows of houses, and he parked the car. They walked hunch-shouldered in the cold to a tall redwood fence enclosing a concrete patio not much bigger than a phone booth. Marilyn pushed the gate aside, let the latch fall behind them, and put her key into the lock on the kitchen door. Two or three flower pots with drooping, unrecognizable plants in them sat on a peeling windowsill beside the door.

"I suppose you think I could afford a nicer place to live, too."

"No, but you do give yourself a long drive to work."

"This place is paid for, Nicholas. It's mine."

She left him sitting under a table lamp with several old copies of *McCall's* and *Cosmopolitan* in front of him on her stonework coffee table and went upstairs to change clothes. She came back down wearing a long-sleeved black jumpsuit with a peach-colored sweater and a single polished-stone pendant at her throat. The heat had kicked on, and the downstairs was cozily warm.

Nicholas stood up. "You've set things up so that I'm going to have to drive your car and you're going to have to navigate. I hope you'll let me buy the gas."

"Why couldn't I drive and you just sit back and enjoy the ride?" Her voice was tight again, with uneasiness and mild disdain. For a products consultant Nicholas didn't seem quite as imaginative as he ought. Liquid Sheers were a rip-off of an idea born out of necessity during World War II, and the "novelties" he'd mentioned in his spiel on Monday were for the most part variations on the standard fare of gift shops and bookstores. He wasn't even able to envision her doing the driving while he relaxed and played the role of a passenger. And *he* was the one who'd come to maturity during the sixties, that fabled decade of egalitarian upheaval and heightened social awareness. . . .

"The real point, Marilyn, is that I wanted to do

something for *you*. But you've taken the evening out of my hands."

All right, she could see that. She relented. "Nicholas, I'm not trying to stage-manage this—this *date*, if that's what it is. I was surprised that you came by the shop. I wasn't ready. And I'm not ready to go out this evening, either—I'm cold and I'm tired. I have a pair of steaks and a bottle of cold duck in the refrigerator, and enough fixings for a salad. Let me make dinner."

"A *pair* of steaks?"

"There's a grocery store off the perimeter highway that stays open night and day. I stopped there last night after work."

"But you didn't think I'd come by today?"

"No. Not really. And despite buying the steaks, I'm not sure I really wanted you to. I know that sounds backwards somehow but it's the truth."

Nicholas ignored this. "But you'll have to cook. I wanted to spare you that. I wanted to do something *for* you."

"Spare me another trip down the highway in my car and the agony of waiting for service in one of this city's snooty night spots."

He gave in, and she felt kindlier toward him. They ate at the coffee table in the living room, sitting on the floor in their stocking feet and listening to an FM radio station. They talked cursorily about sports and politics and movies, which neither of them was particularly interested in anymore; and then, because they had both staked their lives to it, Marilyn lifted the taboo that Nicholas had promised to observe and they talked business. The didn't talk about Liquid Sheers or profit margins or tax shelters, they talked about the involvement of their feelings with what they were doing and the sense of satisfaction that they derived from their work. That was common ground, and the evening passed—as Jane Sidney might have put it—"like sixty."

They were finishing the bottle of cold duck. Nicholas shifted positions, catching his knees with his right arm and rocking back a little.

"Marilyn?"

"Mmm?"

"You would never have let me drive you over here if I hadn't reminded you of this fellow you once knew, would you? This fellow named Jordan? Tell me the truth. No bet-hedging."

Her uneasiness returned. "I don't know."

"Yes, you do. Your answer won't hurt my feelings. I'd like to think that now that you know me a little better my resemblance to this person doesn't matter anymore—that you like me for myself." He waited.

"Okay, then. You're right."

"I'm right," he echoed her dubiously.

"I wouldn't have let you bring me home if you hadn't looked like Jordan. But now that I know you a little better it doesn't make any difference."

Not much, Marilyn told herself. At least I've stopped putting you in a marine uniform and trimming back the hair over your ears. . . . She felt a quiet tenderness for both men, the dead Jordan and the boyish Nicholas Anson who in many ways seemed younger than Jordan ever had. . . . That's because Jordan was almost three years older than you, Odau, and Nicholas is almost twenty years younger. Think a little.

The young man who resembled Jordan Burk drained his glass and hoisted himself nimbly off the floor.

"I'm staying at the Holiday Inn near the airport," he said. "Let me call a cab so you won't have to get out again."

"Cabs aren't very good about answering night calls anymore. The drivers are afraid to come."

"I hate for you to have to drive me, Marilyn." His look was expectant, and she hated to disappoint him.

"Why don't you just spend the night here?" she said.

They went upstairs together, and she was careful to close the door to the bedroom containing the wicker bassinet before following him into her own. They undressed in the greenish light sifting through the curtains from the arc lamp in the elm trees. Her heart raced. Then his body covered its beating, and afterwards she lay staring wide-eyed and bemused at her acoustic ceiling panels as he slept beside her with a hand on her hip. Then she fell asleep too, and woke when her sleeping mind noted that his hand was gone, and sat up to discover that Nicholas was no longer there. The wind in the leafless elms was making a noise like angry surf.

"Nick!" she called.

He didn't answer.

She swung her feet to the carpet, put on her gown, and found him standing in a pair of plaid boxer shorts beside the wicker bassinet. He had put on a desk lamp, and its glow made a pool of light that contained and illuminated everything in that corner of the room. There was no doubt that he had discovered the proof of her monstrousness there, even if he didn't know what it meant.

Instead of screaming or flying at him like a drunken doxy, she sank to the floor in the billow of her dressing gown, shamefully conscious of her restraint and too well satisfied by Nicholas' snooping to be shocked by it. If she hadn't wanted this to happen, she would never have let him come. Or she would have murdered Nicholas in the numb sleep of his fulfillment. Any number of things. But this was what she had wanted.

Confession and surcease.

"I was looking for the bathroom," Nicholas said. "I didn't know where the upstairs bathroom was. But when I saw the baby bed.... well, I didn't know why you'd have a baby bed and—" He broke off.

"Don't explain, Nicholas." She gave him an up-from-under look and wondered what her own appearance must suggest. Age, promiscuousness, dissolution? You grew old, that you couldn't stop. But the others...those were lies. She wanted confession and surcease, that was all, and he was too intent on the bassinet to escape giving them to her, too intent to see how downright *old* she could look at two in the morning. Consumed by years. Consumed by that which life itself is nourished by. Just one of a world of consumer goods.

Nicholas lifted something from the bassinet. He held it

in the palm of one hand. "What is this?" he asked. "Marilyn . . . ?"

"Lithopedion," she said numbly. "The medical term is lithopedion. And lithopedion is the word I use when I want to put myself at a distance from it. With you here, that's what I think I want to do—put myself at a distance from it. I don't know. Do you understand?"

He stared at her blankly.

"It means stone child, Nicholas. I was delivered of it during the first week of December, 1968. A petrified fetus."

"Delivered of it?"

"That's wrong. I don't know why I say that. It was removed surgically, cut from my abdominal cavity. Lithopedion." Finally she began to cry. "Bring him to me."

The unfamiliar man across from her didn't move. He held the stone child questioningly on his naked palm.

"Damn it, Nicholas, I asked you to bring him to me! He's mine! Bring him here!"

She put a fist to one of her eyes and drew it away to find black makeup on the back of her hand. Anson brought her the lithopedion, and she cradled it against the flimsy bodice of her dressing gown. A male child, calcified, with a tiny hand to the side of its face and its eyes forever shut; a fossil before it had ever really begun to live.

"This is Jordan's son," Marilyn told Anson, who was still standing over her. "Jordan's and mine."

"But how could that be? He died during the Pacific campaign."

Marilyn took no notice of either the disbelief in Anson's voice or his unaccountable knowledge of the circumstances of Jordan's death. "We had a honeymoon in the house on Greenbriar while Maggie was off for Christmas," she said, cradling her son. "Then Jordan had to return to his Division. In late March of '43 I collapsed while I was clerking at Satterwhite's. I was stricken with terrible cramps and I collapsed. Maggie drove me home to Greenville, and I was treated for intestinal flu. That was the diagnosis of a local doctor. I was in a coma for a while.

I had to be forcibly fed. But after a while I got well again, and the manager of the notions department at Satterwhite's let me have my job back. I came back to the city."

"And twenty-five years later you had your baby?"

Even the nastiness that Anson imparted to this question failed to dismay her. "Yes. It was an ectopic pregnancy. The fetus grew not in my womb, you see, but in the right Fallopian tube—where there isn't much room for it to grow. I didn't know, I didn't suspect anything. There were no signs."

"Until you collapsed at Satterwhite's?"

"Dr. Rule says that was the fetus bursting the Fallopian tube and escaping into the abdominal cavity. I didn't know. I was twenty years old. It was diagnosed as flu, and they put me to bed. I had a terrible time. I almost died. Later in the year, just before Thanksgiving, Jordan was killed at Tarawa, and I wished that I had died before him."

"He never lived to see his son," Anson said bitterly.

"No. I was frightened of doctors. I'm still frightened by them. But in 1965 I went to work for the Creightons at Capitol Square, and when I began having severe pains in my side a couple of years later, they *made* me go to Dr. Rule. They told me I'd have to give up my job if I didn't go." Marilyn brought a fold of her nightgown around the calcified infant in her arms. "He discovered what was wrong. He delivered my baby. A lithopedion, he said. . . . Do you know that there've been only a few hundred of them in all recorded history? That makes me a freak, all my love at the beck and call of a father and son who'll never be able to hear me." Marilyn's shoulders began to heave and her mouth fell slack to let the sounds of her grief work clear. "A freak," she repeated, sobbing.

"No more a freak than that thing's father."

She caught Anson's tone and turned her eyes up to see his face through a blur of tears.

"Its father was Jordan Burk," Anson told her. "My father was Jordan Burk. He even went so far as to *marry* my mother, Miss Odau. But when he discovered she was pregnant, he deserted her to enlist in a Division bound for combat. And he came here first and found another pretty piece to slip it to before he left. You."

"No," Marilyn said, her sobs suddenly stilled.

"Yes. My mother found Burk in this city and asked him to come back to her. He pleaded his overmastering love for another woman and refused. *I* was no enticement at all—I was an argument for remaining with you. Once during her futile visit here Burk took my mother into Satterwhite's by a side-street entrance and pointed you out to her from one of the mezzanines. The 'other woman' was prettier than she was, my mother said. She gave up and returned home. She permitted Burk to divorce her without alimony while he was in the Pacific. Don't ask me why. I don't know. Later my mother married a man named Samuel Anson and we moved with him to California. . . . That thing in your arms, Miss Odau, is my half-brother."

It was impossible to cry now. Marilyn could hear her voice growing shrill and accusative. "That's why you asked me to lunch yesterday, isn't it? And why you asked me to dinner this evening. A chance for revenge. A chance to defile a memory you could have easily left untouched." She slapped Anson across the thigh, harmlessly. "I didn't know anything about your mother or you! I never suspected and I wasn't responsible! I'm not that kind of freak! Why have you set out to destroy both me and one of the few things in my life I've truly been able to cherish? Why do you turn on me with a nasty 'truth' that doesn't have any significance for me and never can? What kind of vindictive jackal are you?"

Anson looked bewildered. He dropped onto his knees in front of her and tried to grip her shoulders. She shook his hands away.

"Marilyn, I'm sorry. I asked you to lunch because you called me Jordan, just like you let me drive you home because I resembled him."

"'Marilyn?' What happened to 'Miss Odau?'"

"Never mind that." He tried to grip her shoulders again, and she shook him off. "Is my crime greater than yours? If I've spoiled your memory of the man who fathered me, it's because of the bitterness I've carried against him for as long as I can remember. My intention wasn't to hurt you. The 'other woman' that my mother always used to talk about, even after she married Anson, has always been an abstract to me. Revenge wasn't my motive. Curiosity, maybe. But not revenge. Please believe me."

"You have no imagination, Nicholas."

He looked at her searchingly. "What does that mean?"

"It means that if you'd only. . . . Why should I explain this to you? I want you to get dressed and take my car and drive back to your motel. You can drop it off at Summerstone tomorrow when you come to get your rental car. Give the keys to one of the girls, I don't want to see you."

"Out into the cold, huh?"

"Please go, Nicholas. I might resort to screaming if you don't."

He rose, went into the other room, and a few minutes later descended the carpeted stairs without saying a word. Marilyn heard the flaring of her Nova's engine and a faint grinding of gears. After that, she heard nothing but the wind in the skeletal elm trees.

Without rising from the floor in her second upstairs bedroom, she sang a lullaby to the fossil child in her arms. "Dapples and greys," she crooned. "Pintos and bays, / All the pretty little horses. . . ."

It was almost seven o'clock of the following evening before Anson returned her key case to Cissy Campbell at the cash computer up front. Marilyn didn't hear him or see him, and she was happy that she had been in her office when he at last came by. The episode was over. She hoped that she never saw Anson again, even if he was truly Jordan's son—and she believed that Anson understood her wishes.

Four hours later she pulled into the carport at Brookmist and crossed the parking lot to her small patio. The redwood gate was standing open. She pulled it shut behind her and set its latch. Then, inside, she felt briefly on the verge of swooning because there was an odor in the air like that of a man's cologne, a fragrance Anson had worn. For a moment she considered running back onto the patio and shouting for assistance. If Anson was upstairs waiting for her, she'd be a fool to go up there alone. She'd be a fool to go up there at all. Who could read the mind of an enigma like Anson?

He's not up there waiting for you, Marilyn told herself. He's been here and gone.

But why?

Your baby, Marilyn—see to your baby. Who knows what Anson might have done for spite? Who knows what sick destruction he might have—

"Oh, God!" Marilyn cried aloud. She ran up the stairs unmindful of the intensifying smell of cologne and threw the door to her second bedroom open. The wicker bassinet was not in its corner but in the very center of the room. She ran to it and clutched its side, very nearly tipping it over.

Unharmed, her and Jordan's tiny child lay on the satin bolster she had made for him.

Marilyn stood over the baby trying to catch her breath. Then she moved his bed back into the corner where it belonged. Not until the following morning was the smell of that musky cologne dissipated enough for her to forget that Anson—or someone—had been in her house. Because she had no evidence of theft, she rationalized that the odor had drifted into her apartment through the ventilation system from the townhouse next to hers.

The fact the the bassinet had been moved she conveniently put out of her mind.

Two weeks passed. Business at Creighton's Corner Boutique was brisk, and if Marilyn thought of Nicholas Anson at all, it was to console herself with the thought that by now he was back in Los Angeles. A continent away. But on the last weekend before Christmas, Jane Sidney told Marilyn that she thought she had seen Anson going through the center of one of Summerstone's largest department stores carrying his samples case. He looked tan and happy, Jane said.

"Good. But if he shows up here, I'm not in. If I'm waiting on a customer and he comes by, you or Terri will have to take over for me. Do you understand?"

"Yes, ma'am."

But later that afternoon the telephone in her office rang, and when she answered it, the voice coming through the receiver was Anson's.

"Don't hang up, Miss Odau. I knew you wouldn't see me in person, so I've been reduced to telephoning."

"What do you want?"

"Take a walk down the mall toward Davner's. Take a walk down the mall and meet me there."

"Why should I do that? I thought that's why you phoned."

Anson hung up.

You can wait forever, then, she told him. The phone didn't ring again, and she busied herself with the onion-skin order forms and bills of lading. It was hard to pay attention to them, though.

At last she got up and told Jane she was going to stroll down the mall to stretch her legs. The crowd was shoulder to shoulder. She saw old people being pushed along in wheelchairs and, as if they were dogs or monkeys, small children in leather harnesses. There were girls whose legs had been painted with Liquid Sheers, and young men in Russian hats and low-heeled shoes who made no secret of their appreciation of these girls' legs. The benches lining the shaft at the center of the promenade were all occupied, and the people sitting on them looked fatigued and irritable.

A hundred or so yards ahead of her, in front of the jewelry store called Davner's, there was a Santa Claus and a live reindeer.

She kept walking.

An odd display caught Marilyn's eye. She did a double-take and halted amid the traffic surging in both directions around her.

"Hey," a man said. He shoved past.

The shop window to her right was lined with eight or ten chalk-white effigies not much longer than her hand. They were eyeless. A small light played on them like the revolving blue strobe on a police vehicle. A sign in the window said: *Stone Children for Christmas, from Latter-Day Novelties*. Marilyn put a hand to her mouth and made a gagging sound that no one else on the mall paid any mind. She spun around. It seemed that Summerstone itself was swaying under her. Across from the gift shop, on one of the display cases of the bookstore located there, were a dozen more of these minute statuettes. Tiny figures, tiny feet, tiny eyeless faces. She looked down the collapsing mall and saw still another window displaying replicas of her and Jordan's baby. And in the windows that they weren't displayed, they were endlessly reflected.

Tiny fingers, tiny feet, tiny eyeless faces.

"Anson!" Marilyn shouted hoarsely, trying to find something to hang on to. "Anson, God damn you! God *damn* you!" She rushed on the gift-shop window and broke it with her fists. Then, not knowing what else to do, she withdrew her hands—with their worn oxblood nail polish—and held them bleeding above her head. A woman screamed, and the crowd fell back from her aghast.

In front of Davner's, only three or four stores away now, Nicholas Anson was stroking the head of the live reindeer. When he saw Marilyn, he gave her a friendly boyish smile.

The Man Who Was
Heavily into Revenge
by Harlan Ellison

Harlan Ellison steadfastly contends that his stories aren't science fiction, and with a few exceptions he is of course quite correct. Even when he appears in such a "hard-core" science fiction magazine as Analog, *as he did with the story below, he's usually writing pure fantasy. (Sometimes he may use a few words that have the ring of science, which serves the purpose of allowing a science fiction editor to feel more comfortable in running his latest fantasy.)*

Labels aren't important to Ellison; he prefers to be known simply as a writer. And he is certainly that.

William Weisel pronounced his name why-*zell*, but many of the unfortunates for whom he had done remodeling and construction pronounced it *weasel*.

He had designed and built a new guest bathroom for Fred Tolliver, a man in his early sixties who had retired from the active life of a studio musician with the foolish belief that his fifteen thousand dollar-per-year annuity would sustain him in comfort. Weisel had snubbed the original specs on the job, had substituted inferior materials for those required by the codes, had used cheap Japanese pipe instead of galvanized or stressed plastic, had eschewed lath and plaster for wallboard that left lumpy seams, had skirted union wages by ferrying in green card workers from Tijuana every morning by dawn light, had—in short—done a spectacularly crummy job on Fred Tolliver's guest bathroom. That was the first mistake.

And for all of this ghastly workmanship, Weisel had overcharged Fred Tolliver by nine thousand dollars. That was the second mistake.

Fred Tolliver called William Weisel. His tone was soft and almost apologetic. Fred Tolliver was a gentle man, not given to fits of pique or demonstrations of anger. He asked Weisel politely to return and set matters to rights. William Weisel laughed at Fred Tolliver and told him that he had lived up to the letter of the original contract, that he would do nothing. That was the third mistake.

Putatively, what Weisel said was true. Building inspectors had been greased and the job had been signed off: legal according to the building codes. Legally, William Weisel was in the clear; no suit could be brought. Ethically it was a different matter. But even threats of revocation of license could not touch him.

Nonetheless, Fred Tolliver had a rotten guest bathroom, filled with leaks and seamed walls that were already cracking and bubbles in the linoleum from what was certainly a break in the hot water line and pipes that clanked when the faucets were turned on, if they could *be* turned on.

Fred Tolliver asked for repairs more than once.

After a while, William Weisel's wife, Belle, who often acted as his secretary, to save a few bucks when they didn't want to hire a Kelly Girl, would not put through the calls.

Fred Tolliver told her, softly and politely, "Please convey to Mr. Weisel—" and he pronounced it why-*zell*, "—my feelings of annoyance. Please advise him that I won't stand for it. This is an awful thing he's done to me. It's not fair, it's not right."

She was chewing gum. She examined her nails. She had heard this all before: married to Weisel for eleven years: all of this, many times. "Lissen, Mistuh Tollivah, whaddaya want *me* to do about it, *I* can't do nothing about it, y'know. I only work here. I c'n tell 'im, that's *all* I c'n do, is tell 'im you called again."

"But you're his wife! You can see how he's robbed me!"

"Lissen, Mistuh Tollivah, I don't haveta lissen to this!"

It was the cavalier tone, the utterly uncaring tone: impertinent, rude, dismissing him as if he were a crank, a weirdo, as if he weren't asking only for what was due him. It was like a goad to an already maddened bull.

"This isn't fair!"

"I'll tell 'im, I'll tell 'im. Jeezus, I'm hanging up now."

"I'll get even! I will! There has to be justice—"

She dropped the receiver into its rest heavily, cracking her gum with annoyance, looking ceilingward like one massively put-upon. She didn't even bother to convey the message to her husband.

And that was the biggest mistake of all.

The electrons dance. The emotions sing. Four billion, resonating like insects. The hive mind of the masses. The emotional gestalt. The charge builds and builds, surging down the line seeking a focus. A weakest link through which to discharge itself. Why this focus and not that? Chance, proximity, the tiniest fracture for leakage. You, I, him, her. Everyman, Anyman; the crap shoot selection is whatever man or woman born of man and woman whose rage at *that* moment is *that* potent.

Everyman: Fred Tolliver. Unknowing confluence.

He pulled up at the pump that dispensed supreme, and let the Rolls idle for a moment before shutting it off. When the attendant leaned in at the window, Weisel smiled around his pipe and said, "Morning, Gene. Fill it up with extra."

"Sorry, Mr. Weisel," Gene said, looking a little sad, "but I can't sell you any gas."

"Why the hell not? You out?"

"No, sir; just got our tanks topped off last night. Still can't sell you any."

"Why the hell not?!"

"Fred Tolliver doesn't want me to."

Weisel stared for a long moment. He couldn't have heard correctly. He'd been gassing up at this station for eleven years. He didn't even know they *knew* that creep Tolliver. "Don't be an asshole, Gene. Fill the damned tank!"

"I'm sorry, sir. No gas for you."

"What the hell is Tolliver to you? A relative or something?"

"No, sir. I never met him. Wouldn't know him if he drove in right now."

"Then what . . . what the hell . . . I—I—"

But nothing he could say would get Gene to pump one liter of gas into the Rolls.

Nor would the attendants at the next *six* stations down the avenue. When the Rolls ran out, a mile from his office, Weisel *almost* had time to pull to the curb. Not quite. He ran dry in the middle of Ventura Boulevard and tried to turn toward the curb, but though traffic had been light around him just a moment before, somehow it was now packing itself bumper-to-bumper. He turned his head wildly this way and that, dumbfounded at how many cars had suddenly pulled onto the boulevard around him. He could not get out of the crunch. It wouldn't have mattered. Improbably, for this non-business area, for the first time in his memory, there were *no* empty parking spaces at the curb.

Cursing foully, he put it in neutral, rolled down the window so he could hold the steering wheel from outside, and got out of the silent Rolls. He slammed the door, cursing Fred Tolliver's every breath, and stepped away from the car. He heard the hideous rending of irreplaceable fabric. His five hundred dollar cashmere suit jacket had been caught in the jamb.

A large piece of lovely fabric, soft as a doe's eye, wondrously ecru - closer - to - beige - than - fawn - colored, tailor-made for him in Paris, his most favorite jacket hung like slaughtered meat from the door. He whimpered; an involuntary sob of pain.

Then: "What the hell is going *on*!" he snarled, loud enough for pedestrians to hear. It was not a question, it was an imprecation. There was no answer; none was required; but there was the sound of thunder far off across the San Fernando Valley. Los Angeles was in the grip of a two-year drought, but there was a menacing buildup of soot-gray clouds over the San Bernardinos.

He reached in through the window, tried to turn the wheel toward the curb, but with the engine off the power steering prevented easy movement. But he strained and strained...and something went snap! in his groin. Incredible pain shot down both legs and he bent double, clutching himself. Flashbulbs went off behind his eyes. He stumbled around in small circles, holding himself awkwardly. Many groans. Much anguish. He leaned against the Rolls, and the pain began to subside; but he had broken something down there. After a few minutes he was able to stand semi-erect. His shirt was drenched with sweat. His deodorant was wearing off. Cars were swerving around the Rolls, honking incessantly, drivers swearing at him. He had to get the Rolls out of the middle of the street.

Still clutching his crotch with one hand, jacket hanging from him in tatters, beginning to smell very bad, William Weisel put his shoulder to the car, grabbed the steering wheel and strained once again; the wheel went around slowly. He readjusted himself, excruciating pain pulsing through his pelvis, put his shoulder against the window post and tried to push the behemoth. He thought of compacts and tiny sports cars. The Rolls moved a fraction of an inch, then slid back.

Sweat trickled into his eyes, making them sting. He huffed and lunged and applied as much pressure as the pain would permit. The car would not move.

He gave up. He needed help. *Help!*

Standing in the street behind the car, clutching his groin, jacket flapping around him, smelling like something ready for disposal, he signaled wildly for assistance with his free hand. But no one would stop. Thunder rolled around the Valley, and Weisel saw what looked like a pitchfork of lightning off across the flats where Van Nuys, Panorama City, and North Hollywood lay gasping for water.

Cars thundered down on him and swerved at the very last moment, like matadors performing a complicated *veronica*. Several cars seemed to speed up, in fact, as they approached him, and he had the crazy impression the drivers were hunched over the wheels, lips skinned back from clenched teeth, like rabid wild things intent on killing him. Several nearly sideswiped him. He barely managed to hobble out of the way. One Datsun came so close that its side-view mirror ripped a nasty, raw gash down the entire right side of the Rolls. He cursed and gesticulated and pleaded. No one would stop. In fact, one fat woman leaned out of her window as her husband zoomed past, and she yelled something nasty. He caught only the word "Tolliver!"

Finally, he just left it there, with the hood up like a mouth of a hungry bird.

He walked the mile to his office, thinking he would call the Automobile Club to come and tow it to a station where it could be filled. He didn't have the time or patience to walk to a gas station, get a can of fuel, and return to fill the tank. During the mile-long walk he even had time to wonder if he would be *able* to buy a can of gasoline.

Tolliver! God *damn* that old man!

There was no one in the office.

It took him a while to discover that fact, because he couldn't get an elevator in his building. He stood in front of one after another of the doors, waiting for a cage to come down, but they all seemed determined to stop at the second floor. Only when other passengers waited, did an elevator arrive, and then he was always in front of the wrong one. He would dash to the open door, just as the others entered, but before he could get his hand into the opening to stop the retarder bar from slamming against the frame, the door would seem to slide faster, as if it possessed a malevolent intelligence. It went on that way for ten minutes, till it became obvious to him that something was terribly, hideously, inexplicably wrong.

So he took the stairs.

(On the stairs he somehow slipped and skinned his right knee as one of the steps caught his heel and tore it off his right shoe.)

Limping like a cripple, the tatters of his jacket flapping around him, clutching his groin, blood seeping through his pants to stain, he reached the eleventh floor and tried to open the door. It was, of course, for the first time in the thirty-five-year history of the building, locked.

He waited fifteen minutes and the door suddenly opened as a secretary, carrying some papers up one flight to the Xerox center, came boiling through. He barely managed to catch the door on its pneumatic closer. He stumbled frantically onto the eleventh floor, and like a man emerging gratefully from a vast desert to find an oasis, he fled down the corridor to the offices of the Weisel Construction Corporation.

There was no one in the office.

It was not locked. Was, in fact, wholly unattended and wide open to thieves, if such had chosen that office for plundering. The receptionist was not there, the estimators were not there, not even Belle, his wife, who served as secretary when he didn't want to hire a Kelly Girl, was there.

However, she had left him a note:

I'm leaving you. By the time you read this I will have already been to the bank and emptied the joint account. Don't try to find me. Goodbye.

Weisel sat down. He had the beginnings of what he was certain was a migraine, though he had never had a migraine in his life. He didn't know whether, in the vernacular of the United States Army, to shit or go blind.

He was not a stupid man. He had been given more than sufficient evidence that something malevolent and purely anti-Weisel was floating across the land. It was out to get him...had, in fact, *already* gotten him...had, in fact, made a well-ordered and extremely comfortable life turn into a nasty, untidy, redolent pile of doggie-doo.

And it was named *Tolliver* .

Fred Tolliver...! How the hell...? Whom does he know that could...? How did he...?

None of the questions reached a conclusion. He could not even formulate them. Clearly, this was insanity. No one he knew, not Gene at the gas station, not the people in the cars, not Belle, not his staff, not the *car door* or the building's *elevators* even knew who Tolliver was! Well, Belle knew, but what the hell did she have to do with *him*?

Okay, so it *wasn't* going so good with Belle. So they

hadn't really reconciled that innocent little thing he'd had with the lab technician at Mt. Sinai. So what? That was no reason for her to ditch a good thing. *Damn that Tolliver!*

He slammed his hand onto the desk, missed slightly, caught the edge and drove a thick splinter of wood into the fat of his palm, at the same time scattering the small stack of telegrams across his lap and the floor.

Wincing with pain, he sucked at the splinter till it came out. He used one of the telegram envelopes to blot the blood from his hand.

Telegrams?

He opened the first one. The Bank of America, Beverly Hills branch 213, was pleased to advise him they were calling due his loans. All five of them. He opened the second one. His broker, Shearson Hayden Stone, Inc., was overjoyed to let him know that all sixteen of the stocks in which he had speculated heavily, on margin, of course, had virtually plummeted off the big board and he had to come up with seventy-seven thousand dollars by noon today or his portfolio was wiped out. It was a quarter to eleven by the wall clock. (Or had it, inexplicably, stopped?) He opened the third one. He had failed his est class and Werner Erhard himself had sent the telegram, adding in what Weisel took to be an unnecessarily gloating tone, that Weisel had "no human potential worth expanding." He opened the fourth one. His Wassermann had come back from Mt. Sinai. It was positive. He opened the fifth one. The Internal Revenue Service was ecstatic at being able to let him know they were planning to audit his returns for the past five years, and were seeking a loophole in the tax laws that permitted them to go back further, possibly to the start of the Bronze Age.

There were others, five or six more. He didn't bother opening them. He didn't want to learn who had died, or that the state of Israel had discovered Weisel was, in actuality, Bruno "The Butcher" Krutzmeier, a former prison guard at Mauthausen, personally responsible for the deaths of three thousand Gypsies, Trade Unionists, Jews, Bolsheviks, and Weimar democrats, or that the U.S. Coast and Geodetic Survey Department was gleefully taking this opportunity to advise him that the precise spot over which he sat was expected to collapse into the magma at the center of the Earth and by the way we've canceled your life insurance.

He let them lie.

The clock on the wall had, to be sure, stopped dead. In fact, the electricity had been turned off.

The phone did not ring. He picked it up. Of course. It—like its friend the clock—was stone dead.

Tolliver! Tolliver! How was he *doing* all this?

Such things simply *do not* happen in an ordered universe of draglines and scoop-shovels and reinforced concrete.

He sat and thought dark, murderous thoughts about that old sonofabitch, Fred Tolliver.

A 747 boomed sonically overhead and the big heavy-plate window of his eleventh floor office cracked, splintered, and fell in around his feet.

Unknowing confluence of resonating emotions, Fred Tolliver sat in his house, head in hands, miserable beyond belief, aware only of pain and anger. His cello lay on its back on the floor beside him. He had tried playing a little today, but all he could think of was that terrible man Weisel, and the terrible bathroom that was filling with water, and the terrible stomach pains his feelings of hatred were giving him.

Electrons resonate. So do emotions.

Speak of "damned places" and one speaks of locations where powerful emotional forces have been penned up. One cannot doubt, if one has ever been inside a prison where the massed feelings of hatred, deprivation, claustrophobia, and brutalization have seeped into the very stones. One can feel it. Emotions resonate: at a political rally, a football game, an encounter group, a rock concert, a lynching.

There are four billion people in the world. A world that has grown so complex and uncaring with systems and brutalization of individuals because of the inertia produced by those systems' perpetuation of self, that merely to live is to be assaulted daily by circumstances.

Electrons dance. The emotions sing. Four billion, resonating like insects. The charge is built up; the surface tension is reached; the limit of elasticity is passed; the charge seeks release; the focus is sought: the weakest link, the fault line, the most frangible element, AnyTolliver, EveryTolliver.

Like the discharge of a lightning bolt, the greater the charge on the Tolliver, the greater its tendency to escape. The force of the four billion driving the electrons in their mad dance away from the region of highest excess toward the region of greatest deficiency. Pain as electromotive force. Frustration as electric potential. The electrons jump the insulating gap of love and friendship and kindness and humane behavior and the power is unleashed.

Like the discharge of the lightning bolt, the power seeks and finds its focus, leaps the gap, and the bolt of energy is unleashed.

Does the lightning rod know it is draining off the dangerous electrical charge? Is there sentience in a Leyden jar? Does not the voltaic pile continue to sleep while current is drawn off? Does the focus know it has unleashed the anger and frustration of the four billion?

Fred Tolliver sat in misery, the cello forgotten, the pain of having been cheated, of being impotent against the injustice, eating at his stomach. His silent scream: at that moment the most dominant in the entire universe. Chance. It could have been anyone; or perhaps, as Chesterton said, "Coincidences are a spiritual sort of puns."

His phone rang. He did not move to pick up the receiver. It rang again. He did not move. His stomach burned and roiled. There was a scorched-earth desperation in him. Nine *thousand* dollars overcharge. Thirty-seven hundred dollars by the original contract. Twelve thousand seven hundred dollars. He had had to take a second mortgage on the house. Five more months than the estimated two Weisel had said it would take to complete the job. Seven months of filth and plaster dust and inept workmen tramping through his little house with mud and dirt and dropping cigarette butts on his floor.

I'm sixty-two years old, he thought, frantically. *My God, I'm an old man. A moment ago I was just middle-aged, and now I'm an old man. . . . I never felt old before. It's good Betsy never lived to see me like this; she would cry. But this thing with the bathroom is a terrible thing, an awful thing, it's made me an old man, poor, in financial straits; and I don't know how to save myself. He's ruined my life. . . . he's killed me. . . . I'll never be able to get even, to put away a little . . . if the thing with the knees gets any worse, there could be big doctor bills, specialists maybe . . . the Blue Cross would never cover it . . . what am I going to do, please God help me . . . what am I going to do?*

He was an old man, retired and very tired, who had thought he could make it through. He had figured it out so he could just barely slide through. But the pains in the backs of his knees had begun three years before, and though it had not flared up in sixteen months, he remembered how he would simply fall down, suddenly, ludicrously, fall down: the legs prickling with pins and needles as though he had sat cross-legged for a long time. He was afraid to think about the pains too much. They might come back if he thought about them too much.

But he didn't really believe that thinking about things could make them happen. Thinking didn't make things change in the real world. Fred Tolliver did not know about the dance of the emotions, the resonance of the electrons. He did not know about a sixty-two-year-old lightning rod that leaked off the terror and frustration of four billion people, all crying out silently just as Fred Tolliver cried out. For help that never came.

The phone continued to ring. He did not think about the pain he had felt in the backs of his knees, as recently as sixteen months ago. He did not think about it, because he did not want it to return. It was only a low-level throbbing now, and he wanted it to stay that way. He didn't want to feel pins and needles. He *wanted* his money back. He *wanted* the sound of gurgling under the floor of the guest bathroom to stop. *He wanted William Weisel to make good.*

He answered the phone. It rang once too often for him to ignore it.

"Hello?" ·

"Mr. Tolliver? Is that you?"

"Yes, this is Fred Tolliver. Who's calling?"

"Evelyn Hand, I· haven't heard from you about my violin, and I'm going to need it late next week...."

He had forgotten. In all the anguish with Weisel, he had forgotten Evelyn Hand and her damaged violin. And she had paid him already.

"Oh, my gosh, Miss Hand, I'm awfully sorry! I've just had the most awful business going on these last months, a man built me a guest bathroom, and he overcharged me nine thousand dollars, and it's all broken and..."

He stopped. This was unbecoming. He coughed with embarrassment, giving himself a moment to gather his composure. "I'm just as terribly sorry and ashamed as I can be, Miss Hand. I haven't had a chance to get to the repairs. But I know you need it a week from today...."

"A week from *yesterday*, Mr. Tolliver. Thursday, not Friday."

"Oh. Yes, of course. Thursday." She was a nice woman, really. Very slim, delicate fingers and a gentle, warm voice. He had thought perhaps they might go to the Smorgasbord for a meal, and they might get to know each other. He wanted companionship. It was so necessary; now, particularly, it was so necessary. But the memory of Betsy was always there, singing softly within him; and he had said nothing to Evelyn Hand.

"Are you there, Mr. Tolliver?"

"Uh, yes. Yes, of course. Please forgive me. I'm so wrought-up these days. I'll get to it right away. Please don't you worry about it."

"Well, I *am* rather concerned." She hesitated, as though reluctant to speak. She drew a deep breath and plunged on: "I did pay you in advance for the repairs, because you said you needed the money for bills, and..."

He didn't take offense. He understood perfectly. She had said something that otherwise she would have considered *déplacé*, but she was distraught and wanted to make the point as firmly as she could without being overly offensive.

"I'll get to it today, Miss Hand; I promise."

It would take time. It was a good instrument, a fine, old Gagliano. He knew he could finish the repairs in time if he kept at it without distraction.

Her tone softened. "Thank you, Mr. Tolliver. I'm sorry to have bothered you, but . . . you understand."

"Of course. Don't give it a thought. I'll call as soon as it's ready. I'll give it special attention, I promise."

"You're very kind."

They said their good-byes and he stopped himself from suggesting dinner when the violin was ready. There was always time for that later, when appropriate. When the business with the bathroom was settled.

And that brought him back to the state of helpless fury and pain. That terrible man, Weisel!

Unknowing confluence of four billion resonating emotions, Fred Tolliver sat with head in hands; as the electrons danced.

Eight days later, in a filthy alley behind a boarded-up supermarket that had begun as a sumptuous gilt-and-brocade movie house in 1924, William Weisel sat in filth, trying to eat the butt of a stale loaf of pumpernickel he had stolen from a garbage can. He weighed ninety-seven pounds, had not shaved in seven days, his clothes were stained and torn rags, his shoes had been stolen while he slept, four days earlier, in the doorway outside the Midnight Mission, his eyes were rheumy, and he had developed a terrible, wracking cough. The angry crimson weal on his left forearm, where the bolt of lightning had just grazed him, seemed to be infected. He gagged on the bread, realizing he had missed one of the maggots, and threw the granitelike butt across the alley.

He was incapable of crying. He had cried himself out.

He knew, at last, that there was no way to save himself. On the third day, he had tried to get to Tolliver, to beg him to stop; to tell him he would repair the bathroom; to tell him he would build him a new house, a mansion, a palace, *anything*! Just stop this terror! *Please!*

But *he* had been stopped. He could not *get* to Tolliver. The first time he had set his mind to seeing the old man, he had been arrested by a California Highway Patrol officer who had him on his hot sheet for having left the Rolls in the middle of Ventura Boulevard. Weisel had managed to escape on foot, somehow, miraculously.

The second time he had been attacked by a Doberman while skulking through back yards. He had lost his left pant leg below the knee.

The third time he had actually gotten as far as the street on which Tolliver's house sat, but a seven-car pileup had almost crushed him beneath tons of thundering metal, and he had fled, fearing an aircraft carrier might drop from the sky to bury him.

He knew now that he could not even make amends, that it was inertial, and that he was doomed.

He lay back, waiting for the finish. But it was not to be that easy. The song of the four billion is an unending symphony of incredible complexity. As he lay there, a derelict stumbled into the alley, saw him, and pulled the straight razor from his jacket pocket. He was almost upon him when William Weisel opened his eyes. He saw the rusty blade coming for his throat, had a moment of absolute mind-numbing horror wash over him, spasmed into shock, and did not hear the sound of the cop's service revolver as the derelict—who had serviced over a dozen other such bums as Weisel in this same manner—was blown in half.

He woke in the drunk tank, looked around, saw the company to which he had been condemned, knew that if he lived it would be through years of horror, and began tearing off strips of rags from what remained of his clothing.

When the attendant came to turn the men out into the exercise area, he found William Weisel hanging from the bars of the door, eyes bulging, tongue protruding like a charred leaf from his mouth. What he could not reconcile was that no one in the cell had even shouted, nor raised a hand to stop Weisel. That, and the look of voiceless anguish on the dead man's face, as though he had glimpsed, just at the instant of death, a view of an *eternity* of voiceless anguish.

The focus could direct the beam, but it could not heal itself. At the very moment that Weisel died, Fred Tolliver—still unaware of what he had done—sat in his home, realizing finally that the contractor had done him in. He could never repay the note, would perhaps have to get work again in some studio, and probably would be unable to do it with sufficient regularity to save the house. His twilight years would be spent in some dingy apartment. The modest final hope of his life had been denied him: he would not be able to just simply get by in peace. It was a terrible lonely thing to contemplate.

The phone rang.

He picked it up wearily. "Yes?"

There was a moment of silence, then the voice of Miss Evelyn Hand came across the line, icily, "Mr. Tolliver, this is Evelyn Hand. I waited all day yesterday. I was unable to participate in the recital. Please have my violin waiting for me, repaired or not."

He was too stunned, too depressed, even to be polite. "Okay."

"I want you to know you have caused me great pain, Mr. Tolliver. You are a very unreliable and evil man. I want you to know I'm going to take steps to rectify this matter. You have taken money from me under false pretenses, you have ruined a great opportunity I had, and you have caused me unnecessary anguish. You will have to pay for your irresponsibility; there must be justice. I will make certain you pay for what you've done!"

"Yes. Yes, of course," he said, dimly, faintly.

He hung up the receiver and sat there.

The emotions sang, the electrons danced, the focus shifted, and the symphony of frustration went on.

Fred Tolliver's cello lay unattended at his feet. He would never get through, just barely slide through. He felt the excruciating pain of pins and needles in his legs.

"No snowflake in an avalanche ever feels responsible."
S.J. LEC

The Gunslinger
by Stephen King

*Stephen King is famous as the author of a string of
best-selling fantasy novels, most recently* The Stand.
*It's probable, though, that he's never before written a
story as unusual as this compelling novelette
about . . . um . . . six-guns and sorcery?*

I

The man in black fled across the desert, and the
gunslinger followed.

The desert was the apotheosis of all deserts, huge,
standing to the sky for what might have been parsecs in all
directions. White; blinding; waterless; without feature
save for the faint, cloudy haze of the mountains which
sketched themselves on the horizon and the devil-grass
which brought sweet dreams, nightmares, death. An
occasional tombstone sign pointed the way, for once the
drifted track that cut its way through the thick crust of
alkali had been a highway and coaches had followed it.
The world had moved on since then. The world had
emptied.

The gunslinger walked stolidly, not hurrying, not
loafing. A hide waterbag was slung around his middle like
a bloated sausage. It was almost full. He had progressed
through the *khef* over many years, and had reached the
fifth level. At the seventh or eighth, he would not have
been thirsty; he could have watched his own body
dehydrate with clinical, detached attention, watering its
crevices and dark inner hollows only when his logic told
him it must be done. He was not seventh or eighth. He was
fifth. So he was thirsty, although he had no particular
urge to drink. In a vague way, all this pleased him. It was
romantic.

Below the waterbag were his guns, finely weighted to

his hand. The two belts crisscrossed above his crotch. The
holsters were oiled too deeply for even this Philistine sun
to crack. The stocks of the guns were sandalwood, yellow
and finely grained. The holsters were tied down with
rawhide cord, and they swung heavily against his hips.
The brass casings of the cartridges looped into the
gunbelts twinkled and flashed and heliographed in the
sun. The leather made subtle creaking noises. The guns
themselves made no noise. They had spilled blood. There
was no need to make noise in the sterility of the desert.

His clothes were the no-color of rain or dust. His shirt
was open at the throat, with a rawhide thong dangling
loosely in hand-punched eyelets. The pants were seam-
stretched dungarees of no particular make.

He breasted a gently rising dune (although there
was no sand here; the desert was hardpan, and even the
harsh winds that blew when dark came raised only an
aggravating harsh dust like scouring powder) and saw the
kicked remains of a tiny campfire on the lee side, the side
which the sun would quit earliest. Small signs like this,
once more affirming the man in black's essential
humanity, never failed to please him. His lips stretched in
the pitted, flaked remains of his face. He squatted.

He had burned the devil-grass, of course. It was the
only thing out here that *would* burn. It burned with a
greasy, flat light, and it burned slow. Border dwellers had
told him that devils lived even in the flames. They burned
it but would not look into the light. They said the devils
hypnotized, beckoned, would eventually draw the one
who looked into the fires. And the next man foolish
enough to look into the fire might see you.

The burned grass was criss-crossed in the now-familiar
ideographic pattern, and crumbled to gray senselessness
before the gunslinger's prodding hand. There was nothing
in the remains but a charred scrap of bacon, which he ate
thoughtfully. It had always been this way. The gunslinger
had followed the man in black across the desert for two
months now, across the endless, screamingly monotonous purgatorial wastes, and had yet to find spoor other
than the hygienic sterile ideographs of the man in black's

campfires. He had not found a can, a bottle, a waterskin
(the gunslinger had left four of those behind, like dead
snakeskins).

—Perhaps the campfires are a message, spelled out
letter by letter. *Take a powder.* Or, *The end draweth nigh.*
Or maybe even, *Eat at Joe's.* It didn't matter. He had no
understanding of the ideograms, if they were ideograms.
And the remains were as cold as all the others. He knew he
was closer, but did not know how he knew. That didn't
matter either. He stood up, brushing his hands.

No other trace; the wind, razor-sharp, had of course
filed away even what scant tracks the hardpan held. He
had never even been able to find his quarry's droppings.
Nothing. Only these cold campfires along the ancient
highway and the relentless range-finder in his own head.

He sat down and allowed himself a short pull from the
waterbag. He scanned the desert, looked up at the sun,
which was now sliding down the far quadrant of the sky.
He got up, removed his gloves from his belt, and began to
pull devil-grass for his own fire, which he laid over the
ashes the man in black had left. He found the irony, like
the romance of his thirst, bitterly appealing.

He did not use the flint and steel until the remains of
the day were only the fugitive heat in the ground beneath
him and a sardonic orange line on the monochrome
western horizon. He watched the south patiently, toward
the mountains, not hoping or expecting to see the thin
straight line of smoke from a new campfire, but merely
watching because that was a part of it. There was nothing.
He was close, but only relatively so. Not close enough to
see smoke at dusk.

He struck his spark to the dry, shredded grass and lay
down upwind, letting the dreamsmoke blow out toward
the waste. The wind, except for occasional gyrating
dust-devils, was constant.

Above, the stars were unwinking, also constant. Suns
and worlds by the million. Dizzying constellations, cold
fire in every primary hue. As he watched, the sky washed
from violet to ebony. A meteor etched a brief, spectacular
arc and winked out. The fire threw strange shadows as the

devil-grass burned its slow way down into new patterns—
not ideograms but a straightforward crisscross vaguely
frightening in its own no-nonsense surety. He had laid his
fuel in a pattern that was not artful but only workable. It
spoke of blacks and whites. It spoke of a man who might
straighten bad pictures in strange hotel rooms. The fire
burned its steady, slow flame, and phantoms danced in its
incandescent core. The gunslinger did not see. He slept.
The two patterns, art and craft, were welded together. The
wind moaned. Every now and then a perverse downdraft
would make the smoke whirl and eddy toward him, and
sporadic whiffs of the smoke touched him. They built
dreams in the same way that a small irritant may build a
pearl in an oyster. Occasionally the gunslinger moaned
with the wind. The stars were as indifferent to this as they
were to wars, crucifixions, resurrections. This also would
have pleased him.

II

He had come down off the last of the foothills leading the
donkey, whose eyes were already dead and bulging with
the heat. He had passed the last town three weeks before,
and since then there had only been the deserted coach
track and an occasional huddle of border dwellers' sod
dwellings. The huddles had degenerated into single
dwellings, most inhabited by lepers or madmen. He found
the madmen better company. One had given him a
stainless steel Silva compass and bade him give it to Jesus.
The gunslinger took it gravely. If he saw Him, he would
turn over the compass. He did not expect to.

Five days had passed since the last hut, and he had
begun to suspect there would be no more when he topped
the last eroded hill and saw the familiar low-backed sod
roof.

The dweller, a surprisingly young man with a wild
shock of strawberry hair that reached almost to his waist,
was weeding a scrawny stand of corn with zealous

abandon. The mule let out a wheezing grunt and the dweller looked up, glaring blue eyes coming target-center on the gunslinger in a moment. He raised both hands in curt salute and then bent to the corn again, humping up the row next to his hut with back bent, tossing devil-grass and an occasional stunted corn plant over his shoulder. His hair flopped and flew in the wind that now came directly from the desert, with nothing to break it.

The gunslinger came down the hill slowly, leading the donkey on which his waterskins sloshed. He paused by the edge of the lifeless-looking cornpatch, drew a drink from one of his skins to start the saliva, and spat into the arid soil.

"Life for your crop."

"Life for your own," the dweller answered and stood up. His back popped audibly. He surveyed the gunslinger without fear. What little of his face that was visible between beard and hair seemed unmarked by the rot, and his eyes, while a bit wild, seemed sane.

"I don't have anything but corn and beans," he said. "Corn's free, but you'll have to kick something in for the beans. A man brings them out once in a while. He don't stay long." The dweller laughed shortly. "Afraid of spirits."

"I expect he thinks you're one."

"I expect he does."

They looked at each other in silence for a moment.

The dweller put out his hand. "Brown is my name."

The gunslinger shook his hand. As he did so, a scrawny raven croaked from the low peak of the sod roof. The dweller gestured at it briefly:

"That's Zoltan."

At the sound of its name the raven croaked again and flew across to Brown. It landed on the dweller's head and roosted, talons firmly twined in the wild thatch of hair.

"Screw you," Zoltan croaked brightly. "Screw you and the horse you rode in on."

The gunslinger nodded amiably.

"Beans, beans, the musical fruit," the raven recited, inspired. "The more you eat, the more you toot."

"You teach him that?"

"That's all he wants to learn, I guess," Brown said. "Tried to teach him The Lord's Prayer once." His eyes traveled out beyond the hut for a moment, toward the gritty, featureless hardpan. "Guess this ain't Lord's Prayer country. You're a gunslinger. That right?"

"Yes." He hunkered down and brought out his makings. Zoltan launched himself from Brown's head and landed, flittering, on the gunslinger's shoulder.

"After the other one, I guess."

"Yes." The inevitable question formed in his mouth: "How long since he passed by?"

Brown shrugged. "I don't know. Time's funny out here. More than two weeks. Less than two months. The bean man's been twice since he passed. I'd guess six weeks. That's probably wrong."

"The more you eat, the more you toot," Zoltan said.

"Did he stop off?" the gunslinger asked.

Brown nodded. "He stayed supper, same as you will, I guess. We passed the time."

The gunslinger stood up and the bird flew back to the roof, squawking. He felt an odd, trembling eagerness. "What did he talk about?"

Brown cocked an eyebrow at him. "Not much. Did it ever rain and when did I come here and had I buried my wife. I did most of the talking, which ain't usual." He paused, and the only sound was the stark wind. "He's a sorcerer, ain't he?"

"Yes."

Brown nodded slowly. "I knew. Are you?"

"I'm just a man."

"You'll never catch him."

"I'll catch him."

They looked at each other, a sudden depth of feeling between them, the dweller upon his dust-puff-dry ground, the gunslinger on the hardpan that shelved down to the desert. He reached for his flint.

"Here." Brown produced a sulfur-headed match and struck it with a grimed nail. The gunslinger pushed the tip of his smoke into the flame and drew.

"Thanks."

"You'll want to fill your skins," the dweller said, turning away. "Spring's under the eaves in back. I'll start dinner."

The gunslinger stepped gingerly over the rows of corn and went around back. The spring was at the bottom of a hand-dug well, lined with stones to keep the powdery earth from caving. As he descended the rickety ladder, the gunslinger reflected that the stones must represent two years' work easily—hauling, dragging, laying. The water was clear but slow-moving, and filling the skins was a long chore. While he was topping the second, Zoltan perched on the lip of the well.

"Screw you and the horse you rode in on," he advised.

He looked up, startled. The shaft was about fifteen feet deep: easy enough for Brown to drop a rock on him, break his head, and steal everything on him. A crazy or a rotter wouldn't do it; Brown was neither. Yet he liked Brown, and so he pushed the thought out of his mind and got the rest of his water. What came, came.

When he came through the hut's door and walked down the steps (the hovel proper was set below ground level, designed to catch and hold the coolness of the nights), Brown was poking ears of corn into the embers of a tiny fire with a hardwood spatula. Two ragged plates had been set at opposite ends of a dun blanket. Water for the beans was just beginning to bubble in a pot hung over the fire.

"I'll pay for the water, too."

Brown did not look up. "The water's a gift from God. Pappa Doc brings the beans."

The gunslinger grunted a laugh and sat down with his back against one rude wall, folded his arms and closed his eyes. After a little, the smell of roasting corn came to his nose. There was a pebbly rattle as Brown dumped a paper of dry beans into the pot. An occasional *tak-tak-tak* as Zoltan walked restlessly on the roof. He was tired; he had been going sixteen and sometimes eighteen hours a day between here and the horror that had occurred in Tull, the last village. He had been afoot for the last twelve days; the mule was at the end of its endurance.

Tak-tak-tak.

Two weeks, Brown had said, or as much as six. Didn't matter. There had been calendars in Tull, and they had remembered the man in black because of the old man he had healed on his way through. Just an old man dying with the weed. An old man of thirty-five. And if Brown was right, the man in black had lost ground since then. But the desert was next. And the desert would be hell.

Tak-tak-tak.

—Lend me your wings, bird. I'll spread them and fly on the thermals.

He slept.

III

Brown woke him up five hours later. It was dark. The only light was the dull cherry glare of the banked embers.

"Your mule has passed on," Brown said. "Dinner's ready."

"How?"

Brown shrugged. "Roasted and boiled, how else? You picky?"

"No, the mule."

"It just laid over, that's all. It looked like an old mule." And with a touch of apology: "Zoltan et the eyes."

"Oh," He might have expected it. "All right."

Brown surprised him again when they sat down to the blanket that served as a table by asking a brief blessing: Rain, health, expansion to the spirit.

"Do you believe in an afterlife?" The gunslinger asked him as Brown dropped three ears of hot corn onto his plate.

Brown nodded. "I think this is it."

IV

The beans were like bullets, the corn tough. Outside, the prevailing wind snuffled and whined around the ground-

level eaves. He ate quickly, ravenously, drinking four
cups of water with the meal. Halfway through, there was a
machine-gun rapping at the door. Brown got up and let
Zoltan in. The bird flew across the room and hunched
moodily in the corner.

"Musical fruit," he muttered.

Afterward, the gunslinger offered his tobacco.

—Now. Now the questions will come.

But Brown asked no questions. He smoked and looked
at the dying embers of the fire. It was already noticeably
cooler in the hovel.

"Lead us not into temptation," Zoltan said suddenly,
apocalyptically.

The gunslinger started as if he had been shot at. He was
suddenly sure that it was an illusion, all of it (not a dream,
no; an enchantment), that the man in black had spun a
spell and was trying to tell him something in a
maddeningly obtuse, symbolic way.

"Have you been through Tull?" he asked suddenly.

Brown nodded. "Coming here, and once to sell corn. It
rained that year. Lasted maybe fifteen minutes. The
ground just seemed to open and suck it up. An hour later
it was just as white and dry as ever. But the corn—God,
the corn. You could see it grow. That wasn't so bad. But
you could *hear* it, as if the rain had given it a mouth. It
wasn't a happy sound. It seemed to be sighing and
groaning its way out of the earth." He paused. "I had
extra, so I took it and sold it. Pappa Doc said he would,
but he would have cheated me. So I went."

"You don't like town?"

"No."

"I almost got killed there," the gunslinger said
abruptly.

"That so?"

"I killed a man that was touched by God," the
gunslinger said. "Only it wasn't God. It was the man in
black."

"He laid you a trap."

"Yes."

They looked at each other across the shadows, the
moment taking on overtones of finality.

—*Now* the questions will come.

But Brown had nothing to say. His smoke was a smoldering roach, but when the gunslinger tapped his poke, Brown shook his head.

Zoltan shifted restlessly, seemed about to speak, subsided.

"May I tell you about it?" the gunslinger asked.

"Sure."

The gunslinger searched for words to begin and found none. "I have to flow," he said.

Brown nodded. "The water does that. The corn, please?"

"Sure."

He went up the stairs and out into the dark. The stars glittered overhead in a mad splash. The wind pulsed steadily. His urine arched out over the powdery cornfield in a wavering stream. The man in black had sent him here. Brown might even be the man in black himself. It might be—

He shut the thoughts away. The only contingency he had not learned how to bear was the possibility of his own madness. He went back inside.

"Have you decided if I'm an enchantment yet?" Brown asked, amused.

The gunslinger paused on the tiny landing, startled. Then he came down slowly and sat.

"I started to tell you about Tull."

"Is it growing?"

"It's dead," the gunslinger said, and the words hung in the air.

Brown nodded. "The desert. I think it may strangle everything eventually. Did you know that there was once a coach road across it?"

The gunslinger closed his eyes. His mind whirled crazily.

"You doped me," he said thickly.

"No. I've done nothing."

The gunslinger opened his eyes warily.

"You won't feel right about it unless I invite you," Brown said. "And so I do. Will you tell me about Tull?"

The gunslinger opened his mouth hesitantly and was

surprised to find that this time the words were there. He began to speak in flat bursts that slowly spread into an even, slightly toneless narrative. The doped feeling left him, and he found himself oddly excited. He talked deep into the night. Brown did not interrupt at all. Neither did the bird.

V

He had bought the mule in Pricetown a week earlier, and when he reached Tull, it was still fresh. The sun had set an hour earlier, but the gunslinger had continued traveling, guided by the town glow in the sky, then by the uncannily clear notes of a honky-tonk piano playing *Hey Jude*. The road widened as it took on tributaries.

The forests had been gone long now, replaced by the monotonous flat country: endless, desolate fields gone to timothy and low shrubs, shacks, eerie, deserted estates guarded by brooding, shadowed mansions where demons undeniably walked; leering, empty shanties where the people had either moved on or had been moved along, an occasional dweller's hovel, given away by a single flickering point of light in the dark, or by sullen, inbred clans toiling silently in the fields by day. Corn was the main crop, but there were beans and also some peas. An occasional scrawny cow stared at him lumpishly from between peeled alder poles. Coaches had passed him four times, twice coming and twice going, nearly empty as they came up on him from behind and bypassed him and his mule, fuller as they headed back toward the forests of the north.

It was ugly country. It had showered twice since he had left Pricetown, grudgingly both times. Even the timothy looked yellow and dispirited. Ugly country. He had seen no sign of the man in black. Perhaps he had taken a coach.

The road made a bend, and beyond it the gunslinger clucked the mule to a stop and looked down at Tull. It was at the floor of a circular, bowl-shaped hollow, a shoddy jewel in a cheap setting. There were a number of lights, most of them clustered around the area of the music. There looked to be four streets, three running at right angles to the coach road, which was the main avenue of the town. Perhaps there would be a restaurant. He doubted it, but perhaps. He clucked at the mule.

More houses sporadically lined the road now, most of them still deserted. He passed a tiny graveyard with moldy, leaning wooden slabs overgrown and choked by the rank devil-grass. Perhaps five hundred feet further on he passed a chewed sign which said: TULL

The paint was flaked almost to the point of illegibility. There was another further on, but the gunslinger was not able to read that one at all.

A fool's chorus of half-stoned voices was rising in the final protracted lyric of *Hey Jude*—"Naa naa-naa naa-na-na-na . . . hey, Jude . . ." —as he entered the town proper. It was a dead sound, like the wind in the hollow of a rotted tree. Only the prosaic thump and pound of the honky-tonk piano saved him from seriously wondering if the man in black might not have raised ghosts to inhabit a deserted town. He smiled a little at the thought.

There were a few people on the streets, not many, but a few. Three ladies wearing black slacks and identical middy blouses passed by on the opposite boardwalk, not looking at him with pointed curiosity. Their faces seemed to swim above their all-but-invisible bodies like huge, pallid baseballs with eyes. A solemn old man with a straw hat perched firmly on top of his head watched him from the steps of a boarded-up grocery store. A scrawny tailor with a late customer paused to watch him by; he held up the lamp in his window for a better look. The gunslinger nodded. Neither the tailor nor his customer nodded back. He could feel their eyes resting heavily against the low-slung holsters that lay against his hips. A young boy, perhaps thirteen, and his girl crossed the street a block up, pausing imperceptibly. Their footfalls raised little hanging clouds of dust. A few of the streetside lamps worked, but their glass sides were cloudy with congealed oil. Most had been crashed out. There was a livery, probably depending on the coach line for its survival. Three boys were crouched silently around a marble ring drawn in the dust to one side of the barn's gaping maw, smoking cornshuck cigarettes. They made long shadows in the yard.

The gunslinger led his mule past them and looked into the dim depths of the barn. One lamp glowed sunkenly, and a shadow jumped and flickered as a gangling old man in bib overalls forked loose timothy hay into the hay loft with huge, grunting swipes of his fork.

"Hey!" the gunslinger called.

The fork faltered and the hostler looked around waspishly. "Hey yourself!"

"I got a mule here."

"Good for you."

The gunslinger flicked a heavy, unevenly milled gold piece into the semidark. It rang on the old, chaff-drifted boards and glittered.

The hostler came forward, bent, picked it up, squinted at the gunslinger. His eyes dropped to the gunbelts and he nodded sourly.

"How long you want him put up?"

"A night. Maybe two. Maybe longer."

"I ain't got no change for gold."

"I'm not asking for any."

"Blood money," the hostler muttered.

"What?"

"Nothing." The hostler caught the mule's bridle and led him inside.

"Rub him down!" The gunslinger called. The old man did not turn.

The gunslinger walked out to the boys crouched around the marble ring. They had watched the entire exchange with contemptuous interest.

"How is it hanging?" the gunslinger asked conversationally.

No answer.

"You dudes live in town?"

No answer.

One of the boys removed a crazily tilted twist of cornshuck from his mouth, grasped a green cat's-eye marble, and squirted it into the dirt circle. It struck a croaker and knocked it outside. He picked up the cat's-eye and prepared to shoot again.

"There a restaurant in this town?" the gunslinger asked.

One of them looked up, the youngest. There was a huge cold sore at the corner of his mouth, but his eyes were still ingenuous. He looked at the gunslinger with hooded brimming wonder that was touching and frightening.

"Might get a burger at Sheb's."

"That the honky-tonk?"

The boy nodded but didn't speak. The eyes of his playmates had turned ugly and hostile.

The gunslinger touched the brim of his hat. "I'm grateful. It's good to know someone in this town is bright enough to talk."

He walked past, mounted the boardwalk, and started down toward Sheb's, hearing the clear, contemptuous voice of one of the others, hardly more than a childish treble: "Weed-eater! How long you been screwin' your sister, Charlie? Weed-eater!"

There were three flaring kerosene lamps in front of Sheb's, one to each side and one nailed above the drunk-hung batwing doors. The chorus of *Hey Jude* had petered out, and the piano was plinking some other old ballad. Voices murmured like broken threads. The gunslinger paused outside for a moment, looking in. Sawdust floor, spittoons by the tipsy-legged tables. A plank bar on sawhorses. A gummy mirror behind it, reflecting the piano player, who wore the inevitable gartered white shirt and who had the inevitable piano-stool slouch. The front of the piano had been removed so you could watch the wooden keys whonk up and down as the contraption was played. The bartender was a straw-haired woman wearing a dirty blue dress. One strap was held with a safety pin. There were perhaps six townies in the back room, juicing and playing Watch Me apathetically. Another half-dozen were grouped loosely about the piano. Four or five at the bar. And an old man

with wild gray hair collapsed at a table by the doors. The
gunslinger went in.

Heads swiveled to look at him and his guns. There was
a moment of near silence, except for the oblivious piano
player, who continued to tinkle. Then the woman
mopped at the bar, and things shifted back.

"Watch me," one of the players in the corner said and
matched three hearts with four spades, emptying his
hand. The one with the hearts swore, handed over his bet,
and the next hand was dealt.

The gunslinger approached the bar. "You got ham-
burger?" he asked.

"Sure." She looked him in the eye, and she might have
been pretty when she started out, but now her face was
lumpy and there was a livid scar corkscrewed across her
forehead. She had powdered it heavily, but it called
attention rather than comouflaging. "It's dear, though."

"I figured. Gimme three burgers and a beer."

Again that subtle shift in tone. Three hamburgers.
Mouths watered and tongues licked at saliva with slow
lust. Three hamburgers.

"That would go you five bucks. With a beer."

The gunslinger put a gold piece on the bar.

Eyes followed it.

There was a sullenly smoldering charcoal brazier
behind the bar and to the left of the mirror. The woman
disappeared into a small room behind it and returned
with meat on a paper. She scrimped out three patties and
put them on the fire. The smell that arose was maddening.
The gunslinger stood with stolid indifference, only
peripherally aware of the faltering piano, the slowing of
the card game, the sidelong glances of the barflies.

The man was halfway up behind him when the
gunslinger saw him in the mirror. The man was almost
completely bald, and his hand was wrapped around the
haft of a gigantic hunting knife that was looped onto his
belt like a holster.

"Go sit down," the gunslinger said quietly.

The man stopped. His upper lip lifted unconsciously,
like a dog's, and there was a moment of silence. Then he

went back to his table, and the atmosphere shifted back again.

His beer came in a cracked glass schooner. "I ain't got change for gold," The woman said truculently.

"Don't expect any."

She nodded angrily, as if this show of wealth, even at her benefit, incensed her. But she took his gold, and a moment later the hamburgers came on a cloudy plate, still red around the edges.

"Do you have salt?"

She gave it to him from underneath the bar. "Bread?"

"No." He knew she was lying, but he didn't push it. The bald man was staring at him with cyanosed eyes, his hands clenching and unclenching on the splintered and gouged surface of his table. His nostrils flared with pulsating regularity.

The gunslinger began to eat steadily, almost blandly, chopping the meat apart and forking it into his mouth, trying not to think of what might have been added to it to cut the beef.

He was almost through, ready to call for another beer and roll a smoke when the hand fell on his shoulders.

He suddenly became aware that the room had gone silent again, and he tasted thick tension in the air. He turned around and stared into the face of the man who had been asleep by the door when he entered. It was a terrible face. The odor of the devil-grass was a rank miasma. The eyes were damned, the staring, glaring eyes of those who see but do not see, eyes ever turned inward to the sterile hell of dreams beyond control, dreams unleashed, risen out of the stinking swamps of the unconscious to confront sanity with the grinning, death's-head rictus of utter lunacy.

The woman behind the bar made a small moaning sound.

The cracked lips writhed, lifted, revealing the green, mossy teeth, and the gunslinger thought:—He's not even smoking anymore. He's chewing it. He's really *chewing* it.

And on the heels of that:—He's a dead man. He should have been dead a year ago.

And on the heels of that:—The man in black.

They stared at each other, the gunslinger and the man who peered at the gunslinger from around the rim of madness.

He spoke, and the gunslinger, dumfounded, heard himself addressed in the High Speech:

"The gold for a favor, gunslinger. Just one? For a pretty."

The High Speech. For a moment his mind refused to track it. It had been years—God!—centuries, millenniums; there was no more High Speech, he was the last, the last gunslinger. The others were—

Numbed, he reached into his breast pocket and produced a gold piece. The split, scrabbled hand reached for it, fondled it, held it up to reflect the greasy glare of the kerosene lamps. It threw off its proud civilized glow; golden, reddish, bloody.

"Ahhhhhh . . ." An inarticulate sound of pleasure. The old man did a weaving turn and began moving back to his table, holding the coin at eye level, turning it, flashing it.

The room was emptying rapidly, the batwings shuttling madly back and forth. The piano player closed the lid of his instrument with a bang and exited after the others in long, comic-opera strides.

"Sheb!" The woman screamed after him, her voice an odd mixture of fear and shrewishness, "Sheb, you come back here! Goddammit!"

The old man, meanwhile, had gone back to his table. He spun the gold piece on the gouged wood, and the dead-alive eyes followed it with empty fascination. He spun it a second time, a third, and his eyelids dropped. The fourth time, and his head settled to the wood before the coin stopped.

"There," she said softly, furiously. "You've driven out my trade. Are you satisfied?"

"They'll be back," the gunslinger said.

"Not tonight they won't."

"Who is he?" He gestured at the weed-eater.

"Go—" She completed the command by describing an impossible act of masturbation.

"I have to know," the gunslinger said patiently. "He—"

"He talked to you funny," she said. "Nort never talked like that in his life."

"I'm looking for a man. You would know him."

She stared at him, the anger dying. It was replaced with speculation, then with a high, wet gleam that he had seen before. The rickety building ticked thoughtfully to itself. A dog barked brayingly, far away. The gunslinger waited. She saw his knowledge and the gleam was replaced by hopelessness, by a dumb need that had no mouth.

"You know my price," she said.

He looked at her steadily. The scar would not show in the dark. Her body was lean enough so the desert and grit and grind hadn't been able to sag everything. And she'd once been pretty, maybe even beautiful. Not that it mattered. It would not have mattered if the grave-beetles had nested in the arid blackness of her womb. It had all been written.

Her hands came up to her face and there was still some juice left in her—enough to weep.

"Don't *look*! You don't have to look at me so mean!"

"I'm sorry," the gunslinger said. "I didn't mean to be mean."

"None of you mean it!" She cried at him.

"Put out the lights."

She wept, hands at her face. He was glad she had her hands at her face. Not because of the scar but because it gave her back her maidenhood, if not head. The pin that held the strap of her dress glittered in the greasy light.

"Put out the lights and lock up. Will he steal anything?"

"No," she whispered.

· "Then put out the lights."

She would not remove her hands until she was behind him and she doused the lamps one by one, turning down the wicks and then breathing the flames into extinction. Then she took his hand in the dark and it was warm. She led him upstairs. There was no light to hide their act.

●   ●   ●

VI

He made cigarettes in the dark, then lit them and passed one to her. The room held her scent, fresh lilac, pathetic. The smell of the desert had overlaid it, crippled it. It was like the smell of the sea. He realized he was afraid of the desert ahead.

"His name is Nort," she said. No harshness had been worn out of her voice. "Just Nort. He died."

The gunslinger waited.

"He was touched by God."

The gunslinger said, "I have never seen Him."

"He was here ever since I can remember—Nort I mean, not God." She laughed jaggedly into the dark. "He had a honeywagon for a while. Started to drink. Started to smell the grass. Then to smoke it. The kids started to follow him around and sic their dogs onto him. He wore old green pants that stank. Do you understand?"

"Yes."

"He started to chew it. At the last he just sat in there and didn't eat anything. He might have been a king, in his mind. The children might have been his jesters, and the dogs his princes."

"Yes."

"He died right in front of this place," she said. "He came clumping down the boardwalk—his boots wouldn't wear out, they were engineer boots—with the children and dogs behind him. He looked like wire clothes hangers all wrapped and twirled together. You could see all the lights of hell in his eyes, but he was grinning, just like the grins the children carve into their pumpkins on All-Saints Eve. You could smell the dirt and the rot and the weed. It was running down from the corners of his mouth like green blood. I think he meant to come in and listen to Sheb play the piano. And right in front, he stopped and cocked his head. I could see him, and I thought he heard a coach, although there was none due. Then he puked, and it was black and full of blood. It went right through that grin like sewer water through a grate. The stink was enough to make you want to run mad. He raised up his arms and just threw over. That was all. He died with that grin on his face, in his own vomit."

She was trembling beside him. Outside, the wind kept up its steady whine, and somewhere far away a door was banging, like a sound heard in a dream. Mice ran in the walls. The gunslinger thought in the back of his mind that it was probably the only place in town prosperous enough to support mice. He put a hand on her belly and she started violently, then relaxed.

"The man in black," he said.

"You have to have it, don't you!"

"Yes."

"All right. I'll tell you." She grasped his hand in both of hers and told him.

VII

He came in the late afternoon of the day Nort died, and the wind was whooping up, pulling away the loose topsoil. sending sheets of grit and uprooted stalks of corn windmilling past. Kennerly had padlocked the livery, and the other few merchants had shuttered their windows and laid boards across the shutters. The sky was the yellow color of old cheese and the clouds moved flyingly across it, as if they had seen something horrifying in the desert wastes where they had so lately been.

He came in the rickety rig with a rippling tarp tied across its bed. They watched him come, and old man Kennerly, lying by the window with a bottle in one hand and the loose, hot flesh of his second-eldest daughter's left breast in the other, resolved not to be there if he should knock.

But the man in black went by without hawing the bay that pulled his rig, and the spinning wheels spumed up dust that the wind clutched eagerly. He might have been a priest or a monk; he wore a black cassock that had been floured with dust, and a loose hood covered his head and obscured his features. It rippled and flapped. Beneath the garment's hem, heavy buckled boots with square toes.

He pulled up in front of Sheb's and tethered the horse, which lowered its head and grunted at the ground. Around the back of the rig, he untied one flap, found a weathered saddlebag, threw it over his shoulder, and went in through the batwings.

Alice watched him curiously, but no one else noticed his arrival. The rest were drunk as lords. Sheb was playing Methodist hymns ragtime, and the grizzled layabouts who had come in early to avoid the storm and to attend Nort's wake had sung themselves hoarse. Sheb, drunk nearly to the point of senselessness, intoxicated and horny with his own continued existence, played with hectic, shuttlecock speed, fingers flying like looms.

Voices screeched and hollered, never overcoming the wind but sometimes seeming to challenge it. In the corner Zachary had thrown Amy Feldon's skirts over her head and was painting zodiac signs on her knees. A few other women circulated. A fervid glow seemed to be on all of them. The dull stormglow that filtered through the batwings seemed to mock them, however.

Nort had been laid out on two tables in the center of the room. His boots made a mystical V. His mouth hung open in a slack grin, although someone had closed his eyes and put slugs on them. His hands had been folded on his chest with a sprig of devil-grass in them. He smelled like poison.

The man in black pushed back his hood and came to the bar. Alice watched him, feeling trepidation mixed with the familiar want that hid within her. There was no religious symbol on him, although that meant nothing by itself.

"Whiskey," he said. His voice was soft and pleasant. "Good whiskey."

She reached under the counter and brought out a bottle of Star. She could have palmed off the local popskull on him as her best, but did not. She poured, and the man in black watched her. His eyes were large, luminous. The shadows were too thick to determine their color exactly. Her need intensified. The hollering and whooping went on behind, unabated. Sheb, the worthless gelding, was playing about the Christian Soldiers and somebody had persuaded Aunt Mill to sing. Her voice, warped and distorted, cut through the babble like a dull ax through a calf's brain.

"Hey, Allie!"

She went to serve, resentful of the stranger's silence, resentful of his no-color eyes and her own restless groin. She was afraid of her needs. They were capricious and beyond her control. They might be the signal of the change, which would in turn signal the beginning of her old age—a condition which in Tull was usually as short and bitter as a winter sunset.

She drew beer until the keg was empty, then broached another. She knew better than to ask Sheb; he would come willingly enough, like the dog he was, and would either chop off his own fingers or spume beer all over everything. The stranger's eyes were on her as she went about it; she could feel them.

"It's busy," he said when she returned. He had not touched his drink, merely rolled it between his palms to warm it.

"Wake," she said.

"I noticed the departed."

"They're bums," she said with sudden hatred. "All bums."

"It excites them. He's dead. They're not."

"He was their butt when he was alive. It's not right now. It's..." She trailed off, not able to express what it was, or how it was obscene.

"Weed-eater?"

"Yes. What else did he have?" Her tone was accusing, but he did not drop his eyes, and she felt the blood rush to her face. "I'm sorry. Are you a priest? This must revolt you."

"I'm not and it doesn't." He knocked the whiskey back neatly and did not grimace. "Once more, please."

"I'll have to see the color of your coin first. I'm sorry."

"No need to be."

He put a rough silver coin on the counter, thick on one edge, thin on the other, and she said as she would say later: "I don't have change for this."

He shook his head, dismissing it, and watched absently as she poured again.

"Are you only passing through?" she asked.

He did not reply for a long time, and she was about to repeat when he shook his head impatiently. "Don't talk trivialities. You're here with death."

She recoiled, hurt and amazed, her first thought being that he had lied about his holiness to test her.

"You cared for him," he said flatly. "Isn't that true?"

"Who? Nort?" She laughed, affecting annoyance to cover her confusion. "I think you better—"

"You're soft-hearted and a little afraid," he went on, "and he was on the weed, looking out hell's back door. And there he is, and they've even slammed the door now, and you don't think they'll open it until it's time for you to walk through, isn't it so?"

"What are you, drunk?"

"Mistuh Norton, he dead," the man in black intoned sardonically. "Dead as anybody. Dead as you or anybody."

"Get out of my place." She felt a trembling loathing spring up in her, but the warmth still radiated from her belly.

"It's all right," he said softly. "It's all right. Wait. Just wait."

The eyes were blue. She felt suddenly easy in her mind, as if she had taken a drug.

"See?" he asked her. "Do you see?"

She nodded dumbly and he laughed aloud—a fine, strong, untainted laugh that swung heads around. He whirled and faced them, suddenly made the center of attention by some unknown alchemy. Aunt Mill faltered and subsided, leaving a cracked high note bleeding on the air. Sheb struck a discord and halted. They looked at the stranger uneasily. Sand rattled against the sides of the building.

The silence held, spun itself out. Her breath had clogged in her throat and she looked down and saw both hands pressed to her belly beneath the bar. They all looked at him and he looked at them. Then the laugh burst forth again, strong, rich, beyond denial. But there was no urge to laugh along with him.

"I'll show you a wonder!" he cried at them. But they only watched him, like obedient children taken to see a magician in whom they have grown too old to believe.

The man in black sprang forward, and Aunt Mill drew away from him. He grinned fiercely and slapped her broad belly. A short, unwitting cackle was forced out of her, and the man in black threw back his head.

"It's better, isn't it?"

Aunt Mill cackled again, suddenly broke into cracked sobs, and fled blindly through the doors. The others watched her go silently. The storm was beginning; shadows followed each other, rising and falling on the giant white cyclorama of the sky. A man near the piano with a forgotten beer in one hand made a groaning, grinning sound.

The man in black stood over Nort, grinning down at him. The wind howled and shrieked and thrummed. Something large struck the side of the building and bounced away. One of the men at the bar tore himself free and exited in looping, grotesque strides. Thunder racketed in sudden dry vollies.

"All right," the man in black grinned. "All right, here we go."

He began to spit into Nort's face, aiming carefully. The spittle gleamed in the cut troughs of his forehead, pearled down the shaven beak of his nose.

Under the bar, her hands worked faster.

Sheb laughed, loon-like, and hunched over. He began to cough up phlegm, huge and sticky gobs of it, and let fly. The man in black roared approval and pounded him on the back. Sheb grinned, one gold tooth twinkling.

Others fled. Others gathered in a loose ring around Nort. His face and the dewlapped rooster-wrinkles of his neck and upper chest gleamed with liquid—liquid so precious in this dry country. And suddenly it stopped, as if on signal. There was ragged, heavy breathing.

The man in black suddenly lunged across the body, jackknifing over it in a smooth arc. It was pretty, like a flash of water. He caught himself on his hands, sprang to his feet in a twist, grinning, and went over again. One of the watchers forgot himself, began to applaud, and suddenly backed away, eyes cloudy with terror. He slobbered a hand across his mouth and made for the door.

Nort twitched the third time the man in black went across.

A sound went through the watchers—a grunt—and then they were silent. The man in black threw his head back and howled. His chest moved in a quick, shallow rhythm as he sucked air. He began to go back and forth at a faster clip, pouring over Nort's body like water poured from one glass to another glass. The only sound in the room was the tearing rasp of his respiration and the rising pulse of the storm.

Nort drew a deep, dry breath. His hands rattled and pounded aimlessly on the table. Sheb screeched and exited. One of the women followed him.

The man in black went across once more, twice, thrice. The whole body was vibrating now, trembling and rapping and twitching. The smell of rot and excrement and decay billowed up in choking waves. His eyes opened.

Alice felt her feet propelling her backward. She struck the mirror, making it shiver, and blind panic took over. She bolted like a steer.

"I've given it to you," the man in black called after her, panting. "Now you can sleep easy. Even *that* isn't irreversible. Although it's...so...goldamned...*funny!*" And he began to laugh again. The sound faded as she raced up the stairs, grunting and heaving, not stopping until the door to the three rooms above the bar was bolted.

She began to giggle then, rocking back and forth on her haunches by the door. The sound rose to a keening wail that mixed with the wind.

Downstairs, Nort wandered absently out into the storm to pull some weed. The man in black, now the only patron of the bar, watched him go, still grinning.

When she forced herself to go back down that evening, carrying a lamp in one hand and a heavy stick of stovewood in the other, the man in black was gone, rig and all. But Nort was there, sitting at the table by the door as if he had never been away. The smell of the weed was on him, but not as heavily as she might have expected.

He looked up at her and smiled tentatively. "Hello, Allie."

"Hello, Nort." She put the stovewood down and began lighting the lamps, not turning her back to him.

"I been touched by God," he said presently. "I ain't going to die no more. He said so. It was a promise."

"How nice for you, Nort." The spill she was holding dropped through her trembling fingers and she picked it up.

"I'd like to stop chewing the grass," he said. "I don't enjoy it no more. It don't seem right for a man touched by God to be chewing the weed."

"Then why don't you stop?"

Her exasperation startled her into looking at him as a man again, rather than an infernal miracle. What she saw was a rather sad-looking specimen only half-high, looking hangdog and ashamed. She could not be frightened by him anymore.

"I shake," he said. "And I want it. I can't stop. Allie, you was always so good to me—" he began to weep. "I can't even stop peeing myself."

She walked to the table and hesitated there, uncertain.

"He could have made me not want it," he said through the tears. "He could have done that if he could have made me be alive. I ain't complaining. . . . I don't want to complain. . . ." He stared around hauntedly and whispered, "He might strike me dead if I did."

"Maybe it's a joke. He seemed to have quite a sense of humor."

Nort took his poke from where it dangled inside his shirt and brought out a handful of grass. Unthinkingly she knocked it away and then drew her hand back, horrified.

"I can't help it, Allie, I can't—" and he made a crippled dive for the poke. She could have stopped him, but she made no effort. She went back to lighting the lamps, tired although the evening had barely begun. But nobody came in that night except old man Kennerly, who had missed

everything. He did not seem particularly surprised to see
Nort. He ordered beer, asked where Sheb was, and pawed
her. The next day things were almost normal, although
none of the children followed Nort. The day after that, the
catcalls resumed. Life had gotten back on its own sweet
keel. The uprooted corn was gathered together by the
children, and a week after Nort's resurrection, they
burned it in the middle of the street. The fire was
momentarily bright and most of the barflies stepped or
staggered out to watch. They looked primitive. Their
faces seemed to float between the flames and the ice-chip
brilliance of the sky. Allie watched them and felt a pang of
fleeting despair for the sad times of the world. Things had
stretched apart. There was no glue at the center of things
anymore. She had never seen the ocean, never would.

"If I had *guts*," she murmured, "If I had guts, guts,
guts . . ."

Nort raised his head at the sound of her voice and
smiled emptily at her from hell. She had no guts. Only a
bar and a scar.

The fire burned down rapidly and the barflies came
back in. She began to dose herself with the Star Whiskey,
and by midnight she was blackly drunk.

VIII

She ceased her narrative, and when he made no
immediate comment, she thought at first that the story
had put him to sleep. She had begun to drowse herself
when he asked: "That's all?"

"Yes. That's all. It's very late."

"Um." He was rolling another cigarette.

"Don't get crumbs in my bed," she told him, more
sharply than she had intended.

"No."

Silence again, as if all possible words between them
had been exhausted. The tip of his cigarette winked off
and on.

"You'll be leaving in the morning," she said dully.

"I should. I think he's left a trap for me here. A snare."

"Don't go," she said.

"We'll see."

He turned on his side away from her, but she was comforted. He would stay. She drowsed.

On the edge of sleep she thought again about the way Nort had addressed him, in that strange talk. She had not seen him express emotion before or since. Even his lovemaking had been a silent thing, and only at the last had his breathing roughened and then stopped for a minute. He was like something out of a fairytale or a myth, the last of his breed in a world that was writing the last page of its book. It didn't matter. He would stay for a while. Tomorrow was time enough to think, or the day after that. She slept.

IX

In the morning she cooked him grits which he ate without comment. He shoveled them into his mouth without thinking about her, hardly seeing her. He knew he should go. Every minute he sat here the man in black was further away—probably into the desert by now. His path had been undeviatingly south.

"Do you have a map?" he asked suddenly, looking up.

"Of the town?" She laughed. "There isn't enough of it to need a map."

"No. Of what's south of here."

Her smile faded. "The desert. Just the desert. I thought you'd stay for a little."

"What's south of the desert?"

"How would I know? Nobody crosses it. Nobody's tried since I was here." She wiped her hands on her apron, got potholders, and dumped the tub of water she had been heating into the sink, where it splashed and steamed.

He got up.

"Where are you going?" She heard the shrill fear in her voice and hated it.

"To the stable. If anyone knows, the holster will." He put his hands on her shoulders. The hands were warm. "And to arrange for my mule. If I'm going to be here, he should be taken care of. For when I leave."

But not yet. She looked up at him. "But you watch that Kennerly. If he doesn't know a thing, he'll make it up."

When he left she turned to the sink, feeling the hot, warm drift of her grateful tears.

X

Kennerly was toothless, unpleasant, and plagued with daughters. Two half-grown ones peeked at the gunslinger from the dusty shadows of the barn. A baby drooled happily in the dirt. A full-grown one, blonde, dirty, sensual, watched with a speculative curiosity as she drew water from the groaning pump beside the building.

The hostler met him halfway between the door to his establishment and the street. His manner vacillated between hostility and a craven sort of fawning—like a stud mongrel that has been kicked too often.

"It's bein' cared for," he said and before the gunslinger could reply, Kennerly turned on his daughter: "You get in, Soobie! You get right the hell in!"

Soobie began to drag her bucket sullenly toward the shack appended to the barn.

"You meant my mule," the gunslinger said.

"Yes, sir. Ain't seen a mule in quite a time. Time was they used to grow up wild for want of 'em, but the world has moved on. Ain't seen nothin' but a few oxen and the coach horses and . . . Soobie, I'll whale you, 'fore God!"

"I don't bite," the gunslinger said pleasantly.

Kennerly cringed a little. "It ain't you. No, sir, it ain't *you*." He grinned loosely. "She's just naturally gawky. She's got a devil. She's wild." His eyes darkened. "It's coming to Last Times, mister. You know how it says in the Book. Children won't obey their parents, and a plague'll be visited on the multitudes."

The gunslinger nodded, then pointed south. "What's out there?"

Kennerly grinned again, showing gums and few sociable yellow teeth. "Dwellers. Weed. Desert. What else?" He cackled, and his eyes measured the gunslinger coldly.

"How big is the desert?"

"Big." His grin was serious, Kennerly endeavored to look serious. But the layers of secret humor and fear and ingratiation vied beneath the skin in a moiling confusion.

"Maybe three hundred miles. Maybe a thousand. I can't tell you, mister. There's nothing out there but devil-grass and maybe demons. That's the way the other fella went. The one who fixed up Norty when he was sick."

Kennerly kept grinning. "Well, well. Maybe. But we're growed-up men, ain't we?"

"But you believe in demons."

Kennerly looked affronted. "That's a lot different."

The gunslinger took off his hat and wiped his forehead. The sun was hot, beating steadily. Kennerly seemed not to notice. In the thin shadow by the livery, the baby girl was gravely smearing dirt on her face.

"You don't know what's after the desert?"

Kennerly shrugged. "Some might. The coach ran through part of it fifty years ago. My pap said so. He used to say 'twas mountains. Others say an ocean . . . a green ocean with monsters. And some say that's where the world ends. That there ain't nothing but lights that'll drive a man blind and the face of God with his mouth open to eat them up."

"Drivel," the gunslinger said shortly.

"Sure it is." Kennerly cringed again, hating, fearing, wanting to please.

"You see my mule is looked after." He flicked Kennerly another coin, which Kennerly caught on the fly.

"Surely. You stayin' a little?"

"I guess I might."

"That Allie's pretty nice when she wants to be, ain't she?"

"Did you say something?" The gunslinger asked remotely.

Sudden terror dawned in Kennerly's eyes, like twin moons coming over the horizon. "No, sir, not a word. And I'm sorry if I did." He caught sight of Soobie leaning out a window and whirled on her. "I'll whale you now, you little slut-face! 'Fore God! I'll—"

The gunslinger walked away, aware that Kennerly had turned to watch him, aware of the fact that he could whirl and catch the hostler with some true and untinctured emotion distilled on his face. He let it slip. It was hot. The only sure thing about the desert was its size. And it wasn't all played out in this town. Not yet.

XI

They were in bed when Sheb kicked the door open and came in with the knife.

It had been four days, and they had gone by in a blinking haze. He ate. He slept. He made sex with Allie. He found that she played the fiddle and he made her play it for him. She sat by the window in the milky light of daybreak, only a profile, and played something haltingly that might have been good if she had been trained. He felt a growing (but strangely absentminded) affection for her and thought this might be the trap the man in black had left behind. He read dry and tattered back issues of magazines with faded pictures. He thought very little about everything.

He didn't hear the little piano player come up—his reflexes had sunk. That didn't seem to matter either, although it would have frightened him badly in another time and place.

Allie was naked, the sheet below her breasts, and they were preparing to make love.

"Please," she was saying. "Like before, I want that, I want—"

The door crashed open and the piano player made his ridiculous, knock-kneed run for the sun. Allie did not scream, although Sheb held an eight-inch carving knife in his hand. Sheb was making a noise, an inarticulate

blabbering. He sounded like a man being drowned in a
bucket of mud. Spittle flew. He brought the knife down
with both hands, and the gunslinger caught his wrists and
turned them. The knife went flying. Sheb made a high
screeching noise, like a rusty screen door. His hands made
fluttering marionette movements, both wrists broken.
The wind gritted against the window. Allie's glass on the
wall, faintly clouded and distorted, reflecting the room.

"She was mine!" He wept. "She was mine first! Mine!"

Allie looked at him and got out of bed. She put on a
wrapper, and the gunslinger felt a moment of empathy for
a man who must be seeing himself coming out on the far
end of what he once had. He was just a little man, and
gelded.

"It was for you," Sheb sobbed. "It was only for you,
Allie. It was you first and it was all for you. I—ah, oh
God, dear God—" The words dissolved into a paroxysm
of unintelligibilities, finally to tears. He rocked back and
forth, holding his broken wrists to his belly.

"Shhh. Shhh. Let me see." She knelt beside him.
"Broken. Sheb, you donkey. Didn't you know you were
never strong?" She helped him to his feet. He tried to hold
his hands to his face, but they would not obey, and he
wept nakedly. "Come on over to the table and let me see
what I can do."

She led him to the table and set his wrists with slats of
kindling from the fire box. He wept weakly and without
volition, and left without looking back.

She came back to the bed. "Where were we?"

"No," he said.

She said patiently, "You knew about that. There's
nothing to be done. What else is there?" She touched his
shoulder. "Except I'm glad that you are so strong."

"Not now," he said thickly.

"I can make you strong—"

"No," he said. "You can't do that."

●   ●   ●

XII

The next night the bar was closed. It was whatever passed for the Sabbath in Tull. The gunslinger went to the tiny, leaning church by the graveyard while Allie washed tables with strong disinfectant and rinsed kerosene lamp chimneys in soapy water.

An odd purple dusk had fallen, and the church, lit from the inside, looked almost like a blast furnace from the road.

"I don't go," Allie had said shortly. "The woman who preaches has poison religion. Let the respectable ones go."

He stood in the vestibule, hidden in a shadow, looking in. The pews were gone and the congregation stood (he saw Kennerly and his brood; Castner, owner of the town's scrawny dry-goods emporium and his slat-sided wife; a few barflies; a few "town" women he had never seen before; and, surprisingly, Sheb). They were singing a hymn raggedly, *a cappella*. He looked curiously at the mountainous woman at the pulpit. Allie had said: "She lives alone, hardly ever sees anybody. Only comes out on Sunday to serve up the hellfire. Her name is Sylvia Pittston. She's crazy, but she's got the hoodoo on them. They like it that way. It suits them."

No description could take the measure of the woman. Breasts like earthworks. A huge pillar of a neck overtopped by a pasty white moon of a face, in which blinked eyes so large and so dark that they seemed to be bottomless tarns. Her hair was a beautiful rich brown and it was piled atop her head in a haphazard, lunatic sprawl, held by a hairpin big enough to be a meat skewer. She wore a dress that seemed to be made of burlap. The arms that held the hymnal were slabs. Her skin was creamy, unmarked, lovely. He thought that she must top three hundred pounds. He felt a sudden red lust for her that made him feel shaky, and he turned his head and looked away.

"Shall we gather at the river,
The beautiful, the beautiful,

> The riiiver,
> Shall we gather at the river,
> That flows by the Kingdom of
>   God."

The last note of the last chorus faded off, and there was a moment of shuffling and coughing.

She waited. When they were settled, she spread her hands over them, as if in benediction. It was an evocative gesture.

"My dear little brothers and sisters in Christ."

It was a haunting line. For a moment the gunslinger felt mixed feelings of nostalgia and fear, stitched in with an eerie feeling of *deja vu* —he thought: I dreamed this. When? He shook it off. The audience—perhaps twenty-five all told—had become dead silent.

"The subject of our meditation tonight is The Interloper." Her voice was sweet, melodious, the speaking voice of a well-trained soprano.

A little rustle ran through the audience.

"I feel," Sylvia Pittston said reflectively, "I feel that I know everyone in The Book personally. In the last five years I have worn out five Bibles, and uncountable numbers before that. I love the story, and I love the players in that story. I have walked arm in arm in the lion's den with Daniel. I stood with David when he was tempted by Bathsheba as she bathed at the pool. I have been in the fiery furnace with Shadrach, Meshach, and Abednego. I slew two thousand with Samson and was blinded with St. Paul on the road to Damascus. I wept with Mary at Golgotha."

A soft, shurring sigh in the audience.

"I have known and loved them. There is only one—*one* —" she held up a finger—"only one player in the greatest of all dreams that I do not know. Only *one* who stands outside with his face in the shadow. Only *one* that makes my body tremble and my spirit quail. I fear him. I don't know his mind and I fear him. I fear The Interloper."

Another sigh. One of the women had put a hand over her mouth as if to stop a sound and was rocking, rocking.

"The Interloper who came to Eve as a snake on its

belly, grinning and writhing. The Interloper who walked among the Children of Israel while Moses was up on the Mount, who whispered to them to make a golden idol, a golden calf, and to worship it with foulness and fornication."

Moans, nods.

"The Interloper! He stood on the balcony with Jezebel and watched as King Ahaz fell screaming to his death, and he and she grinned as the dogs gathered and lapped up his life's blood. Oh, my little brothers and sisters, watch thou for The Interloper."

"Yes, O Jesus—" The man the gunslinger had first noticed coming into town, the one with the straw hat.

"He's always been there, my brothers and sisters. But I don't know his mind. And you don't know his mind. Who could understand the awful darkness that swirls there, the pride like pylons, the titanic blasphemy, the unholy glee? And the madness! The cyclopean, gibbering madness that walks and crawls and wriggles through men's most awful wants and desires?"

"O Jesus Savior—"

"It was *him* who took our Lord up on the mountain—"

"Yes—"

"It was *him* that tempted him and shewed him all the world and the world's pleasures—"

"*Yesss*—"

"It's *him* that will come back when Last Times come on the world...and they are coming, my brothers and sisters, can't you feel they are?"

"*Yesss*—"

Rocking and sobbing, the congregation became a sea; the woman seemed to point at all of them, none of them.

"It's *him* that will come as the Antichrist, to lead men into the flaming bowels of perdition, to the bloody end of wickedness, as Star Wormwood hangs blazing in the sky, as gall gnaws at the vitals of the children, as women's wombs give forth monstrosities, as the works of men's hands turn to blood—"

"Ahhh—"

"Ah, God—"

"Gawwwwwwwww—"

A woman fell on the floor, her legs crashing up and down against the wood. One of her shoes flew off.

"It's *him* that stands behind every fleshly pleasure ...*him*! The Interloper!"

"Yes, Lord!"

A man fell on his knees, holding his head and braying.

"When you take a drink, who holds the bottle?"

"The Interloper!"

"When you sit down to a faro or a Watch Me table, who turns the cards?"

"The Interloper!"

"When you riot in the flesh of another's body, when you pollute yourself, who are you selling your soul to?"

"In—"

"—ter—"

"Oh, Jesus...Oh—"

"—loper—"

"—Aw...Aw...Aw..."

"And who is he?" She screamed (but calm within, he could sense the calmness, the mastery, the control, the domination. He thought suddenly, with terror and absolute surety: he has left a demon in her. She is haunted. He felt the hot ripple of sexual desire again through his fear.)

The man who was holding his head crashed and blundered foward.

"I'm in hell!" He screamed up at her. His face twisted and writhed as if snakes crawled beneath his skin. "I done fornications! I done gambling! I done weed! I done *sins*! I—" But his voice rose skyward in a dreadful, hysterical wail that drowned articulation. He held his head as if it would burst like an overripe cantaloupe at any moment.

The audience stilled as if a cue had been given, frozen in their half-erotic poses of ecstasy.

Sylvia Pittston reached down and grasped his head. The man's cry ceased as her fingers, strong and white, unblemished and gentle, worked through his hair. He looked up at her dumbly.

"Who was with you in sin?" She asked. Her eyes looked into his, deep enough, gentle enough, cold enough to drown in.

"The . . . the Interloper."

"Called who?"

"Called Satan." Raw, oozing whisper.

"Will you renounce?"

Eagerly: "Yes! Yes! Oh, my Jesus Savior!"

She rocked his head; he stared at her with the blank, shiny eyes of the zealot. "If he walked through that door—" she hammered a finger at the vestibule shadows where the gunslinger stood—"would you renounce him to his face?"

"On my mother's name!"

"Do you believe in the eternal love of Jesus?"

He began to weep. "Your fucking-A I do—"

"He forgives you that, Jonson."

"Praise God," Jonson said, still weeping, unaware of what he had said or done.

"I know he forgives you just as I know he will cast out the unrepentant from his palaces and into the place of burning darkness."

"Praise God." The congregation, drained, spoke it solemnly.

"Just as I know this Interloper, this Satan, this Lord of Flies and Serpents will be cast down and crushed . . . will you crush him if you see him, Jonson?"

"Yes and praise God!" Jonson wept.

"Will you crush him if you see him, brothers and sisters?"

"Yess . . ." Sated.

"If you see him sashaying down Main St. tomorrow?"

"Praise God . . ."

The gunslinger, amused and unsettled at the same time, faded back out the door and headed for town. The smell of the desert was clear in the air. Almost time to move on. Almost.

● ● ●

XIII

In bed again.

"She won't see you," Allie said. She sounded frightened. "She doesn't see anybody. She only comes out on Sunday evenings to scare the hell out of everybody."

"How long has she been here?"

"Twelve years or so. Let's not talk about her."

"Where did she come from? Which direction?"

"I don't know." Lying.

"Allie?"

"I don't know!"

"Allie?"

"All right! All right! She came from the dwellers! From the desert!"

"I thought so." He relaxed a little. "Where does she live?"

Her voice dropped a notch. "If I tell you, will you make love to me?"

"You know the answer to that."

She sighed. It was an old, yellow sound, like turning pages. "She had a house over the knoll in back of the church. A little shack. It's where the . . . the real minister used to live until he moved out. Is that enough? Are you satisfied?"

"No. Not yet." And he rolled on top of her.

XIV

It was the last day, and he knew it.

The sky was an ugly, bruised purple, weirdly lit from above with the first fingers of dawn. Allie moved about like a wraith, lighting lamps, tending the corn fritters that spluttered in the skillet. He had loved her hard after she had told him what he had to know, and she had sensed the coming end and had given more than she had ever given, and she had given it with desperation against the coming of dawn, given it the tireless energy of sixteen. And she was pale this morning, on the brink of menopause again.

She served him without a word. He ate rapidly, chewing, swallowing, chasing each bite with hot coffee. Allie went to the batwings and stood staring out at the morning, at the silent battalions of slow-moving clouds.

"It's going to dust up today."

"I'm not surprised."

"Are you ever?" she asked ironically, and turned to watch him get his hat. He clapped it on his head and brushed past her.

"Sometimes," he told her. He only saw her once more alive.

XV

By the time he reached Sylvia Pittston's shack, the wind had died utterly and the whole world seemed to wait. He had been in desert country long enough to know that the longer the lull, the harder the wind would blow when it finally decided to start up. A queer, flat light hung over everything.

There was a large wooden cross nailed to the door of the place, which was leaning and tired. He rapped and waited. No answer. He rapped again. No answer. He drew back and kicked in the door with one hard shot of his right boot. A small bolt on the inside ripped free. The door banged against a haphazardly planked wall and scared rats into skittering flight. Sylvia Pittston sat in the hall, sat in a mammoth darkwood rocker, and looked at him calmly with those great and dark eyes. The stormlight fell on her cheeks in terrifying half-tones. She wore a shawl. The rocker made tiny squeaking noises.

They looked at each other for a long, clockless moment.

"You will never catch him," she said. "You walk in the way of evil."

"He came to you," the gunslinger said.

"And to my bed. He spoke to me in the Tongue. He—"

"He screwed you."

She did not flinch. "You walk an evil way, gunslinger.

You stand in shadows. You stood in the shadows of the holy place last night. Did you think I couldn't see you?"

"Why did he heal the weed-eater?"

"He was an angel of God. He said so."

"I hope he smiled when he said it."

She drew her lip back from her teeth in an unconsciously feral gesture. "He told me you would follow. He told me what to do. He said you are the Antichrist."

The gunslinger shook his head. "He didn't say that."

She smiled up at him lazily. "He said you would want to bed me. Do you?"

"Yes."

"The price is your life, gunslinger. He has got me with child . . . the child of an angel. If you invade me—" She let the lazy smile complete her thought. At the same time she gestured with her huge, mountainous thighs. They stretched beneath her garment like pure marble slabs. The effect was dizzying.

The gunslinger dropped his hands to the butts of his pistols. "You have a demon, woman. I can remove it."

The effect was instantaneous. She recoiled against the chair, and a weasel look flashed on her face. "Don't touch me! Don't come near me! You dare not touch the Bride of God!"

"Blow it out," the gunslinger said, grinning. He stepped toward her.

The flesh on the huge frame quaked. Her face had become a caricature of crazed terror, and she stabbed the sign of the Eye at him with pronged fingers.

"The desert," the gunslinger said. "What after the desert?"

"You'll never catch him! Never! Never! You'll burn! He told me so!"

"I'll catch him," the gunslinger said. "We both know it. What is beyond the desert?"

"No!"

"Answer me!"

"No!"

He slid forward, dropped to his knees, and grabbed her

thighs. Her legs locked like a vise. She made strange,
lustful keening noises.

"The demon, then," he said.

"No—"

He pried the legs apart and unholstered one of his guns.

"No! No! No!" Her breath came in short, savage
grunts.

"Answer me."

She rocked in the chair and the floor trembled. Prayers
and garbled bits of jargon flew from her lips.

He rammed the barrel of the gun forward. He could
feel the terrified wind sucked into her lungs more than he
could hear it. Her hands beat at his head; her legs
drummed against the floor. And at the same time the huge
body tried to take the invader and enwomb it. Outside
nothing watched them but the bruised sky.

She screamed something, high and inarticulate.

"What?"

"Mountains!"

"What about them?"

"He stops...on the other side...s-s-sweet *Jesus*!
...to m-make his strength. Med-m-meditation, do
you understand? Oh...I'm...I'm..."

The whole huge mountain of flesh suddenly strained
forward and upward, yet he was careful not to let her
secret flesh touch him.

Then she seemed to wilt and grow smaller, and she
wept with her hands in her lap.

"So," he said, getting up. "The demon is served, eh?"

"Get out. You've killed the child. Get out. Get out."

He stopped at the door and looked back. "No child,"
he said briefly. "No angel, no demon."

"Leave me alone."

He did.

XVI

By the time he arrived at Kennerly's, a queer obscurity

had come over the northern horizon and he knew it was
dust. Over Tull the air was still dead quiet.

Kennerly was waiting for him on the chaff-strewn stage
that was the floor of his barn. "Leaving?" He grinned
abjectly at the gunslinger.

"Yes."

"Not before the storm?"

"Ahead of it."

"The wind goes faster than a man on a mule. In the
open it can kill you."

"I'll want the mule now," the gunslinger said simply.

"Sure." But Kennerly did not turn away, merely stood
as if searching for something further to say, grinning his
groveling, hate-filled grin, and his eyes flicked up and
over the gunslinger's shoulder.

The gunslinger sidestepped and turned at the same
time, and the heavy stick of stovewood that the girl Soobie
held swished through the air, grazing his elbow only. She
lost hold of it with the force of her swing and it clattered
over the floor. In the explosive height of the loft,
barnswallows took shadowed wing.

The girl looked at him bovinely. Her breasts thrust with
overripe grandeur at the wash-faded shirt she wore. One
thumb sought the haven of her mouth with dreamlike
slowness.

The gunslinger turned back to Kennerly. The grin was
huge. His skin was waxy yellow. His eyes rolled in their
sockets. "I—" he began in a phlegm-filled whisper and
could not continue.

"The mule," the gunslinger prodded gently.

"Sure, sure, sure," Kennerly whispered, the grin now
touched with incredulity. He shuffled after it.

He moved to where he could watch Kennerly. The
hostler brought the mule back and handed him the bridle.
"You get in an' tend your sister," he said to Soobie.

Soobie tossed her head and didn't move.

The gunslinger left them there, staring at each other
across the dusty, droppings-strewn floor, he with his sick
grin, she with dumb, animal defiance. Outside the heat
was still like a hammer.

XVII

He walked the mule up the center of the street, his boots sending up squirts of dust. His waterbags were strapped across the mule's back.

He stopped at Sheb's, and Allie was not there. The place was deserted, battened for the storm, but still dirty from the night before. She had not begun her cleaning and the place was as fetid as a wet dog.

He filled his tote sack with corn meal, dried and roasted corn, and half of the raw hamburg in the cooler. He left four gold pieces stacked on the planked counter. Allie did not come down. Sheb's piano bid him a silent, yellow-toothed good-bye. He stepped back out and cinched the tote sack across the mule's back. There was a tight feeling in his throat. He might still avoid the trap, but the chances were small. He was, after all, the interloper.

He walked past the shuttered, waiting buildings, feeling the eyes that peered through cracks and chinks. The man in black had played God in Tull. Was it only a sense of the cosmic comic, or a matter of desperation? It was a question of some importance.

There was a shrill, harried scream from behind him, and doors suddenly threw themselves open. Forms lunged. The trap was sprung, then. Men in longhandles and men in dirty dungarees. Women in slacks and in faded dresses. Even children, tagging after their parents. And in every hand there was a chunk of wood or a knife.

His reaction was automatic, instantaneous, inbred. He whirled on his heels while his hands pulled the guns from their holsters, the hafts heavy and sure in his hands. It was Allie, and of course it had to be Allie, coming at him with her face distorted, the scar a hellish, distorted purple in the lowering light. He saw that she was held hostage; the distorted, grimacing face of Sheb peered over her shoulder like a witch's familiar. She was his shield and sacrifice. He saw it all, clear and shadowless in the frozen deathless light of the sterile calm, and heard her:

"He's got me O Jesus don't shoot don't don't *don't*—"

But the hands were trained. He was the last of his breed and it was not only his mouth that knew the High Speech. The guns beat their heavy, atonal music into the air. Her mouth flapped and she sagged and the guns fired again. Sheb's head snapped back. They both fell into the dust.

Sticks flew through the air, rained on him. He staggered, fended them off. One, with a nail pounded raggedly through it, ripped at his arm and drew blood. A man with beard stubble and sweat-stained armpits lunged flying at him with a dull kitchen knife held in one paw. The gunslinger shot him dead and the man thumped into the street. His teeth clicked audibly as his chin struck.

"SATAN!" Someone was screaming: "THE AC-CURSED! BRING HIM DOWN!"

"THE INTERLOPER!" another voice cried. Sticks rained on him. A knife struck his boot and bounced. "THE INTERLOPER! THE ANTICHRIST!"

He blasted his way through the middle of them, running as the bodies fell, his hands picking the targets with dreadful accuracy. Two men and a woman went down, and he ran through the hole they left.

He led them a feverish parade across the street and toward the rickety general store/barber shop that faced Sheb's. He mounted the boardwalk, turned again, and fired the rest of his loads into the charging crowd. Behind them, Sheb and Allie and the others lay crucified in the dust.

They never hesitated or faltered, although every shot he fired found a vital spot and although they had probably never seen a gun except for pictures in old magazines.

He retreated, moving his body like a dancer to avoid the flying missiles. He reloaded as he went, with a rapidity that had also been trained into his fingers. They shuttled busily between gunbelts and cylinders. The mob came up over the boardwalk and he stepped into the general store and rammed the door closed. The large display window to the right shattered inward and three men crowded through. Their faces were zealously blank, their eyes filled with bland fire. He shot them all, and the two that followed them. They fell in the window, hung on the jutting shards of glass, choking the opening.

The door crashed and shuddered with their weight and he could hear *her* voice: "THE KILLER! YOUR SOULS! THE CLOVEN HOOF!"

The door ripped off its hinges and fell straight in, making a flat handclap. Dust puffed up from the floor. Men, women, and children charged him. Spittle and stovewood flew. He shot his guns empty and they fell like ninepins. He retreated, shoving over a flour barrel, rolling it at them, into the barbershop, throwing a pan of boiling water that contained two nicked straight-razors. They came on, screaming with frantic incoherency. From somewhere, Sylvia Pittston exhorted them, her voice rising and falling on blind inflections. He pushed shells into hot chambers, smelling the smells of shave and tonsure, smelling his own flesh as the calluses at the tips of his fingers singed.

He went through the back door and onto the porch. The flat scrubland was at his back now, flatly denying the town that crouched against its huge haunch. Three men hustled around the corner, with large betrayer grins on their faces. They saw him, saw him seeing them, and the grins curdled in the second before he mowed them down. A woman had followed them, howling. She was large and fat and known to the patrons of Sheb's as Aunt Mill. The gunslinger blew her backwards and she landed in a whorish sprawl, her skirt kinked up between her thighs.

He went down the steps and walked backwards into the desert, ten paces, twenty. The back door of the barbershop flew open and they boiled out. He caught a glimpse of Sylvia Pittston. He opened up. They fell in squats, they fell backwards, they tumbled over the railing into the dust. They cast no shadows in the deathless purple light of the day. He realized he was screaming. He had been screaming all along. His eyes felt like cracked ball bearings. His balls had drawn up against his belly. His legs were wood. His ears were iron.

The guns were empty and they boiled at him, transmogrified into an Eye and a Hand, and he stood, screaming and reloading, his mind far away and absent, letting his hands do their reloading trick. Could he hold up a hand, tell them he had spent twenty-five years learning this trick and others, tell them of the guns and the blood that had blessed them? Not with his mouth. But his hands could speak their own tale.

They were in throwing range as he finished, and a stick struck him on the forehead and brought blood in abraded drops. In two seconds they would be in gripping distance. In the forefront he saw Kennerly; Kennerly's younger daughter, perhaps eleven; Soobie; two male barflies; a female barfly named Amy Feldon. He let them all have it, and the ones behind them. Their bodies thumped like scarecrows. Blood and brains flew in streamers.

They halted a moment, startled, the mob face shivering into individual, bewildered faces. A man ran in a large, screaming circle. A woman with blisters on her hands turned her head up and cackled feverishly at the sky. The man whom he had first seen sitting gravely on the steps of the mercantile store made a sudden and amazing load in his pants.

He had time to reload one gun.

Then it was Sylvia Pittston, running at him, waving a wooden cross in each hand. "DEVIL! DEVIL! DEVIL! CHILD-KILLER! MONSTER! DESTROY HIM, BROTHERS AND SISTERS! DESTROY THE CHILD-KILLING INTERLOPER!"

He put a shot into each of the crosspieces, blowing the roods to splinters, and four more into the woman's head. She seemed to accordian into herself and waver like a shimmer of heat.

They all stared at her for a moment in tableau, while the gunslinger's fingers did their reloading trick. The tips of his fingers sizzled and burned. Neat circles were branded into the tips of each one.

There were less of them, now; he had run through them like a mower's scythe. He thought they would break with the woman dead, but someone threw a knife. The hilt struck him squarely between the eyes and knocked him over. They ran at him in a reaching, vicious clot. He fired his guns empty again, lying in his own spent shells. His head hurt and he saw large brown circles in front of his eyes. He missed one shot, downed eleven.

But they were on him, the ones that were left. He fired the four shells he had reloaded, and then they were beating him, stabbing him. He threw a pair of them off his left arm and rolled away. His hands began doing their infallible trick. He was stabbed in the shoulder. He was stabbed in the back. He was hit across the ribs. He was stabbed in the ass. A small boy squirmed at him and made the only deep cut, across the bulge of his calf. The gunslinger blew his head off.

They were scattering and he let them have it again. The ones left began to retreat toward the sand-colored, pitted buildings, and still the hands did their trick, like overeager dogs that want to do their rolling-over trick for you not once or twice but all night, and the hands were cutting them down as they ran. The last one made it as far as the steps of the barber shop's back porch, and then the gunslinger's bullet took him in the back of the head.

Silence came back in, filling jagged spaces.

The gunslinger was bleeding from perhaps twenty different wounds, all of them shallow except for the cut across his calf. He bound it with a strip of shirt and then straightened and examined his kill.

They trailed in a twisted, zigzagging path from the back door of the barber shop to where he stood. They lay in all positions. None of them seemed to be sleeping.

He followed them back, counting as he went. In the general store one man lay with his arms wrapped lovingly around the cracked candy jar he had dragged down with him.

He ended up where he had started, in the middle of the deserted main street. He had shot and killed thirty-nine men, fourteen women, and five children. He had shot and killed everyone in Tull.

A sickish-sweet odor came to him on the first of the dry, stirring wind. He followed it, then looked up and nodded. The decaying body of Nort was spread-eagled atop the plank roof of Sheb's, crucified with wooden pegs. Mouth and eyes were open. A large and purple cloven hoof had been pressed into the skin of his grimy forehead.

He walked out of town. His mule was standing in a clump of weed about forty yards out along the remnant of the coach road. The gunslinger led it back to Kennerly's stable. Outside, the wind was playing a louder tune. He put the mule up and went back to Sheb's. He found a ladder in the back shed, went up to the roof, and cut Nort down. The body was lighter than a bag of sticks. He tumbled it down to join the common people. Then he went back inside, ate hamburgers and drank three beers while the light failed and the sand began to fly. That night he slept in the bed where he and Allie had lain. He had no dreams. The next morning the wind was gone and the sun was its usual bright and forgetful self. The bodies had gone south with the wind. At midmorning, after he had bound all his cuts, he moved on as well.

XVIII

He thought Brown had fallen asleep. The fire was down to a spark and the bird, Zoltan, had put his head under his wing.

Just as he was about to get up and spread a pallet in the corner, Brown said, "There. You've told it. Do you feel better?"

The gunslinger started. "Why would I feel bad?"

"You're human, you said. No demon. Or did you lie?"

"I didn't lie." He felt the grudging admittance in him: he liked Brown. Honestly did. And he hadn't lied to the dweller in any way. "Who are you, Brown? Really, I mean."

"Just me," he said, unperturbed. "Why do you have to think you're such a mystery?"

The gunslinger lit a smoke without replying.

"I think you're very close to your man in black," Brown said. "Is he desperate?"

"I don't know."

"Are you?"

"Not yet," the gunslinger said. He looked at Brown with a shade of defiance. "I do what I have to do."

"That's good then," Brown said and turned over and went to sleep.

XIX

In the morning Brown fed him and sent him on his way. In the daylight he was an amazing figure with his scrawny, burnt chest, pencil-like collarbones and ringleted shock of red hair. The bird perched on his shoulder.

"The mule?" the gunslinger asked.

"I'll eat it," Brown said.

"Okay."

Brown offered his hand and the gunslinger shook it. The dweller nodded to the south. "Walk easy."

"You know it."

They nodded at each other and then the gunslinger walked away, his body festooned with guns and water. He looked back once. Brown was rooting furiously at his little cornbed. The crow was perched on the low roof of his dwelling like a gargoyle.

XX

The fire was down, and the stars had begun to pale off. The wind walked restlessly. The gunslinger twitched in his sleep and was still again. He dreamed a thirsty dream. In the darkness the shape of the mountains was invisible. The thoughts of guilt had faded. The desert had baked them out. He found himself thinking more and more about Cort, who had taught him to shoot, instead. Cort had known black from white.

He stirred again and awoke. He blinked at the dead fire with its own shape superimposed over the other, more geometrical one. He was a romantic, he knew it, and he guarded the knowledge jealously.

That, of course, made him think of Cort again. He didn't know where Cort was. The world had moved on.

The gunslinger shouldered his tote sack and moved with it.

(Thus ends what is written in the first Book of Roland, and his Quest for the Tower which stands at the root of Time.)

A Certain Slant of Light
by Raylyn Moore

Here's a story about a house that has a curse on it...or maybe it doesn't. As the title suggests, it depends on how you look at it.

One of the curious things about that house was that, in past times, things had not been used as they were meant to be used. Locks broken on the kitchen and pantry windows had been replaced not with new locks, but with knives and forks. The main goal, sealing the windows against prowlers and freshening breezes, had been accomplished by stuffing the cracks between the sashes with strips of cloth, and then wedging the tableware into the corners. Of course, the windows were then supposed never to be reopened.

Lace, though preoccupied with the thousand other details of the moving-in, couldn't wait to remove those pieces of bent metal, some of them silver-plated, with family monograms. (There was even one piece of sterling, a pickle fork.) Using a screwdriver, she dug out the rags and opened all the windows that would open. Some of the sashes crashed down again because of broken cords.

But this was an interior, rather shortsighted and carping comment on what was really a splendid old dwelling, the basic excellences of which such minor putterings could never mar, and in the long view the house remained to Lace a dream realized. Brought up among the cliff dwellings of Manhattan, then transplanted to the built-yesterday milieu of metropolitan Southern California, she had gone on yearning for the kind of living she had often read about but experienced just once, briefly, when as a child she had been sent for a part of a summer to a great-aunt who had an old frame house on a quiet street in Prout's Neck.

141

Now Lace had her own old frame house, three stories of it rising in dowdy splendor behind the screening growth of elderly maples on a huge, fenced lot that also had an assortment of mossy outbuildings. It was far too large a place and pointlessly extravagant, unless one happened to believe, as Lace did, that a dream never comes too high.

She spent the first few days (and could have spent weeks) just wandering from floor to floor and room to room, surprised anew at what was behind each closed door, at the end of each twisting staircase and narrow, tributary corridor. What delighted her especially during these excursions was the curious frisson she experienced when entering some forgotten room on an upper floor where nothing moved but dust motes through angling sunbeams and nothing sounded but her own breathing, and yet she would be convinced beyond argument that Something had just been there and gone. Wishful thinking? At least partly that, Lace admitted. For not only had she always wanted such a house, she had wanted one containing just such a hovering Presence, a Thing-in-residence. Wouldn't anyone? And yet it was more than she had dared to hope, for she knew how rare Presences were these days, and how valuable. They were being driven into ever-narrower extremities, of course, by all the senseless destruction of old houses in towns everywhere. Soon they would have no remaining asylum. It taxed credulity beyond the breaking point even to try to imagine a Thing inhabiting a home in Stuyvesant Village or Palos Verdes Estates.

The closest neighbors, who at first failed to recognize the name of Lace's husband, Maynard Hummel, wondered why the new family, with just one daughter, needed such a large house, but they considerately did not wonder aloud. And when Lace made it a point to know them immediately, throwing convention to the winds and turning up at their back door to inquire about trash pickup day and mail deliveries, they talked freely with her about the people who had lived in the house before, showing themselves pleased to be able to answer with authority all Lace's excited questions.

These former occupants had been a large family of unmarried brothers and sisters named Wechsmuth, some of whom had lived to advanced age, but all of whom were now gone, each having left—as Lance was shortly to discover—a clear fossil imprint of his or her existence somewhere in the vast primordial dust of that house that the Hummels then bought.

There had been seven of these spinsters and bachelors, Lace's neighbors told her. Mart, the eldest, the clan chieftain, had been a short, long-armed woman with facial moles growing stiff black bristles. Then came brother Ludy, who since the war (meaning in his case the Spanish-American) had never been quite well, and then Annie, known to the town for some forgotten reason as "the nice one." Arthur and Alice, the twins, were said to have been withdrawn into themselves even from the rest of the family, occupying a castle keep within the greater redoubt, a union within a union.

And there had been Lobithee, a bit dotty in her own way, given to biting off the heads of garden flowers and chewing contemplatively while passersby ogled from the street and God-knew-what thoughts troubled her poor head.

Itsy, the youngest, his Christian name long mislaid, had been a marvelously obese man in a family of thin people and the only one who earned an income. Itsy's was the role of outside monk. He had bought groceries, and answered the doorbell on the rare occasions when it sounded. His job as a casually employed carpenter couldn't have brought in much, but the Wechsmuths required very little. Not only had they never thrown anything away, they also had never permitted anything to wear out, especially clothing. Prodigious experts at making do, they had cannibalized bits and pieces of rusty garments to mend other, equally rusty garments in much the same fashion as they mended the toolshed roof with strips of linoleum left over from the kitchen floor.

Alone of them all, Lobithee had once been married. In her young womanhood (the story went), a local farmboy had proposed and been accepted. The marriage had lasted a day and enough hours into the night to unnerve Lobithee totally. Shaking in a corner like a rabbit in a snare, she had watched her chance to elude the bumbling farmboy, slipping out at last and racing ahead of him back home to her brothers and sisters across several acres of corn stubble on bleeding bare feet.

The Wechsmuths, except for Ludy, had never traveled. They had made no friends. Every incident (though incidents were kept to a minimum) had enhanced their isolation—Lobithee's marriage, Ludy's military service and ensuing malaria, Itsy's accident. (Itsy had toppled from a silo he was roofing and afterward had a characteristic, swiveling limp.)

It was known too that each sister and brother had kept to his or her own section of the big house, cooking meals separately, mostly on alcohol burners, and tending their austere, individual fires in the many fireplaces, all of which were equipped with coal grates. An exception to this rule of separatism was made by the twins, who, it was believed, had a dual household.

Lace returned home satisfied that she now knew everything about her predecessors that was common knowledge in the town. Poking through the house again, she found what she could now identify as one of Itsy's miter boxes being used to block off a mousehole on the second floor, a handmade embroidered corset cover that could have been from Lobithee's trousseau filling one of the window cracks, a prescription bottle with Ludy's name on it, and any number of other things.

And in the garden one day after a summer storm, when the earth was black and loose, a rectangular, flat stone spanning a drainage channel caught Lace's eye. It looked too geometrically regular, too smoothed up for an appearance in that wild, neglected garden. Using a discarded hoe handle, Lace prized it up and discovered its hidden side was inscribed:

SUSAN WECHSMUTH
B. Jan. 6, 1890—D. Dec. 24, 1910
Rest in Jesus

Lace's delight was redoubled. She, a newcomer to town, had discovered an eighth Wechsmuth. She fitted various possible explanations to the offhand use of Susan's headstone in the garden. An error had been made at the monumentmaker's in spelling (she had been Susanne?) or in one of the dates? (It *was* too appalling to believe that a girl born on Twelfthnight would die on Christmas Eve.) A corrected version of the stone had been made but since the error had for some reason not been the fault of the stonemason, the Wechsmuths had been obliged to pay for the ruined monument anyway. They had brought it home—this family that wasted nothing—to use when the first occasion arose that a tombstone would come in handy.

Susan had not been enumerated among the Wechsmuths by Lace's neighbors, of course, because she had died so young she'd been long since forgotten by outsiders. She had not lived on and on in that family of grotesques. Had she foreseen, then, what she was escaping? Taken her own life perhaps because of this dismal vision of a future she could not endure? And then the family, at first forgiving of her act, had been persuaded by the dour Lutheran minister to the harsh conclusion that Susan must lie in an unmarked, suicide's grave? Perhaps even removed the marker after it was installed?

That Susan had known *some*thing before her untimely loss of life was the theory that best satisfied Lace in the end. No one really knew what went on in the minds of young girls. Helen, for instance. It was true that Lace's daughter had literally disappeared into her sixteenth year like a mole into a burrow. One of the reasons for their move had been to see what could be done for Helen by the change, and for Maynard. If very few people remembered Maynard Hummel as a prodigy television writer where they had been living before, they might as well come to a place where he was not known as a person either. Not that it was that simple.

The story they had told one another and the friends they'd left was something of a variation on the truth. After investing fifteen of his best years—he'd started at twenty-two—on the kind of television serial that soars to eminence in a day and then for no reason winks out at the height of the arc, when one's back is momentarily turned, Maynard had been freed by fate to write the book he'd been planning for at least that long. Trouble was the telephone rang all the time in California; people came by. He was getting no work done. Have to move to isolation, buy an island, or what these days passes for one, a big old house in a little town in western Pennsylvania, the town selected almost at random. (Because of the fantastic expense, Maynard had warned that they could move this once, and no more. Lace, he said, must have no second thoughts. "Oh I *won't*," she promised. "It's what I've always wanted. How could I change my mind, ever?")

Of course, the flaw in the myth about the book was the number of years (ten) that had elapsed since the power shift in the industry, the shift that had dumped Maynard and then kept him out. (One of those things, everyone said. Television was funny that way, a power setup that for some was certain to be a knockdown.) Lace, in her narrower reflections, wondered if the real reason they'd moved wasn't because the excuse of the book, no longer believable in their former community, could now be reused credibly and comfortably—a notion as frugal as any of those of the Wechsmuths. Never throw away a perfectly good myth just because it gets a little worn. And back of it all was Lace's hope that there really might be a book. Sometime.

There were moments during the renovating when Lace suspected that it would be impossible after all to remove from the premises the powerful impress of the brothers and sisters, that the house would always be theirs and never hers. Yet when everything was over, she was equally sure the Wechsmuths would have found it hard to recognize their former home. Everything had been vigorously scraped, sanded, and refinished. All deficiencies were repaired with more appropriate materials than before. The woodwork was painted white and some of the more interesting wallpaper had been copied and restored.

The architecture and interior were an uneasy agglomeration of periods out of which Lace chose to preserve features she imagined were Colonial. Coming off particularly well, she thought, were the uncovering and repair of the random-width pegged flooring. It showed to best advantage in the third-story room with many dormer windows, a room now occupied by Maynard, his file cases, his tables, his desk.

Two big rooms on the second floor, joined, were done over especially for Helen, who immediately took to remaining in them much of the time. This left Lace the ground floor for herself, though she still prowled the vacant rooms on the higher levels, relieved to discover that the Thing had not been dislodged—she hoped not even discommoded—by all the activity. In fact, she felt it more strongly than ever, and one day she even imagined it delayed its disappearance out of the room she was about to enter and instead stayed to speak with her.

This happened in the attic, where she had gone one day to store a box of winter blankets. Because the third story rose well into the roof, the attic was tiny, just a single, dim lumber room crouching under the steep slope of the main rafters. And as Lace entered that afternoon, there were the ancient silence piled in drifts, the dust-filtered sunlight slanting palely through a round, high window, and the feeling she had learned to recognize.

"You're making a mistake," said a disapproving voice in her mind, "in taking me so lightly, as if I were just another feature of the property, like the summerhouse in the rear garden or the extra pantry behind the breakfast room. You have been far too casual. You outside people don't appreciate the seriousness of this kind of situation. There are some things one absolutely cannot write off as diversion."

Lace did not reply—partly, she realized, because she was uncertain of the protocol. Should she answer the voice aloud? Or simply think the reply and assume it would be conveyed? But while she was trying to make up her mind, the voice went on.

"In your case the mistake was inevitable because you're

essentially a frivolous woman. The world could be
shattering around you but you wouldn't be likely to see it;
no one so preoccupied with trivialities could. Why hasn't
it ever occurred to you, however, that I might be evil?
You'd better do some research on this kind of phenome-
non before something terrible happens. I feel it's only fair
to warn you that it could happen cumulatively, over a
long period, or suddenly, any day now. But you should
prepare yourself. You have certainly asked for it."

Though Lace waited politely, there was nothing more.
So she shoved the blanket chest to the rear wall of the
lumber room and went back downstairs. The encounter
had cleared up one thing, at least. Ever since she'd found
the tombstone, she had played with the notion that the
Presence might be Susan's restless ghost. Now she knew
better. It was certainly not young Susan Wechsmuth's
voice that had spoken.

No, the Things that live at the bottoms of old wells and
the tops of old houses are old themselves, far older than
anybody's ghost. And she knew beyond doubt now that
this was one of those. Furthermore, contrary to what the
Presence thought, she *had* done some looking into the
matter, since it was a subject that naturally went along
with her interest in old houses in small towns. It was for
this very reason that she *could* take the Thing so casually,
of course. Forewarned is forearmed. No doubt the
Presence had shaped the lives of the Wechsmuths and
those of the people in the house before them. (Had they
been grotesques as well?) But it could not shape Lace's
life, since she knew what to expect. It was the one thing
she must avoid, actually taking the Thing seriously—as
seriously, say, as it demanded to be taken. The frisson was
enjoyable; real fear would be intolerable. It must not
come to that, and there was no reason for it to, so long as
they understood each other—she and It—which she
believed now that they did.

Along with this determination went Lace's new
decision to show the Thing its place by ignoring it for a
while. She would stop moping about the house and
instead act on the resolution she'd made when she first

came to the town. Since she had embraced this way of life, she must live up to it in all ways. One of these ways was to be outgoing, make herself agreeable and acceptable to the townspeople, cause herself (and even more importantly Helen and Maynard) to be invited places.

The difficulty was that the only people she had managed to meet so far were the neighbors who had told her about the Wechsmuths. But they would serve for a beginning. Lace invited them in for coffee and a tour of the house now that the remodeling was accomplished.

These neighbors—a widow and her daughter, an anthropology major home for the summer from graduate school—responded with a show of what seemed to be genuine enthusiasm. The anthropologist daughter added that she looked forward to meeting Helen, whom Lace had mentioned, of course.

So when they arrived, on the appointed morning, Lace set out china cups in the blue-papered breakfast room and said, "Helen's upstairs. If she doesn't come down soon, I'll call her."

"Oh don't do that," Mrs. Bernard said. She was a pursy little woman going a bit stout in her midfifties. "I know how daughters hate being bossed around." And she winked in an exaggerated way at her own daughter, who ignored the signal and remarked:

"How odd it is after all these years to be actually inside this house. I grew up next door, you know, and not only was I never invited in, I never had the guts even to get a close look." Catherine Bernard went on to explain that, going past the house to and from school, she and her friends had titillated one another with dares about going into the Wechsmuth yard, even standing still alone in front of the property. Once they'd been ordered to move on by Mart, who'd made threatening gestures with her long arms from the distant front porch. Catherine, a tall, spectacled, athletic-looking young woman totally different from the mother, laughed at her own reminiscence and accepted her coffee, black, from Lace.

"Hummel, Hummel," Mrs. Bernard burst out suddenly. "Have I told you how familiar your husband's name sounds to me? Not when you first said it. It's only been the past week I've been thinking I'd heard it somewhere before."

So it had come after all, the comment Lace waited for with all new acquaintances, though even so it seemed strangely abrupt in the present context. Yet she was pleased and grateful, even a little relieved. "You remember it from the television shows he used to write." Lace named several of them.

"Oh I used to love those," Mrs. Bernard declared, perhaps just a shade too insistently. "What shows is he writing now?"

"Maynard isn't in television anymore," Lace said. "He can't spare the time from his book."

"How wonderful," Mrs. Bernard said. "I admire anyone who can write a book—so hard to imagine where they get all their ideas. We had a man here in town about six years back, rented the old Whitworth house for a summer. *He* was writing a book."

"Mother, for heaven's sake," Catherine said, and changed the subject. "How does Helen like it here?"

"I don't believe she knows yet. She's hardly been out of the house since we came. She's naturally shy, and a bit overweight. Lacks self-confidence, and in a new situation—" Lace had not meant to go so far, but she felt, suddenly and a bit prematurely, perhaps, with the midmorning sun filling the breakfast room, that the Bernards were her friends.

"I'd be glad to talk with her," Catherine offered. "Tell her about the swimming pool and the tennis. They're the only recreation available here in the summer, but they'd be a start. She could meet people her age at the pool."

"*Would* you?" Lace said gratefully. So one of the results she had secretly hoped for from this meeting had already come. Catherine, a young person, native of the town, knowledgeable, could be no end of help to Helen socially.

Lace examined with calm pleasure the vista into the tangled garden from a window draped crisply in blue linen. She was already proud of the miracles wrought in the house; the garden would be next to receive her attention. She had served hot jam tarts with the coffee, and the odor of sugary pastry clung, a Pennsylvania kind of odor, Lace thought. It went well with the surroundings, anyway. And because she felt comfortable, befriended, Lace began to believe anything was possible. She looked at Catherine and smiled. "How about right now? I'll show you and your mother over the rest of the house, then we can stop by Helen's rooms."

They set off. The Bernards were thoroughly appreciative of the pale paint, the new-old wallpaper, the carved newel post found in the garden toolshed and restored to the terminal of the bannister. The group worked its way through the first floor and prepared to go up. Lace told them about the miter box, the corset cover. Then, after a small pause for dramatic emphasis, she sprang the secret of the tombstone.

She could not have hoped for a better response. "Imagine!" said Catherine. "Isn't it just like the crazy Wechsmuths to use a tombstone to walk on? Do you know who Susan was, Mother?"

"Yes," said Mrs. Bernard, equally awed. "I'd almost forgotten. She was the—uh—idiot, poor girl. And in those days they didn't have the proper kind of care for—well, anyway, I don't really *know*, of course. After all, I was very young then, a child, and the girl was already dead by that time, but the rumor was they kept her locked up in the—"

Lace wanted to hear it all, sad and horrifying though it promised to be (her mind had already flown to the small back bedroom on the third floor where she had discovered a triple lock on the *out*side of the door), but they had by now arrived at Helen's door on the second floor. They had not been especially quiet—had been talking animatedly, in fact—and the exposed plank flooring must have echoed their footfalls. So what happened now didn't seem possible under these circumstances.

There was no answer to the first sharp rapping. Lace made the second raps softer, less demanding. Waiting, she had a moment for a thrust of remorse. Helen had been hidden away in these rooms while she, Lace, expended all her care on the house. Of course, that itself was an effort on Helen's behalf. The deficiency, if deficiency it were, lay in its being an indirect effort. Yet perhaps this visit from Catherine would help make up to Helen for any unmotherly remissness.

It was necessary to knock a third time before the answer came. "Go away!"

Lace spoke in tones that were perhaps unwisely dulcet. "Dear, I'd like you to meet someone." Why *couldn't* she have added, "They're here with me now"? Or would it have made a difference? Surely Helen had known?

"I do not *want* to meet anyone. I particularly do not want to meet any of your godawful hicks from this town, and that goes double for the moronic woman and her ugly daughter from next door. Go away, Lace."

Well, there it was, thought Lace.

The trio withdrew numbly from the newly-white door, walked down the mile stretch of hall and stairs. The Last Mile, Lace realized, had been well called.

Nor was she at all surprised to see Maynard waiting at the foot of the steps. Her executioner. He would finish the job Helen had begun, almost as if they had worked in collusion.

Maynard, who never came down out of his aerie in the morning or at midday, and sometimes not for several days, now stood leaning against the red-and-white paper of the entrance hall, complexion unwholesomely partico-lored by the fanlight. He was dressed in dirty, colorless shorts worn without a shirt, and held an iced-tea glass half full of liquid amber. Lace's hope—as if it mattered anyway, with everything else—was that the Bernards were ingenuous enough to believe the tea glass held iced tea. At the same time she doubted they were.

"How do?" Maynard said maliciously.

Mrs. Bernard recovered herself. "So good to have a famous author for a neighbor, Mr. Hummel. I used to love that series you did, that family series, about the Whatstheirnames—"

Maynard bowed slowly, unbowed equally slowly. "My wife reminded you about it, I suppose. Loyal of her. Did she tell you the big lie about the book too?"

"Well, I understood her to say you're writing a—"

"Ah. Poor Lace. Living in a dream, as always. Romantic. Well, ladies, I can set you straight. What I'm here for. I didn't come to this place to write. I came to rot. A rotter, not a writer. Difference, I think. Though maybe not."

He grew confidential, leaned very close to Mrs. Bernard. Lace thought for a moment he would lay an arm across her neighbor's shoulder. "Want to know who I really am?"

"I'm afraid I—"

"The Tin Woodsman, that's who. Wonderful man, Frank Baum. Some say he was a lush. In one of his more profound utterances, the Tin Woodsman says, 'If I am well oiled, I shall soon be all right again.' What depth, eh? What wit, what a *Weltanschauung*! Now, if Thoreau had ever drunk anything but pond water, *he* could have been the Tin Woodsman."

Maynard laughed all by himself, bowed a second time, fell silent.

Lace led the silent procession around him and down the hall toward the back door. They filed past the breakfast room where an inch of coffee waited, grown cold in the glass pot. A fly droned above two leftover jam tarts.

She saw them out, a ceremonious end to their first and last call. She heard Maynard's unsteady retreat up the front stairs.

Alone now, in full possession of the downstairs, Lace reminded herself that the Bernards would talk; they had talked readily and quite unkindly about the Wechsmuths' fractured lives.

Vividly, she saw how it would be. The Hummels. He on the top floor, their odd daughter whom no one had ever seen on the second. Lace supposed she would become the outside monk.

Sleep Well of Nights
by Avram Davidson

Avram Davidson appeared in the first volume of
The Year's Finest Fantasy *with an adventure of Jack
Limekiller, whose experiences in the almost-real
Central American nation called British Hidalgo are
quite eerie. Here's another very strange adventure in
the series—and no, you certainly don't have to have
read earlier Limekiller stories to understand this one.*

*Its original title has been changed at the request of
the author.*

"Are those lahvly young ladies with you, then?" the Red
Cross teacher asked.

Limekiller evaded the question by asking another, a
technique at least as old as the Book of Genesis. "Which
way did they go?" he asked.

But it did not work this time. "Bless me if I saw them
gow anywhere! They were both just standing on the
corner as I went by."

Limekiller gave up not so easily. "Ah, but which
corner?"

A blank look. "Why... *this* corner."

This corner was the corner of Grand Arawack and
Queen Alexandra Streets in the Town of St. Michael of
the Mountains, capital of Mountains District in the
Colony of British Hidalgo. Fretwork galleries dripping
with potted plants and water provided shade as well as
free shower baths. These were the first and second streets
laid out and had originally been deer trails; Government
desiring District Commissioner Bartholomew "Bajan"
Bainbridge to supply the lanes with names, he had, with
that fund of imagination which helped build the Empire,
called them First and Second Streets: it was rather a while
before anyone in Government next looked at a map and

155

then decided that numbered streets should run parallel to each other and not, as in this instance, across each other. And as the Grand Arawack Hotel was by that time built and as Alexandra (long-suffering consort of Fat Edward) was by that time Queen, thus they were renamed and thus had remained.

"St. Michael's" or "Mountains" Town, one might take one's pick, had once been a caravan city in miniature. The average person does not think of caravan cities being located in the Americas, and, for that matter, neither does anyone else. Nevertheless, trains of a hundred and fifty mules laden with flour and rum and textiles and tinned foods coming in, and with chicle and chicle and chicle going out, had been common enough to keep anyone from bothering to count them each time the caravans went by. The labor of a thousand men and a thousand mules had been year by year spat out of the mouths of millions of North Americans in the form of chewing gum.

So far as Limekiller knew, Kipling had never been in either Hidalgo, but he might have thought to have been if one ignored biographical fact and judged only by his lines,

> *Daylong, the diamond weather,*
> *The high, unaltered blue—*
> *The smell of goats and incense*
> *And the mule-bell tinkling through.*

Across from the hotel stood the abattoir and the market building. The very early morning noises were a series of bellows, bleats, squeals, and screams which drowned out cock-crow and were succeeded by the rattle and clatter of vulture claws on the red-painted corrugated iron roofs. Then the high voices of women cheapening meat. But all of these had now died away. Beef and pork and mutton (sheep or goat) could be smelled stewing and roasting now and then as the mild currents of the air alternated the odors of food with those of woodsmoke. He even thought he detected incense; there was the church spire nearby.

But there were certainly no young ladies around, lovely or otherwise.

There had been no very lengthy mule trains for a very long time.

There had been no flotillas of tunnel boats at the Town Wharf for a long time, either, their inboard motors drawn as high-up in "tunnels" within the vessels as possible to avoid the sand and gravel and boulders which made river navigation so difficult on the upper reaches of the Ningoon. No mule trains, no tunnel boats, no very great quantities of chicle, and everything which proceeded to and from the colonial capital of King Town and St. Michael's going now by truck along the rutted and eroded Frontier Road. No Bay boat could ever, in any event, have gotten higher up the river than the narrows called Bomwell's Boom; and the *Sacarissa* (Jno. Limekiller, owner and Master and, usually—save for Skippy the Cat—sole crew) was at the moment Hired Out.

She had been chartered to a pair of twosomes from a Lake Winnipeg boat club, down to enjoy the long hours of sunshine. Jack had been glad enough of the money but the charter had left him at somewhat of a loss: *leisure* to him had for so long meant to haul his boat up and clean and caulk and paint her: all things in which boatmen delight. Leisure without the boat was something new. Something else.

To pay his currently few debts had not taken long. He had considered getting Porter Portugal to sew a new suit of sails, but old P.P. was not a slot machine; you could not put the price into P.P.'s gifted hands and expect, after a reasonable (or even an unreasonable) period of time, for the sails to pop out. If Port-Port were stone sober he would not work and if dead drunk he *could* not work. The matter of keeping him supplied with just the right flow of old Hidalgo dark rum to, so to speak, oil the mechanism, was a nice task indeed: many boat owners, National, North American, or otherwise, had started the process with intentions wise and good: but Old Port was a crazy-foxy old Port and all too often had drunk them under the table, downed palm and needle, and vanished with the advance-to-buy-supplies into any one of the several stews which flourished on his trade. ("A debt of honor, me b'y," he would murmur, red-eyed sober, long days later. "Doesn't you gots to worry. I just hahs a touch ahv de ague, but soon as I bet-tah. . . .")

So that was *one* reason why John L. Limekiller had eventually decided to forget the new suit of sails for the time being.

Filial piety had prompted him to send a nice long letter home, but a tendency towards muscle spasms caused by holding a pen had prompted him to reduce the n.l.l. to a picture post card. He saw the women at the post office, one long and one short.

"What's a letter *cost*, to St. Michael's?" the Long was asking. "We *could, tele*phone for a reservation," the Short suggested. Jack was about to tell them, unsolicited, how fat the chance was of anybody in St. Michael's having a telephone *or* anything which could be reserved, let alone of understanding what a reservation was—then he took more than a peripheral look at them.

The Long had red hair and was wearing dungarees and a man's shirt. Not common, ordinary, just-plain-red: *cop*per-red. Worn in loops. Her shirt was blue with a faint white stripe. Her eyes were "the color of the sherry which the guests leave in the glass." Or don't, as the case may be. The Short could have had green hair in braids and been covered to her toes in a yashmak for all Jack noticed.

At that moment the clerk had asked him, "What fah you?"—a local, entirely acceptable usage, even commonplace, being higher than "What you want?" and lower than "You does want something?"—and by the time he had sorted out even to his own satisfaction that he wanted postage for a card to Canada and not, say, to send an armadillo by registered mail to Mauritius, and had completed the transaction in haste and looked around, trying to appear casual, they were gone. Clean gone. Where they had been was a bright-eyed little figure in the cleanest rags imaginable, with a sprinkling of white hairs on its brown, nutcracker jaws.

Who even at once declared, "'And now abideth faith,

hope, and charity, these three, and the greatest of these is charity,' you would not deny the Apostle Paul, would you, then, sir?"

"Eh? Uh... no," said Limekiller. Pretense cast aside, craning and gaping all around: *nothing*.

"Anything to offer me?" demanded the wee and ancient, with logic inexorable.

So there had gone a dime. And then and there had come the decision to visit St. Michael of the Mountains, said to be so different, so picturesque, hard upon the frontier of "Spanish" Hidalgo, and where (he reminded himself) he had after all *never been*.

Sometimes being lonely it bothers the way a tiny pebble in the shoe bothers: enough to stop and *do* something. But if one is very lonely indeed, then it becomes an accustomed thing. Only now did Limekiller bethink himself how lonely he had been. The boat and the Bay and the beastie-cat had been company enough. The average National boatman had a home ashore. The two men and two women even now aboard the *Sacarissa* in jammed-together proximity—they had each other. (And even now, considering another definition of the verb *to have* and the possible permutations of two males and two females made him wiggle like a small boy who has to *go—*). There was always, to be sure, the Dating Game, played to its logical conclusion, for a fee, at any one of the several hotels in King Town, hard upon the sea. But as for any of the ladies accompanying him anywhere on his boat...

"*Whattt?* You tink I ahm crazy? *Nut*ting like *dot!*"

Boats were gritty with sand to fill the boggy yards and lanes, smelly with fish. Boats had *no* connotations of romance.

Such brief affairs did something for his prostate gland ("Changing the acid," the English called it), but nothing whatsoever, he now realized, for his loneliness. Nor did conversation in the boatmen's bars, lately largely on the theme of, "New tax law, rum go up to 15¢ a glass, man!"

And so here he was, fifty miles from home, if King

Town was "home"—and if the *Sacarissa* was home
...well, who knew? St. Michael of the Mountains still
had some faint air of its days as a port-and-caravan city,
but that air was now faint indeed. Here the Bayfolk
(Black, White, Colored, and Clear) were outnumbered by
Turks and 'Paniar's, and there were hardly any Arawack
at all. (There seldom were, anywhere out of the sound and
smell of the sea.) There were a lot of old wooden houses,
two stories tall, with carved grillwork, lots of flowering
plants, lots of hills: perhaps looking up and down the hilly
lanes gave the prospects more quaintness and interest,
perhaps even beauty, than they might have had, were they
as level as the lanes of King Town, Port Cockatoo, Port
Caroline, or Lime Walk. And, too, there were the
mountains all about, all beautiful. And there was the
Ningoon River, flowing round about the town in easy
coils, all lovely, too: its name, though Indian in origin,
allowing for any number of easy, Spanish-based puns:

"Suppose you drink de wat-tah here, sah, you *cahn-not*
stay away!"

"En otros paises, señor, otros lugares, dicen mañana.`
Pero, por acá, señor, se dice ningun!"

And so forth.

Limekiller had perambulated every street and lane,
had circumambulated town. Like every town and the one
sole city in British Hidalgo, St. Michael's had no suburbs.
It was clustered thickly, with scarcely even a vacant lot,
and where it stopped being the Town of St. Michael of the
Mountains, it stopped. Abruptly. *Here* was the Incor-
poration; *there* were the farms and fields; about a mile
outside the circumambient bush began again.

He could scarcely beat every tree, knock on every door.
He was too shy to buttonhole people, ask if they had seen
a knockout redhead. So he walked. And he looked. And
he listened. But he heard no women's voices, speaking
with accent from north of the northern border of Mexico.
Finally he grew a little less circumspect.

To Mr. John Paul Peterson, Prop., the Emerging
Nation Bar and Club:

"Say...are there any other North Americans here in
town?"

As though Limekiller had pressed a button, Mr. Peterson, who until that moment had been only amiable, scowled an infuriated scowl and burst out, "What the Hell they want come *here* for? You think them people *crazy*? They got richest countries in the world, which they take good care *keep* it that way; so why the Hell they want come *here*? Leave me ask you one question. Turn your head all round. You see them table? You see them booth? How many people you see sitting and drinking at them table and them booth?"

Limekiller's eyes scanned the room. The question was rhetorical. He sighed. "No one," he said, turning back to his glass.

Mr. Peterson smote the bar with his hand. "Exactly!" he cried. *"No one!* You not bloody damn fool, boy. You have good eye in you head. *Why* you see no one? Because no one can afford come here and drink, is why you see no one. People can scarce afford *eat*! Flour cost nine cent! Rice cost fif*teen* cent! Lard cost thirty-*four* cent! Brown sugar at nine cent and white sugar at eleven! D.D. milk. twen-ty-one cent! And yet the tax going *up*, boy! The tax going *up*!"

A line stirred in Limekiller's mind. "Yes—and, 'Pretty soon *rum* going to cost fifteen cents,'" he repeated. Then had the feeling that (in that case) something was wrong with the change from his two-shillings piece. And with his having made this quotation.

"What you mean, *'fifteen cent'*?" demanded Mr. Peterson, in a towering rage. Literally, in a towering rage; he had been slumped on his backless chair behind the bar, now stood up to his full height . . . and it was a height, too. *"Whattt?'*Fif-*teen*-cent?' You think this some damn dirty liquor booth off in the bush, boy? You think you got *swampy*," referring to backwoods distilled goods, "in you glass? What '*fifteen cent*'? No such *thing*. You got pure Governor Morgan in you glass, boy, never cost less than one shilling, and pretty soon going to be thirty cent, boy: thir-ty-*cent*! And for what? For the Queen can powder her nose with the extra five penny, boy?" Et cetera. Et cetera.

Edwin Rodney Augustine Bickerstaff, Royal British Hidalgo Police (sitting bolt-upright in his crisp uniform beneath a half-length photograph of the Queen's Own Majesty):

"Good afternoon, sir. May I help you, sir?"

"Uh...yes! I was wondering...uh...do you know if there are any North Americans in town?"

Police-sergeant Bickerstaff pondered the question, rubbed his long chin. "Any *North* Americans, you say sir?"

Limekiller felt obliged to define his terms. "Any Canadians or people from the States."

Police-sergeant Bickerstaff nodded vigorously. "Ah, now I understand you, sir. Well. That would be a matter for the Immigration Officer, wouldn't you agree, sir?"

"Why...I suppose. Is *he* in right now?" This was turning out to be more complex than he had imagined.

"Yes, sir. He *is* in. *Un*officially speaking, he is in. *I* am the police officer charged with the duties of Immigration Officer in the Mountains District, sir,"

"Well—"

"Three to four, sir."

Limekiller blinked. Begged his pardon. The police-sergeant smiled slightly. "Every evening from three to four, sir, pleased to execute the duties of Immigration Officer, sir. At the present time," he glanced at the enormous clock on the wall, with just a touch of implied proof, "I am carrying out my official duties as Customs Officer. *Have you anything to declare?*"

And, *So much for that suggestion,* Limekiller thought, a feeling of having only slightly been saved from having made a fool of himself tangible in the form of something warmer than sunshine round about his face and neck.

The middle-aged woman at the Yohan Yahanoglu General Mdse. Establishment store sold him a small bar of Fry's chocolate, miraculously unmelted. Jack asked, "Is there another hotel in town, besides the Grand?"

A touch of something like hauteur came over the still-handsome face of *Sra.* Yohanoglu. "Best you ahsk wan of the men," she said. And, which one of the men? *"Any men,"* said she.

So. Out into the sun-baked street went lonely

Limekiller. Not that lonely at the moment, though, to
want to find where the local hookers hung out. Gone too
far to turn back. And, besides, turn back to *what*?

The next place along the street which was open was the
El Dorado Club and Dancing (its sign, slightly uneven,
said).

Someone large and burly thumped in just before he
did, leaned heavily on the bar, "How much, *rum*?" he
demanded.

The barkeep, a 'Paniard, maybe only one-quarter
Indian (most of the Spanish-speaking Hidalgans were
more than that), gave a slight yawn at this sudden access
of trade. "Still only wan dime," he said. "Lahng as dees
borrel lahst. When necessitate we broach nudder borrel,
under new tox lah, *iay! Pobrecito! Going be fifteen cent!*"

"*¡En el nombre del* Queen!" proclaimed the other new
customer, making the sign of the cross, then gesturing for
a glass to be splashed.

Limekiller made the same gesture.

"What you vex weed de Queen, *varón*?" the barkeeper
asked, pouring two fingers of "clear" into each glass.
"You got new road, meb-be ah beet bum-py, but *new*; you
got new wing on hospital, you got new generator for give
ahl night, electricity: *whattt*? You teenk you hahv ahl
dees, ahn not pay ah new tox? No sotch teeng!"

"*No me hace falta,* 'ahl dees,'" said the other customer.
"*Resido en el* bush, where no hahv not-ting like dot."

The barkeep yawned again. "*Reside en el* bush? Why
you not live like old-time people? Dey not dreenk rum.
Dey not smoke cigarette. Dey not use lahmp-*ile*. Ahn dey
not pay toxes, not dem, no."

"Me no want leev like dot. *Whattt*? You cahl dot
'leev'?" He emptied his glass with a swallow, dismissed
any suggestion that Walden Pond and its tax-free
amenities might be his for the taking, turned to Limekiller
his vast Afro-Indian face. "Filiberto Marín, señor, is de
mahn to answer stranger question. Becahs God *love* de
stranger, señor, ahn Filiberto Marín love *God*. Everybody know Filiberto Marín, ahn if anyone want know
where he is, I am de mahn." Limekiller, having indeed

questions, or at any rate, A Question, Limekiller opened his mouth.

But he was not to get off so easily. There followed a long, *long* conversation, or monologue, on various subjects, of which Filiberto Marín was the principal one. Filiberto Marín had once worked one entire year in the bush and was only home for a total of thirty-two days, a matter (he assured Jack) of public record. Filiberto Marín was born just over the line in Spanish Hidalgo, his mother being a Spanish Woman and his father a British Subject By Birth. Had helped build a canal, or perhaps it was *The* Canal. Had been in Spanish Hidalgo at the time of the next-to-last major revolution, during which he and his sweetheart had absquatulated for a more peaceful realm. Married *in church*! Filiberto Marín and his wife had produced one half a battalion for the British Queen! "Fifteen children—and *puros varónes*! Ahl son, señor! So fahst we have children! Sixty-two year old, and work more tasks one day dan any young man! An I now desires to explain we hunting and fishing to you, becahs you stranger here, so you ignorance not you fahlt, señor."

Limekiller kept his eyes in the mirror, which reflected the passing scene through the open door, and ordered two more low-tax rums; while Filiberto Marín told him how to cast nets with weights to catch mullet in the lagoons, they not having the right mouths to take hooks; how to catch turtle, the *tortuga blanca* and the striped turtle (the latter not being popular locally because it was striped)—

"What difference does the stripe mean, Don Filiberto?"

"*¡Seguro!* Exoctly!!" beamed Don Filiberto, and, never pausing, swept on: how to use raw beef skin to bait lobsters ("Dey cahl him *lobster*, but is really de *langusta*, child of de crayfish."), how to tell the difference in color between saltwater and freshwater ones, how to fix a dory, how to catch tortuga "by dive for him—"

"—You want to know how to cotch croc-o-*dile* by dive for him? Who can tell you? Filiberto Marín will answer dose question," he said, and he shook Limekiller's hand with an awesome shake.

There seemed nothing boastful about the man. Evidently Filiberto Marín *did* know all these things and, out of a pure and disinterested desire to help a stranger, wanted merely to put his extensive knowledge at Jack's disposal. . . .

Of this much, Limekiller was quite clear the next day. He was far from clear, though, as to how he came to get there in the bush where many cheerful dark people were grilling strips of *barbacoa* over glowing coals—mutton it was, with a taste reminiscent of the best old-fashioned bacon, plus . . . well, *mutton*. He did not remember having later gone to bed, let alone to sleep. Nor know the man who came and stood at the foot of his bed, an elderly man with a sharp face which might have been cut out of ivory . . . this man had a long stick . . . a spear? . . . no . . .

Then Limekiller was on his feet. In the moon-speckled darkness he could see very little, certainly not another man. There was no lamp lit. He could hear someone breathing regularly, peacefully, nearby. He could hear water purling, not far off. After a moment, now able to see well enough, he made his way out of the cabin and along a wooden walkway. There was the Ningoon River below. A fine spray of rain began to fall; the river in the moonlight moved like watered silk. *What* had the man said to him? Something about showing him . . . showing him *what*? He could not recall at all. There had really been nothing menacing about the old man.

But neither had there been anything reassuring.

Jack made his way back into the cabin. The walls let the moonlight in, and the fine rain, too. But not so much of either as to prevent his falling asleep again.

Next day, passion—well, that was not exactly the right word—but what was? Infatuation? Scarcely even that. An uncommon interest in, plus a great desire for, an uncommonly comely young woman who also spoke his own language with familiar, or familiar enough, accents—oh, well—Hell!—whatever the *word* was, what-ever his own state of mind had been, next morning had given way to something more like common sense.

Common sense, then, told him that if the young woman (vaguely he amended this to the young women) had intended to come to St. Michael of the Mountains to stay at a hotel ... or wherever it was, which they thought might take a reservation ... had even considered *writing* for the reservation, well, they had not intended to come here at once. In other words: enthusiasm (*that* was the word! ... damn it ...) enthusiasm had made him arrive early.

So, since he was already *there,* he might as well relax and enjoy it.

—He was already *where?*

Filiberto Marín plunged his hands into the river and was noisily splashing water onto his soapy face. Jack paused in the act of doing the same thing for himself, waited till his host had become a trifle less audible—*how* the man could snort!—"Don Fili, what is the name of this place?"

Don Fili beamed at him, reached for the towel. "These place?" He waved his broad hand to include the broad river and the broad clearing, with its scattered fields and cabins. "These place, Jock, *se llame* Pahrot Bend. You like reside here? Tell me, just. I build you house." He buried his face in his towel. Jack had no doubt that the man meant exactly what he said, gave another look around to see what was being so openhandedly—and openheartedly—offered him; this time he looked across to the other bank. Great boles of trees: Immense! Immense! The eye grew lost and dizzy gazing upward toward the lofty, distant crowns. Suddenly a flock of parrots, yellowheads, flew shrieking round and round; then vanished.

Was it some kind of an omen? *Any* kind of an omen? To live here would not be to live just anywhere. He thought of the piss-soaked bogs which made up too large a part of the slums of King Town, wondered how anybody could live *there* when anybody could live *here.* But *here* was simply too far from the sea, and it was to live upon the sunwarm sea that he had come to this small country, so far from his vast own one. Still ... might not be such a bad idea... well, not to *live* here all the time. But... a smaller version of the not-very-large cabins of the hamlet... a sort of country home... as it were... ha-ha... well, why not? Something to think about... anyway.

"Crahs de river, be one nice spot for build you *cabanita*," said Don Filiberto, reading his mind.

"Mmm... what might it cost?" he could not help asking, even though knowing whatever answer he might receive would almost certainly not in the long run prove accurate.

"Cahst?" Filiberto Marín, pulling his shirt over his huge dark torso, considered. Cost, clearly, was not a matter of daily concern. Calculations, muttering from his mouth, living and audible thoughts, struggling to take form: "Cahst... May-be, ooohhh, say-*be* torty dollar?"

"Forty dollars?"

Don Filiberto started to shake his head, reconsidered. "I suppose may-*be*. Not take lahng. May-be one hahf day, collect wild cane for make wall, bay *leaf* for make *techo*, roof. An may-be 'nother hahf day for put everything togedder. Cahst? So: Twenty dollar. Torty dollar. An ten dollar *rum*! Most eeem-por-tont!" He laughed. Rum! The oil which lubricates the neighbors' labors. A house-raising bee, Hidalgo style.

"And the land itself? The cost of the land?"

But Don Fili was done with figures. "What 'cahst of de lond'? Lond not cahṣt nah-ting. Lond belahng to Pike Es-tate."

A bell went ding-a-ling in Limekiller's ear. The Pike Estate. The great Pike Estate Case was the Jarndyce vs. Jarndyce of British Hidalgo. Half the lawyers in the colony lived off it. Was there a valid will? Were there valid heirs? Had old Pike died intestate? *¿Quien sabe?* There were barroom barristers would talk your ears off about the First Codicil and the Second Codicil and the Alleged Statement of Intention and the Holograph Document and all the rest of it. Limekiller had heard enough about the Pike Estate Case. He followed after Don Fili up the bank. Ah, but—

"Well, maybe nobody would bother me *now* if I had a

cabin built there. But what about when the estate is finally settled?"

Marín waved an arm, as impatiently as his vast good nature would allow. "By dot time, *hijo mio*, what you care? You no hahv Squatter Rights by den? Meb-*be* you *dead* by den!"

Mrs. Don Filiberto, part American Indian, part East Indian, and altogether Amiable and Fat, was already fanning the coals on the raised fire-hearth for breakfast.

Nobody was boating back to town then, although earnest guarantees were offered that "by and by somebody" would *be* boating back, for sure. Limekiller knew such sureties. He knew, too, that he might certainly stay on with the Marín family at Parrot Bend until then—and longer—and be fully welcome. But he had after all come to "Mountains" for something else besides rural hospitality along the Ningoon River (a former Commissioner of Historical Sites and Antiquities had argued that the name came from an Indian word, or words, meaning Region of Bounteous Plenty; local Indians asserted that a more literal and less literary translation would be Big Wet). The fine rain of the night before began to fall again as he walked along, and soon he was soaked.

It did not bother him. By the time he got back into town the sun would have come out and dried him. Nobody bothered with oilskins or mackintoshes on the Bay of Hidalgo, nor did he intend to worry about his lack of them here in the Mountains of Saint Michael Archangel and Prince of Israel.

Along the road (to give it its courtesy title) he saw a beautiful flurry of white birds—were they indeed cattle egrets? living in symbiosis, or commensality, with the cattle? was one, indeed, heavy with egg, "blown over from Africa"? Whatever their name or origin, they did follow the kine around, heads bobbing as they, presumably, ate the insects the heavy cloven hooves stirred up. But what did the *cattle* get out of it? Company?

The rain stopped, sure enough.

It was a beautiful river, with clear water, green and bending banks. He wondered how high the highest flood waters came. A "top gallon flood," they called that. Was there a hint of an old tradition that the highest floods would come as high as the topgallant sails of a ship? Maybe.

The rain began again. Oh, well.

An oilcloth serving as door of a tiny cabin was hauled aside and an old woman appeared and gazed anxiously at Jack. "Oh, sah, why you wahk around in dis eager rain?" she cried at him. "Best you come in, *bide,* till eet *stop!*"

He laughed. "It doesn't seem all that eager to me, Grandy," he said, "but thank you anyway."

In a little while it had stopped. *See?*

Further on, a small girl under a tree called, "Oh, see what beauty harse, meester!"

Limekiller looked. Several horses were coming from a stable and down the path to the river; they were indeed beautiful, and several men were discussing a sad story of how the malfeasance of a jockey (evidently not present) had lost first place in a recent race for one of them to the famous Tigre Rojo, the Red Tiger, of which even Limekiller, not a racing buff, had heard.

"Bloody b'y just raggedy-ahss about wid him, an so Rojo win by just a nose. Son of a beach!" said one of the men, evidently the trainer of *the* beauty horse, a big bay.

"—otherwise he beat any harse in British Hidalgo!"

"Oh, yes! Oh, yes, Mr. Ruy!—dot he would!"

Ruy, his dark face enflamed by the memory of the loss, grew darker as he watched, cried, "Goddammit, oh Laard Jesus Christ, b'y! Lead him by de *head* till he *in* de wahter, *den* lead him by rope! When you goin to learn?—an watch out for boulder!—you know what one bloody fool mon want me to do? Want me to *run* harse dis marnin—not even just canter, he want *run* him!—No, *no*, b'y, just let him swim about be de best ting for him—

"Dis one harse no common harse—dis one harse foal by *Garobo*, from Mr. Pike *stud*! Just let him swim about, I say!"

The boy in the water continued, perhaps wisely, to say

nothing, but another man now said, "Oh, yes. An blow aht de cold aht of he's head, too."

Mr. Ruy grunted, then, surveying the larger scene and the graceful sweep of it, he said, gesturing, "I cotch plenty fish in dis river—catfish, twenty-pound tarpon, too. I got nylon *line*, but three week now, becahs of race, I have no time for cotch fish." And his face, which had gradually smoothed, now grew rough and fierce again. "Bloody dom fool jockey b'y purely raggeddy-*ahss* around wid harse!" he cried. The other men sighed, shook their heads. Jack left them to their sorrow.

Here the river rolled through rolling pasture lands, green, with trees, some living and draped with vines, some dead and gaunt but still beautiful. The river passed a paddock of Brahma cattle like statues of weathered grey stone, beautiful as the trees they took the shade beneath, cattle with ears like leaf-shaped spearheads, with wattles and humps. Then came an even lovelier sight: black cattle in a green field with snow-white birds close by among them. Fat hogs, Barbados sheep, water meadows, sweet soft air.

He could see the higher roofs on the hills of the town, but the road seemed to go nowhere near there. Then along came a man who, despite his clearly having no nylon line, had—equally clearly—ample time to fish, carried his catch on a stick. "De toewn, sir? Straight acrahs de savannah, sir," he gestured, "is de road to toewn." And, giving his own interpretation to the text, *I will not let thee go unless thou bless me,* detained Limekiller with blessings of unsolicited information, mostly dealing with the former grandeur of St. Michael's Town, and concluding, "Yes, sir, in dose days hahv t'ree dahnce *hahll*. Twen-ty bar and club! Torkish Cat'edral w'open every day, sah—*every day!*—ahn..." he groped for further evidences of the glorious days of the past, "ahn ah fot fowl, sah, cahst two, t'ree shilling!"

Sic transit gloria mundi.

The room at the hotel was large and bare, and contained a dresser with a clouded mirror, a chair, and a bed with a broad mattress covered in red "brocade"; the sheet, however, would not encompass it. This was standard: the sheet never *would*, except in the highest of high class hotels. And as one went down the scale of classes and the size of the beds diminished so, proportionately, did the sheets: they were *always* too narrow and too short. Curious, the way this was always so. (In the famous, or infamous, Hotel Pelican in King Town, sheets were issued on application only, at an extra charge, for the beds were largely pro forma. The British soldiers of the Right Royal Regiment, who constituted the chief patrons, preferred to ignore the bed and used the *wall*, would you believe it, for their erotic revels. If that was quite the right word.)

There was a large mahogany wardrobe, called a "press" in the best Dickensian tradition, but there were no hangers in it. There was a large bathroom off the hall but no towels and no soap, and the urinal was definitely out of order, for it was tied up with brown paper and string and looked like a twelve-pound turkey ready for the oven.

But all these shortcomings were made up for, by one thing which the Grand Hotel Arawack *did* have: out on the second-story verandah was a wide wooden-slatted swing of antique and heroic mold, the kind one used to see only at Auntie Mary's, deep in the interior of Prince Edward Island or other islands in time.—Did the Hiltons have wide wooden swings on their verandahs? Did the Hiltons have verandahs, for that matter?

Limekiller took his seat with rare pleasure: it was not every damned day that he could enjoy a nostalgia trip whilst at the same time rejoicing in an actual physical trip which was, really, giving him just as much pleasure. For a moment he stayed immobile. (Surely, Great-uncle Leicester was just barely out of sight, reading the Charlottetown newspaper, and damning the Dirty Grits?) Then he gave his long legs a push and was off.

Up! and the mountains displayed their slopes and foothills. *Down!* and the flowery lanes of town came into sight again. And, at the end of the lanes was the open square where stood the flagpole with the Union Jack and the National Ensign flapping in the scented breeze

...and, also, in sight, and well in sight (Limekiller had chosen well) was the concrete bench in front of which the bus from King Town had to disembogue its passengers. If they came by bus, and come by bus they must (he reasoned), being certainly tourists and not likely to try hitching. Also, the cost of a taxi for fifty miles was out of the reach of anyone but a land speculator. No, by *bus*, and there was where the bus would stop.

"Let me help you with your bags," he heard himself saying, ready to slip shillings into the hands of any boys brash enough to make the same offer.

There was only one fly in the ointment of his pleasure.

Swing as he would and as long as he would, no bus came.

"Bus? *Bus*, sir? *No*, sir. Bus ahlready come orlier today. Goin bock in evening. Come ahgain tomorrow."

With just a taste of bitterness, Limekiller said, *"Mañana."*

"¡Ah, Vd, si puede hablar en espanol, señor. Si-señor. Mañana viene el bus, otra vez. —Con el favor de Dios."

An the creek don't rise, thought Limekiller.

Suddenly he was hungry. There was a restaurant in plain sight, with a bill of fare five feet tall painted on its outer wall: such menus were only there for, so to speak, authenticity. To prove that the place was indeed a restaurant. And not a cinema. Certainly no one would ever be able to order and obtain anything which was *not* painted on them.—Besides, the place was closed.

"Be open tonight, sir," said a passerby, observing him observing.

Jack grunted. "Think they'll *have* that tonight?" he asked, pointing at random to *Rost Muttons* and to *Beef Stakes*.

An emphatic shake of the head. "*No*-sir. Rice and beans."

Somewhere nearby someone was cooking something besides rice and beans. The passerby, noticing the stranger's blunt and sunburned nose twitch, with truly Christian kindness said, "But Tía Sani be open now."

"Tía Sani?"

" *Yes*-sir. Miss Sanita. Aunt Sue. Directly down de lane."

Tía Sani had no sign, no giant menu. However, Tía Sani was *open*.

Outside, the famous Swift Sunset of the Tropics dallied and dallied. There was no sense of urgency in Hidalgo, be it British or Spanish. There was the throb of the light-plant generator, getting ready for the night. Watchman, what of the night?—what put *that* into his mind? He swung the screen door, went in.

Miss Sani, evidently the trim grey little woman just now looking up towards him from her stove, did not have a single item of formica or plastic in her spotless place. Auntie Mary, back in P.E.I., would have approved. She addressed him in slow, sweet Spanish. "How may I serve you, sir?"

"What may I encounter for supper, señora?"

"We have, how do they call it in inglés, meat, milled, and formed together? ah! los mitbols! And also a *caldo* of meat with macaroni and verdants. Of what quality the meat? Of beef, señor."

Of course it was cheap, filling, tasty, and good.

One rum afterwards in a club. There might have been more than one, but just as the thought began to form (like a mitbol), someone approached the jukebox and slipped a coin into its slot—the only part of it not protected by a chickenwire cage against violent displays of dislike for whatever choice someone else might make. The management had been wise. At once, NOISE, slightly tinctured with music, filled the room. Glasses rattled on the bar. Limekiller winced, went out into the soft night.

Suddenly he felt sleepy. Whatever was there tonight would be there tomorrow night. He went back to his room, switched the sheet so that at least his head and torso would have its modest benefits, thumped the lumpy floc pillow until convinced of its being a hopeless task, and stretched out for slumber.

The ivory was tanned with age. The sharp face seemed a touch annoyed. The elder man did not exactly *threaten*

Limekiller with his pole or spear, but . . . and why *should*
Limekiller get up and go? Go *where*? For *what*? He had
paid for his room, hadn't he? He wanted to sleep, didn't
he? And he was damned well going to sleep, too. If old
what's-his-name would only let him . . . off on soft green
clouds he drifted. *Up* the river. *Down* the river. Old man
smiled, slightly. And up the soft green mountains. Old
man was frowning, now. Old man was—

"Will you get the Hell *out* of here?" Limekiller shouted,
bolt upright in bed—poking him with that damned—

The old man was gone. The hotel maid was there. She
was poking him with the stick of her broom. The light was
on in the hall. He stared, feeling stupid and slow and
confused. "Eh—?"

"You have bad *dream*," the woman said.

No doubt, he thought. Only—

"Uh, thanks. I—uh. Why did you poke me with the
broomstick? And not just shake me?"

She snorted. "*Whattt?* You theenk I want *cotch* eet?"

He still stared. She smiled, slightly. *He* smiled, slightly,
too. "Are bad dreams contagious, then?" he asked.

She nodded, solemnly, surprised that he should ask.

"Oh. Well, uh, then . . . then how about helping me
have some *good* ones?" He took her, gently, by the hand.
And, gently, pulled. She pulled her hand away. Gently.
Walked towards the open door. Closed it.

Returned.

"Ahl right," she said. "We help each other." And she
laughed.

He heard her getting up, in the cool of the early day.
And he moved towards her, in body and speech. And fell
at once asleep again.

Later, still early, he heard her singing as she swept the
hall, with, almost certainly, that same broom. He burst
out and cheerfully grabbed at her. Only, it wasn't her.
"What you want?" the woman asked. Older, stouter.
Looking at him in mild surprise, but with no dislike or
disapproval.

"Oh, I, uh, are, ah. Ha-ha. Hmm. Where is the other

lady? Here last night? Works here?" He hadn't worded
that as tactfully as he might have. But it didn't seem to
matter.

"She? She not work here. She come help out for just
one night. Becahs my sister, lahst night, she hahv wan lee
pickney—gorl *beh*bee. So I go ahn she stay." The
pronouns were a bit prolix, but the meaning was clear.
"Now she go bock. Becahs truck fah go Macaw Falls di
leave. señor." And, as she looked at the play of expression
on his face, the woman burst into hearty, good-willed
laughter. And bounced down the hall, still chuckling,
vigorously plying her besom.

Oh, *well*.

And they *had* been *good* dreams, too.

Tía Sani was open. Breakfast: two fried eggs, buttered
toast of thick-sliced home-baked bread, beans (mashed),
tea with tinned milk, orange juice. Cost: $1.00, National
Currency—say, 60¢, 65¢, US or Canadian. On the wall,
benignly approving, the Queen, in her gown, her tiara,
and her Smile of State; also, the National Premier, in
open shirt, eyeglasses, and a much broader smile.

Jack found himself still waiting for the bus. *Despite* the
Night Before. See (he told himself), so it *is*n't Just Sex. . . .
Also waiting, besides the retired chicle-tappers and
superannuated mahogany-cutters, all of them authorized
bench-sitters, was a younger and brisker man.

"You are waiting for the bus, I take it," he now said.

"Oh, yes. Yes, I am."

And so was *he*. "I am expecting a repair part for my
tractor. Because, beside my shop, I have a farm. You see
my shop?" He companionably took Limekiller by the
arm, pointed to a pink-washed building with the
indispensable red-painted corrugated iron roof (indispensable because the rains rolled off them and into
immense wooden cisterns) and overhanging gallery.
"Well, I find that I cannot wait any longer, Captain Sneed
is watching the shop for me, so I would like to ahsk you
one favor. *If* you are here. *If* the bus comes. *Would* you be
so kind as to give me a hail?"

Limekiller said, "Of course. Be glad to," suddenly

realized that he had, after all, other hopes for *If* The Bus Come; hastily added, "And if not, I will send someone to hail you."

The dark (but not *local*-dark) keen face was split by a warm smile. "Yes, do.—Tony Mikeloglu," he added, giving Jack's hand a hearty, hasty shake; strode away. (Tony Mikeloglu could trust Captain Sneed not to pop anything under his shirt, not to raid the till, not to get too suddenly and soddenly drunk and smash the glass goods. But, suppose some junior customer were to appear during the owner's absence and, the order being added up and its price announced, pronounce the well-known words, *Ma say, "write eet doeen"*—could he trust Captain Sneed to demand cash and not "write it down?"—no, he could *not*.)

Long Limekiller waited, soft talk floating on around him, of oldtime "rounds" of sapodilla trees and tapping them for chicle, talk of "hunting"—that is, of climbing the tallest hills and scouting out for the telltale reddish sheen which mean mahogany—talk of the bush camps and the high-jinks when the seasons were over. But for them, now, all seasons were over, and it was only that: talk. Great-uncle Leicester had talked a lot, too; only *his* had been other trees, elsewhere.

Still, no bus.

Presently he became aware of feeling somewhat ill at ease, he could not say why. He pulled his long fair beard, and scowled.

One of the aged veterans said, softly, "Sir, de mon *hail*ing you."

With an effort, Limekiller focused his eyes. There. There in front of the pink store building. Someone in the street, calling, beckoning.

"De *Tork* hailing you, sir. Best go see what he want."

Tony Mikeloglu wanted to tell him something? Limekiller, with long strides strolled down to see. "I did not wish to allow you to remain standing in the sun, sir. I am afraid I did not ask your name. Mr. Limekiller?— Interesting name. Ah. Yes. My brother-in-law's brother has just telephoned me from King *Town*, Mr. Limekiller. I am afraid that the bus is not coming today. Break*down*?"

Under his breath, Limekiller muttered something coarse and disappointed.

"Pit-ty about the railroad," a deep voice said, from inside the store. "Klondike to Cape Horn. Excellent idea. Vi-sion. But they never built it. Pit-ty."

Limekiller shifted from one foot to another. Half, he would go back to the hotel. Half, he would go somewhere else. (They, she, no one was coming. What did it matter?) *Any*where. *Where?* But the problem was swiftly solved. Once again, and again without offense, the merchant took him by the arm. "Do not stand outside in the sun, sir. Do come *in*side the shop. In the shade. And have something cold to drink." And by this time Jack was already there. "Do you know Captain Sneed?"

Small, khaki-clad, scarlet-faced. Sitting at the counter, which was serving as an unofficial bar. "I suppose you must have often wondered," said Captain Sneed, in a quarterdeck voice, "why the Spaniard didn't settle British Hidalgo when he'd settled everywhere *else* round about?"

"—Well—"

"Didn't know it was *here*, Old Boy! Couldn't have gotten here if he *did*, you see. First of all," he said, drawing on the counter with his finger dipped in the water which had distilled from his glass (Tony now sliding another glass, tinkling with, could it be?—yes, it was! Ice!—over to Jack, who nodded true thanks, sipped)— "First of all, you see, coming from east to west, there's Pharaoh's Reef—quite enough to make them sheer off south in a bit of a damned hurry, don't you see. Then there's the Anne of Denmark Island's Reef, even bigger! And suppose they'd *sail*ed south to avoid Anne of Denmark Island's Reef? Eh? What would they find, will you tell me that?"

"Carpenter's Reef... unless it's been moved," said Jack.

Sneed gave a great snort, went on, *"Exactly!* Well, then—now, even if they'd missed Pharaoh's Reef and got pahst it... even if they'd missed Anne of Denmark Island's Reef and got pahst it... even if they'd missed Carpenter's Reef and got pahst *it*... why, then there's that great long *Barrier* Reef, don't you see, one of the biggest

in the world. (Of course, Australia's the biggest one. . . .)
No. No, Old Boy. Only the British lads knew the way
through the Reef, and you may be sure that *they* were not
pahssing out the information to the Spaniard, no, ho-ho!"

Well (thought Jack, in the grateful shade of the shop),
maybe so. It was an impressive thought, that, of infinite
millions of coral polyps laboring and dying and
depositing their stony "bones" in order to protect British
Hidalgo (and, incidentally, though elsewhere, Australia)
from "the Spaniard."

"Well!" Captain Sneed obliterated his watery map with
a sweep of his hand. "Mustn't mind *me*, Old Boy. This is
my own King Charles's head, if you want to know. It's just
the damnable *cheek* of those Spaniards there, *there*, in
Spanish Hidalgo, still claiming this blessed little land of
ours as their own, when they had never even set their *foot*
upon it!" And he blew out his scarlet face and actually
said "Herrumph!"—a word which Jack had often seen
but never, till now, actually heard.

And then Tony Mikeloglu, who had evidently gone
through all, all of this many, many times before, said,
softly, "My brother-in-law's brother had just told me on
the telephone from King *Town*—"

"Phantom relay, it has—the telephone, you know—
sorry, Tony, forgive me—what does your damned crook
of a kinsman tell you from King Town?"

". . . tells me that there is a rumor that the Pike Estate
has finally been settled, you know."

Not *again*? *Always* . . . thought Limekiller.

But Captain Sneed said, Don't you believe it! "Oh.
What? 'A rumor,' yes, well, you may believe *that*. Always
a rumor. Why didn't the damned fellow make a proper
will? Eh? For that matter, why don't *you*, Old Christopher?"

There was a sound more like a crackle of cellophane
than anything else. Jack turned to look; there in an
especially shadowy corner was a man even older, even
smaller, than Captain Sneed; and exposed toothless gums
as he chuckled.

"Yes, why you do not, Uncle Christopher?" asked
Tony.

In the voice of a cricket who has learned to speak English with a strong Turkish accent, Uncle Christopher said that he didn't believe in wills.

"What's going to become of all your damned doubloons, then, when you go pop?" asked Captain Sneed. Uncle Christopher only smirked and shrugged. "Where have you concealed all that damned money which you accumulated all those years you used to peddle bad rum and rusty roast-beef tins round about the bush camps? Who's going to get it all, eh?"

Uncle Christopher went *hickle-hickle*. "I know who going get it," he said. *Sh'sh, sh'sh, sh'sh..* His shoulders, thin as a butterfly's bones, heaved his amusement.

"Yes, but *how* are they going to get it? What? How are you going to take care of that? Once you're dead."

Uncle Christopher, with a concluding crackle, said, "I going do like the Indians do. . . ."

Limekiller hadn't a clue what the old man meant, but evidently Captain Sneed had. "What?" demanded Captain Sneed. "Come now, come now, you don't really *believe* all that, do you? You *do*? You do! Tush. Piffle. The smoke of all those bush camps has addled your brains. Shame on you. Dirty old pagan. Disgusting. Do you call yourself a Christian and a member of a church holding the Apostolic Succession? *Stuff!*"

The amiable wrangle went on. And, losing interest in it, Limekiller once again became aware of feeling ill at ease. Or . . . was it . . . could it be? . . . *ill?*

In came a child, a little girl; Limekiller had seen her before. She was perhaps eight years old. *Where* had he seen her?

"Ah," said Mikeloglu, briskly the merchant again. "Here is me best customer. She going make me rich, not true, me Bet-ty gyel? What fah you, *chaparita*?"

White rice and red beans were for her, and some coconut oil in her own bottle was for her, and some tea and some chile peppers (not very much of any of these items, though) and the inevitable tin of milk. (The chief difference between small shops and large shops in St. Michael's was that the large ones had a much larger selection of tinned milk.) Tony weighed and poured, wrapped and tied. And looked at her expectantly.

She untied her handkerchief, knot by knot, and counted out the money. Dime by dime. Penny by penny. Gave them all a shy smile, left. "No fahget me when you rich, me Bet-ty gyel," Tony called after her. "Would you believe, Mr. Limekiller, she is one of the grand*child*ren of old Mr. Pike?"

"Then why isn't she rich already? Did the others get it all?—Oh. I forgot. Estate not settled."

Captain Sneed grunted. "Wouldn't help her even if the damned estate *were* settled. An outside child of an outside child. Couldn't inherit if the courts ever decide that he died intestate, and of course: no mention of her in any will... if there *is* any will..." *An outside child.* How well Jack knew that phrase by now. Marriage and giving in marriage was one thing in British Hidalgo; begetting and bearing of children, quite another thing. No necessary connection. "Do you have any children?" "Well, I has four children." Afterthought: "Ahnd t'ree oetside." Commonest thing in the world. Down here.

"What's wrong with you, Old Boy?" asked Captain Sneed. "You look quite dicky."

"Feel rotten," Limekiller muttered, suddenly aware of feeling so. "Bones all hurt."

Immediate murmurs of sympathy. And: "*Oh,* my. You weren't caught in that rain yesterday morning, were you?"

Jack considered. "Yesterday morning in the daytime. And... before... in the night time, too—Why?"

Sneed was upset. "'*Why?'* Why, when the rain comes down like that, from the north, at this time of year, they call it 'a fever rain'...."

Ah. *That* was what the old woman had called out to him, urging him in out of the drizzle. *Bide,* she'd said. *Not* an "eager" rain—a *fever* rain!

"Some say that the rain makes the sanitary drains overflow. And some say that it raises the mosquitoes. *I* don't know. And some laugh at the old people, for saying that. But *I* don't laugh.... You're not laughing, either, are you? Well. What are we going to do for this man, Mik? Doctor *in,* right now?"

But the District Medical Officer was not in right now. It was his day to make the rounds in the bush hamlets in one half of the circuit. On one other day he would visit the other half. And in between, he was in town holding clinics, walking his wards in the hospital there on one of the hills, and attending to his private patients. Uncle Christopher produced from somewhere a weathered bottle of immense pills which he assured them were quinine, shook it and rattled it like some juju gourd as he prepared to pour them out.

But Captain Sneed demurred. "Best save that till we can be sure that it is malaria. Not they use quinine nowadays. Mmm. No chills, no fever? Mmm. Let me see you to your room at the hotel." And he walked Limekiller back, saw him not only into his room but into his bed, called for "some decent sheets and some blankets, what sort of a kip are you running here, Antonoglu?" Antonoglu's mother, a very large woman in a dress as black and voluminous as the tents of Kedar, came waddling in with sighs and groans and applied her own remedy: a string of limes, to be worn around the neck. The maid aspersed the room with holy water.

"I shall go and speak to the pharmacist," Captain Sneed said, briskly. "What—?" For Limekiller, already feeling not merely rotten but *odd*, had beckoned to him. "Yes?"

Rotten, aching, odd or not, there was something that Limekiller wanted taken care of. "Would you ask anyone to check," he said, carefully. "To check the bus? The bus when it comes in. Two young ladies. One red-haired. When it comes in. Would you check. Ask anyone. Bus. Red-haired. Check. If no breakdown. Beautiful. Would you. Any. Please? Oh."

Captain Sneed and the others exchanged looks.

"Of course, Old Boy. Don't worry about it. All taken care of. Now." He had asked for something. It had not come. "What, not even a thermometer? *What?* Why, what do you *mean,* 'You had one but the children broke it'? *Get another one at once.* Do you wish to lose your license? Never mind. *I* shall get another one at once. *And* speak to the pharmacist. Antonoglu-*khan-um*, the moment he begins to sweat, or his teeth chatter, *send me word*.

"Be back directly," he said, over his shoulder.

But he was not back directly.

Juan Antonoglu was presently called away to take care of some incoming guests from the lumber camps. He repeated Captain Sneed's words to his mother, who, in effect, told him not to tell her how to make yogurt. She was as dutiful as anyone could be, and, after a while, her widower son's children coming home, duty called her to start dinner. She repeated the instructions to the maid, whose name was Purificación. Purificación watched the sick man carefully. Then, his eyes remaining closed, she tiptoed out to look for something certain to be of help for him, namely a small booklet of devotions to the Señor de Esquipulas, whose cultus was very popular in her native republic. But it began to drizzle again: out she rushed to, first, get the clothes off the line and, second, to hang them up in the lower rear hall.

Limekiller was alone.

The mahogany press had been waiting for this. It now assumed its rightful shape, which was that of an elderly gentleman rather expensively dressed in clothes rather old-fashioned in cut, and, carrying a long...*something*...in one hand, came over to Jack's bed and looked at him most earnestly. Almost reproachfully. Giving him a hand to help him out of bed, in a very few moments he had Limekiller down the stairs and then, somehow, they were out on the river; and then...somehow...they were *in* the river. No.

Not exactly.

Not at all.

They were *under* the river.

Odd.

Very odd.

A hundred veiled eyes looked at them.

Such a dim light. Not like anything familiar. Wavering. What was that. A crocodile. *I* am getting *out* of *here*, said Limekiller, beginning to sweat profusely. This was the signal for everyone to let Captain Sneed know. But nobody was there. Except Limekiller. And, of course, the old man.

And, of course, the crocodile.

And, it now became clear, *quite* a number of other creatures. All reptilian. Why was he not terrified, instead of being merely alarmed? He was in fact, now that he came to consider it, not even all that alarmed. The creatures were looking at him. But there was somehow nothing terrifying in this. It seemed quite all right for him to be there.

The old man made that quite clear.

Quite clear.

"Is he delirious?" the redhead asked. Not just plain ordinary red. *Copper*-red.

"I don't have enough Spanish to know if saying '*barba amarilla*' means that you're delirious, or not. Are you delirious?" asked the other one. The Short. Brown hair. Plain ordinary Brown.

"'*Barba amarilla*' means 'yellow beard,'" Limekiller explained. Carefully.

"Then you aren't delirious. I guess. —What does 'yellow beard' mean, in this context?"

But he could only shake his head.

"I mean, we can see that you do have a blond beard. Well, blond in *parts*. Is that your nickname? No."

Coppertop said, anxiously, "His pulse seems so *funny*, May!" She was the Long. So here they were. The Long and the Short of it. Them. He gave a sudden snort of laughter.

"An insane cackle if ever I heard one," said the Short. "Hm, *Hmm*. You're *right*, Felix. It *does* seem so funny. Mumping all *around* the place—Oh, hello!"

Old Mrs. Antonoglu was steaming slowly down the lake, all the other vessels bobbing as her wake reached them. *Very* odd. Because it still *was* old Mrs. Antonoglu in her black dress and not really the old Lake Mickinuckee ferry boat. And this wasn't a lake. Or a river. They were all back in his room. And the steam was coming from something in her hand.

Where was the old man with the sharp face? Tan old

man. Clear. Things were far from *clear*, but—

"What I bring," the old woman said, slowly and carefully and heavily, just the way in which she walked, "I bring 'im to drink for 'ealth, poor sick! Call the . . . call the . . . country *yerba*," she said, dismissing the missing words.

The red-haired Long said, "Oh, good!"

Spoon by bitter spoonful she fed it to him. Sticks of something. Boiled in water. A lot of it dribbled down his beard. "Felix," what an odd name. She wiped it carefully with kleenex.

"But 'Limekiller' is just as odd," he felt it only fair to point out.

"Yes," said the Short. "You certainly are. How did you know we were coming? We weren't sure, ourselves. *Nor* do we know you. Not that it matters. We are emancipated women. Ride bicycles. But we don't smoke cheroots, and we are *not* going to open an actuarial office with distempered walls, and the nature of Mrs. Warren's profession does not bother us in the least: in fact, we have thought, now and then, of entering it in a subordinate capacity. Probably *won't*, though. Still . . ."

Long giggled. Short said that the fact of her calling her Felix instead of *Felicia* shouldn't be allowed to give any wrong ideas. It was just that *Felicia* always sounded so goddamn silly. They were both talking at once. The sound was very comforting.

The current of the river carried them all off, and then it got so very still.

Quite early next morning.
Limekiller felt fine.
So he got up and got dressed. Someone, probably Purificación, had carefully washed his clothes and dried and ironed them. He hadn't imagined everything: there was the very large cup with the twigs of country *yerba* in it. He went downstairs in the early morning quiet, cocking an ear. Not even a buzzard scrabbled on the iron roof. There on the hall table was the old record book used as a register. On the impulse, he opened it. Disappoint-

ment washed over him. *John L. Limekiller, sloop* Sacarissa, *out of King Town.* There were several names after that, all male, all ending in *-oglu*, and all from the various lumber camps round about in the back bush: Wild Hog Eddy, Funny Gal Hat, Garobo Stream. . . .

Garobo.

Struck a faint echo. Too faint to bother with.

But no one named Felix. Or even *Felicia*. Or May. Shite and onions.

There on the corner was someone.

"Lahvly morning," said someone. "Just come from hospital, seeing about the accident victims. Name is Pauls, George Pauls. Teach the Red Cross clahsses. British. You?"

"Jack Limekiller. Canadian. Have you seen two women, one a redhead?"

The Red Cross teacher *had* seen them, right there on that corner, but knew nothing more helpful than that. So, anyway, *that* hadn't been any delirium or dreams, either, *thank God.* (For how often had he not dreamed of fine friends and comely companions, only to wake and know that they had not been and would never be.)

At Tia Sani's. In came Captain Sneed. *"I say!* Terribly sorry! Shameful of me—I don't know how—Well. There'd been a motor accident, lorry overturned, eight people injured, so we all had to pitch in, there in hospital—Ah, by the *way.* I *did* meet your young ladies, thought you'd imagined them, you know—District Engineer gave them a ride from King Town—I told them about you, went on up to hospital, then there was this damned accident—By the time we had taken care of them, poor chaps, fact is, I am *ashamed* to say, I'd forgotten all about you.—But you look all right, now." He scanned Limekiller closely. "Hm, still, you should see the doctor. I wonder. . . ."

He walked back to the restaurant door, looked up the street, looked down the street. *"Doc-tor!*—Here he comes now."

In came a slender Eurasian man; the District Medical Officer himself. (Things were *always* happening like that in Hidalgo. Sometimes it was, "You should see the Premier. Ah, here he comes now. *Prem-ier!*") The D.M.O. felt Limekiller's pulse, pulled down his lower eyelid, poked at spleen and liver, listened to an account of yesterday. Said, "Evidently you have had a brief though severe fever. Something like the one-day flu. Feeling all right now? Good. Well, eat your usual breakfast, and if you can't hold it down, come see me at my office."

And was gone.

"Where are they now? The young women, I mean."

Captain Sneed said that he was blessed if he knew, adding immediately, "Ah. Here they come now."

Both talking at once, they asked Jack if he felt all right, assured him that he looked well, said that they'd spent the night at Government Guest House (there was one of these in every out-district capital and was best not confused with *Government House*, which existed only in the colonial capital itself: the Royal Governor lived there, and he was not prepared to put up guests below the rank of, well, *Go*vernor).

"Mr. Boyd arranged it. We met him in King Town. He was coming here anyway," said Felix, looking long and lovely. "He's an engineer. He's...how would you describe him, May?"

"He's an engin*eer*," May said.

Felix's sherry-colored eyes met Limekiller's. "Come and live on my boat with me and we will sail the Spanish Main together and I will tell you all about myself and frequently make love to you," he said at once. Out loud, however, all he could say was, "Uh...thanks for wiping my beard last night...uh...."

"Don't mention it," she said.

May said, "I want lots and lots of exotic foods for breakfast." She got two fried eggs, buttered toast of thick-sliced, home-baked bread, beans (mashed), tea, orange juice. "There is nothing *like* these exotic foods," she said.

Felix got egg on her chin. Jack took his napkin and wiped. She said that turnabout was fair play. He said that one good turn deserved another. She asked him if he had ever been to Kettle Point Lagoon, said by They to be beautiful. A spirit touched his lips with a glowing coal.

"I am going there today!" he exclaimed. He had never heard of it.

"Oh, good! Then we can all go together!"

Whom did he see as they walked towards the river, but Filiberto Marín. Who greeted him with glad cries, and a wink, evidently intended as compliments on Jack's company. "Don Fili, can you take us to Kettle Point Lagoon?"

Don Fili, who had at once begun to nod, stopped nodding. "Oh, Juanito, only wan mon hahv boat which go to Kettle Point Lagoon, ahn dot is Very Big Bakeman. He get so *vex*, do anybody else try for go dot side, none ahv we odder boatmen adventure do it. But I bring you to him. May-be he go today. *Veremos.*"

Very Big Bakeman, so-called to distinguish him from his cousin, Big Bakeman, was very big indeed. What he might be like when "vex," Limekiller (no squab himself) thought he would pass up knowing.

Bakeman's was the only tunnel boat in sight, probably the only one still in service. His answer was short. "Not before Torsday, becahs maybe not enough wah-teh get me boat ahcross de bar. *Tors*day," he concluded and, yawning, leaned back against the cabin. Monopolists the world over see no reason to prolong conversation with the public.

Felix said something which sounded like, "Oh, spit," but wasn't. Limekiller blinked. *Could* those lovely lips have uttered That Word? If so, he concluded without much difficulty, he would learn to like it. *Love* it. "Don Fili will take us to," he racked his brains, "somewhere just as interesting," he wound up with almost no pause. And looked at Don Fili, appealingly.

Filiberto Marín was equal to the occasion. "*Verdad.* In wan leetle while I going up de Right Branch. *Muy linda.* You will have pleasure. I telling Juanito about it, day before yesterday."

Limekiller recalled no such conversation, but he would have corroborated a deal with the devil, rather than let her out of his sight for a long while yet. He nodded knowingly. "Fascinating," he said.

"We'll get that nice lady to pack us a lunch."

Jack had a quick vision of Tía Sani packing them fried eggs, toast, beans, tea, and orange juice. But that nice lady fooled him. Her sandwiches were immense. Her eggs were deviled. She gave them *empenadas* and she gave them "crusts"—pastries with coconut and other sweet fillings— and then, behaving like aunts the whole world over, she ladled soup into a huge jar and capped it and handed it to Limekiller with the caution to hold it like *this* so that it didn't leak. . . . Not having any intention to have his hands thus occupied the whole trip, he lashed it and shimmed it securely in the stern of Marín's boat.

He had barely known that the Ningoon River *had* two branches. Parrot Bend was on the left one, then. The dory, or dugout, in use today was the largest he had seen so far. Captain Sneed at once decided it had room enough for him to come along, too. Jack was not overjoyed at first. The elderly Englishman was *a decent sort*. But he talked, damn it! *How* he talked. Before long, however, Limekiller found he talked to May, which left Felix alone to talk to Jack.

"John Lutwidge Limekiller," she said, having asked to see his inscribed watch. "there's a *name*. Beats Felicia Fox." *He* thought "fox" of all words in the world the most appropriate for her. He didn't say so. "—Why Lutwidge?"

"Lewis Carroll? Charles Lutwidge Dodgson, his real name? Distant cousin. Or so my Aunty Mary used to say."

This impressed her, anyway a little. "And what does Limekiller mean? How do you kill a lime? And *why*?"

"You take a limestone," he said, "and you burn it in a kil*n*. Often pronounced kill. Or, well, you *make* lime, for cement or whitewash or whatever, by burning stuff. Not just limestone. Marble. Oyster shells. Old orange rinds, maybe, I don't know, I've never done it. Family *name*," he said.

She murmured, "I see. . . ." She wound up her sleeves. He found himself staring, fascinated, at a blue vein in the inside of her arm near the bend. Caught her gaze. Cleared his throat, sought for something subject-changing and ever so interesting and novel to say. "Tell me about yourself," was what he found.

She gave a soft sigh, looked up at the high-borne trees. There was another blue vein, in her *neck*, this time. Woman was one mass of sexy *veins*, damn it! He would simply lean over and he would kiss—"Well, I was an Art Major at Harrison State U. and I said the Hell with it and May is my cousin and she wanted to go someplace, too, and so we're here.... Look at the *bridge!*"

They looked at its great shadow, at its reflection, broken by the passing boat into wavering fragments and ripples. The bridge loomed overhead, so high and so impressive in this remote place, one might forget that its rotting road-planks, instead of being replaced, were merely covered with new ones...or, at the least, newer ones. "In ten years," they heard Captain Sneed say, "the roadbed will be ten feet tall...if it lasts that long."

May: "Be sure and let us know when it's going to fall and we'll come down and watch it. Ffff-*loppp!*—Like San Luis Rey."

"Like *whom*, my dear May?"

The river today was at middle strength: shallow-draft vessels could and still did navigate, but much dry shingle was visible near town. Impressions rushed in swiftly. The day was neither too warm nor too wet, the water so clear that Limekiller was convinced that he could walk across it. Felix lifted her hand, pointed in wordless wonder. There, on a far-outlying branch of a tree over the river was an absolutely monstrous lizard of a beautiful buff color; it could not have been less then five full feet from snout to end of tail, and the buff shaded into orange and into red along the spiky crenelations on the spiny back ridge. He had seen it before. *Had* he seen it before? He *had* seen it before.

"Iguana!" he cried.

Correction was polite but firm. "No, sir, Juanito. Iguana is *embra,* female. Dat wan be *macho.* Male. *Se llama 'garobo.'....*"

Something flickered in Limekiller's mind. "¡*Mira!*

¡*Mira!* Dat wan dere, *she* be iguana!" And that one there, smaller than the buff dragon, was of a beautiful blue-green-slate-grey color. "Usual," said Filiberto, "*residen en* de bomboo t'icket, which is why de reason is call in English, 'Bomboo chicken'...."

"You *eat* it?"—Felix.

"Exotic *food*, exotic *food*!"—May.

"*Generalmente*, only de hine leg ahn de tail. But is very good to eat de she of dem when she have egg, because de egg so very nice eating, in May, June; but even noew, de she of dem have red egg, nice and hard. *Muy sabroso.*"

Jack turned and watched till the next bend hid the place from sight. After that he watched for them—he did not know why he watched for them, were they watching for *him*?—and he saw them at regular intervals, always in the topmost branches: immense. Why so high? Did they eat insects? And were there more insect to be taken, way up there? They surely did not eat *birds*? Some said, he now recalled in a vague way, that they ate only leaves; but were the top leaves so much more succulent? Besides, they seemed not to be eating anything at all, not a jaw moved. Questions perhaps not unanswerable, but, certainly, at the moment unanswered. Perhaps they had climbed so high only for the view: absurd.

"Didn't use to *be* so many of them, time was.—Eh, Fil?" asked Captain Sneed. ("Correct, Copitan. Not.") "Only in the pahst five, six years... it seems. Don't *know* why...."

But whatever, it made the river even more like a scene in a baroque faëry tale, with dragons, or, at least, dragonets, looking and lurking in the gigant trees.

The bed of the river seemed predominantly rocky, with some stretches of sand. The river ran very sinuously, with banks tending towards the precipitate, and the east bank was generally the higher. "When river get high," explained Don Fili, "she get white, ahn come up to de crutch of dem tree—" he pointed to a fork high up. "It can rise in wan hour. Ahn if she rise in de night, we people cahn loose we boat. Very... *peligroso*... dangerous—¡*Jesus María!* Many stick tear loose wid roots ahn ahl, even big stick like dot wan," he pointed to another massy trunk.

Here and there was open land, *limpiado,* "cleaned," they said hereabouts, for "cleared." *"Clear...."* Something flickered in Limekiller's mind as he recollected this. Then it flickered away. There seemed, he realized, feeling odd about it, that quite a lot of flickering was and had been going on his mind. Nothing that would come into focus, though. The scenes of this Right Branch, now: why did they persist in seeming...almost...familiar? ...when he had never been here before?

"What did you say just then, Don Fili?" he demanded, abruptly, not even knowing why he asked.

The monumental face half turned. *"!Que?* What I just say, Juanito? Why...I say, too bod I forget bring ahlong my fisga, my pike...take some of dem iguana, garobo, cook dem fah you.—Fah *we,*" he amended, as one of the women said, *Gik.*

"We would say, 'harpoon'": Captain Sneed, judiciously. "Local term: 'pike.'"

The penny dropped. "Pike! Pike! It was a pike!" cried Limekiller. His body shook, suddenly, briefly. *Not* a lance or a spear. A pike!

They turned to look at him. Abashed, low-voiced, he muttered, "Sorry. Nothing. Something in a dream..." Shock was succeeded by embarrassment.

Felix, also low-voiced, asked, "Are you feverish again?" He shook his head. Then he felt her hand take his. His heart bounced. Then—Oh. She was only feeling his pulse. Evidently it felt all right. She started to release the hand. He took hers. She let it stay.

Captain Sneed said, "Speaking of Pike. All this land, all of it, far as the eye can reach, is part of the Estate of the Late Leopold Albert Edward Pike, you know, of fame and story and, for the last five or six years, since he died, of interminable litigation. He made a great deal of money, out of all these precious hardwoods, and he put it all back into land—Did I know him? Of *course* I knew him! That is," he cleared his throat, "as well as *any*one knew him. Odd chap in a multitude of ways. *Damn*ably odd...."

Of course that was not the end of the subject.

"Mr. Pike, he *reetch*. But he no di *trust* bonks. He say, bonks di go *bust,* mon. People say he'm, now-ah-days, bonks ahl *in*sure. Mr. Pike, he di say, Suh-pose *in*sure company di go bust, too? *¿Ai, como no?* Ahn he di say ah good word. He di say, 'Who shall guard de guards demselves?' "

Some· one of the boatmen, who had theretofore said nothing, but silently plied his paddle, now spoke. "Dey say... Meester Pike... dey say, he *deal....*" And his voice dropped low on this last word. Something went through all the boatmen at that. It was not exactly a shudder. But it was *there*.

Sneed cleared his throat again as though he were going to cry *Stuff!* or *Piffle!* Though what he said was, "Hm, I wouldn't go *that* far. He was pagan enough not to believe in our Devil, let alone try to deal with him. He did, well, he did, you know, study things better left unstudied ... *my* opinion. Indian legends of a certain sort, things like that. Called it 'the *Old* Wisdom'...."

Limekiller found his tongue. "Was he an Englishman?"

The matter was considered; heads were shaken. "He mosely *Blanco*. He *lee* bit *Indio*. And he hahv some lee bit *Block* generation in he'm too."

Sneed said, "His coloring was what they call in The Islands, *bright*. Light, in other words, you would say. Though color makes no difference here. Never *did*."

Marín added, "What dey cahl Light, here we cahl Clear." He gestured towards shore, said, "Lime*stone*." Much of the bankside was composed of that one same sort of rock, grey-white and in great masses, with many holes and caves: limestone was susceptible to such water-caused decay. In Yucatan the water had corroded deep pits in it, immense deep wells and pools.

"Now, up ahead," said Captain Sneed, "towards the right bank of the river is a sort of cove called Crocodile Pool—No No, ladies, no need for alarm. Just stay in the boat. And almost directly opposite the cove, is what's called the Garobo Church; you'll see why."

Often in the savannahs they saw the white egrets with

the orange bills, usually ashore amidst the cattle. Another kind of egret seemed to prefer the sand and gravel bars and the stumps or sawyers in midstream, and these were a distinctive shade of blue mixed with green, though lighter than the blue-green of the iguanas. Something like a blackbird took its perch and uttered a variety of long, sweet notes and calls.

Swallows skimmed and brighter colored birds darted and drank. And like great sentinels in livery, the great buff garobo-dragons peered down from the tall trees and the tall stones. Clouds of lemon-yellow and butter-yellow butterflies floated round the wild star-apples. *Here*, the stones lay in layers, like brickwork; *there*, the layers were warped and buckled, signs—perhaps—of some ancient strain or quake. But mostly, mostly, the stone rose and loomed and hung in bulbous worm-eaten masses. And over them, among them, behind them and between them, the tall cotton trees, the green-leaved cedars, the white-trunked Santa Maria, and the giant wild fig.

"Now, as to how you *catch* the crocodile," Captain Sneed answered an unasked question; "simple: one man stays in the dory and paddles her in a small circle, one or two men hold the *rope—*"

"—rope tie around odder mahn belly," Marín said.

"*Quite* so. And that chap *dives*. Machete in his *teeth*. And he ties up the croc and then he *tugs*. And then they haul them *up*,...you see. Simple."

Felix said, "Not *that* simple!"

May said, "Seems simple enough to me. Long as you've got a sound set of teeth."

Limekiller knew what was coming next. He had been here before. That was a mistake about his never having been here before, of course he had been here; never mind, Right Branch, Left Branch; or how else could he know? Down the steepy bluff a branch came falling with a crash of its *Crack*! falling with it; and the monstrous garobo hit the water with a tremendous sound and spray. It went *down* and it did not come up and it did not come *up*.

And then, distant but clear: the echo. And another echo. And—but that was too many echoes. Jack, who had been looking back, now turned. Spray was still flying up, falling down. *Ahead:* One after another the garobo were falling into the river. And then several at once, together. And then—

"Call *that,* 'The Garobo Church,'" said Captain Sneed.

That was an immense wild fig tree, hung out at an impossible angle; later, Limekiller was to learn that it had died of extreme age and of the storm which finally brought half of its roots out of the ground and forward into the water and canted it, thus, between heaven, earth, and river. It was a skeletal and spectral white against the green *green* of the bush. Three separate and distinct ecologies were along that great tangled length of great gaunt tree: at *least* three!—things crept and crawled, leaped and lurched or lay quiescent, grew and decayed, lived and multiplied and died—and the topmost branches belonged to the iguana and the garobo—

—that were now abandoning it, as men might abandon a threatened ship. Crash! Crash! Down they came, simply letting go and falling. *Crash!*

Sound and spray.

"Won't the crocodiles *eat* them?" cried Felix, tightening her hold on Jack's hand.

The boatmen, to whom this was clearly no new thing, all shook their heads, said No.

"Dey goin *wahrn* he'm, *el legarto,* dot we comin. So dot he no come oet. So cahn tehk *care. Horita el tiene cuidado.*"

"Tush," said Sneed. "Pif-fle. Damned reptiles are simply getting out of our way, *they* don't know that we haven't any pike. Damned old creepy-crawlies...."

Only the sound of their crashings, no other sound now, and Limekiller, saying in a calm flat voice, "Yes, of course," went out of his shirt and trousers and into the river.

He heard the men cry out, the women scream. But for one second only. Then the sounds muffled and died away. He was in the river. He saw a hundred eyes gazing at him. He swam, he felt bottom, he broke surface, he came up on his hands and knees. He did not try to stand. He was

under the river. He was someplace else. Some place with a
dim, suffused, wavering light. An odd place. A very odd
place. With a very bad smell. He was alone. No, he was
not. The garobo were all around and about him. The
crocodile was very near up ahead of him. Something else
was there, and he knew it had crawled there from the
surface through a very narrow fissure. And some *thing*
else was there. *That!* He had to take it and so he took it,
wrenching it loose. It squilched, but it came. The
crocodile gazed at him. The garobo moved aside for him.
He backed away. He was in the water again. He—

"Into the *boat,* for Christ's sake!" old Sneed was
shouting, his red face almost pale. The boatmen were
reaching out to him, holding hands to be grasped by him,
smacking the waters with their paddles and banging the
paddles against the sides of the boat. The women looked
like death. He gasped, spat, trod water, held up
something—

—then it was in the boat. Then, all grace gone, he was
half in and half out of the boat, his skin scraping the hard
sides of it, struggling, being pulled and tugged, wet skin
slipping....

He was in the boat.

He leaned over the side, and, as they pulled and
pressed, fearful of his going back again, he vomited into
the waters.

Captain Sneed had never been so angry. "Well, what
did you *expect* crocodile's den to smell like?" he
demanded. "Attar of roses? Damndest foolishest crack-
brainedest thing I ever saw—!"

Felix said, smoothing Jack's wet, wet hair, "*I* think it
was *brave!*"

"You know nothing whatsoever about it, my dear
child!—No, damn it, don't keep waving that damned old
pipkin pot you managed to drag up, you damned Canuck!
Seven hours under fire at Jutland, and I never had such an
infernal shock, it was reckless, it was heedless, it was
thoughtless, it was devil-may-care and a louse for the
hangman; what was the *reas*on for it, may I ask? To

impress *whom*? Eh? *Me?* These good men? These young women? Why did you *do* it?"

All Limekiller could say was, "I dreamed that I had to."

Captain Sneed looked at him, mouth open. Then he said, almost in a mutter, "Oh, I say, poor old boy, he's still rambling, ill, *look*ed well enough, must have the *fever....*" He was a moment silent. Then he blinked, gaped; almost in a whisper, he asked, "You *dreamed....* Whom did you *see* in your dream?"

Limekiller shrugged. "Don't know who.... Oldish man. Sharp face. Tan. Old-fashioned · clothes. Looked like a sort of a dandy, you might say."

And Captain Sneed's face, which had gone from scarlet to pink and then to scarlet again, now went muddy. They distinctly heard him swallow. Then he looked at the earthenware jar with its faded umber pattern. Then, his lips parting with a sort of dry smack: "... perhaps it *isn't* stuff and piffle, then...."

Ashore.

Sneed had insisted that the police be present. It was customary in Hidalgo to use the police in many ways not customary in the northern nations: to record business agreements, for instance, in places where there were no lawyers. And to witness. Sergeant Bickerstaff said that he agreed with Sneed. He said, also, that he had seen more than one old Indian jar opened and that when they were not empty they usually contained mud and that when they did not contain *mud* they usually contained "grahss-*seed*, cahrn-*ker*-nel, thing like that. Never find any gold in one, not before *my* eye, no, sirs and ladies—But best you go ahead and open it."

The cover pried off, right-tight to the brim was a mass of dark and odorous substance, pronounced to be wild beeswax.

The last crumble of it evaded the knife, sank down into the small jar, which was evidently not filled but only plugged with it. They turned it upside down and the crumble of unbleached beeswax fell upon the table. And so did something else.

"Plastic," said May. "To think that the ancient Indians had invented plastic. Create a furor in academic circles. Invalidate God knows how many patents."

Sergeant Bickerstaff, unmoved by irony, said, "Best unwrap it, Captain."

The plastic contained one dead wasp or similar insect, and two slips of paper. On one was written, in a firm old-fashioned hand, the words, *Page 36, Liber 100, Registers of Deeds of Gift, Mountains District.* The other was more complex. It seemed to be a diagram of sorts, and along the top and sides of it the same hand had written several sentences, beginning, *From the great rock behind Crocodile Cove and proceeding five hundred feet due North into the area called Richardson's Mahogany Lines. . . .*

It was signed, *L.A.E. Pike.*

There was a silence. Then Felix said, not exactly jumping up and down, but almost, her loops of coppery hair giving a bounce, "A treasure map! Jack! Oh, *good*!"

So far as he could recall, she had never called him by name before. His heart echoed: *Oh, good!*

Captain Sneed, pondering, seemingly by no means entirely recovered from his several shocks, but recovered enough, said:

"Too late to go poking about in the bush, today. First thing tomorrow, get some men, some machetes, axes, shovels—Eh?"

He turned to Police-sergeant Bickerstaff, who had spoken softly. And now repeated his words, still softly. But firmly. "First thing, sir. First thing supposed to be to notify the District Commissioner. Mister Jefferson Pike."

He was of course correct. As Captain Sneed agreed at once. Limekiller asked, "Any relation to the late Mr. Leopold Pike?" Bickerstaff nodded. "He is a bahstard son of the late Mr. Leopold Pike." The qualifying adjective implied neither insult nor disrespect. He said it as calmly, as mildly, as if he had said step-son. Cousin. Uncle. It was merely a civil answer to a civil question. A point of identification had been raised, been settled.

D.C. Jefferson Pike was taller than his father had been,

but the resemblance, once suggested, was evident. If any thoughts of an estate which he could never inherit were in his mind, they were not obvious. "Well, this is something new," was all his initial comment. Then, "I will ask my chief clark.... Roberts. Fetch us Liber 100, Register of Deeds of Gift. Oh, and see if they cannot bring some cups of tea for our visitors, please."

The tea was made and half drunk before Roberts, who did not look dilatory, returned, wiping dust and spiderwebs off the large old book. Which was now opened. Pages turned. "Well, well," said the District Commissioner. "This *is* something new!

"Don't know how they came to overlook *this*," he wondered. "The lawyers," he added. "*Who* registered it? Oh. Ahah. I see. Old Mr. Athelny; been dead *several* years. And always kept his own counsel, too. Quite proper. Well." He cleared his throat, began to read:

> I, Leopold Albert Edward Pike, Woodcutter and Timber Merchant, Retired, a resident of the Town of Saint Michael of the Mountains, Mountains District, in the Colony of British Hidalgo, and a British subject by birth...do execute this Deed of Gift...videlicet one collection of gold and silver coins, not being Coin of the Realm or Legal Tender, as follows, Item, one hundred pieces of eight reales, Item, fifty-five gold Lewises or louis d'or, Item...

He read them all, the rich and rolling old names, the gold moidores and gold mohurs, the golden guineas, the silver byzants and all the rest, as calmly as though he were reading off an inventory of office suplies; came finally to:

> and all these and any others which by inadvertancy may not be herein listed which are found in the same place and location I do hereby give and devise to one Elizabeth Mendoza also known as Betty Mendoza a.k.a. Elizabeth Pike a.k.a. Betty Pike, an infant now resident in the aforesaid

Mountains District, which Gift I make for good and
sufficient reason and of my own mere whim and
fancy. . . .

Here the D.C. paused, raised his eyes, looked at
Captain Sneed. Who nodded. Said, "His own sound and
voice. Yes. How *like* him!"

. . . and fancy; the aforesaid collection of gold and
silver coins being secured in this same District in a
place which I do not herein designate or describe
other than to say that it be situate on my own
freehold lands in this same District. And if anyone
attempt to resist or set aside this my Intention, I do
herewith and hereafter declare that he, she or they
shall not sleep well of nights.

After he had finished, there was a long pause. Then
everybody began to talk at once. Then—

Sneed: Well, suppose we shall have to inform the
lawyers, but don't see what *they* can do about it. Deed was
executed whilst the old fellow was alive and has nothing
to *do* with any question of the estate.

D.C. Pike: I quite agree with you. *Un*officially, of
course. Officially, all I am to do is to make my report. The
child? Why, yes, of course I know her. She is an outside
child of my brother Harrison, who died even before the
late Mr. Pike died. The late Mr. Pike seemed rather fond
of her. The late Mr. Pike did, I believe, always give
something to the child's old woman to keep her in clothes
and find her food. As we ourselves have sometimes done,
as best we could. But of course this will make a difference.

Sneed: As it *should*. As it *should*. He had put you big
chaps to school and helped you make your own way in the
world, but this was a mere babe. Do you suppose that he
knew that such an estate was bound to be involved in
litigation and that was why he tried to help the child with
all this . . . this *treasure* business?

Marín: Mis-tah Pike, he ahlways give ah lahf ahn he

say, nobody gweyn molest *he* treasure, *seguro*, no, becahs he di set such watchies roun ah-bote eet as no mahn adventure fi trifle wid day.

May: I can't help feeling that it's someone's cue to say, *"This all seems highly irregular."*

Roberts, Chief Clerk (softly but firmly): Oh, no, Miss. The Stamp Tax was paid according to regulations, Miss. *Everything seems in regular order, Miss.*

Watchies. A "watchie" was a watchman, sometimes registered as a private constable, thus giving him . . . Jack was not sure exactly what it gave him: except a certain status. But it was obvious that this was not what "the late Mr. Pike" had had in mind.

Finally, the District Commissioner said, "Well, well. Tomorrow is another day.—Richardson's Mahogany Lines! *Who* would have thought to look there? Nobody! It took eighty years after Richardson cut down all the mahogany before it was worthwhile for anybody to go that side again. And . . . how long since the late Mr. Pike cut down the last of the 'new' mahogany? Ten to fifteen years ago. So it would be sixty-five to seventy-five years before anybody would have gone that side again. Even to *look*. Whatever we may find there would not have been stumbled upon before then, we may be sure. Well, Well.

"Sergeant Bickerstaff, please take these gentlemen's and ladies' statements. Meanwhile, perhaps we can have some further cups of tea. . . ."

Taking the statement, that action so dearly beloved of police officials wherever the Union Jack flies or has flown, went full smoothly. That is, until the moment (Limekiller later realized it was inevitable, but he had not been waiting for it, then), the moment when Sgt. Bickerstaff looked up, raised his pen, asked, "And what made you go and seek for this Indian jar, sir, which gave the clue to this alleged treasure, Mr. Limekiller? That is, in other words, how did you come to know that it was there?"

Limekiller started to speak. Fell silent beyond possibility of speech. But not Captain Sneed.

"He knew that it was there because Old Pike had

dreamed it to him that it was there," said Captain Sneed.

Bickerstaff gave a *deep* nod, raised his pen. Set it down. Lifted it up. Looked at Jack. "This is the case, Mr. Limekiller, sir?"

Jack said, "Yes, it is." He had, so suddenly, realized it to be so.

"Doubt" was not the word for the emotion on the police-sergeant's face. "Perplexity," it was. He looked at his superior, the District Commissioner, but the District Commissioner had nothing to advise. It has been said by scholars that the Byzantine Empire was kept alive by its bureaucracy. Chief Clerk Roberts cleared his throat. In the tones of one dictating a routine turn of phrase, he produced the magic words.

"*'Acting upon information received,'*" he said, "*'I went to the region called Crocodile Cove, accompanied by,'* and so carry on from there, Sergeant Bickerstaff," he said.

In life, if not in literature, there is always anticlimax. By rights—by dramatic right, that is—they should all have gone somewhere and talked it all over. Talked it all out. And so tied up all the loose ends. But in fact there was nowhere for them all to go and do this. The police were finished when the statement was finished. District Officer Pike, who had had a long, hard day, did not suggest further cups of tea. Tía Sani's was closed. The Emerging Nation Bar and Club was closed, and in the other clubs and bars local usage and common custom held that the presence of "ladies" was contra-indicated: so did common sense.

Wherever Captain Sneed lived, Captain Sneed was clearly not about to offer open house. "Exhausted," he said. And looked it. "Come along, ladies, I will walk along with you as far as the Guest House. Limekiller. Tomorrow."

What should Limekiller do? Carry them off to his landing at the Grand Arawack? Hospitality at Government Guest House, that relic of days when visitors, gaunt and sore from mule transport, would arrive at an even smaller St. Michael's, hospitality there was reported to be

of a limited nature; but surely it was better than a place
where the urinals were tied up in brown paper and string?
(—Not that *they'd* use them anyway, the thought
occurred.)

May said, "Well, if you get sick again, yell like Hell for
us."

Felix said, reaching out her slender hand, whose every
freckle he had come to know and love, she said, *"Will you
be all right, Jack?"* Will you be all right, Jack? Not, mind
you, *You'll be all right, Jack.* It was enough. (And if it
wasn't, this was not the time and place to say what would
be.)

"I'll be all right," he assured her.

But, back on his absurdly sheeted bed, more than
slightly fearful of falling asleep at all, the river, the
moment he closed his eyes, the river began to unfold
before him, mile after beautiful and haunted mile. But this
was a fairly familiar effect of fatigue. He had known it to
happen with the roads and the wheatfields, in the Prairie
Provinces.

It was on awakening to the familiar cockeling chorus
of, *I make the sun to rise!* that he realized that he had not
dreamed at all.

St. Michael's did not have a single bank; and, what was
more—or less—it did not have a single lawyer. Attorneys
for the Estate (alerted perhaps by the telephone's
phantom relay) arrived early. But they did not arrive early
enough . . . early enough to delay the digging. By the time
the first lawyeriferous automobile came spinning to a stop
before the local courthouse, the expedition was already
on its way. The attorney for the Estate requested a delay,
the attorneys for the several groups of claimants
requested a delay. But the Estate's local agent had already
given a consent, and the magistrate declined to set it aside.
He did not, however, forbid them to attend.

· Also in attendance was one old woman and one small
girl. Limekiller thought that both of them looked
familiar. And he was right. One was the same old woman
who had urged him in out of the "fever rain." The other

was the child who had urged him to see "the beauty harse" and had next day made the meager purchases in Mikeloglu's shop ... whom the merchant had addressed as "Bet-ty me gyel," and urged her (with questionable humor) not to forget him when she was rich.

The crocodile stayed unvexed in his lair beneath the roots of the old Garobo Tree, though, seemingly, half the dragons along the river had dived to alert him.

To walk five hundred feet, *as a start*, is no great feat if one is in reasonable health. To cut and hack and ax and slash one's way through bush whose clearings require to be cleared twice a year if they are not to vanish: this is something else. However, the first five hundred feet proved to be the hardest (and hard enough to eliminate all but the hardiest of the lawyers). At the end of that first line they found their second marker: a lichen-studded rock growing right out of the primal bones of the earth. From there on, the task was easier. Clearly, though "the late Mr. Pike" had not intended it to be impossible, he had intended it to be difficult.

Sneed had discouraged, Marín had discouraged, others had discouraged May and Felix from coming: uselessly. Mere weight of male authority having proven to be obsolescent, Captain Sneed appealed to common sense. "My dear ladies," he pleaded, "can either of you handle a machete? Can either of you use an ax? Can—"

"Can either of us carry food?" was May's counter-question.

"*And* water?" asked Felix. "Both of us can," she said.

"Well, good for both of you," declared Captain Sneed, making an honorable capitulation of the fortress.

May had a question of her own. "Why do we all have to wear *boots*?" she asked, when there are hardly any wet places along here."

"Plenty tommy*goff*, Mees."

"Tommy Goff? Who is *he*?"

"Don't know who *he* was, common enough name, though, among English-speaking people in this part of the Caribbean. Don't know why they named a snake after the chap, either...."

A slight pause. "A... snake...?"

"And *such* a snake, too! The dreaded fer-de-lance, as they call it in the French islands."

"Uhh... *Pois*onous?"

Sneed wiped his sweating head, nodded his Digger-style bush hat. "*Dead*ly poisonous. If it's in full venom, bite can kill a horse. Sometimes *does*. So do be exceedingly cautious. Pleas**e**."

There was a further word on the subject, from Filiberto Marín. *"En castellano, se llame 'barba amarilla.'"*

This took a moment to sink in. Then one of the North Americans asked, "Doesn't that mean 'yellow beard'?"

"Quite right. In fact, the tommygoff's other name in English is 'yellow jaw.' But the Spanish is, literally, yes, it's yellow *beard*."

All three North Americans said, as one, *"Oh."* And looked at each other with a wild surmise.

The noises went on all around them. *Slash*—! *Hack*—! And, *Chop! Chop! Chop!* After another moment, May went on, "Well, I must say that seems like quite a collection of watchies that your late Mr. Leopold Pike appointed. Crocodiles. Poison serpents. What else. Oh. Do garobo *bite*?"

"Bite your nose or finger off if you vex him from the front; yes."

May said, thoughtfully, "I'm not sure that I really *like* your late Mr. Leopold Pike—"

Another flash of daytime lightning. Limekiller said, and remembered saying it the day before in the same startled tone, videlicet: "Pike! Pike!" Adding, this time, *"Fer-de-lance...!"*

Felix gave him her swift look. Her face said, No, he was not feverish.... Next she said, "'*Fer*,' that's French for 'iron,' and ...Oh. I see. Yes. Jesus. *Fer-de-lance*, lance-iron, or spear-head. Or spear-*point*. Or—"

"Or in other words," May wound up, *"Pike*.... You dreamed that, too, small John?"

He swung his ax again, nodded. *Thunk*. "Sort of... one way or another." *Thunk*. "He had a, sort of a, pike with him." *Thunk*. "Trying to get his point—ha-ha—across.

Did I dream the snake, too? Must have... I guess...."
Thunk.

"No. I do *not like* your late Mr. Leopold Pike."

Sneed declared a break. Took sips of water, slowly,
carefully. Wiped his face. Said, "You might have liked
Old Pike, though. A hard man in his way. Not without a
sense of humor, though. And ... after all ... he hasn't hurt
our friend John Limekiller... has he? Old chap Pike was
simply trying to do his best for his dead son's child. May
seem an odd way, to us. May *be*. Fact o'the matter: *Is*.
Why didn't he do it another way? Who's to say. Didn't
have too much trust in the law and the law's delays. I'll
sum it up. *Pike liked to do things in his own way.* A lot of
them were Indian ways. *Old* Indian ways. Used to burn
copal gum when he went deer hunting. *Al*ways got his
deer. And as for *this* little business, well ... the old Indians
had no probate courts. What's the consequence? How
does one guarantee that one's bequest reaches one's
intended heir?

"Why ... one *dreams* it to him! Or, for that matter, *her*.
In this case, however, the *her* is a small child. So—"

One of the woodsmen put down his tin cup, and,
thinking Sneed had done, said to Limekiller, "Mon, you
doesn't holds de ox de same way we does. But you holds
eet well. Where you learns dis?"

"Oh..." said Limekiller, vaguely, "I've helped cut
down a very small part of Canada without benefit of chain
saw. In my even younger days." Would he, too, he
wondered, in his even older days, would he too ramble on
about the trees he had felled?—the deeds he had done?

Probably.

Why not?

A wooden chest would have moldered away. An iron
one would have rusted. Perhaps for these reasons the
"collection of gold and silver coins, not being Coin of the
Realm or Legal Tender," had been lodged in more Indian
jars. Larger ones, this time. An examination of one of
them showed that the contents were as described. Once
again the machetes were put to use; branches, vines,
ropes, were cut and trimmed. Litters, or slings, rough but

serviceable, were made. Was some collective ethnic unconscious at work here? Had not the Incas, Aztecs, Mayas, ridden in palanquins?

Now for the first time the old woman raised her voice. "Ahl dis fah *you*, Bet-ty," she said, touching the ancient urns. "Bet-tah food. Fah *you*. Bet-tah house. Fah *you*, Bet-tah school. Fah *you*." Her gaze was triumphant. *"Ahl dis fah you!"*

One of the few lawyers who had not dropped out along the long, hard way, had a caveat. "Would the Law of Treasure Trove apply?" he wondered. "In which case, the Crown would own it. Although, to be sure, where there is no attempt at concealment The Crown would allow a finder's fee ... Mr. Limekiller ... ?"

And if anyone attempt to resist or set aside this my Intention, I do herewith and hereafter declare that he, she, or they shall not sleep well of nights. . . .

Limekiller said, "I'll pass."

And Captain Sneed cried, "Piffle! Tush! Was the Deed of Gift registered, or was it not? Was the Stamp Tax paid, or was it not?"

One of the policemen said, "If you have the Queen's head on your paper, you cahn't go wrong."

"Nol. con.," the lawyer said. And said no more.

That had been that. The rest were details. (One of the details was found in one of the large jars: another piece of plastic-wrapped paper, on which was written in a now-familiar hand, *He who led you hither, he may now sleep well of nights.*) And in the resolution of these other details the three North Americans had no part. Nor had Marín and friends: back to Parrot Bend they went. Nor had Captain Sneed. "Holiday is over," he said. "If I don't get back to my farm, the wee-wee ants will carry away my fruit. Come and visit, all of you. Whenever you like. Anyone will tell you where it is," he said. And was gone, the brave old Digger bush-hat bobbing away down the lane: wearing an invisible plume.

And the major (and the minor) currents of life in St. Michael of the Mountains went on—as they had gone on for a century without them.

There was the inevitable letdown.

May said, with a yawn, "I need a nice, long rest. And I know just where I'm going to find it. *After* we get back to King Town. I'm going to take a room at that hotel near the National Library."

Felix asked, "Why?"

"*Why?* I'll be like a kid in a candy warehouse. Do you realize that on the second floor of the National Library is the largest collection of 19th century English novels which I have ever seen in any one place? EVerything EVer written by EVerybody. Mrs. Edgeworth, Mrs. Trollope, Mrs. Gaskell, Mrs. Oliphant, Mrs. This and Mrs. That."

"Mrs. That. *I* remember *her*. Say, she wasn't bad at all—"

"No, she *was*n't. Although, personally, I prefer Mrs. This."

Felix and Limekiller found that they were looking at each other. *Speak now*, he told himself. *Aren't you tired of holding your own piece?* "And what are you going to be doing, then?" he asked.

She considered. Said she wasn't sure.

There was a silence.

"Did I tell you about my boat?"

"*No*. You didn't." Her look at him was a steady one. She didn't seem impatient. She seemed to have all the time in the world. "Tell me all about your boat," she said.

Selenium Ghosts of
the Eighteen Seventies
by R. A. Lafferty

*R. A. Lafferty's stories are frequently impossible to
categorize—Theodore Sturgeon has suggested that
they should be called, not science fiction or fantasy,
but simply lafferties. A worthy thought, as you'll see
when you read this totally bizarre account of the first
great series of television dramas, produced in 1873 by
Aurelian Bentley and starring the remarkably
resourceful actress Clarinda Calliope.*

Even today, the "invention" of television is usually
ascribed to Paul Nipkow of Germany, and the year is
given as 1884. Nipkow used the principle of the variation
in the electrical conductivity of selenium when exposed to
light, and he used scanning discs as mechanical effectors.
What else was there for him to use before the development
of the phototube and the current-amplifying electron
tube? The resolution of Nipkow's television was very poor
due to the "slow light" characteristics of selenium
response and the lack of amplification. There were,
however, several men in the United States who transmit-
ted a sort of television before Nipkow did so in Germany.

Resolution of the images of these even earlier
experimenters in the field (Aurelian Bentley, Jessy Polk,
Samuel J. Perry, Gifford Hudgeons) was even poorer
than was the case with Nipkow. Indeed, none of these
pre-Nipkow inventors in the television field is worthy of
much attention, except Bentley. And the interest in
Bentley is in the content of his transmissions and not in his
technical ineptitude.

It is not our object to enter into the argument of who
really did first "invent" television (it was not Paul

Nipkow, and it probably was not Aurelian Bentley or Jessy Polk either); our object is to examine some of the earliest true television dramas in their own queer "slow light" context. And the first of those "slow light" or selenium ("moonshine") dramas were put together by Aurelian Bentley in the year 1873.

The earliest art in a new field is always the freshest and is often the best. Homer composed the first and freshest, and probably the best, epic poetry. Whatever cave man did the first painting, it remains among the freshest as well as the best paintings ever done. Aeschylus composed the first and best tragic dramas, Euclid invented the first and best of the artful mathematics (we speak here of mathematics as an *art* without being concerned with its accuracy or practicality). And it may be that Aurelian Bentley produced the best of all television dramas in spite of their primitive aspect.

Bentley's television enterprise was not very successful despite his fee of one thousand dollars per day for each subscriber. In his heyday (or his hey-month, November of 1873), Bentley had fifty-nine subscribers in New York City, seventeen in Boston, fourteen in Philadelphia, and one in Hoboken. This gave him an income of ninety-one thousand dollars a day (which would be the equivalent of about a million dollars a day in today's terms), but Bentley was extravagant and prodigal, and he always insisted that he had expenses that the world wotted not of. In any case, Bentley was broke and out of business by the beginning of the year 1874. He was also dead by that time.

The only things surviving from *The Wonderful World of Aurelian Bentley* are thirteen of the "slow light" dramas, the master projector, and nineteen of the old television receivers. There are probably others of the receivers around somewhere, and persons coming onto them might not know what they are for. They do not look much like the television sets of later years.

The one we use for playing the old dramas is a good kerosene-powered model which we found and bought for eighteen dollars two years ago. If the old sets are ever properly identified and become collectors' items, the price on them may double or even triple. We told the owner of the antique that it was a chestnut roaster, and with a proper rack installed it could likely be made to serve as that.

We bought the master projector for twenty-six dollars. We told the owner of that monster that it was a chicken incubator. The thirteen dramas in their canisters we had for thirty-nine dollars total. We had to add formaldehyde to activate the dramas, however, and we had to add it to both the projector and the receiver; the formaldehyde itself came to fifty-two dollars. I discovered soon that the canisters with their dramas were not really needed, nor was the master projector. The receiver itself would repeat everything that it had ever received. Still and all, it was money well spent.

The kerosene burner activated a small dynamo that imposed an electical grid on the selenium matrix and awakened the memories of the dramas.

There was, however, an oddity in all the playbacks. The film-fix of the receiver continued to receive impressions so that every time a "slow light" drama is presented it is different, because of the feedback. The resolution of the pictures *improves* with use and is now much clearer and more enjoyable than originally.

The librettos of the first twelve of the thirteen Bentley dramas are not good, not nearly as good as the librettos of the Jessy Polk and the Samuel J. Perry dramas later in the decade. Aurelian Bentley was not a literary man; he was not even a completely literate man. His genius had many gaping holes in it. But he was a passionately dramatic man, and these dramas which he himself devised and directed have a great sweep and action to them. And even the librettos from which he worked are valuable for one reason. They tell us, though sometimes rather ineptly and vaguely, what the dramas themselves are all about. Without these outlines, we would have no idea in the world of the meaning of the powerful dramas.

There was an unreality, a "ghostliness," about all the dramas, as though they were made by sewer light underground: or as if they were made by poor quality moonlight. Remember that the element *selenium* (the metal that is not a metal), the chemical basis of the dramas, is named from *Selene*, the moon.

Bentley did not use "moving pictures" of quickly succeeding frames to capture and transmit his live presentation dramas. Although Muybridge was in fact working on the zoopraxiscope (the first "moving picture" device) at that very time, his still incomplete work was not known to Aurelian Bentley. Samuel J. Perry and Gifford Hudgeons did use "moving picture" techniques for their primitive television dramas later in the decade; but Bentley, fortunately perhaps, did not. Each of Bentley's thirty-minute live dramas, however it appeared for the first time in the first television receiver, was recorded in one single matrix or frame: and, thereafter, that picture took on a life and growth of its own. It was to some extent independent of sequence (an effect that has been attempted and failed of in several of the other arts); and it had a free way with time and space generally. This is part of the "ghostliness" of the dramas, and it is a large part of their power and charm. Each drama was one evolving moment outside of time and space (though mostly the scenes were in New York City and in the Barrens of New Jersey).

Of course there was no sound in these early Bentley dramas, but let us not go too far astray with that particular "of course." "Slow sound" as well as "slow light" is a characteristic of selenium response, and we will soon see that sound did in fact creep into some of the dramas after much replaying. Whether their total effects were accidental or by design, these early television dramas were absolutely unique.

The thirteen "slow light" dramas produced by Aurelian Bentley in the year 1873 (the thirteenth of them, the mysterious *Pettifogers of Philadelphia*, lacks Bentley's "Seal of Production," and indeed it was done after his death: and yet he appears as a major character in it) the thirteen were these:

1. *The Perils of Patience, a Damnable Chase.* In this, Clarinda Calliope, who was possibly one of the greatest

actresses of American or world drama, played the part of Patience Palmer in the title role. Leslie Whitemansion played the role of Simon Legree. Kirbac Fouet played the part of "the Whip," a sinister character. X. Paul McCoffin played the role of "the Embalmer." Jaime del Diablo played "the Jesuit," one of the most menacing roles in all drama. Torres Malgre played "the Slaver," who carried the forged certificate showing that Patience had a shadow of black blood and so might be returned to slavery on Saint Croix. Inspiro Spectralski played "the Panther" (Is he a Man? Is he a Ghost?), who is the embodiment of an evil that is perhaps from beyond the world. Hubert Saint Nicholas played the part of "the Guardian," who is really a false guardian.

This *Damnable Chase* is really a galloping allegory. It is the allegory of good against evil, of light against darkness, of inventiveness against crude obtuseness, of life against death, of openness against intrigue, of love against hatred, of courage against hellish fear. For excitement and intensity, this drama has hardly an equal. Time and again, it seemed that the Embalmer, striking out of the dark, would stab Patience with his needle full of the dread embalming fluid and so trap her in the rigidity of living death. Time and again, it seemed that the Whip would cut the flesh of Patience Palmer with his long lash with viper poison on its iron tip that would bring instant death. At every eventuality, it seemed as though Simon Legree or the Slaver would enslave her body, or the Jesuit or the Panther would enslave her soul. And her mysterious Guardian seems always about to save her, but his every attempt to save her has such reverse and disastrous effects as to cast doubt on the honesty and sincerity of the Guardian.

A high point of the drama is the duel of the locomotives that takes place during a tempestuous night in the West Orange Switching Yards. Again and again, Patience Palmer is all but trapped on railroad trestles by thundering locomotives driven by her adversaries (the West Orange Switching Yards seem to consist almost entirely of very high railroad trestles). Patience finally gets control of a locomotive of her own on which to escape, but the locomotives of her enemies thunder at her from every direction so that she is able to switch out of their way only at the last brink of every moment.

The Embalmer attempts to stab her with his needleful of embalming fluid every time their locomotives pass each other with double thunder and only inches to spare. The Whip tries to lash her with his cruel lash with its poisoned tip; and the Slaver threatens her with the outreached forged certificate of color, and only by fantastic cringing can she cringe back far enough to keep from being touched by it as their locomotives roar past each other in opposite directions.

It seems impossible that the racing locomotives can come so close and not hit each other, with their dazzling switching from track to track. And then (oh, God save us all!) the Panther (Is he a Man? Is he a Devil?) has leapt from his own locomotive to that of Patience Palmer: he is behind her on her own locomotive, and *she does not see him.* He comes closer—

But the climax of *The Perils of Patience* is not there in the West Orange Switching Yards. It is at a secret town and castle in the Barrens of New Jersey, a castle of evil repute. In this place the enemies of Patience were assembling a gang of beaters (slack-faced fellows with their tongues cut out), and they were readying blood-hounds to hunt Patience down to her death. She somehow obtains a large wagon piled high with hay and pulled by six large and high-spirited horses. With this, she boldly drives, on a stormy night, into the secret town of her enemies and down that jagged road (there was a lightning storm going on that made everything seem jagged) at the end of which was the castle itself. The bloodhounds leap high at her as she passes, but they cannot pull her from the wagon.

But the Panther (Is he a Man? Is he a Beast?) has leapt onto her hay wagon behind her, and *she does not see him.* He comes closer behind her—

But Patience Palmer is already making her move. Driving unswervingly, carrying out her own intrepid plan, at that very moment she raises a key in her hand very high into the air. This draws the lightning down with a stunning flash, and the hay wagon is set ablaze. Patience leaps clear of the flaming hay wagon at the last possible moment, and the blazing, hurtling inferno crashes into the tall and evil castle to set it and its outbuildings and its whole town ablaze.

This is the flaming climax to one of the greatest chase dramas ever.

This final scene of *The Perils* will be met with often later. Due to the character of the "slow light" or selenium scenes, this vivid scene leaks out of its own framework and is superimposed, sometimes faintly, sometimes powerfully, as a ghost scene on all twelve of the subsequent dramas.

2. *Thirsty Daggers, a Murder Mystery.* This is the second of the Aurelian Bentley television dramas of 1873. Clarinda Calliope, one of the most talented actresses of her time, played the part of Maud Trenchant, the Girl Detective. The actors Leslie Whitemansion, Kirbac Fouet, X. Paul McCoffin, Jaime del Diablo, Torres Malgre, Inspiro Spectralski, and Hubert Saint Nicholas played powerful and menacing roles, but their identities and purposes cannot be set exactly. One must enter into the bloody and thrilling spirit of the drama without knowing the details.

More even than *The Perils of Patience* does *Thirsty Daggers* seem to be freed from the bonds of time and sequence. It is all one unfolding moment, growing always in intensity and intricacy, but not following a straight line of action. And this, accompanied by a deficiency of the libretto, leads to confusion.

The libretto cannot be read. It is darkened and stained. Chemical analysis has revealed that it is stained with human blood. It is our belief that Bentley sent the librettos to his clients decorated with fresh human blood to set a mood. But time has spread the stains, and almost nothing can be read. This is, however, a highly interesting drama, the earliest murder mystery ever done for television.

It is nearly certain that Maud Trenchant, the Girl Detective, overcomes all the menaces and solves all the crimes, but the finer details of this are forever lost.

3. *The Great Bicycle Race*, the third of the Bentley television dramas, has that versatile actress Clarinda Calliope playing the lead role of July Meadowbloom in this joyful and allegorical "journey into summertime." It is in *The Great Bicycle Race* that sound makes its first appearance in the Bentley dramas. It is the sounds of all outdoors that are heard in this drama, faintly at first, and more and more as time goes on. These are country and village sounds; they are county-fair sounds. Though the sounds seem to be an accidental intrusion (another ghostly side-play of the selenium response magic), yet their quality lends belief to the evidence that the full and original title of this drama was *The Great Bicycle Race, a Pastoral.*

But there are other sounds, sometimes angry, sometimes imploring, sometimes arrogant and menacing— more about them in a bit.

Sheep and cattle sounds are all through the play; goat and horse and swine sounds; the rattle of ducks and geese; all the wonderful noises of the countryside. There are birds and grasshoppers, windmills and wagons, people calling and singing. There are the sounds of carnival barkers and the chants of gamblers and shills. There are the shrieks and giggles of young people.

And then there are those intrusive sounds of another sort, the separate overlay. These seem to be mostly indoor sounds, but sometimes they are outdoor grandstand sounds also, bristling talk in the reserved shadows of crowd noise and roaring.

"No, no, no. I'll not be had. What sort of girl do you think I am?"

"All these things I will give you, Clarie. No one else would give you so much. No one else would ever care so much. But now is the time for it. Now is the summer of our lives. Now we cut hay."

"Let's just see the price of a good hay barn first, Aurie.

Let's just get some things down on paper right now. We are talking about a summertime check that is as big as all summer. And we are talking about a much larger settlement to back up the other seasons and years."

"Don't you trust me, Clarie?"

"Of course I trust you, Bentie babe. I trust that you will get that trust fund that we are talking about down on paper today. I am a very trusting woman. I believe that we should have a trust fund to cover every condition and circumstance."

Odd talk that, to be mixed in with the sounds of *The Great Bicycle Race*.

The race was in conjunction with the Tri-county Fair, which counties were Camden, Gloucester, and Atlantic. The bicycle racers rode their twenty-mile course every afternoon for five afternoons, and careful time was kept. There was betting on each day's race, but there was bigger betting on the final winner with the lowest total time for the five days, and the kitty grew and grew. From the great fairground grandstand, one could see almost all of the twenty-mile course that the riders rode, or could follow it by the plumes of dust. The grandstand was on high ground and the whole countryside was spread out before it. Cattle and mules were paraded and judged in front of that grandstand, before and during and after that daily race; then the race (for the approximate hour that it took to run it) was the big thing. There were seven drivers in the race, and all of them were world famous:

1. Leslie Whitemansion drove on a Von Sauerbronn "Special" of fine German craftsmanship. This machine, popularly known as the "whizzer," would get you there and it would bring you back. It was very road-worthy and surprisingly fast.

2. Kirbac Fouet was on an Ernest Michaux Magicien, a splendid machine. It had a socket into which a small sail might be fitted to give greater speed in a favorable wind.

3. X. Paul McCoffin was on a British Royal Velocipede. There are two things that may be remarked about the British Royal: it had solid rubber tires (the first rubber-tired bicycle ever), and it had class. It had that

cluttered austerity of line that only the best of British products have.

4. Jaime del Diablo was on a Pierre Lallement "Boneshaker" with its iron-tired wooden wheels, the front one much larger than the rear.

5. Torres Malgre was on an American-built Richard Warren Sears Roadrunner, the first all-iron machine. "The only wood is in the heads of its detractors" was an advertising slogan used for the Roadrunner.

6. Inspiro Spectralski (Is he a Man? Is he a Cannon Ball?) was riding a McCracken's Comet. This comet had won races at several other county fairs around the state.

7. Hubert Saint Nicholas had a machine such as no one in the state had ever seen before. It was a French *bicyclette* named the Supreme. The bicyclette had the pedals fixed to drive the *back* wheel by the ingenious use of a chain and sprocket wheel, and so was not, strictly speaking, a bicycle at all. The true bicycles of the other six racers had the pedals attached directly to the *front* wheels. There was one syndicate of bettors who said the bicyclette had a mechanical advantage, and that Hubert would win on it. But other persons made jokes about this rig whose back wheel would arrive before its front wheel and whose driver would not arrive before the next day.

It was on these great riders that all the six-shot gamblers around were wagering breath-taking sums. It was for them that sports came from as far away as New York City.

Clarinda Calliope played the role of Gloria Goldenfield, the beauty queen of the Tri-county Fair in this drama. But she also played the role of the "Masked Alternate Rider of Number Seven." (All the racing riders had their alternates to ride in their places in case of emergency.) And Clarinda also played a third role, that of Rakesly Rivertown, the splurging gambler. Who would ever guess that the raffish Rakesly was being played by a woman? The author and director of *The Great Bicycle Race* did not know anything about Clarinda playing these latter two roles.

The grandstand, the bandstand, the pleasures of a

country carnival in the summertime! And the "slow smells" of the selenium-directed matrix just becoming ripe and evocative now! Smell of sweet clover and timothy hay, of hot horses pulling buggies or working in the fields, smells of candy and sausage and summer squash at the eating places at the fair, smells of dusty roads and of green money being counted out and thumped down on betting tables for the bicycle race!

And then again there was the override of intrusive voices breaking in on the real summer drama by accident.

"Clarie, I will do handsomely by you in just a day or so. I have placed very, very heavy bets on the bicycle race, and I will win. I am betting against the wildest gambler in this part of the country, Rakesly Rivertown, and we will have the bet up to a cool million with one more raise. He is betting the field against number seven. And number seven will win."

"I have heard that this Rakesly Rivertown is about the sharpest gambler anywhere, and that he has a fine figure and makes an extraordinary appearance."

"A fine figure! Why, the fraud is shaped like a girl! Yes, he is a sharp gambler, but he doesn't understand mechanics. Number seven, the Supreme, has a rear-wheel drive with a gear-ratio advantage. Hubert Saint Nicholas, who is riding number seven, is just toying with the other riders so far to get the bets higher, and he can win whenever he wants to. I will win a million dollars on the race, my love. And I will give it to you, if you act a little bit more like my love."

"Surely your love for me should transcend any results of a bicycle race, Aurie. If you really loved me, and if you contemplated making such a gift to me, you would make it today. That would show that your appreciation and affection are above mere fortune. And, if you can't lose, as you say that you cannot, you will have your money in the same amount won back in two days' time, and you will have made me happy two days longer."

"All right, I guess so then, Clarie. Yes, I'll give it to you today. Right now. I'll write you a check right now."

"Oh, you are a treasure, Aurie. You are a double

treasure. You can't guess how double a treasure you are!"

The wonderful Tri-county Fair was near its end, and its Great Bicycle Race with it. It was the last day of the race. Hubert Saint Nicholas on number seven, the Supreme, the French bicyclette with the mechanical advantage, was leading the field by only one minute in total elapsed time going into that last day's racing. There were those who said that Hubert could win any time he wanted to, and that he stayed so close only to keep the bets a-growing.

And the bets did grow. The mysterious gambler with the fine figure and the extraordinary appearance, Rakesly Rivertown, was still betting the field to win against number seven. And a still more mysterious gambler, working through agents, was betting on number seven to *place*, but not to win. These latter bets were quickly covered. Number seven would *win*, unless some terrible calamity overtook that entry; and, in the case of such terrible calamity, number seven would not finish second, would not finish at all most likely.

The seven intrepid racers were off on their final, mad, twenty-mile circuit. Interest was high, especially with the moneyed gamblers who followed the riders from the grandstand with their binoculars. At no place was the winding, circuit course more than four miles from the grandstand; and there were only three or four places, not more than three hundred yards in all, where the racers were out of sight of the higher tiers of the grandstand. One of those places was where Little Egg Creek went through Little Egg Meadow. Something mysterious happened near Little Egg Creek Crossing that neither the libretto nor the enacted drama itself makes clear.

Hubert Saint Nicholas, riding the French bicyclette, number seven, the Supreme, with the rear-wheel drive and the mechanical advantage, was unsaddled from his mount and knocked unconscious. The race master later had officially entered this incident as, "A careless rider knocked off his bicycle by a tree branch," though Hubert swore that there wasn't a tree branch within a hundred yards of that place.

"I was slugged by a lurker in the weeds," Hubert said.

"It was a criminal and fraudulent assault and I know who did it." Then he cried, "Oh, the perfidy of women!" This latter seemed to be an unconnected outcry; perhaps Hubert had suffered a concussion.

Fortunately (for whom?) the alternate rider for number seven, the Mysterious (though duly certified) Masked Rider, was in the vicinity of the accident and took control of the bicyclette, the Supreme, and continued the race. But number seven, though having a one-minute lead ere the race began, did not win. Number seven did come in second though in total elapsed time.

The Great Bicycle Race is a quaint little drama, with not much plot, but with a pleasant and bucolic atmosphere that grows more pleasant every time the drama is played back. It is a thoroughly enjoyable "Journey into Summertime."

And there were a few more seconds of those intrusive "ghost" voices breaking into the closing moments of the pastoral drama.

"Clarie, I have been took bad, for a big wad, and I don't know how it happened. There is something funny about it all. There was something funny and familiar about that Masked Alternate Rider for number seven. (I swear that I know him from somewhere!) And there has always been something double funny and familiar about that gambler Rakesly Rivertown. [I swear and be damned if I don't know *him* from somewhere!]"

"Don't worry about it, Aurie. You are so smart that you will have all that money back in no time at all."

"Yes, that's true, I will. But how can I write and produce and direct a drama and then get taken in it and now know what happened?"

"Don't worry about it, Aurie."

I myself doubt very much whether Aurelian Bentley knew about the "slow sounds" from nowhere-town that sometimes broke into the playing of his dramas, much less the "slow smells" which now began to give the dramas a character all their own.

4. *The Voyages of Captain Cook* was the fourth of the

Bentley-produced television dramas of the year 1873. In this, Clarinda Calliope played the role of Maria Masina, the Queen of Polynesia. If *The Great Bicycle Race* was a journey into summertime, *The Voyages of Captain Cook* was a journey into tropical paradise.

Hubert Saint Nicholas played Captain Cook. Inspiro Spectralski (Is he a Man? Is he a Fish?) played the Shark God. Leslie Whitemansion played the Missionary. X. Paul McCoffin played the Volcano God. Torres Malgre played the God of the Walking Dead. Jaime del Diablo played Kokomoko, the bronzed surf boy and lover boy who was always holding a huge red hibiscus bloom between his white teeth.

The people of the South Sea Islands of the Captain Cook drama were always eating possum and sweet potatoes and fried chicken (a misconception) and twanging on little banjoes (another misconception) and talking southern U. S. Darky Dialect (but these ghost voices were not intended to be heard on the television presentation).

The complete libretto for *The Voyages of Captain Cook* has survived, which makes us grateful for those that have not survived for several of the dramas. The story is replete. It is better to disregard the libretto with its simultaneous curses invoked by the Shark God, the Volcano God, and the God of the Walking Dead, and to give oneself over to the charm of the scenery, which is remarkable, considering that it was all "filmed," or "selenium-matrixed," in the salt swamps of New Jersey.

The anomalous intrusive voices are in this drama again, as they will be in all the subsequent dramas.

"A 'South Sea bubble,' yes, that's what I want, Aurie, one that can't burst. Use your imagination [you have so very much of it] and your finances [you have so very much of those] and come up with something that will delight me."

"I swear to you, Clarie, as soon as my finances are in a little better order, I will buy any island or group of islands in the Pacific Ocean for you. Do you hear me, Clarie? I will give you any island or group you wish, Hawaii, Samoa, Fiji. Name it and it is yours."

"So many things you promise! But you don't promise them on paper, only on air. Maybe I will find a way to make the air retain the promises you make."

"Not on paper, not on air, Clarie, but in real life. I will make you the real and living Queen of Polynesia."

The essence of the South Sea appeal is just plain charm. It may be that this Bentley drama, *The Voyages of Captain Cook*, was the original charm bush whence so many things bloomed. No, in things of this sort, it is not necessary that a scion ever be in contact with its source or even know its source. Without the *Voyages* would there ever have been a Sadie Thompson, would there have been a Nellie Forbush? Would there have been a Nina, daughter of Almayer? Well, they wouldn't have been as they were if Clarinda Calliope hadn't, in a way, played them first. Would there have been a *White Shadows of the South Seas* if there hadn't first been *The Voyages of Captain Cook*? No, of course there wouldn't have been.

5. *Crimean Days* was the fifth of the Aurelian Bentley television dramas. In this, the multitalented Clarinda Calliope played the role of Florence Nightingale, of Ekmek Kaya, a Turkish lady of doubtful virtue who was the number-four wife and current favorite of the Turkish admiral, of Chiara Maldonado, a young lady camp follower with the army of Savoy, of Katya Petrova, who was a Russian princess as well as a triple spy, and of Claudette Boudin, a French lady journalist. Clarinda also masqueraded as Claudette's twin brother Claude, a colonel with the French forces, and as such she led the French to a surprising victory over the Russians at Eupatoria. The unmasqueraded Claude himself was played by Apollo Mont-de-Marsan, a young actor making his first appearance in the Bentley dramas.

The Crimean War was the last war in which the field officers of all sides (Leslie Whitemansion was a British officer, Kirbac Fouet was a French, Jaime del Diablo was an officer of the forces of Savoy, Torres Malgre was the Turkish admiral, Inspiro Spectralski was a general of the Czar, X. Paul McCoffin was a special observer of the Pope), after their days of tactical maneuver and sometimes bloody conflict, would dress for dinner and have formal dinner together. And it was at these dinners that Clarinda Calliope, in her various guises, shone.

There was a wonderful and many-leveled table intrigue, and I believe that more and more of it will come through every time the drama is replayed. And it was here in this drama that one of the most strange of the Bentley-effect phenomena first appeared. There is unmistakable evidence that some of the subvocalizations (thoughts) of the people were now to be heard as "slow sound," which was really selenium-triggered "slow thought." Some of these manifestations were the role thoughts of the actors so strangely vocalized (Clarinda Calliope, for instance, could not speak or think in any tongues except English and her own Pennsylvania Dutch in normal circumstances; but in her triple spy roles we find her thinking out loud in Turkish and Greek and Russian); and other of the vocalizations are the real thoughts of the actors (the amazingly frank intentions of Leslie Whitemansion and of the new Apollo Mont-de-Marsan as to their lady loves of the evening after they should have received their two-dollar actors' fee for the day).

It was a wonderful play and too intricate to be described. This one above all, has to be seen. But again there was the anomalous intrusion of voices that were not a part of the scenes of the play;

"Get rid of that Greek Wop kid, Clarie. I told him he was fired, and he said that he would stick around and work for nothing. He said he loved the fringe benefits. What are fringe benefits? I told him I'd run him off, and he said that this was the free state of New Jersey and that no one would run him off. I won't have him around."

"Oh, Aurie, there isn't any Greek Wop kid. That was me playing that role too. Am I not talented to play so many roles? And you *will not* fire me from this role. I will continue to play it, and I will be paid for it. It isn't the principle of the thing either: it's the two dollars."

"Yes, I understand that much about you. But you say that was you playing the part of that smart-mouth Apollo Dago Greek? That couldn't be. I've seen you both at the same time. I've seen you two together too many times. I've seen you smooching each other."

"Ah, Aurie, that was quite an advance technique and illusion, not to mention double exposure, that I used there. What other actress could play both roles at once and get away with it?"

"Your techniques and illusions are becoming a little bit too advanced, Clarie. And do not be so sure that you *are* getting away with it."

All through *Crimean Days,* there was some tampering with history going on for dramatic effect. The Light Brigade, for instance, was successful in its famous charge and it won a great victory. But the final outcome of the war was left in doubt. Aurelian Bentley had somehow become a strong partisan of the Russians and he refused to show them being finally defeated by the allies.

6. *Ruddy Limbs and Flaming Hair* is the sixth of the Bentley television dramas. In this piece, the dramatic Clarinda Calliope plays the part of Muothu, the Maid of Mars, for the Ruddy Limbs and Flaming Hair are on the planet Mars itself. There are some fantastic elements in this piece, as well as amazing scientific accuracy. There is, in fact, a technical precocity that is really stunning. Aurelian Bentley has foreseen circumstances that even the scientific community did not then see, and he has dealt with those circumstances.

He posits, for instance, an atmosphere composed mostly of an eno-magnetized, digammated, attenuated form of oxygen. Being eno-magnetized, that atmosphere would naturally cling to its planet even though the gravity would not be strong enough to retain it otherwise. Being digammated, it would produce no line in the Martian spectrum, would have no corona or optical distortion effect, and could in no way be detected from Earth. And yet a human Earthling would be able to breathe it freely.

This was a good-natured utopian drama of total realization and happiness. The Ruddy Limbs and Flaming Hair apply both allegorically to the planet Mars and literally to the highly dramatic Clarinda Calliope as Muothu. Muothu displayed rather more of the ruddy limbs than were ordinarily shown on Earth, but it was explained that customs on Mars were different.

Ruddy Limbs and Flaming Hair was the last of the dramas in which the apparently tormented and disturbed Aurelian Bentley still showed the strong hand of the master as scenarist, dramaturgist, director, and producer generally. After this we come to the four "Trough of the Wave" dramas, and then the three bewildering and hectic displays on the end of the series.

7. *The Trenton Train Robbery* is the seventh of the Bentley television dramas, and the first of the four "Trough" plays where Aurelian Bentley and his effects are sunken in the slough of despond and have lost their brightness and liveliness and hope. We will pass through them quickly.

In the *Train Robbery*, the peerless Clarinda Calliope plays Roxana Roundhouse, the daughter of the slain locomotive engineer Timothy (Trainman) Roundhouse. Armed with a repeating rifle, a repeating shotgun, a repeating pistol, and a few pocket-sized bombs, Roxana rides the rods of the crack Trenton Express in the effort to catch or kill the murderers of her father. These murderers have sworn that they will rob that very Trenton Express again.

And Roxana Roundhouse does catch or kill all the murderers of her father. In spite of some good shots of landscapes rushing by, this is not one of Aurelian Bentley's best efforts.

And again the voices of unknown persons creep into the drama:

"You've already flayed me, Clarie, and scraped both sides of my pelt for whatever might cling to it. What more do you want from me? Go away with your lover and leave me alone." And then in a fuzzier voice (apparently the "thought voice" made vocal) the same person said or thought: "Oh, if only she *would* go away from me, then I might have a chance! For I will never be able to go away from her."

"Grow more skin, Aurie," the other voice said. "I'm not

nearly finished fleecing you and flaying you. Oh, don't look so torn up, Aurie. You know I could never love anyone except you. But a little token of our love is required now and then, and especially now, today. Yes, I know you are going to use your old line, 'I gave you a million dollars last week,' but, Aurie, that *was* last week. Yes, I know that you have expenses that the world wots not of. So do I. Believe me, Aurie, I wouldn't ask for these tokens of affection if I didn't want them." And then in a fuzzier voice, a "thought voice," the same person said or thought: "I'll never get another fish like this one and I sure can't afford to lose him. But gentle handling doesn't get it all the time. When the hook in him shows signs of working loose a bit, it has to be set in again with a very hard jerk on the line."

8. *Six Guns on the Border* is the eighth of the Bentley television dramas. In this drama, Clarinda Calliope (is there no end to her versatility?) plays the part of Conchita Allegre, the half-breed Apache and Mexican girl, on the Arizona border, during the Mexican War. Conchita hates the American soldiers who are invading that area. She has them come to her secretly, with promises of love, and then she has them ambushed and killed. She kills many of them herself with her own six gun, and she makes antimacassars out of their skins. The sort of gentlemen that Conchita really likes use a lot of oil on their hair so Conchita needs a lot of anitmacassars at her house.

But there are a few of the American officers so awkward and oafish that Conchita simply can't stand to have much to do with them, not even long enough to seduce them and have them killed. These horrible specimens are:

Captain James Polk (played by Leslie Whitemansion).

General Zachary Taylor (played by Kirbac Fouet).

Captain Millard Fillmore (played by X. Paul McCoffin).

Captain Franklin Pierce (played by Jaime del Diablo).

Captain James Buchanan (played by Torres Malgre).

Captain Abraham Lincoln (played by Inspiro Spectralski).

Captain Andrew Johnson (played by Apollo Mont-de-Marsan).

Captain Sam Grant (played by Hubert Saint Nicholas).

There was a lot of historical irony in this play, but maybe it belonged somewhere else.

There was a lot of "Comedy of Manners" stuff in it but it falls a little flat, mostly because the eight oafish officers spared by Conchita were too unmannerly to be in a comedy of manners.

Aurelian Bentley came near the bottom of his form in this piece. But for the energy of Clarinda Calliope (she played five other parts besides that of Conchita) there would have been hardly any drama at all.

And, as always, there were those intrusive voices hovering over the playbacks.

"Clarie, believe me! Believe me! Believe me! I will do all these things for you. I promise it."

"Yes, you promise it to the earless walls and to the earless me. Promise it to the pen and ink and paper here."

"Get rid of that Apollo kid first, Clarie."

"You get rid of him. You have a lot of rough-looking men around."

9. *Clarence Greenback, Confidence Man* was the ninth of the Aurelian Bentley television dramas. Hubert Saint Nicholas played the role of Clarence Greenback, the casino owner. It was the first time that Clarinda Calliope had not played the lead role in a drama. Is it possible that Clarinda had somehow slipped? Or was this another instance of the left lobe of Aurelian Bentley having lost its cunning, and casting badly. The talented prestidigitator of drama did not have his sure touch nowadays. Oh sure, Clarinda played many other roles in the drama, but she did not have the lead role.

Clarinda played the role of Gretchen, the sweep-out girl at the casino. She played the role of Maria, the mounting-block girl in the street outside the casino. She played the role of Elsie, the chimney-sweep girl. She played the part of Hennchen, the scullery maid in the third and vilest kitchen of the casino. She played the part of Josephine, the retriever who had to gather up the shattered bodies of the suicides below Suicide Leap Window of the casino and take them to East Potters' Field and dig their graves and bury them. Elsie made a good thing out of her job, from the gold teeth of the late patrons of the casino, but the dramatist and producer did not know about the good thing she had here.

There were hazards in all these different roles.

"No, of course we can't put out the fires for you to clean the chimneys," said Leslie Whitemansion, who was in charge of fireplaces and chimneys at the casino. "Clean them hot." And it was very hot working inside those tall chimneys with the fires roaring below, and Elsie the chimney-sweep girl suffered.

For keeping a copper coin that she found while sweeping out the casino, the sadist Baron von Steichen (played by X. Paul McCoffin) had Gretchen hung by her thumbs and flogged.

And Maria, the mounting-block girl, who had to stand in the muddy street outside the casino and bend her back for the gentlemen to step on her when they mounted or dismounted their horses, she had it worse on the muddy days. Oh, the great muddy boots of those men!

"Maybe they're trying to tell me something," Clarinda Calliope spoke or thought (by slow talk-thought). "I do like subtle people." But a good actress can play any role, and Clarinda has her revenge today. Hardly anyone remembers the plot of *Clarence Greenback, Confidence Man,* but everybody remembers the tribulations of those pretty little servant girls.

And then there were those other intrusive voices of the overlay. It was almost as if they belonged in another sort of drama.

"Clarie, this has to stop. Not counting the special gifts, and they're fantastic, I'm giving you ten times as much as the President of the United States is making."

"I'm ten times as good at acting as he is. And how about *my* special gifts?—and they're fantastic. Why do you have all the private detectives running around the last couple of days? To spy on me?"

"To spy on everything and everyone. To save my life.

Frankly, Clarie, I am afraid of being murdered. I have premonitions of being killed, with a knife, always with a knife."

"Like in *Thirsty Daggers, a Murder Mystery?* That one wasn't really very well worked out, and I believe it's one of the things bothering you. Your undermind is looking for a better solution, I believe, for a neater murder. It is seeking to enact a more artistic murder. I believe it will do it. I believe you will come up with quite an artistic murder for yourself. There are good murders and bad murders, you see."

"Clarie, I don't intend to let myself be killed at all, not by either a good or a bad murder."

"Not even for art's sake? It seems it would be worth it, for the perfect murder, Aurie."

"Not when *I'm* the murdered one, Clarie."

Then, a moment later, the female person said or thought something further, in a "slow thought-voice."

"Sometimes persons have perfection thrust upon them in spite of themselves. An artful murder for Aurie would make up for a lot of the bad art that he's been guilty of lately."

10. *The Vampires of Varuma* was the tenth of the Aurelian Bentley television dramas. This is the fourth and last of the "Trough of the Wave" dramas, which show Bentley's dramatic powers in almost complete decline and himself mightily disoriented. Yet, in this bottoming-out, there is a curious resurrection of his powers in a slightly different form. His sense of plotting and story movement did not return yet, but his sense of dramatic horror as motive force was resurrected to its highest pitch.

Clarinda Calliope played Magda the peasant maid, Miss Cheryl Somerset, the governess from England, and the Princess Irene of Transylvania. All three of these had been traveling to Castel Khubav on rational errands by the regular coach of the road; and each of the three had seen all the other passengers dismount hastily, and had then experienced the coach horses being whipped ahead frantically by an invisible coachman, or by no coachman at all. And each of these ladies had arrived, on successive days, in the apparently driverless coach, not at Castle Khubav, but at the dread Castle Beden. And inside the Castle Beden were the seven ("no, not seven, eight" was written into the libretto in a weirdly different hand) insane counts in their castle of evil. These were:

Count Vladmel, played by Leslie Whitemansion.

Count Igork, played by Kirbac Fouet.

Count Lascar, played by X. Paul McCoffin.

Count Chort, played by Jaime del Diablo.

Count Sangressuga, played by Torres Malgre.

Count Letuchaya, played by Inspiro Spectralski (Is he a Man? Is he a Bat?).

Count Ulv, played by Hubert Saint Nicholas.

And then there is another one added in the libretto in that weirdly different hand:

Count Prividenne, played by Apollo Mont-de-Marsan. There is a slip-up here somewhere. Apollo is supposed to have been "gotten rid of," to have shuffled off the mortal coil, and the sheriff's report said that he died of indigestion. But if Apollo has not been "gotten rid of" then certain money was paid in vain.

The seven (or eight) evil counts are sometimes conventional counts in evening clothes and monocles. And sometimes they are huge bat-winged creatures flitting ponderously down the lightning-lit corridors of Castle Beden. The castle, in fact, is the main character in the drama. It does not have formal lighting, as it is lit by lightning all twenty-four hours of every night (there is no daylight at Castle Beden). The floors and walls howl and chains rattle constantly. The counts have sometimes conventional six-inch-long eyeteeth, and then suddenly they will have hollow fangs eighteen inches long and deadly. And there is a constant lot of howling and screaming for what is supposed to be a silent television drama.

A flying count will suddenly fold his bat wings and land on the broad bosom of one of the three maidens and have into her throat with his terrible blood-sucking fangs. And every time it happens, there is a horrible flopping and screeching.

The voice of Clarinda Calliope is heard loud and clear

and real in a slow angry sound.

"Dammit, Aurelian, that's real blood they're taking out of my throat."

And came the suave voice of the master dramatist Aurelian Bentley (but the voices shouldn't be breaking in like this):

"Right, Clarie. It is on such verisimilitude that I have built my reputation as a master."

Clarinda, in her three roles, seemed to lose quite a bit of blood as the drama went on, and she fell down more and more often. And the drama was a howling and bloody success, no matter that the story line was shattered in a thousand pieces—for each piece of it was like a writhing blood snake that gluts and gloats.

And then, after the drama itself was ended in a spate of final blood, there came those intrusive voices that seemed to be out of some private drama.

"Aurie, if you are worrying about being killed, how about providing for me before it happens?"

"I leave you half of my kingdom, ah, estate, Clarie, right off the top of it. My word is good for this. And stop falling down."

"I'm weak. It took a lot out of me. Yes, your written word is good on this, Aurie, if it is written and attested to in all the right places. Let's take care of that little detail right now."

"Clarie, my spoken promise is enough, and it is all that I will give. I hereby attest that half of my estate, off the top, belongs to you. Let the eared walls of this room be witnesses to what I say, Clarie. If the walls of this room will swear to it, then surely they will be believed. Now don't bother me for a few days. I will be busy with something else. And stop falling down. It's annoying."

The female person then said or thought something in a fuzzy thought-voice:

"Yes, I believe I *can* make the walls of this room attest for me when the time comes. (I might have to put in another amplifying circuit to be sure.) And I believe that the attesting walls will be believed."

The male person then said or thought something in a fuzzy thought-voice:

"I have Miss Adeline Addams now. Why should I care about this Calliope clown? It's irritating the way she keeps turning chalk-white and falling down. I never saw anyone make such a fuss over nine quarts of blood. But now I am on a new and more glorious dawn road. Is it not peculiar how a man will fall in love with one woman and out of love with another one at the same time?"

11. *The Ghost at the Opera* is the eleventh of the Aurelian Bentley television dramas in the year 1873. *The Ghost* is based on Verdi's *Il Trovatore*, but Bentley's production is quite original for all that. The role of Leonora is played by Miss Adeline Addams. But the same role is also played by Clarinda Calliope, who was originally selected to play the role by herself. This business of having two different persons playing the same role creates a certain duality, one might almost say a certain duplicity, in the drama.

The "Ghost" is the doubling: it is the inept and stumbling Clarinda trying again and again to sing parts of the Leonora role and failing in it totally and being jerked off stage by the stage manager's crook; and it is the beautiful and brimming genius Adeline Addams coming on and performing the same role brilliantly. This provides the "cruel comedy" that is usually lacking in Verdi; for, without cruelty, only a limited success is ever possible in opera. But Clarinda took some very bad falls from the stageman's crook jerking her off her feet, and besides she was still weak and falling down from all the blood she had lost in her roles in *The Vampires of Varuma*. She was suffering.

"Why do you go through with it, Clarinda?" Hubert Saint Nicholas asked her once in an outside-of-the-play-itself voice. "Why do you allow yourself to be tortured and humiliated like that?"

"Only for the money," Clarinda was heard to say. "Only for the actor's fee of four dollars a day. I am clear broke and I am hungry. But if I can stick it out to the end of the opera, I will have four dollars tonight for my wages."

"Four dollars, Clarinda? The rest of us get only two

dollars a day. Are you playing another role that I don't know about?"

"Yes, I am also playing the role of Wilhelmia, the outhouse cleaner."

"But I thought that you had millions from that old tyrant, Clarinda."

"It's gone, Hubie, all gone. I had expenses that the world wotted not of. I gave Apollo most of the money when I was in love with him. And I gave the rest of it to him today to do a special favor for me."

"You gave the money to him today? But he was buried yesterday."

"Time seems to go faster as we get older, doesn't it?"

Meanwhile, back on the opera stage, a new Verdi was being hammered out. Leslie Whitemansion was playing Manrico. X. Paul McCoffin was playing Ferrando. Hubert Saint Nicholas was playing Count di Luni. Apollo Mont-de-Marsan was playing the ghost. But was there a ghost in the libretto besides the double ghost of the two females playing the same role? Yes there was; there was a real ghost in the libretto. It was written in there in a queer "other" hand, really a "ghostly" hand, and it wrote that Apollo was playing the role of the ghost.

So the merry comic opera went along almost to its end. It was just when Manrico was being led to the executioner's block and the evil Count di Luni was gloating in triumph, when everything was finally being shaped up in that drama that had some pleasure for everybody, that a horrible thing happened in one of the loges or boxes that overhung the stage.

Aurelian Bentley was knifed there in his box at the opera. Oh God, this was murder! "Your mind is looking for a better solution, I believe, for a neater murder." Oh, that had been the voice of another sort of ghost. But now, to be slain by the ghost of a man dead only a day or two, and in the presence of several thousands of persons here! (For it was, possibly, none other than Apollo Mont-de-Marsan, who had been "gotten rid of," who was getting rid of Aurelian Bentley.) And again: "There are good murders and bad murders, you see.... It seems it would

be worth it, for art's sake, for the perfect murder."
Aurelian Bentley was stabbed to death in his box at the
opera there, but even he had to admit, with some
appreciation, as he went, that it was done with art.

And immediately, as the opera on stage came to its
great conclusion, there welled up cries of "Author,
Author, Bentley, Bentley!"

Then the dying (or more likely dead) man rose for the
last time, bowed formally, and tumbled out of his box and
onto his face on the stage, stark dead, and with the thirsty
(now slaked) dagger twinkling between the blades of his
shoulders.

What other man had ever made such an exit from or on
life's stage! That was Theater! That was Drama!

12. *An Evening in Newport* was intended to be the
twelfth of the Bentley television dramas. But it was never
produced; possibly because of the death of its producer. It
exists only as libretto.

This was a high society "drama of manners," as Miss
Adeline Addams knew it, as Aurelian Bentley with his
quick mind and quick mimicry knew it from his brief
brushes with it. But does not a drama or comedy of
manners depend largely on the quip and the arch
aphorism? How could it be done in silent presentation?

By art, that's how it might be done: by the perfect art of
the silent mimes, and Aurelian Bentley was master of that
art. By the gestures, by the facial implications, by great
silent acting this might be done. Was there any witticism
that Adeline Addams could not express with her talented,
high society face? Was there any devastating riposte that
she could not give with her autocratic hands? It was never
tested, but Aurelian believed that she was pretty good.

On the lower level, *An Evening in Newport* was a
one-sided duel between Mistress Adeline Addams of
Newport, and Clarinda Calliope, playing the role of
Rosaleen O'Keene, a low, vicious, ignorant, filthy,
bad-mannered, fifth parlor maid newly arrived from
Ireland. It was a stacked set in favor of Adeline-Adela.

On the higher level, the drama was the passionate

portrayal of the total love of a beautiful and wealthy and intelligent and charming and aristocratic young lady (Adeline-Adela) for a man of surpassing genius and ineffable charm, a man of poise and power and heroic gifts, a man the like of whom will hardly appear once in a century. The drama was supposed to take on a note of hushed wonder whenever this man was mentioned, or so the libretto said. The libretto does not identify this exceptional man, but our own opinion is that the librettist, Aurelian Bentley, intended this hardly-once-in-a-century man, the object of the torrid and devoted love of Miss Adeline Addams, to be himself, Aurelian Bentley.

But *An Evening in Newport*, intended to be the surpassing climax of that first and still unsurpassed television series, was never produced.

13. *Pettifoggers of Philadelphia* is the noncanonical, apocryphal, thirteenth apocalypse of *The Wonderful World of Aurelian Bentley*, that first and greatest television series. There is no libretto to it. There is no formal production, and it does not carry the Bentley "Seal of Production." But it does repose in one of the old television receivers, the one that was Aurelian's own control receiver, the one that was in Aurelian's own luxurious den where he spent so many hectic hours with Clarinda Calliope and later with Adeline Addams. It reposes there, and it may be seen and heard there.

Though Bentley was already dead when these scenes were ordered and live-presented, yet he walks in them and talks in them. The experience of hearing the thoughts and words of a hovering dead man spoken out loud and of seeing him as if in the flesh is a shattering but dramatic one.

The setting and sole scene of *Pettifoggers of Philadelphia* is that same luxurious den of Aurelian Bentley's, first placed under court seal, but then opened for a meeting which, as one of the parties to it stated, could not validly be held anywhere else. A probate judge was present, and pettifoggers representing several of the parties, and two of the parties themselves. It was a hearing on the disposition of the estate of Aurelian Bentley, or what might be left of that estate, he having died without having made a will. But one of the parties, Clarinda Calliope, insisted that Bentley *had* made a will, that the will was in this particular room and no other, that the will in fact *was* this room and the eared and tongued walls of it.

There seemed to be several meetings in this room superimposed on one another, and they cannot be sorted out. To sort them out would have been to destroy their effect, however, for they achieved syntheses of their several aspects and became the true meeting that never really took place but which contained all the other meetings in one theatrical unity.

The pettifogger of a second cousin once removed was there to present the claim of that distant person, as next of kin, to the estate of Aurelian Bentley.

The pettifogger of Adeline Addams of Newport was there to present the claim of Adeline to the estate, claims based on in *irrefutable promise*. This irrefutable promise was the marriage license for Aurelian Bentley and Adeline Addams. It was not signed or witnessed, of course. The marriage, the pettifogger said, had been scheduled to take place on a certain night after the presentation of an opera, that was contained in a television drama, that was contained in a riddle. But Aurelian Bentley had been killed during that opera, which voided the prospect of marriage, but did not void the promise.

There were pettifoggers there for the different creditors. And all the pettifoggers were from Philadelphia.

And there was Clarinda Calliope representing herself (as Portia, she insisted, and not as a pettifogger), and she claimed rights by a promise too big and too intricate to be put on paper.

There was the probate judge of the private hearing who ambled around the luxurious den flipping a silver dollar in the air and humming the *McGinty's Saloon Waltz*.

"Oh, stop flipping that silly silver dollar and get on with the matter of the probate," Miss Adeline Addams complained to that nitwit judge.

"The silver dollar is the matter of the probate," the judge said. "The dollar is important. It is the soul and body of what this is all about."

The piles of paper began to accumulate on the tables there. There were the documents and attestations of the distant next of kin, of Adeline Addams, and of the creditors in their severalty. And not one scrap of paper did Clarinda Calliope put forward.

"Enough, enough," said the judge after the flood of paper had narrowed down to a trickle. "Stop the paper," but he didn't stop flipping that silver dollar or humming the *McGinty's Saloon Waltz.* "All a-sea that's going a-sea. Miss Calliope, it is time you laid a little evidence on the table if you are to be a party of these hearings."

"My evidence is too large and too living to lay on the table," Clarinda said. "But listen, and perhaps look! Due to the magic of the selenium 'slow response' principle, and to the walls of this very room being wired parallel to the receiver in this room, we may be able to bring to you a veritable reconstruction of past words and avowals and persons."

And pretty soon the voice of the once-in-a-century man began, ghostly at first, and then gradually taking on flesh.

"Oh, Aurelian!" Adeline Addams squealed. "Where *are* you?"

"He is here present, in this room where he spent so many wonderful hours with me," Clarinda said. "All right, Aurie baby, talk a little bit clearer and start materializing."

"All these things I will give you, Clarie," came the voice of Aurelian Bentley, and Bentley was there in shadow form himself. "No one else would give you so much. No one else would ever care so much...trust me, Clarie."

Aurelian Bentley was standing there solidly now. It was a three-dimensional projection or re-creation of him, coming into focus from all the eared and eyed and remembering walls of the room that was wired in parallel to the television receiver. Aurelian stood in the midst of them there in his own luxurious den.

"Clarie, I will do handsomely by you...a million dollars, my love, and I will give it to you." Oh, these were startling and convincing words coming from the living ghost there!

"I swear to you, Clarie... I will buy any island or group of islands in the Pacific Ocean for you... Hawaii, Samoa, Fiji. Name it and it's yours."

What man ever made such tall promises and with such obvious sincerity?

"Not on paper, not on air, Clarie, but in real life. I will make you the real and living queen."

If they will not listen to one risen from the dead, whom will they listen to?

"Clarie, believe me, believe me, believe me! I will do all things for you. I promise it." How are you going to top something like that?

"I leave you...my kingdom, ah, estate, Clarie. My word is good for that."

It was all in the bag, and the drawstring was being tightened on the bag.

"I hereby attest that...my estate...belongs to you. Let the eared walls of this room be witnesses to what I say, Clarie. If the walls of this room will swear to it, then surely they will be believed."

The image of Aurelian Bentley disappeared, and his sound was extinguished with a sharp snipping sound. Adeline Addams was putting a scissors back into her handbag.

"I've meant to find out what that wire there was for several times," she said. "That sort of shuts is all off when the wire is cut, doesn't it?"

"Here, here, you are guilty of destroying my evidence," Clarinda Calliope said. "You can go to prison for that! You can burn in fire for that!"

A sudden flaming hay wagon with a wild woman driving it rushed into the room and seemed about to destroy everyone in the room. Everyone cringed from it except Clarinda and the probate judge. The flaming hay wagon did crash into all the people of the room, but it did them no damage. It was only a scene from one of the earlier plays. You didn't think that Clarinda had only one circuit in that room, did you? But several of the persons were shaken by the threat.

"Good show," said the probate judge. "I guess it wins, what there is left to win."

"No, no," Adeline cried. "You can't give her the *estate*?"

"What's left of it, sure," said the judge, still flipping the silver dollar.

"It isn't the principle either," said Clarinda, "it's the dollar." She plucked the silver dollar out of the air as the probate judge was still flipping it.

"This *is* the entire residue of the estate, isn't it?" she asked to be sure.

"Right, Calliope, right," the judge said. "That's all that was left of it."

He continued to flip an invisible coin into the air, and he whistled the last, sad bars of the *McGinty's Saloon Waltz*.

"Anybody know where a good actress can get a job?" Clarinda asked. "Going rates, two dollars a day per role." She swept out of the room with head and spirits high. She was a consummate actress.

The other persons fade out into indistinct sounds and indistinct shadows in the old kerosene-powered television receiver.

The prospects of retrieval and revival of the first and greatest of all television series, *The Wonderful World of Aurelian Bentley*, recorded and produced in the year 1873, are in grave danger.

The only true and complete version of the series reposes in one single television receiver, Aurelian Bentley's own control receiver, the one that he kept in his own luxurious den where he spent so many happy hours with his ladies. The original librettos are stored in this set: they are, in fact, a part of this set and they may not, for inexplicable reasons, be removed to any great distance from it.

All the deep and ever-growing side talk, "slow talk," is

in this set. (All the other sets are mute.) All the final drama *Pettifoggers of Philadelphia* is recorded in this set and is in none of the others. *There is a whole golden era of television recorded in this set.*

I bought this old kerosene-burning treasure from its last owner (he did not know what it was: I told him that it was a chestnut roaster) for eighteen dollars. Now, by a vexing coincidence, this last owner has inherited forty acres of land with a fine stand of chestnut trees, and he wants the chestnut roaster back. And he has the law on his side.

I bought it from him, and I paid him for it, of course. But the check I gave him for it was hotter than a selenium rectifier on a shorted circuit. I have to make up the eighteen dollars or lose the receiver and its stored wealth.

I have raised thirteen dollars and fifty cents from three friends and one enemy. I still need four dollars and a half. Oh wait, wait, here is ninety-eight cents in pennies brought in by the "Children for the Wonderful World of Aurelian Bentley Preservation Fund." I still need three dollars and fifty-two cents. Anyone wishing to contribute to this fund had best do so quickly before this golden era of television is forever lost. Due to the fussiness of the government, contributions are not tax-deductible.

It is worth preserving as a remnant of that early era when there were giants on the earth. And, if it is preserved, someday someone will gaze into the old kerosene-powered receiver and cry out in astonishment in the words of the Greatest Bard:

"—what Poet-race
Shot such Cyclopean arches at the stars?"

The Treasure of Odirex
by Charles Sheffield

*Charles Sheffield is one of the best new writers to enter
the sf and fantasy field in many years. (His first novel,
Sight of Proteus, was published in 1978; another novel
and a collection of shorter stories are scheduled for
this year.) The following novella shows his talents in
full force: he tells a fascinating story, and he can
surprise us. Not least surprising about this story is the
fact that its hero is an obese, nearly toothless man
approaching middle age. But he is a hero, as any
student of the history of science will recognize: his
name is Erasmus Darwin.*

"The fever will break near dawn. If she wakes before that,
no food. Boiled water only, if she asks for drink. I will
infuse a febrifuge now, that you can give in three hours
time if she is awake and the fever has not abated."

The speaker rose heavily from the bedside and moved
to the fireplace, where oil lamps illuminated the medical
chest standing on an oak escritoire. He was grossly
overweight, with heavy limbs and a fat, pock-marked
face, and a full mouth from which the front teeth had long
been lost. The jaw was jowly, and in need of a razor. Only
the eyes belied the impression of coarseness and past
disease. They were grey and patient, with a look of deep
sagacity and a profound power of observation.

The other man in the room had been standing
motionless by the fire, his eyes fixed on the restless form
of the young woman lying on the bed. Now he bit his lip,
and shook his head.

"I wish you could stay the night, Erasmus. It is
midnight now. Are you sure that the fever will lessen?"

"As sure as a man can be, Jacob, when we deal with
disease. I wish I could stay, but there is a bad case of

puerperal fever in Rugeley that I must see tonight. Already the ways are becoming foul."

He looked ruefully down at his leather leggings, spattered with drying mud from the late November rain. "If anything changes for the worse, send Prindle after me. And before I go I'll leave you materials for tisanes, and instructions to prepare them."

He began to select from the medical chest, while his companion walked to the bedside and gazed unhappily at his wife as she tossed in fevered sleep. The man was tall and lean, with a dark, sallow complexion, deeply lined and channeled. Long years of intense sunlight had stamped a permanent frown on his brow, and a slight, continuous trembling in his hands told of other legacies of foreign service.

Erasmus Darwin looked at him sympathetically as he sorted the drugs he needed, then took paper and quill and prepared careful written instructions for their use.

"Attend now, Jacob," he said, as he sanded the written sheets. "There is one preparation here that I would normally insist on administering myself. These are dried tubers of aconite, cut fine. You must make an infusion for three hundred pulse beats, then let it cool before you use it. It serves as a febrifuge, to reduce fever, and also as a sudorific, to induce sweating. That is good for these cases. If the fever should continue past dawn, here is dried willow bark, for an infusion to lower body temperature."

"After dawn. Yes. And these two?" Jacob Pole held up the other packets.

"Use them only in emergency. If there should be convulsions, send for me at once, but give this as a tisane until I arrive. It is dried celandine, together with dried flowers of silverweed. And if there is persistent coughing, make a decoction of these, dried flowers of speedwell."

He looked closely at the other man and nodded slightly to himself as he saw the faint hand tremor and yellowish eyes. He rummaged again in the medical chest.

"And here is one for you, Jacob." He raised his hand, stifling the other's protest. "Don't deny it. I saw the signs again when I first walked in here tonight. Malaria and

Jacob Pole are old friends, are they not? Here is cinchona, Jesuit-bark, for your use. Be thankful that I have it with me—there's little enough call for it on my usual rounds. Rheumatism and breech babies, that's my fate."

During his description of the drugs and their use, his voice had been clear and unhesitating. Now, at the hint of humor, his usual stammer was creeping back in. Jacob Pole was glad to hear it. It meant that the physician was confident, enough to permit his usual optimistic outlook to re-emerge.

"Come on, then, Erasmus," he said. "Your carriage should still be ready and waiting. I can't tell you how much I appreciate what you've done for us. First Milly, and now Elizabeth. One life can never repay for two, but you know I'm ready should you ever need help yourself."

The two men took a last look at the sleeping patient, then Jacob Pole picked up the medical chest and they left the room. As they did so, the housekeeper came in to maintain the vigil on Elizabeth Pole. They walked quietly past her, down the stairs and on to the front of the silent house. Outside, the night sky was clear, with a gibbous moon nearing the full. A hovering ground mist hid the fields, and the distant lights of Lichfield seemed diffuse and deceptively close. The sulky was waiting, the old horse standing patiently between the shafts and munching quietly at her nosebag.

"That's strange." Jacob Pole paused in his work of removing the mare's nosebag. He looked down the road to the south. "Do you hear it, Erasmus? Unless my ears are going, there's a horseman coming this way, along the low road."

"Coming here?"

"Must be. There's no other house between here and Kings Bromley. But I don't expect visitors at this hour. Did you promise to make any calls that way?"

"Not tonight."

They stood in silence as the faint jingling of harness grew steadily louder. The rider who at last came into view seemed to be mounted on a legless horse, smoothly breasting the swirling ground mist. The Derbyshire clay, still slick and moist from the afternoon rain, muffled the sound of the hooves. The rider approached like a phantom. As he grew closer they could see him swaying a little in the saddle, as though half-asleep. He cantered up to them and pulled aside the black face-cloth that covered his nose and mouth.

"I'm seeking Dr. Darwin. Dr. Erasmus Darwin." The voice was soft and weary, with the flat vowels of a northcountryman.

"Then you need seek no further." Jacob Pole stepped forward. "This is Dr. Darwin, and I am Colonel Pole. What brings you here so late?"

The other man stiffly dismounted, stretching his shoulders and bowing at the waist to relieve the cramped muscles of a long ride. He grunted in relief, then turned to Darwin.

"Your housekeeper finally agreed to tell me where you were, Doctor. My name is Thaxton, Richard Thaxton. I must talk to you."

"An urgent medical problem?"

Thaxton hesitated, looking warily at Jacob Pole. "Perhaps. Or worse." He rubbed at the black stubble on his long chin. "'Canst thou not minister to a mind diseased?'"

"Better perhaps than Macbeth could." Erasmus Darwin stood for a moment, head hunched forward on his heavy shoulders. "Who suggested that you come to me?"

"Dr. Warren."

"Warren of London?" Darwin's voice quickened with interest. "I doubt that I can do anything for you that he cannot. Why did he not treat your problem himself?"

Again the other man hesitated. "If Dr. Warren is an old friend, I fear that I bring you bad news. He can no longer sustain his practice. His health is failing, and he confided in me his belief that he is consumptive."

"Then that is bad news indeed." Darwin shook his head sadly. "To my mind, Warren is the finest diagnostician in Europe. If he has diagnosed consumption in himself, the prospect is bleak indeed."

"He holds you to be his master, especially in diseases of the mind. Dr. Darwin, I have ridden non-stop from London, and I must get back to Durham as soon as possible. But I must talk with you. Dr. Warren offers you as my only hope."

Thaxton's hands were trembling with weariness as they held the bridle. Darwin scrutinized him closely, measuring the fatigue and the despair.

"We will talk, Mr. Thaxton, never fear. But I cannot stay here to do it. There is an urgent case of childbed fever six miles west of here. It cannot wait." He gestured at the carriage. "However, if you would be willing to squeeze into the sulky with me, we could talk as we travel. And there is a hamper of food there, that you look to be sorely in need of."

"What about my horse?"

"Leave that to me." Jacob Pole stepped forward. "I'll see he gets a rub-down and feed. Erasmus, I suggest that you come back here when you are done, and take some rest yourself. I can send one of the servants over to Lichfield, to tell your household that they can reach you here."

"Aye. It bids fair to be a long night. Say that I will be home before sunset tomorrow. This is a bad time of year for fevers and agues."

"No need to tell me that, Erasmus." Jacob Pole smiled ruefully and looked at his own shaking hand, as the other two men climbed into the carriage. As they moved off into the mist, he stirred himself with an effort and led the horse slowly to the stables at the rear of the house.

"It is a long and confusing story, Dr. Darwin. Bear with me if it seems at first as though I am meandering."

Food and brandy had restored Thaxton considerably. Both men had made good use of the hamper of food and drink balanced between them on their knees. Darwin wiped his greasy hands absent-mindedly on his woollen shawl, and turned his head to face Richard Thaxton.

"Take your time. Detail is at the heart of diagnosis, and in the absence of the patient—since it is clear that you are not he—the more that you can tell me, the better."

"Not 'he', Doctor. She. Three years ago my wife, Anna, went to see Dr. Warren. At that time we were living in the heart of London, hard by St. Mary le Bow. She had been feeling lacking in strength, and was troubled by a racking cough."

"With bleeding?"

"Thank God, no. But Dr. Warren was worried that she might become phthisic. He recommended that we move away from the London style of life, to one with more of country ways and fresh air."

Darwin nodded approvingly. "Warren and I have seldom disagreed on diagnosis, and less still on treatment. You took his advice?"

"Of course. We moved back to my family home, Heartsease, near Milburn in Cumbria."

"I know the area. Up in the high Fell country. Clean air, and clear sun. A good choice. But did it fail?"

"Not for my wife's general health, no. She became stronger and more robust. I could see the improvement, month by month. Then—about one year ago—there came another problem. She began to see visions."

Erasmus Darwin was silent for a long moment, while the carriage rolled steadily along the gravelled roads. "I see," he said at last. "Invisible to others, I take it?"

"Invisible to all, save Anna. Our house stands north of Milburn, facing out across Cross Fell. Late at night, in our bedroom, when the Helm stands on the Fell and the wind is strong from the north, she sees phantom lights moving on the Fell slopes, and hears crying in the wind."

"You have looked for them yourself?"

"I, and others. I have brought our servants upstairs to look also. We see nothing, but Anna is persistent."

"I see." Darwin paused again, reflective, then shrugged. "Even so, it does not sound like a matter for serious concern. She believes that she can see what you cannot. What harm is there in a will-o-the-wisp? It does not interfere with your life."

"It did not." Thaxton turned directly to Darwin, intense and troubled. "Until three months ago. Then

Anna found a book in Durham telling of the early history of our part of the country. Cross Fell had another name, long ago. It was known as Fiends Fell. According to legend, it was re-named Cross Fell when St. Augustine came with a cross to the Fell and drove out the fiends. But Anna says that she has seen the fiends herself, on two occasions. By full moonlight, and only when the Helm is on the Fell."

"Twice now you have mentioned the Helm. What is it?"

"Dense cloud, like a thunder-head. It sits as a bank, crouching over the top of Cross Fell. It does not move away, even when the wind sweeping from the top of the Fell is strong enough in Milburn to overturn carts and uproot trees. Anna says that it is the source of the fiends."

Darwin nodded slowly. The two men rode on in silence for a while, both deep in thought.

"Nothing you have said so far suggests the usual mental diseases," Darwin said at last. "But the human mind is more complicated than we can guess. Tell me, has your wife any other fears or fancies? Any other fuel for her beliefs?"

"Only more legends." Thaxton shrugged apologetically. "There are other legends of the Fell. According to the writings of Thomas of Appleby, in Roman times a great king, Odirex, or Odiris, lived in the high country of the Fells. He acquired a great treasure. Somehow, he used it to banish the Romans from that part of the country, completely, so that they never returned."

"What was his treasure?"

"The legend does not tell. But according to Thomas of Appleby, Odirex hid his treasure on Cross Fell. Local folk say that it is there to this day, guarded by the fiends of the fell. Anna says that she has seen the guardians; that they are not of human form; and that they live on Cross Fell yet, and will sometime come down again."

Darwin had listened to this very closely, and was now sitting upright on the hard seat of the carriage. "A strange tale, indeed, and one that I have not heard before in all my reading of English myth and legend. Odirex, eh? A name to start trains of thought, if we will but remember our

Latin. *Odii Rex*—the King of Hate. What else does Thomas of Appleby have to say about the King of Hate's Treasure?"

"Only that it was irresistible. But surely, Dr. Darwin, you are not taking these tales seriously? They are but the instruments that are turning my wife's mind away from sanity."

"Perhaps." Darwin relaxed and hunched low in his seat. "Perhaps. In any case, I would have to see your wife to make any real decision as to her condition."

"I can bring her here to see you, if you wish. But I must do it under some subterfuge, since she does not know that I am seeking assistance for her condition. As for money, I will pay any fee that you ask."

"No. Money is not an issue. Also, I want to see her at your home in Milburn." Darwin appeared to have made up his mind about something. "Look, I now have the responsibilities of my practice here, and as you can see they are considerable. However, I have reason to make a visit to York in a little more than two weeks time. I will have another doctor, my *locum tenens*, working here in my absence. If you will meet me in York, at a time and place that we must arrange, we can go on together to Milburn. Then perhaps I can take a look at your Anna, and give you my best opinion on her—and on other matters, too."

Darwin held up his hand, to stem Thaxton's words. "Now, no thanks. We are almost arrived. You can show your appreciation in a more practical way. Have you ever assisted in country medicine, two hours after midnight? Here is your chance to try it."

"The roof of England, Jacob. Look there, to the east. We can see all the way to the sea."

Darwin was leaning out of the coach window, holding his wig on with one hand and drinking in the scenery, as they climbed slowly up the valley of the Tees, up from the eastern plain that they had followed north from the Vale of York. Jacob Pole shivered in the brisk east wind that blew through the inside of the coach, and huddled deeper into the leather greatcoat that hid everything up to his eyes.

"It's the roof, all right, blast it. Close that damn window. No man in his right mind wants to be out on the roof in the middle of December. I don't know what the devil I'm doing up here, when I could be home and warm in bed."

"Jacob, you insisted on coming, as you well know."

"Maybe. You can be the best doctor in Europe, Erasmus, and the leading inventor in the Lunar Club, but you still need a practical man to keep your feet on the ground."

Darwin grinned, intoxicated by the clear air of the fells. "Of course. The mention of treasure had nothing to do with it, did it? You came only to look after me."

"Hmph. Well, I wouldn't go quite so far as to say that. Damn it all, Erasmus, you know me. I've dived for pearls off the eastern Spice Islands; I've hunted over half the Americas for El Dorado; I've scrabbled after rubies in Persia and Baluchistan; and I've dug for diamonds all the way from Ceylon to Samarkand. And what have I got out of it? A permanent sunburn, a bum that's been bitten by all the fleas in Asia, and a steady dose of malaria three times a year. But I could no more resist coming here, when I heard Thaxton talk about Odirex's treasure, than you could . . . stop philosophizing."

Darwin laughed aloud. "Ah, you're missing the point, Jacob. Look out there." He waved a brawny arm at the Tees Valley, ascending with the river before them. "There's a whole treasure right here, for the taking. If I knew how to use them, there are plants for a whole new medical pharmacopoeia, waiting for our use. I'm a botanist, and I can't even name half of them. Hey, Mr. Thaxton." He leaned further out of the coach, looking up to the driver's seat above and in front of him.

Richard Thaxton leaned perilously over the edge of the coach. "Yes, Dr. Darwin?"

"I'm seeing a hundred plants here that don't grow in the

lowlands. If I describe them to you, can you arrange to get me samples of each?"

"Easily. But I should warn you, there are many others that you will not even see from the coach. Look." He stopped the carriage, swung easily down, and went off to a mossy patch a few yards to one side. When he came back, bare-headed, dark hair blowing in the breeze, he carried a small plant with broad leaves and a number of pale green tendrils with blunt, sticky ends.

"There's one for your collection. Did you ever see or hear of anything like this?"

Darwin looked at it closely, smelled it, broke off a small piece of a leaf and chewed it thoughtfully. "Aye, I've not seen it for years, but I think I know what it is. Butterwort, isn't it? It rings a change on the usual order of things—animals eat plants, but this plant eats animals, or at least insects."

"That's right." Thaxton smiled. "Good thing it's only a few inches high. Imagine it ten feet tall, and you really have a 'Treasure of Odirex' that could have scared away the Romans."

"Good God." Jacob Pole was aghast. "You don't really think that there could be such a thing, do you—up on Cross Fell?"

"Of course not. It would have been found long ago—there are shepherds up there every day, you know. They'd have found it."

"Unless it found them," said Pole gloomily. He retreated even further into his greatcoat. Thaxton climbed back into the driver's seat and they went on their way. The great expanse of the winter fells was spreading about them, a rolling sea of copper, sooty black and silver-grey. The land lay bleak, already in the grip of winter. At last, after three more hours of steady climbing, they came to Milburn. Thaxton leaned far over again, to shout into the interior of the coach. "Two more miles, and we'll be home."

The village of Milburn was small and windswept, a cluster of stone houses around the church and central common. Thaxton's coach seemed too big, out of scale with the mean buildings of the community. At the crossroads that led away to the neighboring village of Newbiggin, Thaxton halted the carriage and pointed to the great mass of Cross Fell, lying to the north-east. Darwin looked at it with interest, and even Jacob Pole, drawn by the sight of his potential treasure-ground, ventured out of his huddle of coats and shawls.

After a couple of minutes of silent inspection of the bleak prospect, rising crest upon crest to the distant, hidden summit, Thaxton shook the reins to drive on.

"Wait—don't go yet!" Darwin's sudden cry halted Thaxton just as he was about to start the coach forward.

"What is it, Dr. Darwin? Is something the matter?"

Darwin did not reply. Instead, he opened the carriage door, and despite his bulk swung easily to the ground. He walked rapidly across the common, where a boy about ten years old was sitting by a stone milestone. The lad was deformed of feature, with a broad, flattened skull and deep-set eyes. He was lightly dressed in the cast-off rags of an adult, and he did not seem to feel the cold despite the biting breeze.

The child started up at Darwin's approach, but did not run away. He was less than four feet tall, heavy-chested and bow-legged. Darwin stood before him and looked at him with a professional eye.

"What is it, Erasmus?" Jacob Pole had dismounted also and come hurrying after. "What's his disease?"

Darwin had placed a gentle hand on the boy's head and was slowly turning it from side to side. The child, puzzled but reassured by Darwin's calm manner and soft touch, permitted the examination without speaking.

"It is not disease, Jacob." Darwin shook his head thoughtfully. "At first I thought it must be, but the lad is quite healthy. Never in my medical experience have I seen such a peculiar physiognomy. Look at the strange bone structure of the skull, and the curious regression of the jaw. And see that odd curve, in the relation of the thoracic and cervical vertebrae." Darwin puffed out his full lips, and ran a gentle finger over the child's lumpy forehead. "Tell me, my boy, how old are you?"

The child did not reply. He looked at Darwin with soft, intelligent eyes, and made a strange, strangled noise high in his throat.

"You'll get no reply from Jimmy," said Thaxton, who had followed behind the other two men. "He's mute—bright enough, and he'll follow any instructions. But he can't speak."

Darwin nodded, and ran his hand lightly over the boy's throat and larynx. "Yes, there's something odd about the structure here, too. The hyoid bone is malformed, and the thyroid prominence is absent. Tell me, Mr. Thaxton, are the boy's parents from these parts of Cumbria?" Darwin smiled encouragingly at the lad, though his own lack of front teeth made that more frightening than reassuring. A piece of silver, pressed into the small hand, was more successful. The boy smiled back tentatively, and pointed upwards towards the Fell.

"See, he understands you very well," said Thaxton. "His mother is up on Dufton Fell, he says." He turned away, drawing the other two men after him, before he continued in a low voice. "Jimmy's a sad case. His mother's a shepherdess, Daft Molly Metcalf. She's a poor lass who doesn't have much in the way of wits. Just bright enough to tend the sheep, up on Dufton Fell and Cross Fell."

"And the father?" asked Darwin.

"God only knows. Some vagrant. Anyway, Jimmy's not much to look at, but his brain is all right. He'll never be much more than a dwarf, I fear, but there will always be work for him here in the village. He's trustworthy and obedient, and we've all grown used to the way he looks."

"He's certainly no beauty, though," said Jacob Pole. "That's a strange deformity. You know what he reminds me of? When I was in the Spice Islands, there was a creature that the Dutch called the Orange-Lord, or Orang-Laut, or some such name. It lived in the deep forest, and it was very shy, but I once saw a body that the natives brought in. The skull and bone structure reminded me of your Jimmy."

"It's a long way from the Spice Islands to Cross Fell, Colonel," said Thaxton. "And you can guess what Anna

has been saying—that Daft Molly was impregnated by a
fiend of the Fell, some diabolical incubus, and Jimmy is
the devilish result. What do you think of that, Dr.
Darwin?"

Erasmus Darwin had been listening absent-mindedly,
from time to time turning back for another look at the
boy. "I don't know what to think yet, Mr. Thaxton," he
finally replied. "But I can assure you of one thing. The
only way that a human woman bears children is from
impregnation by a human male. Your wife's chatter about
an incubus is unscientific piffle."

"Impregnation is not always necessary, Doctor. Are
you not forgetting the virgin birth of Our Lord, Jesus
Christ?"

"Don't get him started on that," said Jacob Pole
hastily. "or we'll be here all day. You may not know it,
Mr. Thaxton, but this is Erasmus Darwin, the doctor, the
inventor, the philosopher, the poet, the everything—
except the Christian."

Thaxton smiled. "I had heard as much, to tell the truth,
from Dr. Warren. 'If you are wise,' he said, 'you will not
dispute religion with Dr. Darwin. If you are wiser yet, you
will not dispute anything with him.'"

The men climbed back into the coach and drove slowly
on through Milburn, to Thaxton's house north of the
village. Before they went inside the big, stone-built
structure, they again took a long look at Cross Fell, rising
vast to the north-east.

"It's clear today," said Thaxton. "That means that the
Helm won't be on the Fell—Anna won't be seeing or
hearing anything tonight. Dr. Darwin, I don't know what
your diagnosis will be, but I swear to God that the next
twenty-four hours will be the hardest for me of any that I
can remember. Come in, now, and welcome to Heartsease."

Darwin did not speak, but he patted the other man
sympathetically on the shoulder with a firm hand. They
walked together to the front door of the house.

"They are taking an awfully long time." Richard

Thaxton rose from his seat by the fire and began to pace the study, looking now and again at the ceiling.

"As they should be," said Jacob Pole reassuringly. "Richard, sit down and relax. I know Erasmus, and I've seen him work many times in the past. He has the greatest power of observation and invention of any man I ever met. He sees disease where others can see nothing—in the way a man walks, or talks, or stands, or even lies. And he is supremely thorough, and in the event of dire need, supremely innovative. I owe to him the lives of my wife, Elizabeth, and my daughter Milly. He will come down when he is satisfied, not before."

Thaxton did not reply. He stood at the window, looking out at the inscrutable bulk of Cross Fell. A strong north-east wind, harsh and gusting, bent the leafless boughs of the fruit trees in the kitchen garden outside the study window, and swirled around the isolated house.

"See up there," he said at last. "The Helm is growing. In another two hours the top of the Fell will be invisible."

Pole rose also and joined him by the window. At the top of the Fell, a solid bank of roiling cloud was forming, unmoved by the strengthening wind. As they watched, it grew and thickened, shrouding the higher slopes and slowly moving lower.

"Will it be there tonight?" asked Pole.

"Until dawn. Guarding the treasure. God, I'm beginning to talk like Anna. It's catching me, too."

"Has there ever been any real treasure on the Fell? Gold, or silver?"

"I don't know. Lead, there surely is. It has been mined since Roman times, and there are mine workings all over this area. As for gold, I have heard much talk of it, but talk is easy. I have never seen nuggets, or even dust."

Jacob Pole rubbed his hands together. "That's meat and drink to me, Richard. Fiends or no fiends, there's nothing I'd like better than to spend a few days prospecting around Cross Fell. I've travelled a lot further than this, to places a good deal more inhospitable, on much less evidence. Yes, and I've fought off a fair number of fiends, too—human ones."

"And you have found gold?"

Pole grimaced. "Pox on it, Richard, you would ask me that. Never, not a pinch big enough to cover a whore's modesty. But luck can change at any time. This may be it."

Richard Thaxton pushed his fingers through his black, bushy hair, and smiled at Jacob Pole indulgently. "I've often wondered what would take a man to the top of Cross Fell in mid-winter. I think I've found out. One thing I'll wager, you'll not get Dr. Darwin to go with you. He's carrying a bit too much weight for that sort of enterprise."

As he spoke, they heard the clump of footsteps on the stairs above them. Thaxton at once fell silent and his manner became tense and somber. When Erasmus Darwin entered, Thaxton raised his eyebrows questioningly but did not speak.

"Sane as I am," said Darwin at once, smiling. "And a good deal saner than Jacob."

"—or than you, Richard," added Anna Thaxton, coming in lightly behind Darwin. She was a thin, dark-haired woman, with high cheekbones and sparkling grey eyes. She crossed the room and put her arms around her husband. "As soon as Dr. Darwin had convinced himself that I was sane, he confessed to me that he was not really here to test me for a consumptive condition, but to determine my mental state. Now—" she smiled smugly "—he wants to do some tests on *you*, my love."

Richard Thaxton pressed his wife to him as though he meant to crack her ribs. Then her final words penetrated, and he looked at her in astonishment.

"Me! You're joking. I've seen no fiends."

"Exactly," said Darwin. He moved over to the table by the study window, where an array of food dishes had been laid out. "You saw nothing. For the past hour, I have been testing your wife's sight and hearing. Both are phenomenally acute, especially at low levels. Now I want to know about yours."

"But others were present when Anna saw her fiends. Surely we are not all blind and deaf."

"Certainly, all are not. But Anna tells me that when she

saw and heard her mysteries on Cross Fell, it was night and you alone were with her upstairs. You saw and heard nothing. Then when you brought others, they also saw and heard nothing. But they came from lighted rooms downstairs. It takes many minutes for human eyes to acquire their full night vision—and it is hard for a room full of people, no matter how they try, to remain fully silent. So, I say again, how good are *your* eyes and ears?"

"—and I tell you, they are excellent!" exclaimed Thaxton.

"—and I tell you, they are indifferently good!" replied Anna Thaxton. "Who cannot tell a rook from a blackbird at thirty paces, or count the sheep on Cross Fell?"

They still held each other close, arguing across each other's shoulder. Darwin looked on with amusement, quietly but systematically helping himself to fruit, clotted cream, Stilton cheese, and West Indian sweetmeats from the side table.

"Come, Mr. Thaxton," he said at last. "Surely you are not more prepared to believe that your wife is mad, than believe yourself a little myopic? Short-sightedness is no crime."

Thaxton shrugged. "All right. All right." He held his wife at arms' length, his hands on her shoulders. "Anna, I've never won an argument with you yet, and if Dr. Darwin is on your side I may as well surrender early. Do your tests. But if you are right, what does that mean?"

Darwin munched on a candied quince, and rubbed his hands together in satisfaction. "Why, then we no longer have a medical problem, but something much more intriguing and pleasant. You see, it means that Anna is *really* seeing something up on Cross fell, when the Helm sits on the upland. And that is most interesting to me—be it fiends, fairies, hobgoblins, or simple human skullduggery. Come, my equipment for the tests is upstairs. It will take about an hour, and we should be finished well before dinner."

As they left, Jacob Pole went again to the window. The Helm had grown. It stood now like a great, grey animal, crouching at the top of Cross Fell and menacing the nearer lowlands. Pole sighed.

"Human skullduggery?" he said to Anna Thaxton. "I hope not. I'll take fiends, goblins, and all—if the Treasure of Odirex is up there with them. Better ghouls and gold together, than neither one."

"Tonight? You must be joking!"

"And why not tonight, Mr. Thaxton? The Helm sits on the Fell, the night is clear, and the moon is rising. What better time for Anna's nocturnal visitants?"

Richard Thaxton looked with concern at Darwin's bulk, uncertain how to phrase his thought. "Do you think it wise, for a man of your age—?"

"—forty-six," said Darwin.

"—your age, to undergo exertion on the Fell, at night? You are not so young, and the effort will be great. You are not—lissom; and it—"

"I'm fat," said Darwin. "I regard that as healthy. Good food wards off disease. This world has a simple rule: eat or be eaten. I am not thin, and less agile than a younger man, but I have a sound constitution, and no ailment but a persistent gout. Jacob and I will have no problem."

"Colonel Pole also?"

"Try and stop him. Right, Jacob? He's been lusting to get up on that Fell, ever since he heard the magic word 'treasure,' back in Lichfield. Like a youth, ready to mount his first—er—horse."

"I've noticed that," said Anna Thaxton. She smiled at Darwin. "And thank you, Doctor, for tempering your simile for a lady's ears. Now, if your mind is set on Cross Fell tonight, you will need provisions. What should they be?"

Darwin bowed his head, and smiled his ruined smile. "I have always observed, Mrs. Thaxton, that in practical decision-making, men cannot compare with women. We will need food, shielded lamps, warm blankets, and tinder and flint."

"No weapons, or crucifix?" asked Richard Thaxton.

"Weapons, on Cross Fell at night, would offer more danger to us than to anyone else. As for the crucifix, it has been my experience that it has great influence—on those who are already convinced of its powers. Now, where on the Fell should we take up our position?"

"If you are going," said Thaxton suddenly, "then I will go with you. I could not let you wander the Fell, alone."

"No. You must stay here. I do not think that we will need help, but if I am wrong we rely on you to summon and lead it. Remain here with Anna. We will signal you—three lantern flashes from us will be a call for help, four a sign that all is well. Now, where should we position ourselves? Out of sight, but close to the lights you saw."

"Come to the window," said Anna Thaxton. "See where the spur juts out, like the beak of an eagle? That is your best waiting point. The lights show close there, when the fiends of the Fell appear. They return there, before dawn. You will not be able to see the actual point of their appearance from the spur. Keep a watch on our bedroom. I will show a light there if the fiends appear. When that happens, skirt the spur, following west-ward. After a quarter of a mile or so the lights on the Fell should be visible to you."

As she was speaking, the sound of the dinner gong rang through the house.

"I hope," she continued, "that you will be able to eat something, although I know you must be conscious of the labors and excitement of the coming night."

Erasmus Darwin regarded her with astonishment. "Something? Mrs. Thaxton. I have awaited the dinner bell for the past hour, with the liveliest anticipation. I am famished. Pray, lead the way. We can discuss our preparations further while we dine."

"We should have brought a timepiece with us, Erasmus. I wonder what the time is. We must have been here three or four hours already."

"A little after midnight, if the moon is keeping to her usual schedule. Are you warm enough?"

"Not too bad. Thank God for these blankets. It's colder than a witch's tit up here. How much longer? Suppose they don't put in an appearance at all? Or the weather changes? It's already beginning to cloud up a little."

"Then we'll have struggled up here and been half frozen for nothing. We could never track them with no moon. We'd kill ourselves, walking the Fell blind."

The two men were squatted on the hillside, facing south-west towards Heartsease. They were swaddled in heavy woollen blankets, and their exhaled breath rose white before them. In the moonlight they could clearly see the village of Milburn, far below, etched in black and silver. The Thaxton house stood apart from the rest, lamps showing in the lower rooms but completely dark above. Between Darwin and Pole sat two shielded oil lanterns. Unless the side shutters were unhooked and opened, the lanterns were visible only from directly above.

"It's a good thing we can see the house without needing any sort of spyglass," said Pole, slipping his brass brandy flask back into his coat after a substantial swig. "Holding it steady for a long time when it's as cold as this would be no joke. If there are fiends living up here, they'll need a fair stock of Hell-fire with them, just to keep from freezing. Damn those clouds."

He looked up again at the moon, showing now through broken streaks of cover. As he did so, he felt Darwin's touch on his arm.

"There it is, Jacob," he breathed. "In the bedroom. Now, watch for the signal."

They waited, tense and alert, as the light in the window dimmed, returned, and dimmed again. After a longer absence, it came back once more, then remained bright.

"In the usual place, where Anna hoped they might be," said Darwin. "Show our lantern, to let Thaxton know we've understood their signal. Then let's be off, while the moon lights the way."

The path skirting the tor was narrow and rocky, picked out precariously between steep screes and jagged outcroppings. Moving cautiously and quietly, they tried to watch both their footing and the fell ahead of them. Jacob Pole, leading the way, suddenly stopped.

"There they are," he said softly.

Three hundred yards ahead, where the rolling cloud

bank of the Helm dipped lower to meet the broken slope of the scarp face, four yellow torches flickered and bobbed. Close to each one, bigger and more diffuse, moved a blue-green phosphorescent glow.

The two men edged closer. The blue-green glows gradually resolved themselves to squat, misshapen forms, humanoid but strangely incomplete.

"Erasmus," whispered Jacob. "They are headless!"

"I think not," came the soft answer. "Watch closely, when the torches are close to their bodies. You can see that the torch light reflects from their heads—but there is no blue light shining there. Their bodies alone are outlined by it."

As he spoke, a despairing animal scream echoed over the Fell. Jacob Pole gripped Darwin's arm fiercely.

"Sheep," said Darwin tersely. "Throat cut. That bubbling cry is blood in the windpipe. Keep moving towards them, Jacob. I want to get a good look at them."

After a moment's hesitation, Pole again began to move slowly forward. But now the lights were moving steadily uphill, back towards the shrouding cloud bank of the Helm.

"Faster, Jacob. We've got to keep them in sight and be close to them before they go into the cloud. The light from their torches won't carry more than a few yards in that."

Darwin's weight was beginning to take its toll. He fell behind, puffing and grunting, as Pole's lanky figure loped rapidly ahead, around the tor and up the steep slope. He paused once and looked about him, then was off uphill again, into the moving fog at the edge of the Helm. Darwin, arriving at last at the same spot, could see no sign of him. Chest heaving, he stopped to catch his breath.

"It's no good." Pole's voice came like a disembodied spirit, over from the left of the hillside. A second later he suddenly emerged from the cloud bank. "They vanished into thin air, right about here. Just like that." He snapped his fingers. "I can't understand how they could have gone so fast. The cloud isn't so thick here. Maybe they can turn to air."

Darwin sat down heavily on a flat-topped rock. "More likely they snuffed their torches."

"But then I'd still have seen the body-glow."

"So let's risk the use of the lanterns, and have a good look round here. There should be some trace of them. It's a long way back to Heartsease, and I don't fancy this climb again tomorrow night."

They opened the shutters of the lanterns, and moved cautiously about the hillside. Darwin knew that the Thaxtons would be watching from Heartsease, and puzzling over what they had seen. He interrupted his search long enough to send a signal: four lantern flashes—all goes well.

"Here's the answer." Jacob Pole had halted fifty feet away, in the very fringe of the Helm. "I ought to have guessed it, after the talk that Thaxton and I had earlier. He told me yesterday that there are old workings all over this area. Lead, this one, or maybe tin."

The mine shaft was set almost horizontally into the hillside, a rough-walled tunnel just tall enough for a crouching man. Darwin stooped to look at the rock fragments inside the entrance.

"It's lead," he said, holding the lantern low. "See, this is galena, and this is blue fluorspar—the same Blue John that we find back in Derbyshire. And here is a lump of what I take to be barytes—heavy spar. Feel the weight of it. There's been lead mines up here on the Fell for two thousand years, since before the Romans came to Britain, but I thought they were all disused now. Most of them are miles north and east of this."

"I doubt that this one is being used for lead mining," replied Jacob Pole. "And I doubt if the creatures that we saw are lead miners. Maybe it's my malaria, playing up again because it's so cold here." He shivered all over. "But I've got a feeling of evil when I look in that shaft. You know the old saying: iron bars are forged on Earth, gold bars are forged in Hell. That's the way to the treasure, in there. I know it."

"Jacob, you're too romantic. You see four poachers

killing a sheep, and you have visions of a treasure trove. What makes you think that the Treasure of Odirex is gold?"

"It's the natural assumption. What else would it be?"

"I could speculate. But I will wager it is not gold. That wouldn't have served to get rid of the Romans. Remember the Danegeld—that didn't work, did it?"

As he spoke, he was craning forward into the tunnel, the lantern held out ahead of him.

"No sign of them in here." He sniffed. "But this is the way they went. Smell the resin? That's from their torches. Well, I suppose that is all for tonight. Come on, we'd best begin the descent back to the house. It is a pity we cannot go further now."

"Descent to the house? Of course we can follow them, Erasmus. That's what we came for, isn't it?"

"Surely. But on the surface of the Fell, not through pit tunnels. We lack ropes and markers. But now that we know exactly where to begin, our task is easy. We can return here tomorrow with men and equipment, by daylight—perhaps we can even bring a tracking hound. All we need to do now is to leave a marker here, that can be seen easily when we come here again."

"I suppose you're right." Pole shrugged, and turned disconsolately for another look at the tunnel entrance. "Damn it, Erasmus, I'd like to go in there, evil or no evil. I hate to get this far and then turn tail."

"If the Treasure of Odirex is in there, it has waited for you for fifteen hundred years. It can wait another day. Let us begin the descent."

They retraced their steps, Jacob very reluctantly, to the downward path. In a few dozen paces they were clear of the fringes of the Helm. And there they stopped. While they had examined the entrance to the mine, the cloud cover had increased rapidly. Instead of seeing a moon shining strongly through light, broken cloud they were limited to occasional fleeting glimpses through an almost continuous mass of clouds.

Jacob Pole shrugged, and looked slyly at Darwin. "This is bad, Erasmus. We can't go down in this light. It would be suicide. How long is it until dawn?"

"Nearly four hours, at a guess. It's bad luck, but we are only a week from winter solstice. There's nothing else for it, we must settle down here and make the best of it, until dawn comes and we have enough light to make a safe descent."

"Aye, you're right." Jacob Pole turned and looked thoughtfully back up the hill. "Since we're stuck here for hours, Erasmus, wouldn't it make sense to use the time, and take a quick look inside the entrance of the mine? After all, we do have the lanterns—and it may well be warmer inside."

"Or drier, or any other of fifty reasons you could find for me, eh?" Darwin held his lantern up to Pole's face, studying the eyes and the set of the mouth. He sighed. "I don't know if you're shivering now with excitement or malaria, but you need warmth and rest. I wonder now about the wisdom of this excursion. All right. Let us go back up to the mine, on two conditions: we descend again to Heartsease at first light, and we take no risks of becoming lost in the mine."

"I've been in a hundred mines, all over the world, and I have yet to get lost in one. Let me go first. I know how to spot weak places in the supports."

"Aye. And if there's treasure to be found—which I doubt—I'd not be the one to deprive you of the first look."

Jacob Pole smiled. He placed one lantern on the ground, unshuttered. "Let this stay here, so Richard and Anna can see it. Remember, we promised to signal them every three hours that all is well. Now, let's go to it—fiends or no fiends."

He turned to begin the climb back to the abandoned mine. As he did so, Darwin caught the expression on his face. He was nervous and pale, but in his eyes was the look of a small child approaching the door of a toyshop.

On a second inspection, made this time with the knowledge that they would be entering and exploring it, the mine tunnel looked much narrower and the walls less secure. Jacob, lantern partially shuttered to send a narrow beam forward, led the way. They went cautiously into the interior of the shaft. After a slight initial upward slant, the tunnel began to curve down, into the heart of the hill. The walls and roof were damp to the touch, and every few yards small rivulets of water ran steadily down the walls, glistening like a layer of ice in the light of the lantern. Thirty paces on, they came to a branch in the tunnel. Jacob Pole bent low and studied the uneven floor.

"Left, I think," he whispered. "What will we do if we meet the things that live here?"

"You should have asked the question before we set out," replied Darwin softly. "As for me, that is exactly what I am here for. I am less interested in any treasure."

Jacob Pole stopped, and turned in the narrow tunnel. "Erasmus, you never cease to amaze me. I know what drives *me* on, what makes me willing to come into a place like this at the devil's dancing-hour. And I know that I'm in a cold sweat of fear and anticipation. But why aren't *you* terrified? Don't you think a meeting with the fiends would carry great danger for us?"

"Less danger than you fear. I assume that these creatures, like ourselves, are of natural origin. If I am wrong on *that*, my whole view of the world is wrong. Now, these fiends hide on the Fell, and they come out only at night. There are no tales that say they kill people, or capture them. So I believe that *they* fear *us*—far more than we fear them."

"Speak for yourself," muttered Pole.

"Remember," Darwin swept on, "when there is a struggle for living space, the stronger and fiercer animals drive out the weaker and more gentle—who then must perforce inhabit a less desirable habitat if they are to survive. For example, look at the history of the tribes that conquered Britain. In each case—"

"Sweet Christ!" Jacob Pole looked round him nervously. "Not a lecture, Erasmus. This isn't the time or the place for it. And not so loud! I'll take the history lesson some other time."

He turned his back and led the way into the left branch of the tunnel. Darwin sniffed, then followed. He was almost fat enough to block the tunnel completely, and had to walk very carefully. After a few steps he stopped again and looked closely at a part of the tunnel wall that had been shored up with rough timbers.

"Jacob, bring the light back for a moment, would you? This working has been used recently—new wood in some of the braces. And look at this."

"What is it?"

"Sheep wool, caught on the splintered wood here. It's still dry. We're on the correct path all right. Keep going."

"Aye. But what now?"

Pole pointed the beam from the lantern ahead to where the tunnel broadened into a domed chamber with a smooth floor. They walked forward together. At the other side of the chamber was a deep crevasse. Across it, leading to a dark opening on the other side, ran a bridge of rope guides and wooden planks, secured by heavy timbers buttressed between floor and ceiling. Pole shone his lantern across the gap, into the tunnel on the other side, but there was nothing to be seen there. They walked together to the edge.

"It looks sturdy enough. What do you think, Erasmus?"

"I think we have gone far enough. It would be foolhardy to risk a crossing. What lies below?"

Pole swung the lantern to throw the beam downward. The pit was steep-sided. About eight feet below the brink lay black, silent water, its surface smooth and unrippled. To right and left, the drowned chasm continued as far as the lantern beam would carry. Pole swung the light back to the bridge, inspecting the timbers and supporting ropes.

"Seems solid to me. Why don't I take a quick look at the other side, while you hold the lantern."

Darwin did not reply at once. He was staring down into the crevasse, a puzzled frown on his heavy face.

"Jacob, cover the lantern for a moment. I think I can see something down there, like a faint shining."

"Like gold?" The voice was hopeful. Pole shuttered the lantern and they stared in silence into the darkness. After a few moments, it became more visible to them. An eerie, blue-green glow lit the pit below, beginning about three feet below the lip and continuing to the water beneath. As their eyes adjusted, they began to see a faint pattern to the light.

"Jacob, it's growing there. It must be a moss, or a fungus. Or am I going blind?"

"It's a growth. But how can a living thing glow like that?"

"Some fungi shine in the dark, and so do some animals—glow-worms, and fireflies. But I never heard of anything like this growth. It's in regular lines—as though it had been set out purposely, to provide light at the bridge. Jacob, I must have a sample of that!"

In the excited tone of voice, Pole recognized echoes of his own feelings when he thought about hunting for treasure. Darwin knelt on the rocky floor, then laboriously lowered himself at full length by the side of the chasm.

"Here, let me do that, Erasmus. You're not built for it."

"No. I can get it. You know, this is the same glow that we saw on the creatures on Cross Fell."

He reached over the edge. His groping fingers were ten inches short of the highest growth. Grunting with the effort, Darwin took hold of the loose end of a trailing rope from the bridge, and levered himself farther over the edge.

"Erasmus, don't be a fool. Wait until we can come back here tomorrow, with the others."

Darwin grunted again, this time in triumph. "Got it."

The victory was short-lived. As he spoke, the hemp of the rope, rotted by many years of damp, disintegrated in his grasp. His body, off-balance, tilted over the edge. With a startled oath and a titanic splash, Darwin plunged head-first into the dark water beneath.

"Erasmus!" Jacob Pole swung around and groped futilely in the darkness for several seconds. He at last located the shuttered lantern, opened it and swung its beam onto the surface of the pool. There was no sign of Darwin. Pole ripped off his greatcoat and shoes. He stepped to the edge, hesitated for a moment, then took a deep breath and jumped feet-first into the unknown depths of the black, silent pool.

"More than three hours now. They should have signalled."

"Perhaps they did." Richard Thaxton squinted out of the window at the dark hillside.

"No. The lantern has been steady. I'm worried, Richard. See, they set it exactly where the lights of the fiends disappeared into the Helm." Anna shook her head unhappily. "It must be freezing up on Cross Fell tonight. I just can't believe that they would sit there for three hours without moving or signalling, unless they were in trouble."

"Nor can I." Thaxton opened the window and stuck his head out. He stared at the bleak hillside. "It's no good, Anna. Even when the moon was up I couldn't see a thing up there except for the lantern—and I can only just see that when you tell me where to look. Let's give it another half hour. If they don't signal, I'll go up after them."

"Richard, be reasonable. Wait until dawn. You'll have an accident yourself if you go up there in the dark—you know your eyes aren't good enough to let you be sure-footed, even by full moonlight."

The freezing wind gusted in through the open window. Thaxton pulled it closed. "At dawn. I suppose you're right. I'd best check the supplies now. I'll take medicine and splints, but I hope to God we won't be needing them." He stood up. "I'll tell two of the gardeners that we may have to make a rescue trip on the Fell at first light. Now, love, you try and get some sleep. You've been glued to that window most of the night."

"I will." Anna Thaxton smiled at her husband as he left the room. But she did not move from her vigil by the window, nor did her eyes move from the single point of light high on the bleak slopes of Cross Fell.

The first shock was the cold of the water, enfolding and piercing his body like an iron maiden. Jacob Pole gasped as the air was driven from his lungs, and flinched at the thought of total immersion. Then he realized that he was still standing, head clear of the surface. The pool was less than five feet deep.

He moved around in the water, feeling with his stockinged feet until he touched a soft object on the bottom. Bracing himself, he filled his lungs and submerged to grope beneath the surface. The cold was frightful. It numbed his hands instantly, but he grasped awkwardly at Darwin's arm and shoulder, and hoisted the body to the level of his own chest. Blinking water from his eyes, he turned the still form so that its head was clear of the surface. Then he stood there shuddering, filled with the awful conviction that he was supporting a corpse.

After a few seconds, Darwin began to cough and retch. Pole muttered a prayer of relief and hung on grimly until the spasms lessened.

"What happened?" Darwin's voice was weak and uncertain.

"You fell in head-first. You must have banged your head on the bottom." Pole's reply came through chattering teeth. His arms and hands had lost all feeling.

"I'm sorry, Jacob." Darwin was racked by another spell of coughing. "I behaved like an absolute fool." He roused himself. "Look, I can stand now. We'd better get out of here before we freeze."

"Easier said then done. Look at the height of the edge. And I see no purchase on either side."

"We'll have to try it anyway. Climb on my shoulders and see if you can reach."

Scrabbling with frozen hands on the smooth rock face, Pole clambered laboriously to Darwin's shoulders, leaned against the side of the pit and reached upwards. His straining fingertips were a foot short of the lip. He felt in vain for some hold on the rock. Finally he swore and slid back into the icy water.

"No good. Can't reach. We're stuck."

"We can't afford to be. An hour in here will kill us. This water must be snow-melt from the Fell. It's close to freezing."

"I don't give a damn where it came from—and I'm well

aware of its temperature. What now, Erasmus? The feeling is going out of my legs."

"If we can't go up, we must go along. Let's follow the pool to the left here."

"We'll be moving away from the lantern light up there."

"We can live without light, but not without heat. Come on, Jacob."

They set off, water up to their necks. After a few yards it was clear that the depth was increasing. They reversed their steps and moved in the other direction along the silent pool. The water level began to drop gradually as they went, to their chests, then to their waists. By the time it was down to their knees they had left the light of the lantern far behind, and were wading on through total darkness. At last, Jacob Pole bent forward and touched his fingers to the ground.

"Erasmus, we're out of the water completely. It's quite dry underfoot. Can you see anything?"

"Not a glimmer. Stay close. We don't want to get separated here."

Pole shivered violently. "I thought that was the end. What a way to have gone—stand until our strength had gone, then down, like trapped rats in a sewer pipe."

"Aye. I didn't care for the thought. 'O Lord, methought what pain it was to drown, what dreadful noise of waters in my ears, what sights of ugly death within my eyes.' At least poor Clarence smothered in a livelier liquid than black Fell water. Jacob, do you have your brandy flask? Your hand is ice."

"Left it in my greatcoat, along with the tinder and flint. Erasmus, I can't go much further. That water drained all my strength away."

"Pity there's not more flesh on your bones." Darwin halted and placed his hand on Pole's shoulder, feeling the shuddering tremors that were shaking the other's skinny frame. "Jacob, we have to keep moving. To halt now is to die, until our clothes become dry. Come, I will support you."

The two men stumbled blindly on, feeling their way

along the walls. All sense of direction was quickly lost in the labyrinth of narrow, branching tunnels. As they walked, Darwin felt warmth and new life slowly begin to diffuse through his chilled body. But Pole's shivering continued, and soon he would have fallen without Darwin's arm to offer support.

After half an hour more of wandering through the interminable tunnels, Darwin stopped again and put his hand to Pole's forehead. It burned beneath his touch.

"I know, 'Rasmus, you don't need to tell me." Pole's voice was faint. "I've felt this fever before—but then I was safe in bed. I'm done for. No Peruvian-bark for me here on Cross Fell."

"Jacob, we *have* to keep going. Bear up. I've got cinchona in my medical chest, back at the house. We'll find a way out of here before too long. Just hang on, and let's keep moving."

"Can't do it." Pole laughed. "Wish I could. I'm all ready for a full military funeral, by the sound of it. I can hear the fife and drum now, ready to play me out. They're whispering away there, inside my head. Let me lie down, and have some peace. I never warranted a military for my exit, even if it's only a ghostly one."

"Hush, Jacob. Save your strength. Here, rest all your weight on me." Darwin bent to take Pole's arm across his shoulder, supported him about the waist, and began to move forward again. His mood was somber. Pole needed medical attention—promptly—or death would soon succeed delirium.

Twenty seconds later, Darwin stopped dead, mouth gaping and eyes staring into the darkness. He was beginning to hear it, too—a faint, fluting tone, thin and ethereal, punctuated by the harsh deeper tone of drums. He turned his head, seeking some direction for the sound, but it was too echoing and diffuse.

"Jacob—can you tell me where it seems to be coming from?"

The reply was muttered and unintelligible. Pole, his body fevered and shaken with ague, was not fully conscious. Darwin had no choice but to go forward again, feeling his way along the damp, slick walls with their occasional timber support beams. Little by little, the sound was growing. It was a primitive, energetic music, shrill pan-pipes backed by a taut, rhythmic drum-beat. At last Darwin also became aware of a faint reddish light, flickering far along the tunnel. He laid Pole's semi-conscious body gently on the rocky floor. Then, light-footed for a man of his bulk, he walked silently towards the source of the light.

The man-made tunnel he was in emerged suddenly into a natural chimney in the rock, twenty yards across and of indefinite height. It narrowed as it went up and up, as far as the eye could follow. Twenty feet above, on the opposite side from Darwin, a broad, flat ledge projected from the chimney wall.

Darwin stepped clear of the tunnel and looked up. Two fires, fuelled with wood and peat, burned on the ledge and lit the chimney with an orange-red glow. Spreading columns of smoke, rising in a slight updraft, showed that the cleft in the rock served as a chimney in the other sense. Behind the fires, a group of dark figures moved on the ledge to the wild music that echoed from the sheer walls of rock.

Darwin watched in fascination the misshapen forms that provided a grotesque back-drop to the smoky, flickering fires. There was a curious sense of regularity, of hypnotic ritual, in their ordered movements. A man less firmly rooted in rational convictions would have seen the fiends of Hell, capering with diabolic intent, but Darwin looked on with an analytical eye. He longed for a closer view of an anatomy so oddly distorted from the familiar human form.

The dancers, squat and shaggy, averaged no more than four feet in height. They were long-bodied and long-armed, and naked except for skirts and head-dresses. But their movements, seen through the curtain of smoke and firelight, were graceful and well-coordinated. The musicians, set back beyond the range of the firelight, played on and the silent dance continued.

Darwin watched, until the urgency of the situation

again bore in on him. Jacob had to have warmth and proper care. The dancers might be ferocious aggressors, even cannibals; but whatever they were, they had fire. Almost certainly, they would also have warm food and drink, and a place to rest. There was no choice—and, deep inside, there was also the old, overwhelming curiosity.

Darwin walked forward until he was about twenty feet from the base of the ledge. He planted his feet solidly, legs apart, tilted his head back, and shouted up to the dancers.

"It's no good, Anna. Not a sign of them." Richard Thaxton slumped on the stone bench in the front yard, haggard and weary. "They must have gone up, into the Helm. There's not a thing we can do for them until it lifts."

Anna Thaxton looked at her husband with a worried frown. His face was pale and there were dark circles under his eyes. "Love, you did all you could. If they got lost on the Fell, they'd be sensible enough to stay in one place until the Helm moves off the highlands. Where did you find the lantern—in the same place as I saw it last night?"

"The same place exactly. There." Thaxton pointed a long arm at the slope of Cross Fell. "The trouble is, that's right where the Helm begins. We couldn't see much of anything. I think it's thicker now than it was last night."

He stood up wearily and began to walk towards the house. His steps were heavy and dragging on the cobbled yard. "I'm all in. Let me get a hot bath and a few hours sleep, and if the Fell clears by evening we'll go up again. Damn this weather." He rubbed his hand over his shoulder. "It leaches a man's bones to chalk."

Anna watched her husband go inside, then she stooped and began collecting the packages of food and medicine that Richard in his weariness had dropped carelessly to the floor. As she rose, arms full, she found a small figure by her side.

"What is it, Jimmy?" The deformed lad had been leaning by the wall of the house, silent as always, listening to their conversation.

He tugged at her sleeve, then pointed to the Fell. As

usual, he was lightly dressed, but he seemed quite unaware of the cold and the light drizzle. His eyes were full of urgent meaning.

"You heard what Mr. Thaxton said to me?" asked Anna. Jimmy nodded. Again he tugged at her arm, pulling her towards the Fell. Then he puffed out his cheeks and hunched his misshapen head down on his shoulders. Anna laughed. Despite Jimmy's grotesque appearance, he had somehow managed a creditable impersonation of Erasmus Darwin.

"And you think you know where Dr. Darwin is?" said Anna.

The lad nodded once more, and tapped his chest. Again, he pointed to Cross Fell. Anna hesitated, looking back at the house. After the long climb and a frantic four-hour search, Richard was already exhausted. It would serve no purpose to interrupt his rest.

"Let me go inside and write a note for Mr. Thaxton," she said. "Here, you take the food and medicine. We may need them." She handed the packages to Jimmy. "And I'll go and get warm clothing for both of us from the house. How about Colonel Pole?"

Jimmy smiled. He drew himself up to his full height of three-feet nine-inches. Anna laughed aloud. The size and build were wrong, but the angular set of the head and the slightly trembling hands were without question Jacob Pole.

"Give me five minutes," she said. "Then you can lead the way. I hope you are right—and I hope we are in time."

At Darwin's hail, the dancers froze. In a few seconds, pipe and drum fell silent. There was a moment of suspense, while the tableau on the ledge held, a frieze of demons against the dark background of the cave wall. Then the scene melted to wild confusion. The dancers milled about, most hurrying back beyond the range of the firelight, a few others creeping forward to the edge to gaze on the unkempt figure below.

"Do you understand me?" called Darwin.

There was no reply. He cursed softly. How to ask for help, when a common language was lacking? After a few moments he turned, went rapidly back into the tunnel, and felt his way to where Jacob Pole lay. Lifting him gently, he went back to the fire-lit chamber and stood there silently, the body of his unconscious friend cradled in his arms.

There was a long pause. At last, one of the fiends came to the very edge of the ledge and stared intently at the two men. After a second of inspection he turned and clucked gently to his companions. Three of them hurried away into the darkness. When they returned, they bore a long coil of rope which they cast over the edge of the ledge. The first fiend clucked again. He swung himself over the edge and climbed nimbly down, prehensile toes gripping the rope.

At the base he halted. Darwin stood motionless. At last, the other cautiously approached. His face was a devil-mask, streaked with red ochre from mouth to ears—but the eyes were soft and dark, deep-socketed beneath the heavy brow.

Darwin held forward Pole's fevered body. "My friend is sick," he said. The other started back at his voice, then again came slowly closer.

"See, red-man," said Darwin. "He burns with fever." Again, he nodded at Pole's silent form.

The fiend came closer yet. He looked at Pole's face, then put a hesitant hand out to feel the forehead. He nodded, and muttered to himself. He felt for the pulse in Pole's scrawny neck and grunted unhappily.

Darwin looked at him with an approving eye. "Aye, doctor," he said quietly. "See the problem? If we don't get him back home, to where I can give him medicine and venesection, he'll be dead in a few hours. What can you do for us, red-man?"

The fiend showed no sign of understanding Darwin's speech, but he looked at the other with soft, intelligent eyes. Darwin, no Adonis at the best of times, was something to look at. His clothes, wrinkled and smeared, hung like damp rags on his corpulent body. He had lost hat and wig in his descent into the pool, and his face was grimed and filthy from their travels through the tunnels of the mine. On his left hand, a deep cut had left streaks of dried blood along wrist and sleeve.

Darwin stood there steadily, heedless of his appearance. The fiend finally completed his inspection. He took Darwin by the arm and led him to the foot of the ledge. After slipping the rope around Jacob Pole's body and making it fast, he called a liquid phrase to the group above. The fiends on the ledge hoisted Pole to the top and then—with considerably greater effort—did the same for Darwin. The red-smeared fiend shinned up lightly after them. The others, taking the rope with them, quietly hurried away into the dark tunnel that led from the cave.

Together, Darwin and the fiend lifted Jacob Pole and laid him gently on a heap of sheepskins and rabbit furs. The red-man then also hurried away into the darkness. For the first time, Darwin was alone and could take a good look around him on the ledge.

The area was a communal meeting-place and eating-place. Two sheep carcasses, butchered and dressed, hung from a wooden tripod near one of the fires. Pole lay on his pile of furs about ten feet from the other fire, near enough for a comforting warmth to be cast on the sick man. Darwin walked over to the large black pot that nestled in the coals there. He bent over and sniffed it. Hot water. Useful, but not the source of the tantalizing smell that had filled his nostrils. He walked to the other fire, where an identical pot had been placed. He sniffed again. His stomach rumbled sympathetically. It was mutton broth. Darwin helped himself with the clay ladle and sipped appreciatively while he completed his inspection of the ledge.

Clay pots were stacked neatly along the nearer wall. Above them a series of murals had been painted in red and yellow ochre. The figures were stylized, with little attempt at realism in the portrayal of the fiends. Darwin was intrigued to see that many of them were set in forest backgrounds, showing boars and deer mingled with the distorted human figures. The animals, unlike the humanoids, were portrayed with full realism.

The other wall also bore markings, but they were more mysterious—a complex, intertwined network of lines and curves, drawn out in yellow ochre. At the foot of that wall lay a heap of jackets and leggins, made from crudely stitched rabbit skins. Darwin's eye would have passed by them, but he caught a faint bluish gleam from the ones furthest from the fire. He walked over to them and picked one up. It shone faintly, with the blue-green glow that they had seen moving on Cross Fell, and again near the rope bridge.

Darwin took a tuft of fur between finger and thumb, pulled it loose and slipped it into his damp coat pocket. As he did so, the red-man appeared from the tunnel, closely followed by a female fiend. She had a red-streaked face with similar markings, and was carrying a rough wooden box. Giving Darwin a wide berth, she set the box beside Jacob Pole. The red-man brought a clay pot from the heap by the wall, filled it with scalding water from the cauldron by the fire, and opened the wooden box. He seemed absorbed in his actions, completely oblivious to Darwin's presence.

"I see," said Darwin reflectively. "A medicine chest, no less. And what, I wonder, are the prescriptive resources available to the medical practitioner on Cross Fell?" He stooped to watch the red-man at his work.

"That one looks familiar enough. Dried bilberries—though I doubt their efficacy. And this is—what?—bog rosemary? And here is dried tormentil, and blue gentian. Sound enough." He picked up a petal and chewed on it thoughtfully. "Aye, and flowers of violet, and dried holly leaves. You have the right ideas, red-man—I've used those myself in emergency. But what the devil are these others?" He sniffed at the dried leaves. "This could be bog asphodel, and I think these may be tansy and spleenwort. But this?" He shook his head. "A fungus, surely—but surely not fly agaric!"

While he mused, the fiend was equally absorbed. He selected pinches of various dried materials from the chest and dropped them into the scalding water in the clay pot. He muttered quietly to himself as he did so, a soft stream of liquid syllables.

At last he seemed satisfied. Darwin leaned over and sniffed the infusion. He shook his head again.

"It worries me. I doubt that this is any better than prancing around Jacob to ward off evil spirits. But my judgment is worthless with those drugs. Do your best, red-man."

The other looked up at Darwin, peering from under his heavy brows. He smiled, and closed the box. The female fiend picked up the clay pot, while the red-man went to Jacob Pole and lifted him gently to a sitting position. Darwin came forward to help. Between them, they managed to get most of the hot liquid down Pole's throat.

Darwin had thought that the female was naked except for her short skirt. At close quarters, he was intrigued to see that she also wore an elaborately carved necklace. He bent forward for a closer look at it. Then his medical interests also asserted themselves, and he ran a gentle hand along her collar-bone, noting the unfamiliar curvature as it bent towards her shoulder. The woman whimpered softly and shied away from his touch.

At this, the red-man looked up from his inspection of Jacob Pole and grunted his disapproval. He gently laid Pole back on the heap of skins. Then he patted the female reassuringly on the arm, removed her necklace, and handed it to Darwin. He pointed to the red streaks on her face. She turned and went back into the tunnel, and the red-man patted his own cheek and then followed her. Darwin, mystified, was alone again with Pole. The other fiends had shown no inclination to return.

Darwin looked thoughtfully at the remains of the infusion, and listened to Pole's deep, labored breathing. At last, he settled down on a second pile of skins, a few yards from the fire, and looked closely at the necklace he had been given. He finally put it into a pocket of his coat, and sat there, deep in speculation. One theory seemed to have been weakened by recent events.

When the red-streaked fiend returned, he had with him another female, slightly taller and heavier than the first. He grunted in greeting to Darwin and pointed to the single line of yellow ochre on her cheek. Before Darwin could rise, he had turned and slipped swiftly away again into the recesses of the dark tunnel.

The female went over to Pole, felt his brow, and tucked sheepskins around him. She listened to his breathing, then, apparently satisfied, she came and squatted down on the pile of skins, opposite Darwin. Like the other, she wore a brief skirt of sewn rabbit skins and a similar necklace, less heavy and with similar carving. For the first time, Darwin had the chance for a leisured assessment of fiend anatomy, with adequate illumination. He leaned forward and looked at the curious variations on the familiar human theme.

"You have about the same cranial capacity, I'd judge," he said to her quietly. She seemed reassured by his gentle voice. "But look at these supra-orbital arches—they're heavier than human. And you have less cartilage in your nose. Hm." He leaned forward, and ran his hand softly behind and under her ear. She shivered, but did not flinch. They sat, cross-legged, opposite each other on the piled skins.

"I don't feel any mastoid process behind the ear," Darwin continued. "And this jaw and cheek is odd—see the maxilla. Aye, and I know where I've seen that jawline recently. Splendid teeth. If only I had my commonplace book with me. I'd like sketches. Well, memory must suffice."

He looked at the shoulder and rib cage and moved his index finger along them, tracing their lines. Suddenly he leaned forward and plucked something tiny from the female's left breast. He peered at it closely with every evidence of satisfaction.

"*Pulex Irritans*, if I'm any judge. Pity I don't have a magnifying glass with me. Anyway, that seems to complete the proof. You know what it shows, my dear?"

He looked up at the female. She stared back impassively with soft, glowing eyes. Darwin leaned forward again.

"Now, with your leave I'd like a better look at this abdominal structure. Very heavy musculature here—see how well-developed the *rectus abdominis* is. Ah, thank you, that makes inspection a good deal easier." Darwin nodded absently as the female reached to her side and removed her brief skirt of rabbit skins. He traced the line of ribbed muscle tissue to the front of the pelvis. "Aye, and an odd pelvic structure, too. See this. The pubic ramus seems flattened, just at this point." He palpated it gently.

"Here! What the devil are you doing!" Darwin suddenly sat bolt upright. The female fiend sitting before him, naked except for her ornate necklace, had reached forward to him and signalled her intentions in unmistakable terms.

"No, my dear. You mustn't do that."

Darwin stood up. The female stood up also. He backed away from her hurriedly. She smiled playfully and pursued him, despite his protests, round and round the fire.

"There you go, Erasmus. I turn my back on you for one second, and you're playing ring-a-ring-a-rosy with a succubus." Pole's voice came from behind Darwin. It sounded cracked and rusty, like an unoiled hinge, but it was rational and humorous.

The female squeaked in surprise at the unexpected sound. She ran to the heap of furs, snatched up her skirt, and fled back into the dark opening in the wall of the ledge. Darwin, no less surprised, went over to the bed of furs where Pole lay.

"Jacob, I can't believe it. Only an hour ago, you were running a high fever and beginning to babble of green fields." He felt Pole's forehead. "Back down to normal, I judge. How do you feel?"

"Not bad. Damn sight better than I did when we got out of that water. And I'm hungry. I could dine on a dead Turk."

"We can do better than that. Just lie there." Darwin

went across to the other fire, filled a bowl with mutton stew from the big pot, and carried it back. "Get this inside you."

Pole sniffed it suspiciously. He grunted with pleasure and began to sip at it. "Good. Needs salt, though. You seem to be on surprisingly good terms with the fiends, Erasmus. Taking their food like this, without so much as a by-your-leave. And if I hadn't been awakened by your cavortings, you'd be playing the two-backed beast this very second with that young female."

"Nonsense." Darwin looked pained. "Jacob, she simply misunderstood what I was doing. And I fear the red-man mistook the nature of my interest in the other female, also. It should have been clear to you that I was examining her anatomy."

"And she yours." Pole smiled smugly. "A natural preliminary to swiving. Well, Erasmus, that will be a rare tale for the members of the Lunar Society if we ever get back to Lichfield."

"Jacob—" Darwin cut off his protest when he saw the gleeful expression on Pole's face. "Drink your broth and then rest. We have to get you strong enough to walk, if we're ever to get out of this place. Not that we can do much on that front. I've no idea how to find our way back—we'll need the assistance of the fiends, if they will agree to give it to us."

Pole lay back and closed his eyes. "Now this really feels like a treasure hunt, Erasmus. It wouldn't be right without the hardships. For thirty years I've been fly-bitten, sun-baked, wind-scoured, and snow-blind. I've eaten food that the jackals turned their noses up at. I've drunk water that smelled like old bat's-piss. And all for treasure. I tell you, we're getting close. At least there are no crocodiles here. I almost lost my arse to one, chasing emeralds on the Ganges."

He roused himself briefly, and looked around him again. "Erasmus, where are the fiends? They're the key to that treasure. They guard it."

"Maybe they do," said Darwin soothingly. "You rest

now. They'll be back. It must be as big a shock to them as it was to us—more, because they had no warning that we'd be here."

Darwin paused and shook his head. There was an annoying ringing in his ears, as though they were still filled with Fell water from the underground pool.

"I'll keep watch for them, Jacob," he went on. "And if I can. I'll ask them about the treasure."

"Wake me before you do that," said Pole. He settled back and closed his eyes. Then he cracked one open again and peered at Darwin from under the lowered lid. "Remember, Erasmus—keep your hands off the fillies." He lay back with a contented smile.

Darwin bristled, then smiled himself. Jacob was on the mend. He sat down again by the fire, ears still buzzing and singing, and began to look in more detail at the contents of the medical chest.

When the fiend returned he gave Darwin a look that was half-smile and half-reproach. It was easy to guess what the females must have said to him. Darwin felt embarrassed, and he was relieved when the fiend went at once to Pole and felt his pulse. He looked pleased with himself at the result, and lifted Pole's eyelid to look at the white. The empty bowl of stew sitting by Pole's side also seemed to meet with his approval. He pointed at the pot that had contained the infusion of medicaments, and smiled triumphantly at Darwin.

"I know," said Darwin. "And I'm mightily impressed, red-man. I want to know a lot more about the treatment, if we can manage to communicate with each other. I'll be happy to trade my knowledge of medicinal botany for yours, lowland for highland. No," he added, as he saw the other's actions. "That isn't necessary for me."

The fiend had filled another pot with hot water while Darwin had been talking, and dropped into it a handful of dried fungus. He was holding it forward to Darwin. When the latter refused it, he became more insistent. He placed the bowl on the ground and tapped his chest. While Darwin watched closely, he drew back his lips from his

teeth, shivered violently all over, and held cupped hands
to groin and armpit to indicate swellings there. Darwin
rubbed his aching eyes, and frowned. The fiend's mimicry
was suggestive—but of something that seemed flatly
impossible. Unless there was a danger, here on Cross Fell,
of...

The insight was sudden, but clear. The legends, the
King of Hate, the Treasure, the departure of the Romans
from Cross Fell—at once this made a coherent picture,
and an alarming one. He blinked. The air around him
suddenly seemed to swirl and teem with a hidden peril. He
reached forward quickly and took the bowl.

"Perhaps I am wrong in my interpretation, red-man,"
he said. "I hope so, for my own sake. But now I must take
a chance on your good intentions."

He lifted the bowl and drank, then puckered his lips
with distaste. The contents were dark and bitter, strongly
astringent and full of tannin. The red fiend smiled at him
in satisfaction when he lowered the empty bowl.

"Now red-man, to business," said Darwin. He picked
up the medicine chest and walked with it over to the fire.
He hunkered down where the light was best and gestured
to the red fiend to join him. The other seemed to
understand exactly what was in Darwin's mind. He
opened the lid of the box, pulled out a packet wrapped in
sheep-gut, and held it up for Darwin's inspection.

How should one convey the use of a drug—assuming
that a use were known—without words? Darwin prepared
for a difficult problem in communication. Both the
symptoms and the treatment for specific diseases would
have to be shown using mimicry and primitive verbal
exchange. He shook off his fatigue and leaned forward
eagerly to meet the challenge.

Three hours later, he looked away from the red fiend
and rubbed his eyes. Progress was excellent—but
something was very wrong. His head was aching, the
blood pounding in his temples. The buzzing and singing
in his ears had worsened, and was accompanied by a
blurring of vision and a feeling of nausea. The complex

pattern of lines on the cave wall seemed to be moving, to have become a writhing tangle of shifting yellow tendrils.

He looked back at the fiend. The other was smiling—but what had previously seemed to be a look of friendship could equally well be read as a grin of savage triumph. Had he badly misunderstood the meaning of the infusion he had drunk earlier?

Darwin put his hands to the floor and attempted to steady himself. He struggled to rise to his feet, but it was too late. The cave was spiralling around him, the murals dipping and weaving. His chest was constricted, his stomach churning.

The last thing he saw before he lost consciousness was the red-streaked mask of the fiend, bending towards him as he slipped senseless to the floor of the cave.

Seen through the soft but relentless drizzle, Cross Fell was a dismal place. Silver was muted to dreary grey, and sable and copper gleams were washed out in the pale afternoon light. Anna Thaxton followed Jimmy up the steep slopes, already doubting her wisdom in setting out. The Helm stood steady and forbidding, three hundred feet above them—and although she had looked closely in all directions as they climbed, she had seen no sign of Pole and Darwin. She halted.

"Jimmy, how much further? I'm tired, and we'll soon be into the Helm."

The boy turned and smiled. He pointed to a rock a couple of hundred yards away, then turned and pointed upwards. Anna frowned, then nodded.

"All right, Jimmy. I can walk that far. But are you sure you know where to find them?"

The lad nodded, then shrugged.

"Not sure, but you think so, eh? All right. Let's keep going."

Anna followed him upwards. Two minutes later, she stopped and peered at a scorched patch of heather.

"There's been a lantern set down here, Jimmy—and recently. We must be on the right track."

They were at the very brink of the Helm. Jimmy paused for a moment, as though taking accurate bearings, then moved up again into the heavy mist. Anna followed close behind him. Inside the Helm, visibility dropped to a few yards.

Jimmy stopped again and motioned Anna to his side. He pointed to a dark opening in the side of the hill.

"In here, Jimmy? You think they may have gone in, following the fiends?"

The boy nodded and led the way confidently forward into the tunnel. After a moment of hesitation, Anna followed him. The darkness inside quickly became impenetrable. She was forced to catch hold of the shawl that she had given Jimmy to wear, and dog his heels closely. He made his way steadily through the narrow tunnels, with no sign of uncertainty or confusion. At last he paused and drew Anna alongside him. They had reached a rough wooden bridge across a deep chasm, lit faintly from below by a ghostly gleaming on the walls. Far below, the light reflected from the surface of a dark and silent pool.

Jimmy pointed silently to a group of objects near the edge. A lantern, shoes, and a greatcoat. Anna went to them and picked up the coat.

"Colonel Pole's." She looked down at the unruffled water below. "Jimmy, do you know what happened to them?"

The boy looked uncomfortable. He went to look at the frayed end of the trailing rope that hung from the bridge, then shook his head. He set out across the bridge, and Anna again took hold of the shawl. They soon were again in total darkness. This time they seemed to grope their way along for an eternity. The path twisted and branched, moving upward and downward in the depths of the Fell.

At last they made a final turn and emerged without warning into a broad clear area, full of people and lit by flickering firelight. Anna, dazzled after long minutes in total darkness, looked about her in confusion. As her eyes adjusted to the light, she realized with horror that the figures in front of her were not men and women—they were fiends, powerfully-built and misshapen. She looked at the fires, and shivered at what she saw. Stretched out on piles of rough skins lay Erasmus Darwin and Jacob Pole, unconscious or dead. Two fiends, their faces red-daubed and hideous, crouched over Darwin's body.

Anna did not cry out. She turned, twisted herself loose of Jimmy's attempt to restrain her, and ran blindly back along the tunnel. She went at top speed, though she had no idea where her steps might lead her, or how she might escape from the fiends. When it came, the collision of her head with the timber roof brace was so quick and unexpected that she had no awareness of the contact before she fell unconscious to the rocky floor. She was spared the sound of the footsteps that pursued her steadily along the dark tunnel.

Richard Thaxton surfaced from an uneasy sleep. The taste of exhaustion was still in his mouth. He sat up on the bed, looked out at the sky, and tried to orient himself. He frowned. He had asked Anna to waken him at three o'clock for another search of Cross Fell, but outside the window the twilight was already far advanced. It must be well past four, on the grey December afternoon. Could it be that Darwin and Pole had returned, and Anna had simply decided to let him sleep to a natural waking, before she told him the news?

He stood up, went to the dresser, and splashed cold water on his face from the jug there. Rubbing his eyes, he went to the window. Outside, the weather had changed again. The light drizzle of the forenoon had been replaced by a thick fog. He could scarcely see the tops of the trees in the kitchen garden, a faint tangle of dark lines bedewed with water droplets.

The first floor of the house was cold and silent. He thought of going down to the servants' quarters, then changed his mind and went through to the study. The log fire there had been banked high by one of the maids. He picked up Anna's note from the table, and went to read it by the fireside. At the first words, his concern for Darwin and Pole was overwhelmed by fear for Anna's safety. In winter, in a dense Cumbrian fog, Cross Fell could be a deathtrap unless a man knew every inch of its sudden slopes and treacherous, shifting screes.

Thaxton put on his warmest clothing and hurried out into the gathering darkness. In this weather, the safest way up to the Fell would be from the north, where the paths were wider—but the southern approach, although steeper and more treacherous, was a good deal more direct. He hesitated, then began to climb the southern slope, moving at top speed on the rough path that had been worn over the years by men and animals. On all sides, the world ended five yards from him in a wall of mist. The wind had dropped completely, and he felt like a man climbing forever in a small, silent bowl of grey fog. After ten minutes, he was forced to stop and catch his breath. He looked around. The folly of his actions was suddenly clear to him. He should now be on his way to Milburn, to organize a full-scale search party, rather than scrambling over Cross Fell, alone and unprepared. Should he turn now, and go back down? That would surely be the wiser course.

His thoughts were interrupted by a low, fluting whistle, sounding through the fog. It seemed to come from his left, and a good distance below him. The mist made distance and direction difficult to judge. He held his breath and stood motionless, listening intently. After a few seconds it came again, a breathy call that the fog swallowed up without an echo.

Leaving the path, he moved down and to the left, stumbling over the sodden tussocks of grass and clumps of heather, and peering ahead into the darkness. Twice, he almost fell, and finally he stopped again. It was no good, he could not negotiate the side of Cross Fell in the darkness and mist. Exploration would have to wait until conditions were better, despite his desperate anxiety. The only thing to do now was to return to the house. He would rest there as best he could, and be fit for another ascent, with assistance, when weather and light permitted it. Whatever had happened to Anna, it would not help her if he were to suffer injury now, up on the Fell. He began a cautious descent.

At last he saw the light in the upper bedroom of the house shining faintly through the mist below him. Down at ground level, on the left side of the house, he fancied that he could see a group of dim lights, moving in the kitchen garden. That was surprising. He halted, and peered again through the darkness. While he watched, another low whistle behind him was answered, close to the house. The lights grew dimmer. He was gripped by a sudden, unreasoning fear. Heedless of possible falls, he began to plunge full-tilt down the hillside.

The house and garden seemed quiet and normal, the grounds empty. He made his way into the kitchen garden, where he had seen the moving lights. It too seemed deserted, but along the wall of the house he could dimly see three oblong mounds. He walked over to them, and was suddenly close enough to see them clearly. He gasped. Side by side, bound firmly to rough stretchers of wood and leather, lay the bodies of Darwin, Pole, and Anna, all well wrapped in sheepskins. Anna's cold forehead was heavily bandaged, with a strip torn from her linen blouse. Thaxton dropped to his knee and put his ear to her chest, full of foreboding.

Before he could hear the heartbeat he heard Darwin's voice behind him.

"We're here, are we?" it said. "About time, too. I must have dropped off to sleep again. Now, Richard, give me a hand to undo myself, will you. I'm better off than Anna and Jacob, but we're all as sick as dogs. I don't seem to have the strength of a gnat, myself."

"What a sight. Reminds me of the field hospital after a Pathan skirmish." Jacob Pole looked round him with gloomy satisfaction. The study at Heartsease had been converted into a temporary sick-room, and Darwin, Anna Thaxton, and Pole himself were all sitting in armchairs by the fire, swaddled in blankets.

Richard Thaxton stood facing them, leaning on the mantelpiece. "So what happened to Jimmy?" he said.

"I don't know," said Darwin. He had broken one of his own rules, and was drinking a mug of hot mulled wine. "He started out with us, leading the way down while the rest of them carried the stretchers. Then I fell asleep, and I don't know what happened to him. I suspect you'll find him over in Milburn, wherever he usually lives there. He did his job, getting us back here, so he's earned a rest."

"He's earned more than a rest," said Thaxton. "I don't know how he did it. I was up on the Fell myself in that fog, and you couldn't see your hand in front of your face."

"He knows the Fell from top to bottom, Jimmy does," said Anna. "He was almost raised there." She was looking pale, with a livid bruise and a long gash marring her smooth forehead. She shivered. "Richard you've no idea what it was like, following him through the dark in that tunnel, then suddenly coming across the fiends. It was like a scene out of Hell—the smoke, and the shapes. I felt sure they had killed the Colonel and Dr. Darwin."

"They hardly needed to," said Pole wryly. "We came damned close to doing that for ourselves. Erasmus nearly drowned, and I caught the worst fever that I've had since the time that I was in Madagascar, looking for star sapphires. Never found one. I had to settle for a handful of garnets and a dose of dysentery. Story of my life, that. Good thing that Erasmus could give me the medicine, up on the Fell."

"And that was no thanks to me," said Darwin. "The fiends saved you, not me. They seem to have their own substitute for cinchona. I'll have to try that when we get back home."

"Aye," said Pole. "And we'll have to stop calling them fiends. Though they aren't human, and look a bit on the fiendish side—if appearances bother you. Anyway, they did right by me."

Richard Thaxton dropped another log on the fire, and pushed a second tray of meat pasties and mince pies closer to Darwin. "But at least there *are* fiends on Cross Fell," he remarked. "Anna was right and I was wrong. It was a hard way to prove it, though, with the three of you all sick. What I find hardest to believe is that they've been there in the mines for fifteen hundred years or more, and we've not known it. Think, our history means nothing to them. The Norman Conquest, the Spanish Armada—they mean no more to them than last year's rebellion in the American Colonies. It all passed them by."

Darwin swallowed a mouthful of pie, and shook his head. "You're both wrong."

"Wrong? About what?" asked Thaxton.

"Jacob is wrong when he says they are not human, and you are wrong when you say they've been up in the mines for fifteen hundred years."

There was an immediate outcry from the other three.

"Of course they're not human," said Pole.

Darwin sighed, and regretfully put down the rest of his pie, back on the dish. "All right, if you want evidence, I suppose I'll have to give it to you. First, and in my opinion the weakest proof, consider their anatomy. It's different from ours, but only in detail—in small ways. There are many fewer differences between us and the fiends than there are between us and, say, a monkey or a great ape. More like the difference between us and a Moor, or a Chinee.

"That's the first point. The second one is more subtle. The flea."

"You'd better have some more proofs, more substantial than that, Erasmus," said Pole. "You can't build a very big case around a flea."

"You can, if you are a doctor. I found a flea on one of the young females—you saw her yourself, Jacob."

"If she's the one you were hoping to roger, Erasmus, I certainly did. But I didn't see any flea. I didn't have the privilege of getting as close as you apparently did."

"All the same, although you didn't see it, I found a flea on her—our old friend, *pulex irritans*, if I'm a reliable judge. Now, you scholars of diabolism and the world of demons, when did you ever hear of any demon that had fleas—and the same sort of fleas that plague us?"

The other three looked at each other, while Darwin took advantage of the brief silence to poke around one of his back teeth for a piece of gristle that had lodged there.

"All right," said Anna at last. "A fiend had a flea. It's still poor evidence that fiends are *human*. Dogs have fleas, too. Are you suggesting *they* should be called human, too? There's more to humanity than fleas."

"There is," agreed Darwin. "In fact, there's one final test for humanity, the only one I know that never fails."

The room was silent for a moment. "You mean, possession of an immortal soul?" asked Richard Thaxton at last, in a hushed voice.

Jacob Pole winced, and looked at Darwin in alarm.

"I won't get off on the issue of religious beliefs," said Darwin calmly. "The proof that I have in mind is much more tangible, and much more easily tested. It is this: a being is human if and only if it can mate with a known human, and produce offspring. Now, having seen the fiends isn't it obvious to you, Jacob, and to you, Anna, that Jimmy was sired by one of the fiends? One of them impregnated Daft Molly Metcalf, up on the Fell."

Anna Thaxton and Jacob Pole looked at each other. Jacob nodded, and Anna bit her lip. "He's quite right, Richard," she said. "Now I think about it, Jimmy looks just like a cross of a human with a fiend. Not only that, he knows his way perfectly through all the tunnels, and seems quite comfortable there."

"So, my first point is made," said Darwin. "The fiends are basically human, though they are a variation on our usual human form—more different, perhaps, than a Chinaman, but not much more so."

"But how could they exist?" asked Thaxton. "Unless they were created as one of the original races of man?"

"I don't know if there really were any 'original races of man.' To my mind, all animal forms develop and change, as their needs change. There is a continuous succession of small changes, produced I know not how—perhaps by the changes to their environment. The beasts we finally see are the results of this long succession—and that includes Man."

Darwin sat back again, and picked up his pie for a second attack. Pole, who had heard much the same thing several times before, seemed unmoved, but Anna and Richard were clearly uncomfortable with Darwin's statements.

"You realize," said Thaxton cautiously, "that your statements are at variance with all the teachings of the Church—and with the words of the Bible?"

"I do," said Darwin indistinctly, through a mouth crammed full of pie. He held out his mug for a refill of the spiced wine.

"But what of your other assertion, Erasmus?" said Pole. "If the fiends were not on Cross Fell for the past fifteen hundred years, then where the devil were they? And what were they doing?"

Darwin sighed. He was torn between his love of food and his fondness for exposition. "You didn't listen to me properly, Jacob. I never said they weren't about Cross Fell. I said they weren't living in the mine tunnels for fifteen hundred years."

"Then where were they?" asked Anna.

"Why, living on the surface—mainly, I suspect, in the woods. Their murals showed many forest scenes. Perhaps they were in Milburn Forest, south-east of Cross Fell. Think, now, there have been legends of wood-folk in England as long as history has records. Puck, Robin Goodfellow, the dryads—the stories have many forms, and they are very widespread."

"But if they lived in the woods," said Anna. "Why would they move to the mine tunnels? And when did they do it?"

"When? I don't know exactly," said Darwin. "But I would imagine that it was when we began to clear the forests of England, just a few hundred years ago. We began to destroy their homes."

"Wouldn't they have resisted, if that were true?" asked Pole.

"If they were really fiends, they might—or if they were

like us. But I believe that they are a very peaceful people. You saw how gentle they were with us, how they cared for us when we were sick—even though we must have frightened them at least as much as they disturbed us. *We* were the aggressors, we drove them to live in the disused mines."

"Surely they do not propose to live there forever?" asked Anna. "Should they not be helped, and brought forth to live normally?"

Darwin shook his head. "Beware the missionary spirit, my dear. They want to be allowed to live their own lives. In any case, I do not believe they would survive if they tried to mingle with us. They are already a losing race, dwindling in numbers."

"How do you know?" asked Pole.

Darwin shrugged. "Partly guesswork, I must admit. But if they could not compete with us before, they will inevitably lose again in the battle for living-space. I told you on the Fell, Jacob, in all of Nature the weaker dwindle in number, and the strong flourish. There is some kind of selection of the strongest, that goes on all the time."

"But that cannot be so," said Thaxton. "There has not been enough time since the world began, for the process you describe to significantly alter the balance of the natural proportions of animals. According to Bishop Ussher, this world began only four thousand and four years before the birth of Our Lord."

Darwin sighed. "Aye, I'm familiar with the bishop's theory. But if he'd ever lifted his head for a moment, and looked at Nature, he'd have realized that he was talking through his episcopal hat. Why, man, you have only to go and look at the waterfall at High Force, not thirty miles from here, and you will realize that it must have taken tens of thousands of years, at the very least, to carve its course through the rock. The earth we live on is old—despite the good bishop's pronouncement."

Anna struggled to her feet and went over to look out of the window. It was still foggy and bleak, and the Fell was barely visible through the mist. "So they are humans, out there," she said. "I hope, then, that they have some happiness in life, living in the cold and the dark."

"I think they do," said Darwin. "They were dancing when first we saw them, and they did not appear unhappy. And they do come out, at night when the Fell is shrouded in mist—to steal a few sheep of yours, I'm afraid. They always return before first light—they fear the aggressive instincts of the rest of us, in the world outside."

"What should we do about them?" asked Anna.

"Leave them alone, to live their own lives," replied Darwin. "I already made that promise to the red fiend, when we began to exchange medical information. He wanted an assurance from us that we would not trouble them, and I gave it. In return, he gave me a treasure-house of botanical facts about the plants that grow on the high fells—if I can but remember it here, until I have opportunity to write it down." He tapped his head.

Anna returned from the window. She sat down again and sighed. "They deserve their peace," she said. "From now on, if there are lights and cries on the Fell at night, I will have the sense to ignore them. If they want peace, they will have it."

"So, Erasmus, I've been away again chasing another false scent. Damn it, I wish that Thomas of Appleby were alive and here, so I could choke him. All that nonsense about the Treasure of Odirex—and we found nothing."

Pole and Darwin were sitting in the coach, warmly wrapped against the cold. Outside, a light snow was falling as they wound their way slowly down the Tees valley, heading east for the coastal plains that would take them south again to Lichfield. It was three days before Christmas, and Anna Thaxton had packed them an enormous hamper of food and drink to sustain them on their journey. Darwin had opened it, and was happily exploring the contents.

"I could have told you from the beginning," he said, "that the treasure would have to be something special to please Odirex. Ask yourself, what sort of treasure would please the King of Hate? Why was he *called* the King of Hate?"

"Damned if I know. All I care about is that there was nothing there. If there ever was a treasure, it must have been rifled years ago."

Darwin paused, a chicken in one hand and a Christmas pudding in the other. He looked from one to the other, unable to make up his mind.

"You're wrong, Jacob," he said. "The treasure was there. You saw it for yourself—and I had even closer contact with it. Don't you see, *the fiends themselves are the Treasure of Odirex*. Or rather, it is what they bear with them that is the Treasure."

"Bear with them? Sheepskins?"

"Not something you could see, Jacob. *Disease*. The fiends are carriers of plague. That's what Odirex discovered, when he discovered them. Don't ask me how he escaped the effects himself. That's what he used to drive away the Romans. If you look back in history, you'll find there was a big outbreak of plague in Europe, back about the year four hundred and thirty—soon after the Romans left Britain. People have assumed that it was bubonic plague, just like in the Black Death in the fourteenth century, or the Great Plague here a hundred years ago. Now, I am sure that it was not the same."

"Wait a minute, Erasmus. If the fiends carry plague, why aren't all the folk near Cross Fell dead?"

"Because we have been building up immunity, by exposure, for many hundreds of years. It is the process of selection again. People who can resist the plague can survive, the others die. I was struck down myself, but thanks to our improved natural resistance, and thanks also to the potion that the red fiend made me drink, all I had was a very bad day. If I'd been exposed for the first time, as the Romans were, I'd be dead by now."

"And why do you assert that it was not bubonic plague? Would you not be immune to that?".

"I don't know. But I became sick only a few *hours* after

first exposure to the fiends—that is much too quick for bubonic plague."

"Aye," said Pole. "It is, and I knew that for myself if I thought about it. So Odirex used his 'treasure' against the Romans. Can you imagine the effect on them?"

"You didn't see me," said Darwin. "And I only had the merest touch of the disease. Odirex could appear with the fiends, contaminate the Roman equipment—touching it might be enough, unless personal contact were necessary. That wouldn't be too difficult to arrange, either. Then, within twelve hours, the agony and deaths would begin. Do you wonder that they called him *Odii Rex*, the King of Hate? Or that they so feared his treasure that they fled this part of the country completely? But by then it was too late. They took the disease with them, back into Europe."

Pole looked out at the snow, now beginning to settle on the side of the road. He shivered. "So the fiends really are fiends, after all. They may not intend to do it, but they have killed, just as much as if they were straight from Hell."

"They have indeed," said Darwin. "More surely than sword or musket, more secretly than noose or poison. And all by accident, as far as they are concerned. They must have developed their own immunity many thousands of years ago, perhaps soon after they branched off from our kind of humanity."

Jacob Pole reached into the hamper and pulled out a bottle of claret. "I'd better start work on the food and drink, too, Erasmus," he said morosely. "Otherwise you'll demolish the lot. Don't bother to pass me food. The wine will do nicely. I've had another disappointment, and I want to wash it down. Damn it, I wish that once in my lifetime—just once—I could find a treasure that didn't turn to vapor under my shovel."

He opened the bottle, settled back into the corner of the coach seat, and closed his eyes. Darwin looked at him unhappily. Jacob had saved his life in the mine, without a doubt. In return, all that Pole had received was a bitter letdown.

Darwin hunched down in his seat, and thought of all that he had omitted to say, to Jacob and to the Thaxtons. In his pocket, the necklace from the female fiend seemed to burn, red-hot, like the bright red gold from which it was made. Somewhere in their explorations of the tunnels under Cross Fell, the fiends had discovered the gold mine that had so long eluded the other searchers. And it was plentiful enough, so that any fiend was free to wear as much of the heavy gold as he chose.

Darwin looked across at his friend. Jacob Pole was a sick man, they both knew it. He had perhaps two or three more years, before the accumulated ailments from a lifetime of exploration came to take him. Now it was in Darwin's power to satisfy a life's ambition, and reveal to Jacob a true treasure trove, up there on Cross Fell. But Darwin also remembered the look in the red fiend's eyes, when he had asked for peace for his people as the price for his medical secrets. More disturbance would break that promise.

Outside the coach, the snow was falling heavier on the Tees valley. Without doubt, it would be a white Christmas. Darwin looked out at the tranquil scene, but his mind was elsewhere and he felt no peace: Jacob Pole, and the red fiend. Very soon, he knew that he would have to make a difficult decision.

Recommended Reading—1978

T. CORAGHESSAN BOYLE: "Quetzalcóatl Lite." *Quest/78*, December 1978-January 1979.

GLEN COOK: "Ghost Stalk." *Fantasy and Science Fiction*, May 1978.

RONALD ANTHONY CROSS: "The Birds Are Free." *Orbit 20.*

AVRAM DAVIDSON: "The Redward Edward Papers." *The Redward Edward Papers.*

PARKE GODWIN: "The Last Rainbow." *Fantastic*, July 1978.

PETER JACKSON: "Jim Crocker, Prince of Atlantis." *Ariel*, Volume Three.

GARY JENNINGS: "Let Us Prey." *Fantasy and Science Fiction*, June 1978.

M. MENDELSOHN: "Little Goethe." *Fantasy and Science Fiction*, November 1978.

R. FARADAY NELSON: "Nightfall on the Dead Sea." *Fantasy and Science Fiction*, September 1978.

LARRY NIVEN: "Transfer of Power." *Ariel*, Volume Three.

CHARLES OTT: "The Ecologically Correct House." *Universe 8.*

TOM REAMY: "Insects in Amber." *Fantasy and Science Fiction*, January 1978.

DAVID REDD: "Morning." *Fantasy and Science Fiction*, July 1978.

ROBERT F. YOUNG: "The Journal of Nathaniel Worth." *Fantastic*, July 1978.

The Year in Fantasy: 1978
by Susan Wood

Susan Wood is a professor of English at the University of British Columbia, where she teaches courses in science fiction and fantasy, Canadian literature, and children's literature.

1978 seems to have been the year of the barbarians in fantasy fiction. Despite the appearance of some notable new books, additions to series by Zelazny, Kurtz, McCaffrey, L'Engle, and others, and the development of fantasy art, one is overwhelmed by images of mighty thews, flashing swords, horses trekking across wastelands, bobbing breasts, rape, unconvincing sorcery, and all the other trappings of Conan and his brethren.

The Robert E. Howard boom which began in 1977 with the Ace and Berkley reissues of several Conan sagas continued in 1978, and should be fueled in 1979 with yet more reprints. In addition, this year, Donald H. Grant issued a new edition of Howard's *Red Shadows*, "a compilation of all the known Solomon Kane writings" with eight color paintings by Jeff Jones; and Berkley issued *Son of the White Wolf*, a collection of minor Howard stories. Grosset and Dunlap (which controls Ace) introduced a series of large-format illustrated paperbacks with the Conan collection *The Devil In Iron* (with six color paintings by Dan Green), and Andrew Offutt's new *Conan and the Sorcerer,* illustrated by Sanjulian.

Semiliterate series in the "heroic fantasy" mode abounded:

"For the last blazing instant I saw Naghan hoist Fimi onto a mount, leap up with her and slash the gnutrix

301

across the flanks. In a clashing bounding of six legs and flying tassles, the gnutrix raced away.

"Then it was only the leem and me," says the narrator of Alan Burt Akers' *Savage Scorpio*, #16 in the Dray Prescott series (DAW). Other sword-opera titles, which substituted exotic names and formula plots for imagination, included Akers' *Captive Scorpio* (DAW); Lin Carter's *The Pirate of World's End*, "the fifth book of the Gondwane Epic" (DAW); Carter's *Renegade of Callisto*, # 8 in his Jandar of Callisto series (Dell); John Jakes' *Brak: When the Idols Walked* (Pocket Books); Gene Lancour's *Sword For the Empire*, "the third saga of Dirshan, the God-Killer" (Doubleday); Manning Norvil's *Whetted Bronze*, second in the "Odan the Half-God" series (DAW); and Richard Kirk's *Raven: Swordmistress of Chaos* (Corgi), the first in a series of novels featuring an ex-slave in explicit scenes of sex and violence. Other titles abounded; all seemed equally unimaginative and interchangeable, but their popularity with publishers and readers reveals much about the current state of what is marketed in North America as "fantasy." At times it seemed that the only significant event in the field was the fact that the 1978 John Norman production, *Beasts of Gor* (DAW), featured a cover-painting of a woman who was not only unchained, but actually clothed.

More notable titles in the heroic-fantasy and sword-and-sorcery subgenres included Eric Van Lustbader's *Shallows of Night* and *Dai-San* (Doubleday), which completed his Sunset Warrior trilogy, drawing on Japanese martial arts and creating effective alien societies; Alexei and Cory Panshin's *Earth Magic* (Ace), an expansion of their "Son of Black Morca" *Fantastic* serial, with some effective characterization; and Juanita Coulson's *The Web of Wizardry* (Ballantine/Del Rey). Tanith Lee's *Vazkor, Son of Vazkor,* and *Quest for the White Witch* (DAW), sequels to *The Birthgrave*, lacked that book's inventiveness but were, like it, lengthy accounts of sword-and-sorcery and suffering-by-demigods. Lee's gift for creating interesting worlds was more evident in her young-adult fantasy *East of Midnight*

(St. Martin's), the North American edition of a 1977 British release. The prolific Andre Norton added variety to the subgenre with *Quag Keep* (Atheneum), a quest story based on the game Dungeons and Dragons. Her *Trey of Swords* (Grossett) was a weak collection of three linked Witch World stories; and her *Yurth Burden* (DAW) was a formula quest novel involving psionic and arcane powers.

The most interesting of the traditional sword-and-sorcery novels was *The Panorama Egg* by A.E. Silas (DAW). This was literally an "escapist" fantasy, fulfilling an ordinary man's dreams as he became a hero in an alternate world; yet it transcended its standard formulas with good writing, as few 1978 releases did.

Variations on escapist themes, marred by clumsy writing and plotting, were evident in *The Want and the Star* by Pat Wallace (Pocket), an attempt to combine stock fantasy with the bodice-buster romance; and *Coriolanus, The Chariot!* by Alan Yates (Ace), a science fantasy with an obnoxious protagonist, set on the planet Thesbos where the Word of Shakespeare is Law.

Just where does one subgenre end and another begin? "Science fantasy" seems as good a term as any for the numerous books that mixed spaceships with sorcery, or depicted "magic" powers as knowable. Marion Zimmer Bradley's *Stormqueen!* (DAW), her latest Darkover novel, was set in the Ages of Chaos, and depicted a *leronis* attempting to control the *laran* power of a child able to unleash lightning. Bradley originally presented *laran* as an arcane, psionic power; yet here, as in recent novels, she depicted it as a mental/physical force involving the brain's electrical energy, thus knowable and controllable: "scientific" rather than "magic."

The control of mysterious psionic powers was also central to *Lamarchos* and *Irsud* (DAW), Jo Clayton's sequels to *Diadem from the Stars*. Both involved her barbarian heroine, Alyetys, in a variety of misadventures, including the kidnapping of her child; yet they also showed her developing as a character, gaining more control over the diadem which gives her access to the consciousnesses of a warrior, a sorceress, and a singer, as well as to earth-forces. Another DAW author, C.J. Cherryh, continued both her sf series and her science-fantasy series begun with *Gate of Ivrel*. *The Well of Shiuan* involved Cherryh's warrior-woman Morgaine and her companion Nhi Vanye in adventures on a barbarian planet, but focused on a heroic young woman, Jhirun, in the last days of her world. Unfortunately, the book revealed signs of hasty writing and plotting.

The blurring of genre-lines between "sf" and "fantasy" was typical of the best 1978 releases. Anne McCaffrey's *The White Dragon* (Ballantine/Del Rey), third book of her "Dragonriders" series, was "sf" yet featured such fantasy elements as a semi-feudal society and, of course, time-and-space-traveling dragons. Probably most fans care little about genre distinctions; certainly both "fantasy" and "sf" audiences have made the book a bestseller. Though McCaffrey tied up loose ends and left Pern free from the menace of the Threads, she also left room for more adventures in the same world; a third volume in the young-adult "Dragonsinger" series is forthcoming.

Roger Zelazny too ended but did not really conclude his Amber series with the fifth book, *The Courts of Chaos* (Doubleday). Though Amber is a world of magic, Doubleday published the book as "science fiction," further confusing genre terminology. *Saint Camber* by Katherine Kurtz (Ballantine/Del Rey), the fifth and best volume of her Deryni series, was her sequel to *Camber of Culdi*. Kurtz seemed to be developing the arcane Deryni powers, not in the direction of a knowable science, but as something akin to and activated by religious ritual.

Equally unclassifiable was Avram Davidson's *The Redward Edward Papers* (Doubleday), a collection of five previously-published stories and the new title novella—infuriating, disjointed, and displaying Davidson's contagious delight in wit, words, and erudition. Suzy McKee Charnas' *Motherlines* (Berkley) was an outstanding novel which, while technically "sf" set in a post-holocaust future, could also be read as Amazon fantasy. It focused on the former slave Alldera (of *Walk to the End of the World*) as she learned to accept freedom amid two societies populated solely by women.

1978 saw comparatively little traditional fantasy. Phyllis Eisenstein's *Born to Exile* (Arkham House) marked the first hardcover publication of her tales of Alaric the minstrel. Well-written, they held up as a continuous narrative, and point the way to a sequel. Dahlov Ipcar drew on the traditional material of English and Scottish ballads (notably Child 4 and 40) and Norse mythology in *A Dark Horn Blowing* (Viking), an interesting adult fantasy weakened by a shifting point of view.

The best and most unusual of the year's fantasies, however, appeared as an alternate-history novel. Michael Moorcock's *Gloriana: Or the Unfulfill'd Queen* (Allison and Busby) was set in Albion, an alternate-future Elizabethan England which ruled America and part of Asia; and especially in the vast palace of Queen Gloriana, a world in itself. Mannered, lush, intricate, and absorbing, the book acknowledged influences as diverse as Spenser's *Faerie Queene* and Peake's Gormenghast novels.

Attempts to combine humor with fantasy were not notably successful. Lin Carter's *The Wizard of Zao* (DAW) and Robert Asprin's *Another Fine Myth*, illustrated by Polly and Kelly Freas (Starblaze), both involved wizards, exotic animals, cunning assistants, and so on in complicated plots; but their humor was broad and forced. Similar attempts in juvenile fantasy included *Save Sirrushany!* by Betty Baker (Macmillan) and *The Perils of Putney* by Stephen Krensky, illustrated by Jürg Obrist (Atheneum), both send-ups of fantasy and fairy-tale conventions involving heavy-handed satire. Humor was handled rather more deftly by Sheila Rousseau Murphy in *The Flight of the Fox* (Atheneum), part animal-fantasy and part sf, in which a boy, a rat, and a lemming rebuild a model plane.

Diana Wynne Jones's *Drowned Ammet* (Atheneum) was a powerful and convincing young-adult fantasy, the second in a projected series of five novels set in the realm of Dalemark; it centered around the adventures of a young rebel, and a ritual invoking old fertility gods. It was first published in 1977 in England; and a third volume, *Charmed Life*, which appeared this year in Britain from Macmillan, is listed here from Morrow, Madeleine L'Engle's *A Swiftly Tilting Planet* (Farrar, Straus and Giroux) presented the third adventure of Charles Wallace, Meg, and the unicorn Gaudior, in a series which began with the award-winning *A Wrinkle in Time*. Ruth Nichols' *The Left-Handed Spirit* (Atheneum) showed Mariana, a first-century Roman woman, struggling to accept both the healing powers bestowed on her by the god Apollo, and her feelings for the cultured Chinese ambassador who abducted her. This philosophical and psychological novel was the introduction to Nichols' fantasy *Song of the Pearl*.

Joanna Russ also chose a children's tale to show a young woman developing independence and self-awareness. *Kittatinny: A Tale of Magic* (Daughters) was a series of tales in which Kit ran away from home; adopted a faun; met a mother dragon, a Woman Warrior, and a Princess; and had other appropriate adventures which led her to adulthood and sisterhood. Loretta Li contributed full-page line drawings in a "childlike" style to an attractive book that will probably appeal mostly to adults.

Adults deprived of wonder can also indulge in fantasy art books. Last year's bestselling *Gnomes* produced 1978 spinoffs ranging from calendars and jigsaw puzzles to bumper-stickers and a cardboard Gnome House. This year's notable art book was Brian Froud and Alan Lee's *Faeries* (Abrams). The author/illustrators drew on British oral tradition to create an eerie, beautiful, and alien world. Other notable fantasy-art collections included *Sidney H. Sime: Master of Fantasy*, edited by Paul Skeeters (Ward Richie); *Fantasy by Fabian*, edited and published by Gerry de la Ree; *A Dinosaurian Beastiary* by Robert Huntoon (St. Heironymous Press);

and *"...and then we'll get him!"* a collection of Gahan Wilson's cartoons (Richard Marek).

The blurring of the lines between fantasy books and adult comics (fantasy for a post-literate generation?), shown by the popularity of magazines like *Heavy Metal,* was evident in many 1978 books. *Ariel: the Book of Fantasy,* Volumes 3 and 4, edited by Thomas Durwood (Ariel/Ballantine), were large-format paperbacks containing stories, poems, interviews, and artwork ranging from mediocre black-and-white illustrations to stunning two-page multi-colored spreads that dwarfed the text. The same firm also published Richard Corben's *Neverwhere,* a full-color graphic fantasy novel; and *Sorcerers,* edited by Bruce Jones and Armand Eisen, an eighty-page collection of fantasy art.

The Illustrated Roger Zelazny by Zelazny and Gray Morrow, "edited and adapted by Byron Priess" (Baronet), was another large-format "graphic story" collection, featuring Morrow's comic-strip versions of Zelazny stories in a variety of styles. Less successful was *The First Kingdom* by Jack Katz, "The First All-Illustrated Heroic Fantasy Epic," a large-format paperback marking Pocket Books' entry into the "graphic novel" format. Clumsy dialogue and clumsy drawing— lots of distorted naked women, and lumpy male muscles and ribs—destroyed whatever appeal the story may have had.

One of the year's notable fantasies appeared as part of Grosset and Dunlap's new large-format illustrated line. *The Magic Goes Away* by Larry Niven was dressed up with a stock cover by Boris, and interior illustrations by Esteban Moroto, most of which did not add either a sense of wonder or harmony to Niven's short novel. The magic was all in the words. Niven gave an unsentimental picture of a long-ago Earth in which magic, which worked by drawing upon *mana* inherent in the world, was vanishing. Sandra Miesel's lucid essay, "The Mana Crisis," provided an interesting discussion of Niven's development of "logical fantasy."

Another fantasy-related genre, horror fiction, continued to develop strongly in 1978. Notable collections included Harlan Ellison's *Strange Wine* (Harper and Row), fifteen previously uncollected stories; Stephen King's *Night Shift* (Doubleday), containing twenty stories first published between 1970 and 1977; and *Shadows* edited by Charles L. Grant, a collection of thirteen original stories which marked the debut of a promising anthology series. Brian Lumley's novels *The Clock of Dreams* and *Spawn of the Winds* (Jove) used elements of the Lovecraftian mythos in rather clumsy sword-and-sorcery plots; and Les Daniels' *The Black Castle* (Scribners) mixed historical fiction and horror. Chelsea Quinn Yarbro's *Hôtel Transylvania* (St. Martin's) was a blending of comedy of manners, demonism, sadism, and horror in an unusual mixture which introduced a charming vampire-hero of a projected series. The major event in horror fiction, however, was the release of the new Stephen King novel, *The Stand* (Doubleday), set in 1980 when the remnants of humanity make a last stand against evil.

Mike Ashley's *Who's Who in Horror and Fantasy Fiction* (Taplinger) presented 400 brief biographies of major genre writers from the early 18th century onward. A useful book, it is significant as evidence that growing interest in the field has created a demand for such secondary material.

Diana Waggoner's *The Hills of Faraway: A Guide to Fantasy* (Atheneum) promised to fill a need for a basic fantasy bibliography, but proved disappointing. The annotated bibliography, 177 pages long, was ambitious but, as Waggoner noted, incomplete. North American "adult fantasy," current releases, and acknowledged classics received most attention, and the choices and omissions were often curious. Waggoner's 121 pages of introductory material drew upon sources as diverse as Tolkien and Northrop Frye (!) for a critical discussion of fantasy which was poorly formulated and confusing. Her attempt to classify fantasy into eight subgenres could have been useful as a discussion of the many things fantasy can be and what fantasy can do; but it degenerated into pigeonholing and list-making. In the end *The Hills of Faraway* was an example of an excellent idea misapplied, and pointed to the need for real theoretical work in the field.

Franz Rottensteiner's *The Fantasy Book* (Thames and Hudson), part coffee-table illustrated volume and part encyclopedia, was more interesting and useful, both for its historical and critical discussions, as well as its succession of powerful fantasy images—which affect the subconscious directly, as good fantasy does.

Touchstone, edited by James Tucker and Erin McKee (The Mysterious Stranger Press) was "a tribute to Ray Bradbury and Fritz Leiber." It was an attractive *festschrift*, with brief appreciations by Poul Anderson, Robert Bloch, Marion Zimmer Bradley, Harlan Ellison, and others: a celebration rather than a study. Scholarly rather than fan interest in the fantasy field was represented by *Fairy Tales and After: From Snow White to E.B. White* by Roger Sale (Harvard), a study of the classics of children's literature, including the Oz books.

The growth of interest in comtemporary fantasy as a distinct genre was reflected in the growth of specialized conventions. In Britain, the 1978 Fantasycon, organized by the British Fantasy Society, was held in the Imperial Hotel, Birmingham, February 24-26. The Guest of Honor, Stephen King, was unable to attend because of poor health. Ramsey Campbell was Master of Ceremonies. The 1977 British Fantasy Awards were presented in the following categories: Novel—Piers Anthony, *A Spell for Chameleon* (Ballantine); Short Story—Ramsey Campbell, "In the Bag"; Film—Brian de Palma, *Carrie*; Small Press—S. Jones/D. Sutton, *Fantasy Tales 1*; Artwork—Stephen Fabian, *Chacal 2* ("The End of Days"); and Comic—Moench/Ploog/Nino, *Marvel Premiere 38, Weirdworld.*

The fourth World Fantasy Convention was held from October 13-15, 1978 in Fort Worth, Texas, with Guest of Honor Fritz Leiber, Artist Alicia Austin, and Toastmaster Andrew Offutt (replacing Gahan Wilson, who was unable to attend). The World Fantasy Awards (the "Howards") were presented in the following categories: Novel—Fritz Leiber, *Our Lady of Darkness* (Berkley); Short Fiction—Ramsey Campbell, "The Chimney," (*Whispers*); Collection/Anthology—Hugh B. Cave, *Murgunstrumm and Others* (Carcosa); Artist—Lee Brown Coye; Special Award, Pro—E.F. Bleiler; Special Award, Nonpro—Robert Weinberg; and Life Achievement—Frank Belknap Long.

The 36th World Science Fiction Convention (Iguanacon), held in Phoenix, Arizona from August 30 to September 4, also presented two fantasy awards. Poul Anderson won the Gandalf Award for lifetime achievement, and J.R.R. Tolkien's *The Silmarillion* (Allen and Unwin/Houghton Mifflin) won the Gandalf Award as best fantasy book of the year.

Fantasy readers are served by a wide variety of amateur and semi-professional magazines. *Fantasaie*, edited by Ian M. Slater, is the monthly newsletter of the Fantasy Association. The eight to ten pages of book news, articles, and reviews are available from: The Fantasy Association, P.O. Box 24560, Los Angeles, CA 90024; a year's subscription is $6/US, $8/US in Canada, and $10/US elsewhere. *Fantasy Newsletter* is a new monthly publication covering the professional and fan scene in North America and Britain. It is edited by Paul Allen, 1015 W. 36th St., Loveland, CO 80537; a year's subscription is $6/US, $8/US in Canada, $10/US elsewhere. *The Guide to Current Fantasy Fanzines and Semi-Prozines* is edited by Rosemary Pardoe, Flat 2, 38 Sandown Lane, Liverpool 15, U.S. It is available for 25 pence (50 cents), or 3 International Reply Coupons.

The year's major fantasy events, however, will probably turn out not to be any publication, but the North American premieres of Ralph Bakshi's film *Lord of the Rings* (which received mixed reviews after its Los Angeles preview and its opening November 15), and of *Watership Down* (which premiered at Iguanacon to mixed reactions). These, as well as other fantasy films such as *Heaven Can Wait* and *Superman* (and with attendant *LoTR* calendars, illustrated editions, and other spinoffs), will focus public attention on fantasy in 1979. Maybe 1979, like 1977, will be a year of Tolkien imitations rather than Conan-clones.

With exceptions, notably *Faeries, Gloriana, The Magic Goes Away*, and some of the sword-and-sorcery variants, 1978 was a disappointing year for book-length fantasy. C.S. Lewis, writing about the fantasies of William Morris, said: "He seems to retire far from the real world and build a world out of his wishes; but when he has finished the result stands out as a picture of experience ineluctably true." In 1978, the paperback houses, especially, churned out two or three escapist-fantasy titles a month. Yet few offered even half-convincing wish-worlds, worlds genuinely *other*; and fewer still used these worlds to give us some small glimpse of universal human truth.